Redeeming Dust

A political drama from first century Palestine

JACQ MARLOW

malcolm down
PUBLISHING

24 23 22 21 20   7 6 5 4 3 2 1

First published 2020 by Malcolm Down Publishing Ltd.
www.malcolmdown.co.uk

British Library Cataloguing in Publication Data
A catalogue record for this book is available from the British Library.

ISBN 978-1-912863-61-7

Cover design by Angela Selfe
Art direction by Sarah Grace

Printed in the UK

Preface

During a tumultuous period in first-century Palestine, this is a story of four Passovers and an execution. The people groan under the oppressive control of an overbearing Roman empire, whose tax burden and food rationing have made outlaws of some, fanatical for a violent rebellion.

The majority of the land is owned by the puppet kings that do Rome's bidding, whilst a priestly class have their own corrupt means of levying further taxes.

The people dream of freedom, clinging to the hope of a great leader, a Messiah, that will arise and set them free, as their prophets and their history have foretold.

Holy men and sages have come and gone, leaving only forlorn hope, whilst warrior rebel leaders have been ruthlessly snuffed out by Rome's legions.

A man appears from a desert cult to denounce both King and religious leaders, it costs him his life.

A chariot of white stallions stands ready to charge for freedom, but there is no chariot race.

Another man enters an ancient temple with a whip in his hand, but his quest is not for an ancient artefact.

If this were mixed as cocktail, the recipe could perhaps be imagined as follows:

Take two parties religion and one party politic,
mix in a sprinkling of freedom fighters and
stir all into one large foreign empire.
Finally, add one Messiah.
All shaken and stirred.

Politics and religion, if mixed together, is invariably a potent brew. Since ancient times and up to the present day, the results have often resulted in turmoil and conflict.

In the story before you, seen through the eyes of 'John the beloved', the secular politics sometimes fights against the religious politics and sometimes they are mixed together in unholy alliance, as strange bedfellows. But perhaps it has always been this way and always will be, because with both of these two systems, religion and politics, there are always some people who consider the good of their fellow man and the best actions for their world, whilst there are others who seek power within one of these systems, for their own ends, to order or control the lives of others.

"Testimonium Flavianum"
The Testimony of Flavius Josephus (37-100AD)

"About this time there lived Jesus, a wise man, if indeed one ought to call him a man. For he was one who performed surprising deeds and was a teacher of such people as accept the truth gladly. He won over many Jews and many of the Greeks. He was the Messiah. And when, upon the accusation of the principal men among us, Pilate had condemned him to a cross, those who had first come to love him did not cease. He appeared to them spending a third day restored to life, for the prophets of God had foretold these things and a thousand other marvels about him. And the tribe of the Christians, so called after him, has still to this day not disappeared."

***Jewish Antiquities,* 18.3.3 §63**

(Based on the translation of Louis H. Feldman, The Loeb Classical Library.)

The Political Geography of Palestine circa AD20-30

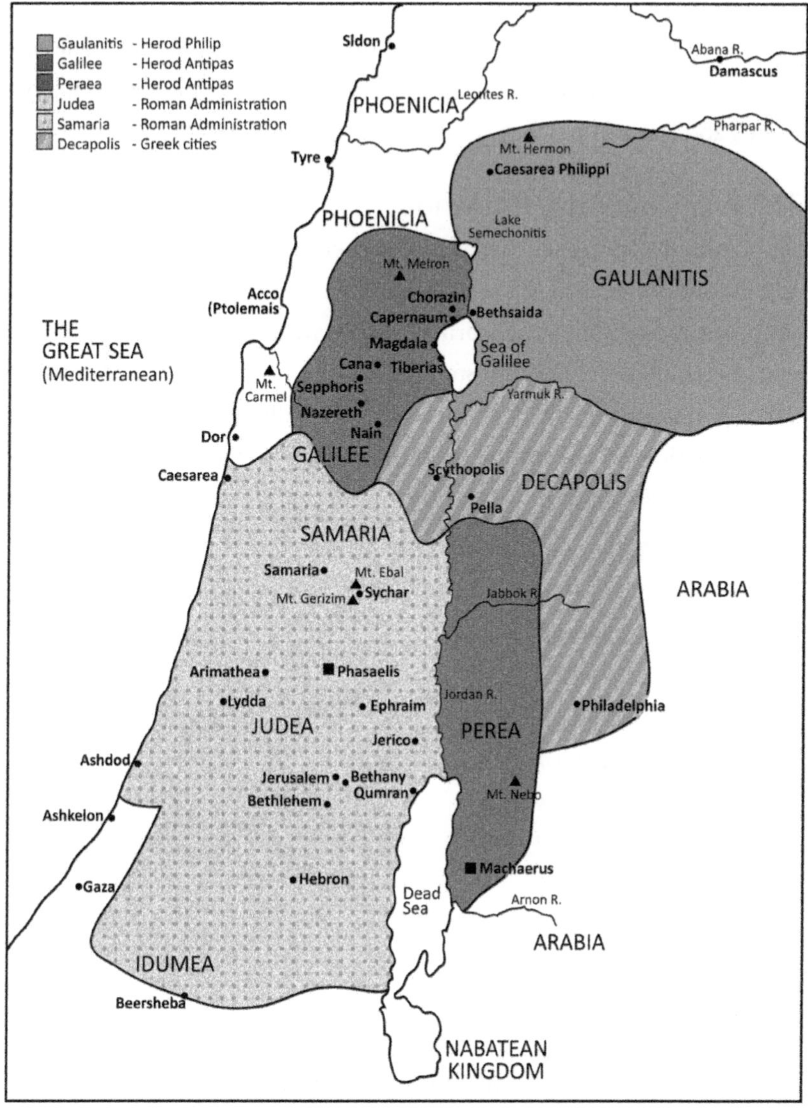

Contents

The chapters and contents are also shown in an appendix, on a four-year timeline, based mainly on the Gospel of Luke, with scripture references. A second appendix shows the Jewish calendar year with the main religious events and festivals.

The first year: Arise the King

First, John the Immerser challenges the social order and causes the people to talk of fulfilment of the long-awaited prophecies of the scriptures, the promise of a Messiah that will bring freedom with a kingdom that will never end. What follows is the baptism of a labourer from a non-descript village called Nazareth, then the first miracle, the first disciples, the first cleansing of the temple at Jerusalem and the meteoric rise of this man, called Jesus, to fame and huge celebrity.

The second year and a half: The Call of the King

He calls himself the fulfilment of ancient prophecies and then calls the twelve 'Apostles' and for eighteen months they both ride and fight a wave of popularity, as they are treated like heroes wherever they go. The

Twelve learn that they have been chosen to be different, taken out of their own people to be a new kingdom under the new king. They struggle to understand that the battle is not to take power by force but to save their own people by winning their hearts and minds. However, problems start to arise and whilst they are treated as heroes wherever they go, the mission is misunderstood by many, including by some of the Twelve themselves. At the end of this time, the Twelve are sent out on their own missionary journeys, but return to adversity.

The third year: Into the Storm

After the political assassination of John the Immerser, beheaded by King Herod Antipas, Jesus begins to warn his disciples of his own coming death. Many people now reject this radical Rabbi as king in the manner he proclaims and the opposition of the religious authorities is growing into a storm. Thus begins what is to be a year of conflict leading up to the final battle, a tumultuous Passover week in Jerusalem.

The Apostles continue to follow he whom they believe to be a true king, as they journey throughout the area of King David's ancient Israel. They travel the length and breadth of their land, homeless, destitute and often hungry, but also moving inexorably on to Jerusalem and the climax of the mission.

1/. Power Declined
2/. Bread and Rations
3/. Total Withdrawal
4/. Face of Stone
5/. Death Foretold
6/. Harbinger
7/. Invasion Force
8/. Triumph Brought Down
9/. The Safe House
10/. Power Displayed
11/. Ruthless Challenge
12/. The Scent of Death

The 'final week': Battle Climax

The Apostles cannot imagine or accept it is their Messiah's last week before his death.

At first, they enter Jerusalem in triumph. Then, they take the temple by storm throwing out all that should not be there. Their Messiah now teaches and heals for all to see and there is open conflict between Jesus and the political and religious elite: the stakes are power or death. Passover, betrayal and crucifixion follow. The disciples go through an emotional wringer of triumph, despair, grief and hope once again.

1/. Triumph or Tears?
2/. Not Fit For Purpose
3/. Tricks, Snares and Woes
4/. Destruction Will Follow
5/. Elijah's Cup
6/. Night Without End
7/. Judgement

King of Heaven and Hell

For six weeks, it is as close to heaven as the Twelve will ever be in this life.

The resurrected Messiah restores his Apostles to faith and hope. The battle has been won and the evidence is there for them to see. The Messiah King has conquered the ultimate enemy; death has been made powerless and he has a new body that will never grow old. He is eternally alive. He leads and teaches them for a further forty days and then gives them their ultimate mission. Because his own nation rejected him, their mission is now to the whole world, to enable all men to break free and defeat the enemy of death. He ascends to His Father, entering heaven as a living man, but they know that one day, that same living man will be back…

Appendices

The First Year: Arise the King

1/. Careful Talk

The dust hung thick and heavy in the air. On this stifling hot summer day, I could taste it with every breath; my eyes itched, my lips and nostrils were encrusted. All day long the legion had marched, trotted and rolled through our town, and every step and hoof beat raised yet more dust to choke us. I hated their dust. They stopped just long enough to drain our spring-water cistern dry before moving on to relieve their garrison at Caesarea. It was as if they bled our land dry.

Mother bustled around the house hanging wet cloths across each window. "They take our grain and expect us to eat the dust of their ten thousand boots instead," she said with much feeling and sneezed behind her veil.

"Why do they have to come through Bethsaida anyway?" my brother seethed.

"Not just our town, James," Father replied. "They will go through every town and village around the lake. It is their grand parade of Roman power, to remind us all we live in the shadow of their eagle."

I took myself away to lay in the darkened inner room, trying to rest before the nights fishing ahead, but sleep would not come. Many thoughts churned through my head; news, speculation, disputed opinions, talk of freedom. The last of the marching boots faded from the street and as the day cooled, so did my temper.

I gave up on sleep and found Father and James tending the vines in the courtyard.

"Father, did you hear the talk at market about the man from the desert," I asked. "They say he is wild in appearance; like one of the Lord God's prophets of old?"

"Yes, I have." He continued to clip away the smaller or malformed bunches, his voice casual, as if my question was the price of fish. "If it is true, he would be the first prophet for hundreds of years."

I pressed on. "Andrew bar Jonas says that he is going to leave Bethsaida to become this man's disciple," I said. "Could a man like this lead us to freedom?"

Father gave the vine his undivided attention. I knew his eyes now struggled but his fingers had the way of many years of practice. "I have listened to a lot of this talk, trying to measure it all in my heart and mind for several days. What freedom can you imagine?"

"Freedom from Rome, of course," said my brother.

"Freedom from taxes for their temples!" I added.

"Hmmm, that would be good." Father moved to another vine. "But would freedom also bring a spiritual awakening in our people?" His eye broke from the vine to penetrate my heart and challenged my thoughts.

"Do you hope for that more than freedom from Rome?" asked James.

"I pray to God for both," replied Father, "freedom to worship and to obey."

"Andrew says this man has a camp on the pools of the Jordan near Jericho, but also retreats to the wilderness," I said.

"I heard the same," said Father. "There will be much speculation at synagogue. I expect there will be some who will go and seek this repentance."

"Wasn't the rebellion of The Maccabeus a spiritual awakening?" asked James. "Then our people shook off the chains of the foreign invaders."

"And our temple was purified from their disgusting rituals," I added, picking up the rake to gather the vine clippings.

"The land was ours for a time, but I would not say this was a time of 'spiritual awakening,'" Father replied, straightening and stretching his back. "The temple was indeed purified from their abominations, but it brought no new direction for the spirits of our people. Nor did it tell us any more than we already knew about the coming of the Messiah."

"You both had many hours with Rabbi Benjamin and Father spent our Sabbath days telling you the many stories of our people," Mother reminded us as she sat with our servant girl, sorting and spinning her wools. "Now you must continue to grow in the Lord's ways and make your way in the world. The men must respect you and you must earn that with fairness and control, in the ways of the law."

I had inherited much of Father's love for our history and the Holy Scriptures and judged this was a moment to venture my question.

"I remember the prophecy that Elijah will precede the Messiah," I said. "These reports of the man from the desert say that he is as Elijah, dressed in animal skin, and with hair and beard that has never been cut. What better time than now for God to show his power than when Rome rules the whole world?"

"The Messiah would free us from the power of Rome," said James. "Our people can be great again, as the days of old."

"James, that may shed a lot of blood," replied Father, pausing from the pruning again to regard us in turn. "However, we should always have faith in God, whichever foreign invader threatens us." He returned to the vine.

"I have also heard that this man performs an immersion in the pools for the forgiveness of sins," I said. "Do the Holy Scriptures speak of a prophet using this sign?"

"Does there need to be such a prophecy, John?" replied Father. "We bathe in the *Mikvah*, to cleanse and prepare ourselves for God's presence before the feast days. What this man offers is cleansing and repentance without the blood sacrifice."

"The Chief Priests will count that as a direct challenge to them," said Mother severely.

"Can there be forgiveness without the shedding of blood?" I asked.

"Of course, blood is to atone for our sins," said Father. "I also heard about his rugged appearance and that his food is the meagre diet the desert offers. It seems that he has spent many years in desert isolation with the Essene cult at Qum'ran, who have turned their back on Jerusalem."

"We are given instructions for Passover and all the festivals in the scriptures though, Father," said James. "So we must attend them. Is this not what the Lord requires?"

"Of course, James, but is it enough to just go to the feast? What else should we do but eat the prescribed food when we are there?"

"We should know these holy days are required by the Lord God," replied James. "And know the reason and time they speak of."

"And also," I added, "that following the rituals is not just with our actions but that our hearts and minds are bought in tune with the Lord's will for our lives and our land."

Father showed us his approval with a generous smile. "Yes indeed, my sons."

"The priests lead us in these feasts, but I have often had to search myself for the deeper meanings that they have not been able to give to me," I said. "What have you experienced at these times, Father?"

Before he could answer, Mother interrupted. "Ah, but now your talk will be deep and meaningful theology. This should be a conversation for you men on the Sabbath day and not now." Her eyes flashed a look of caution that did not match the light tone of her voice.

We all saw it and Father nodded. "Yes, you are right, my dear. A spiritual debate for The Sabbath it should be."

"How are your parents, Deborah?" Mother addressed our servant. "Does your mother recover fully from her illness yet? Today I can look after the meal as it is almost prepared, you should go and attend your family."

Deborah gave her thanks for this kindness and withdrew as Father talked about the vines until the courtyard gate had closed behind her.

"John, you have asked an important question," said Father. "I will now speak about the practice of the temple as I have never done before. The appearance of this man from the desert makes it the time to do this. However, I will not do this at synagogue; only within the walls of our home." He regarded us both. "Do you understand?"

"Is that why Deborah was allowed to go?" said James. "Don't you trust her?"

"Deborah is a good girl, she loves us much as we also love her," Father replied. "It is not a matter of trust. Because she is young and respects us, she may repeat our opinions to her friends. If she passes on what I am about to say, it could be very difficult for us. You must realise that it is dangerous to talk about chief priests and leaders in public if that involves criticism of their actions."

"We could be shunned at synagogue and in the community." My mother's tone was brusque as she tugged at her wool. "And then where would we be? That could ruin the business and everything your father and I have worked for would be gone."

"Your mother fears the worst, but it is right to be cautious," said Father. "Galilee is not so remote from Jerusalem for The Sanhedrin's power to reaches us here, they protect their position and do this in ways that is not always correct. It is a sad part of our history that the prophets we now revere were persecuted by many of the priests of their time."

"The true prophets of the Lord always were," said Mother, tugging at her wool again. "Isaiah was sawn in half, Jeremiah was put down a cistern and even Elijah ran for his life from that wicked Jezebel."

Father paused for a few moments before continuing, his voice as even as ever.

"There are many good priests and there are devout Pharisees in the Sanhedrin who seek God's will in their lives." He regarded us and measured his words with care and purpose. "However, some of the Chief Priests are without Levite birthright and have purchased their position. They make a convenience of Rome to create a smokescreen to hide their own corruption. For many years I have presented my offerings at the temple to obey the God of heaven, but knowing that many of the Priests and the Sanhedrin are using their authority to take money from the people to make themselves rich."

James and I looked at each other with wide eyes and then at Father; we had never heard him talk like this before.

"You mean that when they make us buy their animals and use temple currency, that they are ripping us off?" said James. "I have thought this before but never said it!"

"You use the language of the marketplace, James," Father raised his eyebrows with a wry smile. "But your feelings are correct. We are told our animals are not good enough and forced to buy theirs for the sacrifice and the exchange of money is rigged. The Lord's Temple has become just a common marketplace with the cheating that goes on there."

"Is it just the taking of our money that you think is wrong, Father?" I wanted to use the moment and get to the bottom of his feelings.

"No, that is only a small part of it. What distresses me most is the observances they have invented that are not part of the Law. These petty rules are barriers that prevent our people understanding what their God asks of them. It is a regime to control the masses by the dulling of their senses."

The last vine was clipped and trained; he smiled at Mother. "The Lord will bless us with the fruit of the vine again, my dear. This work has also trained my appetite; can you make use of these vine leaves?"

He looked at me before continuing: "So, John, to return to your question about the prophet from the desert that they call The Immerser. I have respect for the Essenes of Qum'ran because they have separated themselves from all that is wrong in the temple and sought God in poverty and humility. But bear in mind they are not perfect, either: their claim to be 'the true Israel' leads to an unhealthy self-righteousness and there is much danger in that."

2/. Narrow Escape

"John, you are still brooding about the legion." Father soothed me. "Put your hands to work, everyday tasks can be a blessing to bring back normality."

I nodded, picked up a food platter and followed my mother through the courtyard and up the stair. The roof was the only fit place to eat the evening meal, high above the hanging dust, where the evening breeze from the lake would caress our faces. I arranged the cushions, pounding my frustration into each of them.

James joined me to put up the awning; together we angled it over the table, to keep the setting sun out of our eyes. Then it was the ritual of washing our hands and serving our parents with water for theirs. Since we were young, Father had always insisted we did the simple tasks of life, telling us that it would keep us humble. If we had ever complained the work was for the servant, he would dismiss us with a twinkle in his eye, saying that a little work never hurt anyone.

Bethsaida and fishing the lake was my world and, except for the pilgrimages to Jerusalem, all I had ever known. Now in my middle teenage years, I knew my future was opening before me, but the conversation we would have over this evening meal and the events that followed would change me and my world forever.

Father took a deep breath and exhaled long and slowly as he raised his arms. We all followed and paused with faces raised to the heavens and still our mind and body to be in tune with our spirit. This ritual had been a reservoir of peace for me ever since I could remember.

Father spoke in soft reverent tones. He thanked the Lord, his God … for the working day that had been … for the evening to come … for the food before us … for the presence of the Lord as the spiritual food for our hearts … to match the food his world provided. "Amen," we echoed.

We all settled to recline on the soft cushions, Mother arranging her veils for eating.

“Ah, that breeze is indeed blessed,” Father sighed. “As also is this fresh bread.”

“I suppose that we are being subjected to this display of Roman power because The Prefect was forced to back down with his effigies of Caesar,” said my brother with feeling.

“I am sure you are correct, James,” Father replied. “His reputation as a man of cruelty and venality preceded him, but let’s talk of other things: if we allow the legion to spoil our meal and time together, it would only be as to give them a victory.”

He turned to our mother. “You should tell us about your day, my dear. Do you have any news to share?”

“There was other talk that distressed me,” said Mother. “Young Simon bar Mordecai has left home to join the Zealots.”

“Yes, I heard this too,” said Father. “If he believes that joining bandits and ambushing merchants on the road to pay off his family’s debts is easy, he will find it is not so. This brings his parents much grief.”

“He will not be the last,” Mother sighed. “This Roman tax burden creates outlaws from farm boys and he’s now being called ‘Simon the Zealot’.”

“My dear,” replied Father, “I do not think he will easily be radicalised into violent resistance. His parents have always been peaceable and Simon is not the type.”

“Nevertheless, once in the Zealot’s blood-brotherhood he will have no escape,” Mother insisted. “His choice will be between their capture and Rome’s.”

A melancholy fell over our evening meal as I heard the message my parents were sending to my brother and I. I knew Simon well. He was my own age and as boys, we had been together in classes with the Rabbi, although he had been an irregular student. His family were honest and hardworking, but soft negotiators, just not astute enough and easily dominated by the stewards of their landlord, who then purchased their crops at low price.

"Father, you said we need to see this man of the desert and hear his words," I said with a little caution. "The cult at Qum'ran has never raised an army, and I would like to go with Andrew bar Jonas to see this prophet and perhaps to be his disciple for a time."

I saw Mother's eye look up and it was a while before Father replied. "Your mother and I have seen many false Messiahs come and go during our lives."

"Yes, indeed," Mother agreed. "Those fakes created a temporary noise and distraction; they were freedom fighters to some and terrorists to the Romans, who ruthlessly snuffed out both them and their followers."

"Andrew bar Jonas has grown up with a good family around him," said Father. "A family of uncomplicated people, who have given him a strong sense of right and wrong."

"Yes, a good family," said Mother. "But be aware that his decisions will be guided by his instincts and feelings, without the need to think about what confronts him."

"I would also like to hear this 'Immerser', as they call him, but his position is dangerous now he has criticised the King's affairs," said Father. "But he has chosen his place well, this pool of the Jordan is on the route of everyone passing between Galilee and Judea at the southern end of Antipas' kingdom, so he could flee back to Qum'ran or further if he needed to."

We finished the meal; I was sure that Father and Mother were leaving us with a thoughtful silence. As Father rose from the table, we followed and he raised his voice to make a final statement.

"Yes, we yearn for freedom and for the Messiah to come and set us free. My heart rises with hope of a spiritual revival sent by God, but not a waste of life and spilled blood. Still, my mind teaches me to be cautious and to put these things to the test. This man has shown no inclination towards armed rebellion and we can discuss a way for you to seek him, but the journey from Galilee down the Jordan will be no small thing. Remember there will be frontiers to cross. Your brother and I will visit whilst you are there to see for ourselves."

He picked up two platters and gave one to each of us. "That is for tomorrow, but tonight it is time for you, James and John, to be about our business. It will not be good if the men are kept waiting for you. Keep your minds on the fishing tonight, there will be other times for us to talk of prophets and of the Messiah." He embraced us both. "May God be with you this night and give you success, remember Him and thank Him for whatever catch you have, great or small."

"Take the rest of the loaf and share it with the men," Mother told us. "Always remember they get only the daily ration and this will bind their loyalty to you." We embraced Mother with a goodnight and walked out into the warm evening with Father's last instructions in our ears.

* * * *

"You were smooth there!" exclaimed James as we walked through the darkened streets. "However, will Mother let her favourite son go away on his own adventure?" His teeth flashed in the gathering evening as he grinned at me.

"Because she has you, my big brother," I gave him a shove, "lined up to run the business and care for her and Father as their hair goes grey. You've already shown them you're capable in matters of business and of social standing and local politics. A son to be proud of!"

"Oh, you mean I'll stay at home and catch the fish, whilst you travel the world in search of spiritual enlightenment?" he said with another mischievous grin. "The neighbours say you are clever and articulate enough to be a merchant, but are you really a hard commercial animal?" He mimicked the action of counting through a moneybag, but I didn't push him again, I just smiled.

We both knew that I was in some ways our mother's favourite, but it did not cause problems between us. I was very aware of her ambitions for me and even though he would never admit it, James was probably glad that it was not him after all!

"Don't you dream of freedom for our people and our land?" I asked him. "Haven't you thought about this prophet and all those prophets of old confronting the evils of their time?"

"Well, let us first take Father's advice and see if this desert man is indeed a prophet."

"Yes, but you know what I mean," I replied. "I know you'll tell me I'm too young to be a philosopher, but there are so many moral and material wrongs in our world and they irk me."

"I don't dispute it!" said James. "But this man of God will need to get rid of Rome and then their puppet rulers, because those Herod brothers would apply the same tax burden if they could. Then this man will need to sort out the temple grandees, as Father told us. So, tell me young philosopher, which of the three will he do first?" James gave me Father's smile and eye twinkle, which he had perfected after much practice; I scowled back at him in exasperation.

"I don't need to think very far to know that the Herods may just tear themselves apart with this adultery scandal anyway. Either Philip or Antipas could fall, as their outrageous brother already has!"

Now we were approaching the boats and hired men, which forced our discussion to close.

"Greetings, Caleb!" James hailed our foreman. "The Lord be with you!"

"And also with you, young master," came the chorus of reply.

I broke pieces of the loaf amongst them and James added a little oil, waving away the men's gratitude and talking of the nights fishing. Suddenly, one of them said, "Legionaries! Coming over the bank."

"Don't turn or look," James said immediately. "Launch the boats or they will take the bread!"

The rough accent of a Syrian auxiliary hailed us to hold and stay.

"We didn't hear," said James. "Face the lake; push the boats out."

"Don't hurry now," said Caleb. "Just act natural, push and jump in."

"Kneel and paddle," James' voice came cool and calm. "Don't sit and row or you will have to turn to face them, they're not taking any bread from us!"

"I know you Judah-boys 'eard me," the rough voice called after us.

"A Psalm to the Lord!" Caleb called out, and broke gustily into the chant for all to follow.

"You wait 'til I catch you eating more than your daily ration!" Legionaries' sandals crunched on the gravel beach behind us.

"Now the sails," said James, "lots of heaving noises now!"

We melted into the dusk, still triumphantly chewing our bread.

3/. Prophet or Messiah or Fake?

"Repent! Come and be clean in God's sight! Repent and make good!" The prophet stood above his pool and hailed the people. "Bring the sacrifice of your contrite heart. Be clean before God within, as you are cleansed without."

Andrew and I watched our Rabbi, his skin reddened by the sun, the mass of uncut hair and beard and the animal skin that hung from his gaunt body. Day after day, the pilgrims had massed around us, constantly coming and going. It was an amazing sight for two country boys from Galilee.

We had been here for several weeks and still they came from towns and villages I had never heard of. Some sat on surrounding places in watchful indecision; others were in the water asking for the attention of the prophet. In the background, both the guard of Herod Antipas and the Roman Cohorts came and went at regular intervals to report on this mass movement of the people and their wild prophet.

In these weeks of my discipleship, I had learned that The Immerser never spoke to a group but to each individual in turn, telling them that walking away from their sins was not enough; their God required their life to be positive, correct and good. It was always the same script without deviation, I felt as if it had seeped into my soul. Then he would hold them in the ritual immersion for a few moments, and raise them again. Many were visibly moved and sometimes it required two of us to haul an emotional man to the safety of the bank as they called their praises to the God of heaven.

And so it had continued, hour after hour as day followed day under the heat of the sun. We took it in turns to rest but I had become amazed at the unrelenting intensity of The Immerser and wondered that it did not seem to tire him.

Then the day came when Father and James arrived and took a discrete position a little away from the pool. My heart was singing as I saw them; my discipleship was the adventure of my young life, but I had missed home, its comforts and its familiarities. I knew Father would want my report on this wild prophet, to judge if he was just another revolutionary or pseudo-prophet claiming an anointing from God.

The sun had reached its zenith, but still people continued to arrive in the heat of the day and now I saw significant new visitors. I caught Andrew's attention and nodded towards a large group of men in fine robes with servants and pack animals, descending towards our pool.

"Men of the Sanhedrin," I said.

Andrew returned my look with a raised brow and nod. "One look tells me they are both Pharisees and of the Sadducees. They travel together in rivalry to keep an eye on each other," he ended with a wry smile.

I scowled at him in warning to keep his opinions to himself in public as these men made their way straight towards the centre of activity, as those with authority do when they expect others to make way. No more new people came to the water's edge to ask for the immersion.

Andrew and I now communicated only with our expressions. We stood our ground and moved closer to our Rabbi, who remained waist-deep as he went on relentlessly with his task. I kept one eye to the men of the Sanhedrin, who sat in their rival groups and looked down their noses at us, discussing matters between them.

Andrew and I again exchanged glances with the other disciples.

"The challenge must come soon," I said.

"He is ignoring them," said Andrew under his breath. "As if their authority was of no consequence to him."

"Then we do the same." I mouthed back and uttered a silent prayer for my Rabbi; he was about to face an inquisition from the rulers of Jerusalem.

Two men sitting front and central now stood. I knew them by sight and reputation: Shlomo bar Abiram, a Pharisee, and Uri bar Sethur, a Sadducee and one of the High Priests.

The interrogation began, as Shlomo spoke with arrogant manners, "You there, who do you say you are?"

The Immerser straightened and with a flick of his hand dismissed his disciples from the pool; he was going to make his stand alone. Andrew and

I moved up to where Father was and at that moment I was so glad he was there.

The Immerser waded out into the shallows to face his examiners; his gaze scanned across them all.

"I am not the Messiah!" He spoke loud enough to make sure that all people would hear him. I watched the effect as it rippled through both the people and the inquisitors.

"This was the opposite situation for which they came prepared for," Father told us. "If The Immerser had claimed to be a prophet or Messiah, they would have prepared plenty of questions to cross-examine him and discredit him before the people."

I could see it was true, these men of the Sanhedrin were now disconcerted that the ragged peasant before them seemed to have read their minds. The directness of the answer and the instant denial had surprised them.

Two of the priests prodded with the next questions: "Who are you, then? Are you Elijah?"

"I am not!"

My Rabbi continued to stand unmoved in the faces of the men of the Sanhedrin.

I felt the excitement rise in me; I had not seen this before. The Immerser had only shown himself to be a humble ascetic, the servant of God dealing with holiness and peoples sins. Now he stood like a champion, unbending in the face of pressure from the highest authority.

Andrew took a deep breath. "The tables are turning, look: it is now the men of the Sanhedrin who shuffle awkwardly under the pressure."

"The situation rebounds onto them," agreed James. "These men are accustomed to getting all the information they want with one question instead of being faced down. The question now is how are they going to escape with their authority intact before the people?"

I looked at my father. His expression was intense, he was taking it all in, but saying nothing.

Seeing that confrontation was getting them nowhere, one of the council then showed good presence of mind and broke the deadlock with a more accommodating voice. "Then tell us who you are. We have to take an answer back to those who sent us. What do you say about yourself?"

The Immerser's gaze scanned across his interrogators again; the people stood motionless, everyone waited for the answer. The moment seemed to me like an age of emptiness.

When he spoke, it was as a proclamation: "I am 'the voice of someone shouting in the desert: Make a straight path for the Lord to travel!'"

"He quotes from Isaiah the prophet," said Father, breaking his silence. "He is claiming that this prophecy becomes true in him, that he is the fulfilment."

We all nodded and craned our heads forward to see what would happen next.

The parties of the Sanhedrin had closed into two huddles, each discussing this last statement amongst them. The Immerser remained in the shallows, unmoved by the questions or the relentless sun on his head and body. The huddles opened again and Uri the Priest took a step forward; I fancied that he needed to rescue his personal authority.

"If you are not the Messiah nor Elijah nor the Prophet, why do you do this immersion in water for repentance from sins?"

Now The Immerser waded from the pool, bent to seize a branch that lay there, and stood eyeball to eyeball with Uri and Shlomo. "You brood of vipers! Who warned you to flee from the coming wrath? Produce fruit in keeping with repentance." The branch circled through the air. "The axe is already at the root of the trees and every tree that does not produce good fruit will be cut down and thrown into the fire!"

The Immerser stared into the eyes of his inquisitors, his voice hissing across the void between them. "I immerse the people with water, but there is a man you do not know. He will immerse his people with the Holy Spirit and with fire. I have already told you, I am only the preparation; I am not good enough even to untie his sandals."

They stood face to face for a few moments more before the inquisitors looked at each other and withdrew.

The tension eased and a hubbub of excited conversations broke the silence around the pool.

James exhaled between his teeth. "I'd say that was a group decision that it was time to make their escape."

"They certainly have enough to tell their colleagues in Jerusalem," said Andrew with his wistful grin.

It was now late in the day and we watched as The Immerser picked up a skin of water and headed out towards the east followed by his other disciples.

"He needs solitude now," said Father.

We unloaded the pack animal, fetched water, struck a fire and, as we sat in the gathering dusk, discussed the wild prophet and the confrontation we had witnessed.

Andrew was in raptures. "He was fearless in front of them, with his mind set on his mission and on the purpose of God."

"What did you think of The Immerser, Father?" asked James. "Were you impressed by him and how he spoke to those from the Sanhedrin?"

"Who could fail to be impressed by such strength of purpose and directness of answer?" replied Father. "I was very impressed; I have never seen the like. Shlomo and Uri are not men to be trifled with."

"Was he what you imagined one of the prophets of old to be like?" I asked.

"Yes, but not only that," replied Father. "If he had wanted to take a position of authority in Jerusalem, this was his opportunity to find favour with our political and religious leaders. They in turn would have been pleased to recruit him into their ranks, both for credibility with the people and to contain and control his potential threat."

"Yes," said James, sudden realization in his voice, "it was shrewd politics on their part, but it came undone."

Father nodded. "Yes, The Immerser turned them down and instead he showed us all a single-minded purpose of knowing who he is and who he is not. I am willing to accept that this is a prophet sent from God, and yet this still leaves so many questions in my mind unanswered."

We all looked at Father and waited, respectful of the grey hairs on his head and the wisdom that he could impart.

"Let us think through what we heard. Firstly, he has stated that he is neither the Messiah, nor Elijah, nor the Prophet and yet he claims to be preparing a pathway for the Lord. Secondly, he claims to fulfil the words of Isaiah, but I cannot yet work out how this fits with other writings of the prophets." He looked at us all from under his raised and cautious brow, "For we must consider them all. After four hundred years of prophetic silence from the Lord, why has this man come now, at this point in our history?"

We were all bursting with our questions.

"And what about this other man who is already among us and so much greater than him?" asked James.

"Well, he told those from Jerusalem to their face," said Andrew. "They don't know the greater man who will follow."

"So this greater man will not come from among the Pharisees or Sadducees or any of the Levites," I said. "He will be like The Immerser and arise out of a nowhere, but not from Jerusalem."

"No wonder they did not ask any more questions after a rebuke like that!" said James.

"And thirdly," the look on Father's face demanded our respect and we all lowered ours, conscious that our impulsive excitement had not been respectful. "Thirdly, the biggest question in my mind is about the greater man to follow. What sort of man can possess the Holy Spirit in such a manner that he can impart it and indeed immerse people in the Spirit himself? Surely such an anointing could only be given by The Anointed One himself? That is such an unfathomable that I cannot begin to understand it!"

"What will the men of Sanhedrin think of this?" asked James.

"They will spend all night preparing their interrogation to continue tomorrow," said Father.

4/. Speak Truth to Power

"Repent! Repent or face the wrath of God!" The Immerser had arrived with the dawn and stood, statuesque on a tall rock, against a crimson-flecked sky. He appeared to me as much beast as man, with the desert wind flapping the skin against him, as hair and beard streamed across his face. People rolled out of their blankets and burst from their tents with awkward haste to heed his message.

"Men of Judea, ask yourselves: can God favour and protect the blessed land He gave our forefathers!? I tell you He cannot! The King takes his brother's wife in adultery, as she in turn leads him astray from the Law of God!"

I heard us all draw sharp, involuntary breath. "The Immerser has decided," Father said in low voice, "that having rejected a place in Jerusalem, his message will still go there by preaching his sermon to these Pharisees and Sadducees."

"The King's sin pollutes the land and the blessed land will spew him out!" Even at a distance, I could see The Immerser's eyes blaze as his sermon thundered onwards. He was leaving the people in no doubt of what their God thought of the moral corruption at the head of our nation. I tore my gaze from my Rabbi to watch the people as they began to stand and hail his message.

The captain of Antipas' Guard assembled his men with noisy show of force, but faced with the growing fervour of the crowds, seemed indecisive of what to do next. Meanwhile, the Roman cohort commenced a dusty circumnavigation of the area.

The Immerser was oblivious. "And what of you, men of the Sanhedrin? Do you not read the scrolls of the law that tell us of the cost of sexual impropriety at the heart of God's people? Was not the battle at Ai lost for the presence of one single adulterous idol?"

"And they thought they could stand at a safe distance!" gasped James.

"Men of the Sanhedrin," The Immerser projected himself straight at them. "Your sins will find you out. If you do not care for yourselves, should you not care for the souls of these Herod brothers? These two who were once three, the first of which has already had his grievous power removed by Rome and whose father died in the grotesqueness of his piles of sin! Why do you not condemn the King's sin and save his soul?"

Even at a distance, I could see that those from Jerusalem were reeling from this frontal assault on their authority. They clambered to their feet and left in haste. Catcalls from the crowd followed them.

"They are shamed in front of the people!" said Father.

"They have more than they bargained for to report back to their colleagues in Jerusalem," said Andrew.

Father looked just as grim and my thoughts turned back to my Rabbi as his message rumbled on. "Father, The Immerser will not be allowed to live long after such a sermon." The words caught in my throat. "Surely he has signed his own death warrant by denouncing both the King and the temple establishment!"

"His only chance now must be to gather the people as an army and march on Jerusalem," said my brother.

"Then why didn't he arrest those from Jerusalem to prevent them reporting back?" I asked. "The people would have followed his call!"

"They know how some of those men lord it over them," said Andrew.

Father held up his hands for a pause. "I agree it might seem like that from a normal man's perspective, but if The Immerser is a true prophet of God, he is not a normal man. Remember the ancient prophets. None of them ever raised an army, none of them ever needed an army; they had God on their side, and that for them was enough. No, this man will not be interested in the politics or the power of men."

"And this is how he has come to 'prepare the way'?"

"I believe you are correct, James. The Immerser has come to prepare the way for the greater man of God who follows. He already knows he must become less important whilst the greater man rises to even greater fame. If the King or the Sanhedrin imprison him or even kill him, he will not be concerned as long as he has completed the mission for which God sent him." Father's hand again halted our further questions. When he continued, I heard darkness in his voice. "All this has the marks of a political earthquake in our land, and I do not see how that can happen without the iron fist of Rome descending upon us all. If the Herods become inconvenient and ineffective, then Rome will impose direct and brutal rule in Galilee, as they have in Judea."

"So you do not think The Immerser will rise against Rome, sir?" asked Andrew.

"That remains to be seen," Father replied. "For now he has turned his face only towards the King and the Sanhedrin, for whom he is an immediate and unpredictable threat."

"Then they must hope that Rome will remove him?"

"So, not to rise against Rome would be the smart move?"

"Peaceful resistance is possible," said Father. "We have seen it."

"Please explain," I requested.

"Was not the whole nation harnessed together into protest when The Prefect hoisted his effigies of Caesar?"

"Yes, the King, the Sanhedrin, and down to the lowest beggar!" we agreed.

"The Sanhedrin acted well to lead the people in protest, but it also served them well," said Father. "The moral high ground of God and nation is a good distraction from the profiteering many of them practise in the temple."

"Whereas this sermon of The Immerser threatens to expose what they do not want revealed," said my brother.

"Yes, that is the threat the Sanhedrin will see," Father concluded.

The echoes of the sermon were now dying away; I watched the zealous stampede of pilgrims into the water to proclaim repentance for their own sins and to demand The Immerser's attention.

Andrew and I rose to help our comrades to calm the melee and keep order, but James caught my attention and nodded to a group of young men across the pool. "Look, there, do you see Simon bar Mordecai?"

"He must be with a group sent by the Zealots," said Father. "They will want to use The Immerser as a recruiting sergeant for their movement."

"*They'll* tell him to march on Jerusalem!" said Andrew.

"John." Father turned to me. "I want you to make your way around the pool to see if you can greet Simon; show him acceptance and a way back if he needs it in future."

I climbed over the rocks and through the shallows, then out and around the rear of Simon's group. I wanted to get within speaking distance before I was recognised, but he was alert and saw me when I was still thirty paces away. I saw him speak to his comrades in haste and they moved away. I knew that it would be wrong to follow; if the others in Simon's band reported back that he was a hazard to their security and secrecy, then it could be disastrous for him. I joined The Immerser and the others in the pool, calling for repentance and order, so that Simon would see me there with the wild prophet.

Later as the crowds eased, I returned to Father and James. I was still bursting to continue discussing the effect of the Immerser's sermon. "Father, what will happen now? The Immerser must have some plan after preaching such a sermon? He has lighted a fire amongst the people; they will expect more."

"Your brother has asked me the same and my reply is that we can but wait and see where this fire will burn. As I have said, I have many fears. I do not want to miss a great spiritual revival, but I do not want you to be in a place where you are seen to be fanning the flames of political turmoil."

"So I must leave my place with The Immerser?"

"You must be careful. Whilst he remains the humble ascetic it is not dangerous, as long as you realise that the King's Guards will look for a moment to swoop at a time when the crowds do not protect him."

"And if he moves on to Jerusalem?"

"Then you need to be invisible, as just another young man amongst the crowds."

I nodded my understanding.

"I do not want to talk of this anymore at this time." Father looked at us both. "Because I have also come here to seek refreshing for my soul, as the commandments tell me to."

"Here rather than Jerusalem?" asked James.

Father indicated the crowds around the pool. "I do not want to be caught up in an emotional over-reaction, but after the people have eased I will ask to be immersed in repentance of my sins."

We must have looked shocked; I could see it reflected in Father's face. After a moment, James said, "Father, you are a good man, and you have always taught us what is right, why then…?" His voice trailed away, his question unfinished.

"Why do I need to repent of my sins? When I already do this at the temple?" Father finished the question for him. "Are you worried that I have some large and secret sin that you do not know of? No, I do not believe I do. I have always been faithful to your mother and have tried to live a good and peaceful life. But do you think I claim to be without sin? To be perfect in God's sight as he demanded of Abraham?" His eyebrows lifted as he looked at us and I pondered my own life in the silence. "Do we not all sometimes have bad thoughts for our fellow man and even in our own family quarrels? Have we always made sure that we have done all the good we can whenever we have a chance to help our neighbour? These are the reasons that I will ask to be immersed in this pool."

I looked at him and realised I saw my father in new light as emotion swelled within me. Today I would also set aside my desires of freedom and the politics that controlled our nation. I would descend to The Immerser's pool, not as his disciple but to recognise and repent of my sins and seek my God's blessings anew. As Father led us in prayer, I knew we would all do this. I moved away into my own space, finding my own deep places of personal stillness. In those moments, I found much of what I had been seeking when Andrew and I had begun our pilgrimage, and it seemed to me like a vital relief from the high drama of these days, as if the dust had settled in my soul.

5/. The Anointed One

"Look." Andrew pointed. "Who is that?"

The gaunt figure had been working in his usual unhurried but relentless manner as the pilgrims clamoured around him, but now The Immerser had stopped.

I realized that his mood had changed as he waded to face a lone man on the bank. The man who stood there seemed to hold his complete attention and yet he looked very ordinary. In fact he looked like we did, in typical Galilean dress, except poorer. We exchanged quizzical glances with each other and looked on.

"He gave no such attention to those of the Sanhedrin," said James.

"Quiet now," said Father. "Let's see if we can hear what is said."

Every breath was silent as we strained to try and catch the words. There was a discussion about the repentance. The Immerser protested he was not worthy and that he was the one that needed the immersion. The newcomer was insistent he needed this done because God required it and they both waded out into the pool.

"Whoever this man is," said my brother, "he is being given privilege over the masses of pilgrims."

The Immerser lowered the man under the water, paused as if in prayer and then, as he raised him again, it happened: it seemed to me that the sunlight itself had changed.

I was looking at a vision of moving light; it was descending like the beating of wings. I was sure that something about men in the pool seemed to glow even in the bright sunlight. Then I heard the voice, as it rolled all around us, like the whisper of distant thunder that comes floating through the air from far away. "This is my son," it seemed to say. "Listen to him."

I collapsed in a bemused state. I was aware the others around me were the same; was this an earthquake, or something fallen from the heavens? I had no breath in me.

The Immerser remained in the pool with his hands upon the man and then he raised his voice in a proclamation that seemed to echo off the sky. "Behold! The Lamb of God who takes away the sin of the world! I have prepared the way, I came immersing with water so that he could be revealed. This is he who immerses with the Holy Spirit; this is the Son of God!"

"The Son of God!"

"The Son of God?"

The Son of God. The words seemed to echo round and round the pool.

We were statues, boggle-eyed and jaws a-hanging. I felt breathless and weak and groped across to hold James' arm, but he looked as I felt and offered little comfort. Andrew in turn held onto me. Then Father lay reassuring, albeit quivering, hands upon us each in turn.

As my breath returned, I gulped some air and coughed. My gaze scanned across the pool, where many heads were starting to raise from the ground to take in what The Immerser had just said. But if we were hoping for anything more from the newly proclaimed 'Son of God', we were to be disappointed. The man turned and waded out of the pool; his face seemed to be set as stone, like a man with a great task to do and who must concentrate all his determination. Walking straight through the surrounding crowd, as the apparition of the Spirit that had settled upon him seemed to drive him onwards, he went east towards the barren hills of Peraea.

I watched as his image grew smaller and then disappeared in the shimmering heat; I felt the tension ease. For some time nobody moved, then the dispute erupted around the pool.

"To be equal with God himself?"

"The worst of blasphemies!"

"Worthy of death!"

"The Immerser's claim is incredible!"

"How can it be true?"

"It cannot be true!"

For hours the disputes continued, men in groups talking at each other with their arms in air, until dusk fell and exhaustion claimed them.

For most of that night, I lay and watched the canopy of stars above me. The moon made its path across the sky during the hours of my vigil. My eyes tracked the shooting stars and the vision of light played back in my mind over and over. I prayed and tried to reach my God. Desires and expectations enticed me. Power and freedom beckoned me. My father's words and wisdom held me close. What would now happen to my people? What was I getting myself into? I glowed inside with desires of freedom and enlightenment, but my guts churned with fears of upheavals and rebellion. My teenage life in Bethsaida seemed a world away, yet these were the same stars above me as on those nights of fishing.

* * * *

The next day, Father was withdrawn, quiet and thoughtful, whilst James, Andrew and I discussed the events of the last two days over and over again.

James approached him. "I know there is much to think about, Father, but what are you most concerned about?"

"We can do little about revolutions and conflicts, except to pray and prepare," he said. "It is the people that we can help that concern me now."

"Are you thinking about Simon bar Mordecai being among the Zealots?" I asked.

"Yes, I am concerned for him, but we cannot help him now. He will go back to whichever Zealot hideout he was in. We must pray that we will meet again, perhaps in Jerusalem, perhaps at Passover."

"That would be almost a miracle in itself," said James. "To find him amongst millions would be amazing."

"I agree," said Father. "That's why we must pray that God will grant this and also that we may be ready to make contact in the most casual way possible."

"You have other thoughts, Father?" I asked.

"Yes, I have been going back through my memories." He paced another circle. "I have memories of stories from many years ago." He was shaking his head, as if in wonderment. "I was just a boy, too young to ask many questions, only to listen to the talk after synagogue. The stories concerned two women, who told that they had had visitations from angels regarding the children they would bear, both boys that would do great deeds in Israel. Many wondered at these stories, some scoffed at the stories, others said we needed men of God not babies." Father's brow was still furrowed as he ploughed through his field of memories. He paced in slow circles.

"Were the great deeds known in these stories?" I asked.

"No, not the deeds, just the rising and falling of many in Israel," Father replied. "But the circumstances were in themselves miraculous. One woman was already old, beyond childbearing, her husband was a priest and was struck dumb at his time of service in the temple, yet she bore him a boy-child, and … and the woman said that the angel told that her child would walk in the spirit of Elijah."

"And the other?" we all asked, hungry for the rest.

"The other was not born in Galilee. The family had to go away to register for taxes, and afterwards disappeared. Stories that came back from Bethlehem of Judea told of more visitations from angels and Persian Magi who read the signs of the heavens and came to anoint a new king. Then old Herod sent his guard to murder every baby boy in Bethlehem, a slaughter to ensure he had no rival."

Father lapsed into silence again; we left him alone to ponder anew and returned to packing the camp.

I tried to take in all he had said. I knew there was more to come; with the packing done, we waited in respectful but yearning silence.

After some time, he walked back to us. "Do you remember that evening on our roof, when we discussed this prophet of the immersion and also that Elijah must come again before the Messiah?"

"Of course, Father," said James. "We know the scriptures make that clear."

"What are you thinking, Father?" I asked.

"Tell us, please," said Andrew.

"Let us think what the scriptures say about Elijah." He fired a question: "Who was his enemy at that time?"

"King Ahab, who led Israel astray to the worship of the Baal idols," said James. "And his manipulative Queen, who threatened Elijah's life."

"Correct," replied Father. "And yesterday what did we hear The Immerser say in his sermon on the moral state of our nation?"

"He denounced Antipas as an immoral king with a bad wife and that they were leading Israel astray!"

The conclusion of my brother's statement struck home and we all spoke together.

"The Immerser is Elijah?"

"But he denied that to the leaders and in front of all the people!"

"Surely he could not speak such a lie and be a true man of God!?"

"No, indeed," said Father. "I do not believe he lied. He is not literally Elijah, but he is a kind of Elijah. He is, perhaps, a prophet in the spirit of Elijah, as the angel visitation to his mother foretold!"

"So the man he anointed as the 'Son of God' *is the Messiah!?*"

"Perhaps a prophet, perhaps the Messiah, perhaps a madman," said Father in a slow and even voice. "I hope you remember what I said about keeping opinions within the walls of our home and always to couch your words with care when in public."

We three nodded our obedience.

"You are still cautious, Father?"

He paced around in a yet wider circle. "Do you recall what I said, in our discussion at the end of my first day here? What was the biggest question in my mind?"

"It was about what The Immerser said about the greater man to follow?" inquired James.

"About what sort of man could impart the Holy Spirit in such a way as to be able to immerse people," I agreed.

"And yet, we all saw and heard the apparition," said Andrew.

"Indeed, and from the proclamation of that man as the 'Son of God' today," said Father. "I believe this question now has two possible answers."

We waited. He paced.

"The Holy Spirit is of God himself, therefore an immersion of the Spirit, and the divine fire could not come from a mere man, it would have to be done by a 'Son of God.'"

"But Father, that would be..."

"I know! Blasphemy! The same as spoken by The Immerser. Worthy of death, in just the speaking of it! Sin unto damnation, in the very thought, if it were wrong!"

"Then how can it be?"

"He is a man, and yet he would have to be more than a mere man."

"At the same time?"

"Is that possible?"

"No, not unless he is of God, and then all things are possible. Who are we as mere men to put the limitations of our own understanding on the God of ages?"

"Sir," asked Andrew, "what is the other possible answer?"

Father wagged his finger and shook his head at no one in particular, as he paced a yet wider circle. I held my breath watching the darkness of consternation in his face. "The other possibility is that this is the cleverest and most damnable conspiracy imaginable!"

6/. Desert Power Struggle

Whispered talk of the Messiah hummed among the crowds, but no one wanted to consider the blasphemy. The feeling of a growing revolution unsettled me, and some talked of an uprising against Rome, as Father had feared. In recent weeks, The Immerser had moved north up to Jordan and with Herod Antipas' territory of Peraea on the east bank, the only direction of escape would be west into Samaria, but going there was almost unthinkable. I was startled at The Immerser's fearlessness, or was he simply naive of the danger he was in?

Both Rome and Antipas' soldiers were ever present, but they stayed on the edges. It was clear to me that their orders were surveillance rather than confrontation. There was one frightening moment when some of Antipas' Guard surrounded The Immerser, but they too were searching for their own righteousness before God. He looked them in the eye and told them their job was to protect the weak, and not to use their position to threaten and extort.

In the weeks since those epic events during the visit of my father and brother, our lives had returned to the way of the humble ascetic. I revelled in the feeling that I was serving my people, a joy in my spirit. Hours of prayer under the stars became my source of peace and sustained me.

Andrew and I, with other disciples, Joash, Seth and Yossi, were now in the pool working alongside our teacher. The multitudes of pilgrims continued to come to us from all over the Judean countryside and, now we were closer to Galilee, from there as well. I kept a constant watch for Simon or indeed any new groups of young men, but none had appeared.

Then, one morning in the middle of our work, I stopped, aware that our teacher had moved away. I exchanged quizzical glances with Andrew and we followed as he waded out of the water and walked to the top of the bank by the pool.

We followed his stare into the shimmering haze; a figure began to appear. I knew it had to be the 'Son of God'. Some spiritual bond linked these two men. The figure came towards us, walking with unsteady steps. As he came close, I could see the man looked pale, thin and frail, and yet his expression was not haggard. His face was calm, peaceful, and even, yes, even triumphant.

The Immerser spoke quietly. "Behold, the lamb of God who takes away the sins of the world..."

I now saw Andrew's instincts come to the fore as he said, "So must I follow him now?"

My face must have registered the same question, yet unspoken.

Our teacher looked at us both and nodded his shaggy head, with all seriousness. "Go, and follow so closely that you are covered by the dust of his sandals," he replied, as if it was a statement of fact.

We embraced the wild prophet, kissed his forehead, my eyes wet from emotion, and exchanged man-hugs with Joash, Yossi and Seth. Then, collecting our few possessions, we walked after the man from the desert, following at a distance as he headed north up the Jordan valley.

"He's going towards Galilee!" said Andrew.

"He's gaunter than The Immerser. When did he last eat, I wonder?"

Andrew nodded. "We should offer him something. Two days' march is too much in his state. His need is great and we can last until we get home."

"Have you seen we are being followed?" I told him. "Two of Herod's men were sent after us. Look to your right, but don't make it obvious."

"What do they want!?"

"Their captain figured out this is the one anointed by The Immerser, to be his successor."

Then, for the first time, the man seemed to know that we were walking after him and spoke. "What are you looking for?" His voice was a croak through cracked lips.

I thought it a strange statement at first. I would have expected, 'why are you following me?' but then I reflected, we were indeed looking for something: for a Messiah.

"Sir," answered Andrew. "We would like to know, where are you staying?"

"Come and see," the man replied, so we walked closer and offered him some dried figs and dates. "You are starving, Rabbi." Andrew stated the obvious. "I fear your stomach cannot take much, so we will walk with you."

He was detached, as if in a trance, but thanked us. He ate slowly and in silence, chewing out every morsel of goodness, and sipped on water from our skin.

"I believe we saw you at The Immerser's pool some weeks ago, Rabbi?" Andrew ventured.

"Forty days and forty nights," was the reply, before returning to his semi-trance.

I stared at Andrew; the symbolism of what he had just said was not lost on either of us. I mouthed to Andrew, "Forty days and forty nights! A new Moses?"

In reply, Andrew wrinkled his face in puzzlement.

After hours of slow progress, we came to a village not far from the lake and the man came to the house of a relative, who took us in. One guard stayed on surveillance whilst the other went on, presumably to find an inn.

Inside, as we sat down, I screwed up my courage to ask a question. "Rabbi, in the wilderness, were you alone all of that time?"

It took him a few minutes to reply, still the croaked whisper. "Not all the time. I had a visitor, a powerful and important person."

"What did you do together?" Andrew asked.

After another long pause, the answer came. "He offered me satisfaction for my hunger, but really it was for my greed. He offered me status and celebrity. And finally he offered me power." He gesticulated with a sweep of his arm. "Over all the earth."

I felt dumbfounded, but wonderment still drove my next question. "What did you say?"

"I told him it was not his to offer in the first place!"

"Tell us more." I pleaded. So, he did: he told us about his battles with an angel, a fallen angel, called Lucifer.

He spoke like no one else I had ever met before; I was captivated and drained of emotion. Andrew sat shaking his head.

Another question burned within me. "Did we see you anointed with the Spirit of God?"

"It was He that drove me into the desert."

"Are you now … now filled with the Spirit to anoint others?" I watched his eyes in the long pause; they were distant, perhaps towards the future.

"After my battles, I am now in the power of the Spirit. And yet, I am empty, unfulfilled." The man then excused himself, put his head on the floor, and slept.

Our host came with blankets and put a cushion under his head. We learned that the man was Jesus bar Joseph, a carpenter from Nazareth.

"Nazareth, that place of itinerant *tektons* and no synagogue?" said Andrew with lack of subtlety.

"I know the work there will have dried up since Herod Antipas took his court away from Sepphoris," I said to our host. "Will this man return to his wife and family in Nazareth?"

"No," our host told us, "this man has never married."

Andrew and I looked at each other. "The only unmarried man of his age I know is the simpleton of the marketplace who picks up overripe and discarded fruit," I said.

"His life has been one long desert!" said Andrew.

"We need to get home and he is too weak to make that distance."

"We could come back with a boat."

"That would also give Antipas' men the slip!"

* * * *

The next morning we rose with the sun and thanked our host for his hospitality. The cool air caressed the wisps of beard on my face as we marched at a breathless pace, yearning to see our families, our news burning within us.

"I left home expecting an experience of meditation and reflection, prayer and solitude, locusts and honey," I said. "I have loved those times, but my overwhelming memory is of the power, the politics and the apparition of the spirit."

"We heard nothing of Rome or taxes for the temples of their gods," said Andrew. "At least the legions don't march this way as they hunt the Zealots," he added.

"Yesterday we found ourselves following a man of pure wilderness experience, who seldom speaks," I continued. "I need to reconnect myself with our times of solitude, so I can connect with this man."

Andrew just looked overwhelmed. "I need to get home," he said.

"So do I, but not to rejoin normal life and lose what I have gained. I want to touch the inner power that enables a man to survive that long in a spiritual and physical desert. I want to walk close, to be covered in his dust."

After many hours marching around the lake, Bethsaida hove into view. First, we came to Andrew's family. Andrew broke into a trot; I knew he was bursting to share everything with Simon, his elder brother. I knew Simon well from many nights of fishing; he was like Andrew in many ways, genuine but also a little straightforward. The difference between them was that because Simon was the older brother and more concerned with the practical things of life, like putting food on the table and grumbling about paying his taxes.

The level of grumbling would depend on the size of the catch, but we arrived at a good time, Simon had been asleep most of the morning after a night's fishing, but now he was content to be around his jobs. We sat in their yard as Andrew poured out all that had happened during our weeks away.

Simon listened with careful attention until Andrew reached the part about the vision of light and proclamation of the 'Son of God', when his eyebrow raised in alarmed scepticism.

I could see what was going on in Simon's mind. He cared much for his younger brother and whilst he knew that his Andrew was not a liar, Simon was worried that his brother was getting carried away into something he did not understand. It was time for Simon to check out our man. We moved on to my father's house, where it took some time to work through Mother's welcome, and Deborah fetched Father from the market. Then, after what seemed like an eternity, we could sit in private on the roof and tell our story again. This time it was my story to tell, I added some parts of my father's caution about fake or genuine holy men and dangerous whiffs of rebellion and made sure I did not use the word 'Messiah'.

That evening we prepared the nets as all fishermen do, in order not to attract any undue attention, and then slipped away. This time we would not be back with the dawn and headed towards the other side of the lake to look for this Jesus of Nazareth.

I turned the situation over in my mind and wondered what Simon, and indeed Andrew, were thinking. How do you prepare for being introduced to a 'Son of God'? It is difficult not to have some pre-conceived idea of what a person with that level of title of would look like.

As we met again at the relative's house, I watched Simon's eyes and he sized up the ragged and half-starved peasant that Andrew presented to him.

Jesus smiled a broad and easy smile of welcome. His voice had recovered from its desert croak. "You are Simon, son of Jonah; you will be called Peter-the-rock."

I could see that the new Simon Peter was not that impressed, perhaps thinking that his brother had told Jesus about him before, and perhaps this was because he was a big man. However, the meeting had all courtesy and when Jesus announced that he wanted to return to his family in Capernaum, a few hours past our home, Simon Peter offered his boat as far as Bethsaida. We made a backdoor exit and a circuitous route to the lake, leaving Antipas' soldiers none the wiser.

* * * *

As the boat beached back in Bethsaida, it was clear that the tasks of the day had returned to the front of Simon Peter's mind. Searching the countryside for prophets was all very well for his younger brother, but Simon said he must return to his house. Jesus told us he needed to look for someone.

The next time we met Jesus, a man called Philip, who we both knew, was with him. Andrew shared our experiences of The Immerser with him. Philip nodded at each part of the story and in return told us that Jesus had asked him to follow and proclaim 'The Kingdom of God'.

"Proclaim 'The Kingdom of God'?" said Andrew.

"At that moment, there seemed to be nothing more important that I should do." Philip said with certainty in his voice, before leaving with the words, "Now I must find a friend of mine."

"Philip seemed to realise that this Jesus is no ordinary Rabbi," said Andrew.

"Or was he just carried away by talk of 'The Kingdom of God'?" I said. "Are we being drawn into a deception as my father cautioned?"

Andrew shrugged and pulled a puzzled look on his face.

"Have you sometimes wondered," I continued, "how the Scriptures say so many things about the Messiah? Sometimes as a great leader of powerful conquest, sometimes as a humble servant of peace on a donkey? A man of sorrows?"

Andrew looked at me, his face blank. "Your Rabbi was different to mine."

"Have you even sat under the stars at night, to think how all these things might be and how all the hundreds of pieces of prophecy might fit together like a huge puzzle?"

"I just see what is in front of me," said Andrew.

I nodded and smiled for him. "Yes, that's most important," I agreed. "I need to do that as well."

Andrew continued in a low voice, "Could it be that after so many generations have waited for the Messiah that these things will happen in our times?" He stared at me, as if trying to see through me. "He looks so ordinary!"

"On the outside, yes, but do we believe what we saw at the pool?" I reminded him, our heads close together. "That he was anointed with the Spirit from above."

"If he is truly the Messiah, all we have to do is wait," said Andrew with certainty. "He will take his throne in Jerusalem and all men will see the glory of God in him."

"This Jesus will be associated with rebellion against Rome, just by coming from Nazareth," I said. "If he then preaches a Kingdom of God, it seems certain."

"Yes, but it doesn't fit," Andrew replied. "As an ascetic from the desert he is closer to an Essene than a Zealot."

Philip now reappeared with his friend Nathanael, whose first question to Jesus was direct. "I hear that you come from Nazareth, Rabbi!"

Jesus looked straight back at Nathanael and smiled as he said, "A true Israelite, straightforward and no falsehoods!"

"And how do you know me?" Nathanael asked, a little more challenge in his voice.

Jesus gave that easy smile. "I saw you while you were under the fig tree before Philip called you."

I saw Nathanael's eyes widen with surprise as he took a step backwards and then another. "I was on the other side of Bethsaida! Rabbi, you are the Son of God; you are the King of Israel!" He dropped to his knees and reached to kiss Jesus' hand.

"Are you trying to get us crucified?!" Philip moved in front of them. "Herod Antipas' men are already interested and if you are going to proclaim Caesar's equal, then for goodness sake do it quietly and in private!"

Jesus pulled Nathanael to his feet with a man-hug and with look of mystery said, "You believe because I told you I saw you under the fig tree? You'll see greater things, you'll see heaven open, and the angels of God ascending and descending on the Son of Man."

My jaw hung loose, only a Messiah could say such things – or a great fake, or else a madman!

7/. Miraculously Unwilling

In the next few months, as the rumours of Messiah and the scandal of blasphemy rumbled on, I saw many rush to press around him, but Jesus would pass them by, whereas there were others that he would go out of his way to find.

Meanwhile, Herod Antipas' men started patrolling the towns and villages of the lakeshore. In Capernaum, they loitered around the inn and marketplace and offered 'protection' to the synagogue ruler.

In many ways, my new Rabbi was an enigma for me. I had expected anyone proclaimed as the 'Son of God' to start issuing instructions as commands, but he did not. Instead, I heard only an invitation to join his Kingdom for those who had 'eyes to see and ears to hear it'.

Then, as summer moved into autumn, there was an invitation to a wedding between two leading families in the town of Cana. Jesus was to escort his mother to their relatives and that meant we got in as his companions. This would be the society event of the year, the place to see and to be seen.

We arrived to a mansion built in the Greco style and a huge courtyard, filled with light, music and the fragrances of citrus and spices. It was as lavish as we had hoped and the celebration was in full swing, when I noticed Jesus leave our dance and move to where his mother waited with a stance that asked his attention. Supposing that his mother was not well and hoping we would not need to leave, Andrew and I followed at a respectful distance. Instead, we found that Mary was speaking to her son about a problem with the hospitality, gesturing towards the top table and then to the agitated chief steward who stood nearby.

I listened as Mary talked of the great humiliation that was about to fall upon her relatives. "The merchant did not arrive, he was robbed on the road and they have run out of wine!" she explained to Jesus. "You know this will be a great shame upon our relatives and we should help them with this."

"Dear woman," he replied. "This isn't your problem. Don't worry and the situation will resolve itself."

The chief steward then stepped in with his opinion. "This crisis in my Master's house is of your doing, O prophet of the Most High! Those men of the King's Guard followed you here," he said, indicating the soldiers seated in a corner. "They sit there all night drinking what wine remains, when they could have been chasing the *Sicarii* that ambushed my caravan!"

Mary reached and took Jesus' hand; I had seen the look that now flickered in her eye before in my own mother's. She was not going to be put off by her son's gentle rebuttal, it was the look that could tell a son, no matter how old he was, this was important and there was an expectation. Even in the dim light and from under her veil, I saw her eyes search his face. "I have always known you are special, Jesus," she said. "Ever since the planets aligned and the angels spoke and all those people came to us at your birth. Egypt was all a great strain on me and Joseph, now do this thing I ask, please."

Father's stories flooded into my brain, but I had no time to think before Mary's voice changed pitch as she addressed the chief steward with the bossy tone of a family matriarch. "Just do whatever he tells you to do."

I saw Jesus' head drop a little as he sighed to himself. "Bring those vessels and also fetch more water to fill them." The servants looked back at him for a moment, but Jesus had a way that nobody could refuse and so they started to work, shuttling to and from the well.

As I took this all in, I also looked around the courtyard and could see goblets empty of wine; the guests were starting to look peeved and the dancing was winding down. From a glance towards the top table, I could see the bride's father was now feeling most uncomfortable, and the disapproval of the groom's father and mother could be seen in their faces.

Now Jesus turned to the chief steward. "Draw out from the vessels and go and serve it for your Master's approval." The man's eyes were full of fear and apprehension as he looked for a way out. "Sir, I have served my master for a score of years. I am trusted as a friend, and you cannot ask me to do what cannot be done! If I serve water from a washing jar, my master will be a laughing stock as far as Jerusalem and this will be the end of my tenure here!"

I saw Jesus' smile just touch the corners of his mouth as he nodded at the predicament that this wretched man was in. Taking the jug from a servant's hand, he dipped it into the nearest vessel and presented it back to the chief steward, with the same look that said 'right, now go and do what I told you'. It was then that the bouquet of the wine pervaded the air around us, a beautiful, warm aroma, delicious and full-bodied. We lurched forward, our heads knocking together to look at the jug. The steward's eyes bulged as he almost dropped the jug, and some of its wonderful contents spilled out onto the floor. There was a moment of stunned silence and then the other servants started to gabble. Jesus' hand commanded them into silence and he raised a stern voice. "Alright, so go and do what I said." He inclined his head towards the top table.

Andrew and I stood close and watched the chief steward try to maintain his composure as he crossed the courtyard towards the top table. I saw the bride's father stiffen in his seat to prepare himself for the bathing water humiliation, with his face set like stone.

The chief steward reached the table, bowed and lifted the jug to pour from a height so the red wine could be seen by all. Then he stood back to wait for approval, so it could be served to the guests. The scene was almost comical, the bride's father acting as if nothing was out of the ordinary, although his face told a different tale. I wondered if he was trying to work out if this was a trick with coloured water. The next moment his expression changed, and I knew that the aroma of the wine had reached his nostrils; he sipped in cautious wonderment. He and his steward exchanged looks that told me they were now together in amazement and relief. The bride's father smiled and nodded. Andrew and I stood together and watched as all at the top table tasted the new wine, looks of surprise and pleasure spreading across many faces. The groom's father stood, generous in his praise. "This is magnificent wine," he declared. "Most hosts wait until the guests have drunk a few and keep the cheap wine for the end, but you have saved this magnificent vintage until now!"

Now it was our turn. The moment that had held us in its spell was broken and as one, we all grabbed for our goblets and cups and lurched forwards. I knocked heads with Andrew again as others jostling to dip into the vessels. From the first taste, it was the most extraordinary I had ever known; taste rolled across my tongue with smooth blackcurrants, rich pomegranates, tangs of citrus and it just went on and on!

The bride's father was basking in the praise as he looked across toward us, and it was at that moment that the captain of the guard came curiously close and Jesus' voice ended the night for us. "Time to go, and that means now! Mother, you will need to stay here with the family, I will see you are escorted back home."

And that was it, party over! We walked out into the cold night and slept a few hours at the groom's house before Jesus woke us at dawn.

As we trudged through the grey morning, bleary eyed in our Rabbi's wake, I rubbed my head ruefully and then started to giggle.

"What's s'funny?" inquired Andrew.

"Do you have lumps on your head, too? How many times did we knock our heads together, diving to get our cups into that vessel?"

Andrew fingered his forehead, then his mood cracked and he too started to laugh. "And that poor chief steward tried to look so normal and failed so badly!"

We collapsed against one another in helpless mirth, staggering as if we were two drunks with hurting heads; it was too ridiculous to believe and yet we had the bruises to prove it!

Jesus joined our mirth. "You two young men will need to learn how to hold your drink," he mocked, "if you expect me to take you to any more high society weddings."

This continued for some time, until we had relived it all and our mood had calmed. Then Jesus spoke again. "I want you to rejoin your families in Bethsaida for a while and tell the others to disperse as well. I have brought you this far but need to return for my mother." He turned and walked away. It had been so abrupt; Andrew and I stood and watched him disappear before turning towards Bethsaida. Anti-climax crushed me; the miles passed in dreary and unspeaking boredom until we could cross the Herod's border and reach the lakeside. Once at Peter's, I lay on his floor and contemplated the ceiling, too confused to do anything else.

* * * *

It was some days later before Andrew and I could get together with Simon Peter, James, Philip and Nathanael to discuss the events of the wedding.

"Jesus changed it with just a word of command," Andrew told them. "And yet he did it because his mother pressed him into it."

"Then he just dragged us away and sent us back here to stay in hiding for days," I said.

"It's as if Jesus did not want it to be known that he had performed this amazing miracle," said Andrew. "Not that the excitement has died down much!"

"So what does this mean for you?" asked Simon Peter. "What are you going to do now?"

"We disciples agree that he has revealed his glory, we have all put our faith in him," answered Andrew.

"Water to wine is impressive," returned Peter, with sceptical eyebrows. "What next, are we to expect olives into oranges? Is this what a Messiah is supposed to do?"

There were a few guffaws but no one laughed. The mood was serious and Peter, straightforward as ever, had hit the nail on the head.

"We still need to see if this Jesus of Nazareth is Pharisee, Zealot or Essene in his purpose," said Nathanael.

"He's mysterious," said Philip. "Doesn't entrust himself to anyone."

Andrew called for my support. "We also heard his mother talk about signs at his birth and angels. Tell them what you heard, John."

I needed to get my own point across. "Yes, we did, but we also found out about his family. His father was Joseph from Bethlehem and of the house of David."

"My father's opinion," said my brother, "is that, if he is the Messiah, he will take his throne in Jerusalem so that all men will see his glory. Until then, I must be cautious in line with my father's advice. To believe in this Jesus of Nazareth, he must begin to fulfil all of the many prophecies written about the Messiah in the Law and the Prophets."

"I am already confident that he will," replied Andrew.

"He has only talked about the Kingdom," said Philip. "How many wonders will we see when the Messiah establishes the Kingdom?"

"There will be no campaign this side of winter," said Nathanael. "The nation waits for Passover and that gives us time to see what this *tekton* of Nazareth is really made of."

"I want to be there when he starts to fulfil these things," said Andrew. "Then I will come back and tell you so that you can know too," he added to his brother.

"In the meantime, you must keep your feet on the ground and your head in this world and come fishing with me," retorted Peter. "Water into wine for the rich who already eat well doesn't impress me. A Messiah needs to show me he knows about everyday life and its struggles to pay Rome's taxes and survive on their starvation grain ration!"

Then he added, "Listen, I also have some good news to share with you. Mordecai and Esther have great happiness and they have paid some debts." He lowered his voice. "I assume that young Simon-the -Zealot paid them a night-time visit with some money he 'acquired', but it is well not to ask questions!"

We nodded and, wishing each other God's blessing, parted. It would not take very long before three of us would see our Rabbi act in power in the temple at Jerusalem, but it would not be in a way that any of us could have imagined.

8/. Passover, the First

My hopes and fears swirled within whilst my world was changing about me. I lay in the boat and gazed at the twinkling heavens, ever present and stable for me in the cold of the night.

All through that first winter since meeting Jesus, I was still a fisherman, yet now my life was so different.

"Are you doing any work tonight?" My brother's hushed words jerked me back to reality, as his toe prodded my ribs.

"I love this time of year," I said. "When the lake swells with the cold melt-waters and the fish jump as the days warm."

"I'm thinking about catching the fish we need for market."

"The Milky Way arches over us as the Lord God's canopy," I told him. "Our world is a drop in a bucket."

"All you are doing is philosophizing about your pilgrimage with The Immerser and not thinking about fishing," he told me.

"Sins of idleness," I confessed. "Has it really been six months since the wedding at Cana?"

Speculation of the Messiah had circulated at fever pitch in the towns and villages around the lake. Yet the object of the speculation had remained a middle-aged unmarried carpenter, who spoke of a Kingdom and would disappear from sight for several days of prayer vigil. Just once, he had allowed me to go with him; I relived every action, every word, as I cast the net with James and then gathered it in.

Dawn was breaking with the sun over the Golan Heights, its first rays bringing warmth to my skin and an end to our silent fishing. We shipped oars, my muscles feeling stiff as we began to pull for shore.

"What did you talk about on your sojourn with the Rabbi?" Peter's voice came across the water.

"I asked him about the things I do not understand," I said. "He emerged from the wilderness with the power to turn water into wine and yet told Andrew and me that he was empty."

"Empty of what?"

"I still don't know. He said that he has much work to do, before he can be made perfect."

"To walk before God and be perfect," said Father, as if to himself, and stroked his beard.

"Did he say anything else like that?" asked Andrew.

"He said that virtue drains from him with every miracle and he needs the prayer and solitude to replenish it," I said.

"That makes some sense," said James. "No man can be always giving without rest."

"Yes, but he makes it sound like more than just rest," I replied.

"Does he say anything about catching fish to pay Rome's taxes?" asked Peter.

"So why are you now in Capernaum, Peter?" asked my father.

"To be close to him, of course," Peter said, before adding, "and keep an eye on our Andrew."

"Zebedee," asked Andrew, "why, do you think, Jesus has moved to Capernaum?"

"There are several possible reasons I can think of. Every *tekton* at Nazareth who laboured on the mansions of Sepphoris will have followed the work as Herod Antipas moved his court to Tiberias and his face would be known there. Perhaps also because Capernaum is the main town, at the head of the lake."

"Jesus acts as if he will always be a local Rabbi, and yet we all know the huge expectation that hangs over him," said James. "A man proclaimed as 'Son of God' must have bigger ambitions than Capernaum can hold."

"Does The Immerser have more work to do as he prepares the way?" I asked.

"That may be another reason for Capernaum," said Father. "If Jesus was known to keep a close association with the Immerser, he would be in more danger from Herod Antipas and may need to move quickly. Herod Philip's border is close and escape across the lake gives him two possibilities."

"Herod Antipas' stewards must already have told him about the numbers of people crossing his borders," said Andrew. "I see increasing numbers come from outside of Galilee to seek the Rabbi."

"What do you hear in his message?" asked Father.

"He tells us that the 'times are fulfilled' and to 'repent for the Kingdom of God is at hand.'"

"So, what does that message speak of to you?" asked Father again. As I listened, I knew he was preparing us all to take hold of our own lives and seize whatever destiny awaited us.

"It is not just that he says 'the Kingdom of God is here,'" James replied, searching Father's face. "I cannot think of a bigger statement than 'the times are fulfilled'. He is telling us that everything the Law and the Prophets have told our people for centuries is coming to pass, as if he is fulfilling them!"

"So why are we waiting here in Galilee, let alone Capernaum?" Father continued his rhetorical questioning. "He must be in Jerusalem for Passover."

"I think that Cana was the introduction that he did not want," I said. "I saw his reticence to do that miracle; it was for obedience to his mother."

"So he needs some calm and space for his message to be heard," Father concluded for us. "Have his actions attracted the attention of The Prefect or the Herods?"

"No, they are still busy watching The Immerser," agreed James.

"He still 'prepares the way,'" I said. "But the people talk more about this Jesus now."

"Every synagogue in Galilee and all the way to Jerusalem gossips about Jesus' every word since Cana," said Peter. "I do not think the scribes have ever been so busy with demands for newsletters as they are now."

"Yes and that means the Sanhedrin, Shlomo and Uri and their parties will know of all this," said James.

"Their memory will be painful," said Father. "The Immerser told them he was preparing the way for another. They will be preparing for Passover, but not knowing what peasant uprising they may face."

"Rome's Eagle will be staked on the Mount of Olives as usual," said James.

"The Prefect will have his spies working overtime," said Peter. "They will tell him the rumours of the Kingdom of God."

"We can expect legionaries on every corner," said Father. "I will invite Jesus to stay with us and then we can get to know him and see his actions for ourselves."

I was stunned; I could see my brother was too.

"I know," continued Father, "After all I have told you about the risks of being associated with criticism of the Sanhedrin or rebellion against Rome. But Jesus' face is still unknown in Jerusalem, even if his reputation precedes him. I have seen how he conducts himself and I'm confident that he's shrewd enough to keep his whereabouts hidden. John, I want you to continue your pilgrimage with Jesus and bring him to our house with the others, but in ones and twos. James and I will travel with the usual friends so as not to attract attention. I want to take this opportunity to find out more about this man, whether Son of God or deluded carpenter of Nazareth!"

"Yes, Father. I understand."

"In the meantime…" Father's voice had finality. "I rely on you all not to breathe a word of this to anyone."

* * * *

Passover! There was nothing like The Passover. The very earliest memories of my life were asking for the story of The Passover and why this night was different from all others. Passover meant Jerusalem, our house there full of people, and opening the door to see if Elijah were there to herald the coming Messiah.

But this time was different, oh so different! As we all covered the many miles south down the Jordan and then up from Jericho, my imagination told me I was riding a chariot of deliverance to Passover. My chariot had four white stallions: I named them Desire, Expectancy, Power and Freedom. Desire had always been ahead of me, whenever I had seen the legions raise the dust in my hometown and yearned for the freedom of my nation. Now Expectancy rode alongside Desire. If Power and Freedom were to follow, then this must be at Passover.

Passover brought my people together from all over the world, in their hundreds of thousands. Freedom; Passover spoke of freedom for my people, and it was deliverance from the starvation rations of slavery that my people yearned for.

Every Passover that I had known, Father had always brought us to The Holy City early, to prepare the house and bathe in the Mikvah. Now Jesus had brought us in the midst of the people, in order to slip in unnoticed. As we neared Jerusalem, the road had become choked with travelling parties, whole villages of Galilee and Judea on the march, and groups from foreign lands with pack animals and carts. The Songs of Ascent had not ceased all day and I sung them like never before.

The city walls hove into sight and we paused to take in the scene. My eyes scanned across the Kidron valley and its tent city of hundreds of thousands jostling for space, the merchant's camel trains bringing in supplies, all wreathed in the wood-smoke of thousands of fires that flavoured the air and drifted toward me with the bleating of tens of thousands of Passover lambs.

Andrew pointed towards the Mount of Olives. "I would say there is an extra legion this year."

"A cohort at every gate," said Nathanael.

"The Prefect has already caught a whiff of rebellion," said Philip.

"Perhaps the herbs of slavery will not taste so bitter this year," I said.

"Keep your sandals on your feet," said Andrew, and laid an arm across my shoulders. "And your cloak tucked into your belt, we shall run to freedom!"

"And see if Elijah will come to take his cup and the Messiah bid the despotic Prefect of Rome to let his people go, or suffer the pestilence and plagues of torment!" said Nathanael.

"We must move on and be there before the *Shofar* sounds." Jesus called us back to attention.

Andrew clapped me across the shoulder and we began to work our way through the masses. We had a plan to separate from the others, meet by the Sheep Gate and to make it to our house before sunset.

I took the lead for the last part, through the jostling crowds. Wearied by the journey, I looked forward to Father's welcoming kiss, the washing of face and feet and Mother's evening meal, the house warm and familiar.

* * * *

The Sabbath day was an oasis of calm in a city full to overflowing. We were together almost as an extended family. First, the ceremonial cleansing of the Mikvah, then Jesus took his turn to recall the stories from our scriptures in the same way as Father, James, Andrew, Philip, Nathanael and I did. That night, as I lay down, I thought how relaxed and normal Jesus had seemed; he was just another man from a nondescript town visiting his capital city for Passover. Before my brain swirled towards sleep, I remembered the words of Isaiah the prophet written seven hundred years beforehand: "He had no beauty or majesty to attract us to him, nothing in his appearance that we should desire him."

The next morning, I commented on this to Father.

"Yes that would fit with his behaviour," he agreed. "But if this Jesus of Nazareth is to fulfil the prophecies, he must fulfil them all."

"When are you going up to the temple, Father?" asked James.

"I will wait for the young Rabbi, but follow at a distance."

"Will he go to worship or preach his message?" I asked.

"We can only wait and see. He has given us no hint of what his actions may be."

"You think he may take some action?"

"I'm sure there will be things that offend him as they offend me," said Father.

"I remember well what you have told us about the corruption," said James. "The Immerser's confrontation with Shlomo and Uri fills my mind."

My thoughts also went back to The Immerser's pool. "Father, I wonder if Simon bar Mordecai is here somewhere with his Zealot comrades?"

"Yes," said Father, with a thoughtful stroke of his beard. "If he is, it will be difficult to spot him and I am sure there are enough young hotheads ready to ferment trouble with Rome and lead him astray."

9/. Temple Protest

My heart pounded in my chest as we set off through the toiling streets. Jesus was leading our group now instead of walking in our midst as he usually did. For the first time I felt alone without Father and James close by and was glad that my youth made me less conspicuous.

We emerged from the tunnel and into the mass of people and animals in the outer courts. I stood close with Andrew and watched Jesus as he surveyed the scene; before us were the tables of the moneychangers and the sheep and cattle tied in groups. He walked with slow, deliberate strides to the animals and picked up several of the cords discarded there, plaiting them together. As he turned to the moneychangers, I saw anger flare his nostrils and the curl of his upper lip.

"Well, friends," he called to the moneychangers with open distain as he approached the tables, the rope behind his back. "How is the profit today?"

Two or three of them looked at him down their noses to counter the implied accusation. "Good enough!" replied one with a smugness of smile.

The first table cartwheeled backwards, its coins launched through the air; the second kicked away, skidding yards across the paving. The cord-whip swished through the air and lashed the next table, keeping the moneymen at bay. Down the line we saw him advance, one table after another, his actions fast and furious. The moneychangers screamed and were scattered like their coins, crawling across the floor to retrieve them.

I gasped. Andrew, Philip and Nathanael stood with me, open-mouthed at our Rabbi's rampage.

"If The Immerser prepared the way, then this is it!" exclaimed Andrew.

"'Zeal for your house will consume me!'" said Nathanael, quoting from somewhere in the scriptures.

Jesus was not finished and now turned his attention to the animals, loosing them from their ties, his whip droving them all en masse before him. "Get these out of here! How dare you turn my Father's house into a market?"

Chaos reigned; people and animals compressed together in jostling mass, doves and pigeons flew free from their cages. Our Rabbi stood in the middle of the court, the cord-whip circling his head, refusing to let anyone cross. Foam flecked his lips as he proclaimed that he had come to restore prayer and order to God's House.

Across the court, I exchanged wide-eyed looks with James. Whilst we had expected something might happen, the outright aggression had taken us all aback. This was not the Messiah revealed in his temple in glory, which we had discussed before. And then, I was not surprised. I looked at my father, but his face was impassive.

Now I saw that the Chief Priests had called the Temple Guards and were closing in around Jesus. I took it all in. In the background, I could also see Shlomo amongst his fellow Pharisees and Uri of the Sadducees mixed in with some of Herod's court. I marked all the faces around them, that I might remember them.

The voices of the Chief Priests rang out. "What miraculous sign can you show us to prove your authority to do this?" they demanded, in high priestly Hebrew.

Like The Immerser before him, I saw not a flinch from Jesus. "Destroy this temple and I will raise it again in three days." He had replied to them in Hebrew and it spoke to all who heard it.

The Priests looked aghast. "It has taken forty-six years to build this temple and you are going to raise it in three days?"

Excitement coursed through me like a fire. The Immerser had challenged the rule of Jerusalem from his place in the desert and now my Rabbi had faced the authorities in the very centre of their powerbase. However, it was clear Jesus was not staying to dispute with them and as he turned away towards the tunnel, I saw a group of young men separate themselves from the crowd and move towards him. It was then I saw Simon; his short and sturdy frame was distinctive, but he had not seen me. I moved sideways around the edges of the crowd and within a minute, I had caught up with them as they closed on Jesus.

"Greetings, Rabbi," said the leader of the group of men. "I am Barabbas and these are my followers. Our zeal for the removal of these stooges of Rome from our land are as yours."

So, the Zealots were anxious to claim Jesus as their own. I used the moment to work my way towards Simon.

"My work is the Kingdom of God," replied Jesus. "So should yours also be, Barabbas."

"The Immerser has shown our nation the need for a spiritual revolution," returned Barabbas. "Together you and I can bring that to fulfilment in the Kingdom of God, then these half-breed Herods can be deposed and their court of opportunist leeches with them."

My Rabbi had not even looked at the leader or the other young men who swarmed around him and kept striding forward through the crowds. I made my move, my speech as gentle as possible. "Shalom, Simon bar Mordecai, I am pleased to see you."

He started at my familiar voice in his ear and shot a glance around at his comrades, but they had not heard me in the melee. "We must all be careful," I said, trying to build a bridge between us. "The days ahead will be important." Simon looked ill at ease so I tarried no longer and moved on, to make it plain that I was following Jesus.

We left the temple. Jesus led us straight out of the city and up the Mount of Olives, skirting the Legion there, and with the occasional pause to make sure we were not being followed.

I walked close to him. "Rabbi, are you now fulfilled?" I asked. "Today you were what I always imagined a prophet of the Lord to be."

"I must do God's will to be fulfilled, but there is much yet to do."

"Does that fill the emptiness you told me about?"

"The power of his Spirit flows well through my emptiness." He turned his head to look at me. "It is a good lesson for all who would follow."

It was much later, after seeking solitude and prayer, that Jesus asked me to lead us back to the house under darkness. Father had been correct; we could rely on Jesus to maintain our safe house.

Once our guests had settled for the night, we withdrew to the roof and our family discussion began in earnest.

"What did you think of Jesus' actions, Father?" asked James.

"I admit I was taken aback that his actions were so radical, and by the severity of the way he carried it out. At first this seemed to be out of place in our Holy Temple, but we must always use the scriptures for guidance," said Father. "Remember in the time of King David, how he took the sacred bread from the temple? I have asked myself what is more righteous: to have a temple with moneychangers, or to see them swept aside without mercy? In the end, I was much impressed with this Jesus and what he has done. It was, after all, what I had always wanted to see and what I had always hoped a prophet of God would do: to bring God to the people and to bring the people to God and save them from the injustices of a religious system that holds them down."

"Yes, but this wildness has made him enemies," our mother joined in. "Could he have not first reasoned with them and then taken action if they had refused him?"

"I'm sure they would have dismissed him as an uneducated peasant from 'Galilee of the Gentiles,'" I said. "By taking this lone action, he has focused all attention on himself and I feel safer as his disciple."

"How can he build a following when everyone wants to claim him, as we saw those Zealots try to?" added James.

"I agree with you both, your judgements represent the prevailing politics well," said Father. "It seems to me that Jesus' actions were calculated to cause disturbance amongst the temple authorities, but not severe enough to concern the Tribune watching from the Antonia. They will have seen it as a minor religious demonstration in a matter that did not concern them."

"Herod Antipas will hear of it," said James. "What is certain is that Jesus is a straight-talking man of God and with The Immerser, that is two of them in Israel at the same time."

"I managed a few words to Simon bar Mordecai," I said.

"Good," replied Father. "Try to let him see you, but don't press for any more contact for now."

* * * *

In the following days of that Passover week, we watched and followed as Jesus moved among the crowds. Father and James were never far away and at times, I saw Father talking with Pharisees he knew well. I also knew some from previous Passovers and visits to our house. One was a renowned scholar called Nicodemus, always calm and reserved, and a rich merchant, Joseph of Arimathea, who had engaged in more heated conversation following Jesus' rampage.

Jesus had brought a new order to the temple. It was not just that the traders had been banished and the people could take their sacrifices straight to the inner courts. I could see that Jesus was taking God to the people. He sat where the Rabbis of great age and authority would sit, except that his peasant's attire contrasted with their finery. He taught the people from the Law, in Aramaic and without reference to scrolls. He answered their needs and told them that he demonstrated the Lord God's compassion for them, with many miracles of healing and signs of authority. We acted as his eyes and, as the searching Temple Guards came through the crowds, either Andrew or I or one of the others would draw his attention and he moved us all on. We would disappear among the crowds until he took another place.

Once Barabbas and his group caught up with us again, I offered a covert smile, but made no move towards Simon and his ease towards me seemed to grow.

"Tell us, Rabbi," asked Barabbas. "How can the Kingdom you preach be established without the removal of Rome's poison from our land?"

"The 'Son of Man' came to act justly, to love mercy and walk humbly with his God," was Jesus' reply and we moved on again.

Each night, as the Temple Guard closed the day's sacrifice, it was the same careful routine: we would climb the Mount of Olives, skirt around the legions, check for any pursuit, spend time in prayer and make our way back after dark. My conversations with Father, Mother and James continued deep into each night.

"Many people are amazed and in awe of him," I said. "Some try to join us, but he just moves on."

"He knows how people are," said Mother. "He is not trusting of their fickle emotions. Many will join when the times are good and turn away when it gets difficult."

"You are quite right, my dear," affirmed Father. "This Jesus is avoiding himself being at the centre of a personality cult, unlike so many rebel leaders that have come and gone before."

"He always points to the Lord God," I said. "After every healing, he tells them to present themselves before the priests and offer a sacrifice."

"He just seems to be his own man, so strong in conviction and not swayed by the opinions of others," said James, shaking his head. "Do you not find it a paradox that by keeping his movements so unpredictable for the Sanhedrin to follow, they can accuse him of nothing, neither good nor bad, healing nor riot?"

"It cannot be always like this," said Father. "There must be more to come. If he forever kept his anonymity and with his small group of followers, this Jesus would never build the Kingdom of God that he preaches."

All of this time, I could feel myself trying to keep my emotions in check and make sound judgements, as Father schooled me. I felt so privileged and special, wanting to watch and learn from this peasant carpenter who spoke heavenly Hebrew.

It would be three years before we disciples would discuss all of this again, and realise that the temple Jesus had spoken about was not the physical building, and his Kingdom of God was not built of cities and lands. For now, I was being swept along, trying to make sense of my place in it all.

10/. Night Visitors

Late one night of the Passover week, there was a knocking at our door. The servant called to the visitor to identify himself. "I am Nicodemus and I am alone," came the reply. "I wish to speak to the Rabbi of Nazareth."

"I know this Nicodemus," Father said to Jesus. "He is a Pharisee and a good man too. Perhaps some of you also know of him," he continued to Andrew, Philip and Nathanael. "He is a member of the Sanhedrin who is well thought of by many. Rabbi, if you wish to meet him, I am not afraid to have him in my house."

I exchanged the briefest of knowing looks with James; so, this was the result of those conversations in the temple. Father had some political manoeuvres of his own and wanted Nicodemus to evaluate Jesus, or introduce Jesus to a potential ally in high authority, or both.

Jesus nodded. "Thank you, Zebedee. At this time of night, he must have some discreet matter to discuss. I will take him onto your roof; he will feel more private there."

Father kissed Nicodemus in welcome as an old friend and offered the oil for face and beard, as the servant attended his feet. "You will have privacy to speak with the young Rabbi on the roof; my youngest son, John, will guide you."

I lifted the lamp and led up the stairs. If Nicodemus thought I understood only Aramaic, he was wrong. My Hebrew was not fluent, but I knew enough to follow the conversation. I concentrated on appearing as the uninterested teenager as I sat and gazed over the city, but stayed within eavesdropping distance.

"Rabbi, we know you have come from God, for no one could perform the miraculous signs you are doing if God were not with him."

It was a well-prepared opening statement, but Jesus' answer told me that he was no more interested in offers from Pharisees than he had been with Zealots. "I tell you the truth; no one can see the Kingdom of God unless he is born again."

I heard fluent Hebrew. Nicodemus could not have expected this of a peasant *tekton*. A test had been set, but Jesus had not stumbled. More than that, he had answered the question that Nicodemus had not asked; it was to be a conversation of theology, not politics. Like my old Rabbi, The Immerser, this Jesus was not courting allies in authority.

I knew this Nicodemus was a walking library, but for the next few minutes, Jesus led him on a theological dance through his Kingdom of God. It was a birth of flesh, water and spirit; my brain whirled to remember it all.

If the Sanhedrin did indeed believe he was genuine, Jesus asked, why had his actions not been accepted? And just why couldn't Nicodemus understand his theology? He ended with a reference to Moses and the Son of God, and stark choices between good and evil, light and dark, as if that would be easier territory for Nicodemus.

I lead them back down the stairs and Nicodemus disappeared into the night with a parting Shalom, to work through the uncompromising challenges of heaven and earth that Jesus had faced him with. Once again, our discussions went deep into the night.

"Jesus turned down the recognition that was offered," I told Father and James. "In fact, he reversed it in such a way that it was almost shameful to such a senior Rabbi. He used a manner of speech to challenge Nicodemus to leave all that he was. It was as if he were still turning over yet more tables."

"Father, did you open the possibility of meeting Jesus for Nicodemus?" said James.

"Yes, because I thought it would be useful to them both and because I trust Nicodemus. As you could see, he came alone and his discretion keeps our house safe. I did not imagine the Rabbi would be so uncompromising towards my friend."

"Why do you think Nicodemus took the opportunity?"

"There are several possibilities I can think of, following what we saw the Rabbi do in the temple."

"The priests must hate and fear him, do you not think, Father?"

"Yes, and that means they must choose to either resist him or try to recruit him into their fold."

"So you think Nicodemus came here with a message, an olive branch offered by the parties of the Sanhedrin?" asked James. "An offer that would give the Rabbi credibility and influence?"

"That is what I heard," I said.

"It would be a shrewd political move if they could bring him within their fold, then they could control him. Shlomo and Uri are shrewd men and there are many similar in the council. However, I also calculated that Nicodemus wanted to assess for himself if Jesus could be the one Israel is waiting for. This gave him that opportunity without his fellow Pharisees knowing about it. It is difficult for him to take a stand alone in the Sanhedrin if so many are against."

"Or even a mixture of the two?" questioned James. "If he volunteered to do this for the council, it would give him the perfect cover for his own quest."

"My son, you too have a shrewd mind," smiled Father. "We can only guess, but it may be just as you have suggested." Turning to me, he added, "John, I do not think that this Jesus of Nazareth will start a revolution of blood against Rome, and I am confident enough for you to continue with him. However, his zeal for the Kingdom he preaches will continue to pit him against many in the temple whilst many in Israel will desire a king to displace Rome and the Herods. You must consider these risks without the emotion of following a possible Messiah. Do you wish to continue with Jesus yourself?"

"Yes, Father, my heart and my head want this and know that Jesus is important for our people."

"I praise God he has sent us these prophets," put in Mother. "If Jesus of Nazareth is the Messiah, then he can save Israel without need of your help, and if he isn't, then trouble will surely follow him everywhere."

"I promise you I will take care and seek peace with God and remain as inconspicuous as possible," I reassured her. "Andrew will be with me, and Philip and Nathanael are good men, as you now know."

So, the pressures of Passover week eased. The Legions decamped and escorted their Prefect back to Caesarea, well satisfied that Pax Romana had been maintained. The Sanhedrin were bruised but still in control of their temple. The multitudes journeyed back to the towns, villages, and foreign lands they had come from, still dreaming of deliverance from slavery, and with stories of the peasant-Rabbi from Galilee who defied the Sanhedrin and brought them to God with compassion and healings.

* * * *

In the following weeks the travelling became incessant, as Jesus took us from village to village; we lived as vagabonds, often sleeping rough and taking hospitality where we could find it.

Reputation went before us as news of the 'cleansing the temple' had been spread already by all those returning from The Passover. I could see that Jesus had planned this well: having taken God to the people at Passover, this was the springboard to take his message of the Kingdom of God to the people of Judea.

"We will offer the immersion in water for the repentance of sins," Jesus told us. "John the Immerser continues this great work and I want to show our oneness with him." He looked at us. "Andrew and John, I want you to teach us from your experience."

I looked at Philip and Nathanael with some apprehension, aware of my youth in front of them.

"Will you lead us in this, Rabbi?" Andrew asked.

"All service for God should be carried out with humility," Jesus replied. "If you can do this, you are as qualified as anyone."

"I would like to hear about your time with The Immerser," said Philip. "To learn about this repentance he preached."

"Don't be concerned about the skinny whiskers on your chin," Nathanael grinned at me.

Over the following days, my awkwardness of disturbed social order diminished. Philip and Nathanael were good men who focused on the task and on their fellow countrymen, and the result for Andrew and I was that our brotherhood of friendship with them grew.

"More people are now coming to us for immersion and repentance than were going to The Immerser," said Andrew.

"Our Rabbi is the man of the moment!" said Philip.

"I am thinking about Joash, Seth and Yossi," I told Andrew. "Their work must be diminishing as ours grows."

Every Sabbath day, Jesus took his message to a local synagogue, but we could see that the welcome from the synagogue rulers was waning.

"These local Pharisees are under pressure from the Sanhedrin," said Nathanael, "to show they do not approve of Jesus or his ways."

"The whispering against him is constant and insidious," I said.

"No matter," said Philip. "The people still welcome Jesus, thirsty for his words and their sick to be healed."

"I see faces from Shlomo's and Uri's parties, I marked them out in the temple," I told them all. "There is a frequent visitor called Saul, a young disciple of Shlomo's."

"Do you see others?" asked Andrew.

"Chai from Uri's party also monitors our movements," I said. "No doubt keeping an eye on Saul as well as us."

We never tarried long in one place, but kept moving on, and then one day Joash, Seth and Yossi found us. They were desolate, with shocking news to share: Herod's Guard had swooped out of the night, two days past.

"We heard the hoof-beats approaching in the dusk," said Seth. "He told us to stand away from him. The Immerser knew they had come for him."

"He was dragged away between two of them as the others swung their swords at us," said Joash.

"The Immerser now pays for his fearless condemnation of Antipas and Herodias," Yossi told us.

"Where did they take him?"

"The dungeon at Machaerus."

A chill ran through my guts. Andrew and I held our erstwhile comrades to comfort them as their story unfolded, but inside me, my stomach clenched in a knot. The world would not now see The Immerser again; his time was done. I remembered my mother's dramatic statement on the night we first talked about him; it had come to pass, as it had done for those true prophets of old. We kept a prayer vigil through the watches of the night, and next morning Jesus told us the people would now be too frightened to come for immersion and it was time to withdraw to Galilee.

11/. The Foreign Whore

The Damascus Road; it puzzled and unnerved me, only the legions marched this way to Caesarea. Foreign gods also lay over the horizon that I now scanned for the tell-tale dust of the oppressors of my people. The land of Samaria that lay between us and Galilee was a place of half-breeds, foreigners from far-away lands that had adopted our patriarchs, but mixed in a hotchpotch of their own beliefs. I had never been to Samaria. What business could our Rabbi have there?

I held Andrew back at the rear of the group to ask what he thought of this. "Surely this is not right for a prophet," I said. "He seems to be neither concerned about what is expected of him nor the recruitment of more followers."

Andrew confessed he was just as surprised. "I'm just confident that following Jesus is the right thing to do," he said. "Besides, it will be shorter and quicker."

"But that cannot be the reason that our Rabbi is taking us this way. Will he incite Samaria against Rome? Or are we to preach in Caesarea as Jonah did at Ninevah?"

"We've already seen that he doesn't do what we expect him to," Andrew replied. "Think of the wedding at Cana: this was the perfect opportunity to project himself on the public stage and build a following, yet he did just the opposite and hid from view."

"He has his mysteries," I agreed. "But he also explains many things to us when we escape the crowds. If he doesn't explain this and I leave, will you come with me?"

We walked on, recounting the past weeks since Passover, reliving all we had seen and done. By midday, we had reached a well near a Samaritan town called Sychar. Even though I had never been here, I knew it as Jacob's Well from the Sabbath stories of how it had been dug thousands of years ago, by our patriarch.

Jesus said he would like to rest and asked me to keep him company whilst the others went into the town. We had some money, given by benefactors in Judea and needed to replenish food supplies but our Rabbi did not want to mix with the Samaritan townsfolk.

We sat on the large capstone wall of the well and I took my opportunity.

"The arrest of The Immerser was a shock for me, even though I knew it would be inevitable," I said.

"We spent many days together when we were younger," he told me. "We talked often of how Israel should be and the Kingdom that would one day come."

"Did you talk about your place in the Kingdom?"

"Such matters were not clear in my youth," he looked at me with his smile. "John bar Zacharias and I both had to grow in wisdom and in favour with God and men."

"Did you also grow in God's Spirit?" I asked. "Until that day when he drove you into the wilderness."

"Yes, that is also important. I grow when I do God's will."

I screwed up my courage; I needed to understand him more. "How are you now, Rabbi? Are you now filled or empty?"

"There are many portions between full and empty; I have much work yet to do."

"You will grow as you do this work, Rabbi?"

"Yes, but it also drains me."

"Do you grow when you are being emptied?"

He did not answer, but turned his head towards the town. "There is a woman coming to the well."

I saw a woman carrying her water jar alone in the heat of the day. This was a scarlet woman, rejected within her own community, not welcome to come with others in the cooler evening. As she got nearer, I rose to move away, but Jesus remained on the capstone and I stood feeling awkward, expecting him to move with me.

The woman approached but, like me, she tarried with indecision, waiting for Jesus to move. She shot a glance at me, evaluating if I was a threat. I wondered what was going through her head, would she conclude Jesus was blind and I was just his guide?

She sidled to the other side of the capstone and lowered her dipper. As she was just pulling it back up for the second time, Jesus shattered the stiff silence with a very simple request. "Will you give me a drink?"

The woman reeled backward; I stood too stiff to move. I would never have expected a Rabbi to ask his own wife of something in public, but my Rabbi had just done this with a foreign whore.

It took her a few moments to recover, but then I saw a look of mocking defiance come into her eyes, and under her veil, I saw her chin rise as she squared her diminutive shoulders. I was sure I could read her mind: this Jew, this high and mighty Jew, must be desperate with thirst and she had him at her mercy!

"And how can a Jew ask a Samaritan woman for a drink?" she asked, her voice loaded with the sentiment of false honey.

Jesus smiled and didn't answer for a while. I thought he was waiting for her defiance to cool, showing he was not about the take her bait. The woman twirled her dipper in front of him. When his answer did come, it was the same as I had heard to Nicodemus the Pharisee. He answered a question that she had not asked. "If you knew the gift of God and who it is that asks you for a drink, you would have asked him and he would have given you living water."

I watched the stance of her body language. This scarlet woman, who knew how to manipulate men and live by her wits as many tried to use her, was still defiant. The 'high and mighty' Jew who needed a drink was trying to catch her with clever words because he did not want to beg for a drink. Well, she had other ideas and was going to enjoy her moment of power!

"Sir," the voice was still as sweet and beguiling. "You have nothing to draw with and the well is deep. Where can you get this living water?"

Then, when no immediate answer came, she reminded my Rabbi this was her territory and therefore his God didn't have power; our patriarch was her father and it was therefore her well.

But her malevolence did not change Jesus' calm and polite manner. He could give her living water; she could possess it for herself. Then she would never thirst and need the well again.

My guts were still cold as my emotions tried to cope with a situation that should not be happening.

She stood for a few moments and then sauntered up to the well and twirled her dipper again; it was her moment to call the Rabbi's bluff.

"Sir, give me some of this living water, so that I won't get thirsty and have to keep coming here to draw water."

"Go, call your husband and come back."

"I do not have a husband," her chin raised again in terse reply.

Jesus was as calm and cool as the well water. "You are right when you say you have no husband. The fact is, you have had five husbands and the man you now have is not your husband. What you have said is quite true."

She reeled backwards again; the dipper slipped from her fingers and fell to the ground. The prophetic insight had been a direct hit deep into the woman's soul. Once again, she was reduced to the outcast in her home village, loved by no one and taken advantage of by many as she had lurched through life. My Rabbi had dismantled the pretence of her life and yet had not condemned it.

She started to speak again; the honey had vanished and yet she still tried to fight and claw back, because it was all that her life had ever taught her to do. Desperate to switch the conversation away from her own life, she threw back that this was still her land and her god reigned.

Jesus dismissed her unilateral claim, along with the well, the land, her mountain and Jerusalem, telling her that God is spirit and the true worshippers he wanted must worship in spirit and in truth.

Had her world been turned upside down or just the right way up? I knew that my universe had been changed forever; Jerusalem no longer needed to exist! I slumped to the ground broken, exhausted. The gifts God had given to my people had just been shared with the unrighteous Gentiles who would see us deposed from our land again if they could!

The woman was now also finished. She capitulated and just wanted to know more. "I know that Messiah is coming. When he comes, he will explain everything to us."

Jesus delivered the final stroke. "I who speak to you am he."

The Messiah! Why did he not declare it among his own? I boiled inside, I was drained of every emotion as I sat and listened to The Son of God and the foreign harlot. They continued to discuss new life, as two friends do as they sit in the sun.

The others returned, their faces scowled unspoken questions at me. They could see my shock and reflected it, but they said nothing. The woman, meanwhile, left her water jar and ran towards the town. Within minutes, we could hear her shouting and calling and then the hundreds came out to meet Jesus as he lectured us about these new fields of harvest.

Afterwards, as we continued the journey north towards Galilee, Andrew demanded an explanation of me, but I couldn't tell him anything. I bit back and waved his frustration away, telling him I needed to speak with my father.

Andrew could not rest and appealed to Jesus, demanding a reason for preaching and healings among the Samaritans. The reply he got was that God always honoured his covenants and that God had guaranteed to bless all of Abraham's seed, both physical and spiritual.

I heard the answer but I could not process it. All I had ever known was a God who had set us apart from all other nations. A God who had given us a system of laws and justice. A God whose prophets warned us of the barbaric ways of the nations around us.

But a Messiah that made God's blessing available to foreigners without even going to the temple?

I thought of our family concerns for Simon the Zealot being radicalized against Rome and wondered if I, too, was being radicalized. Was this man a Rabbi of God or a psychotic madman?

My mind and guts were still churning over as we crossed the border out of Roman controlled Samaria and back into Galilee. I took off my sandals, banged them together and scrubbed my bare feet in the grass to expunge every trace of foreign dust, then asked Jesus for leave and returned home to Bethsaida. My mood was still black the following day as I crossed the next frontier into Herod Philip's territory.

* * * *

Fishing was my respite; I needed a few nights out on the lake with Father and James to unwind. At first, my story tumbled out without a clear chronology, a disorder of shock highlights, until Father and James helped me get my thoughts in order. Mother's aromatic lentil broth had warmed my stomach and the ballast of home had righted the storm-tossed vessel of my emotions.

Together, we worked through everything after the confrontation with the Chief Priests and synagogue leaders, the peoples' mixture of adoration and fear, and lastly the journey back through Samaria and the meeting at Jacob's Well.

Meanwhile, speculation about 'The Nazarene' continued to circulate at a fever pitch and the market place hummed with the latest news. The most extraordinary tale concerned a Herodian official, who rode the thirty miles from Capernaum to Cana and tore his way through the crowd to find Jesus, begging him from his knees to heal his sick son. The boy was healed despite being many miles away.

Then there was news of a riot as Jesus visited his hometown. Father wrote an urgent message to Simon Peter's new house in Capernaum. We needed to see Andrew and the others again to find out what had happened.

12/. Riot Sermon

Two days later, Andrew, Nathanael and Philip arrived in Bethsaida. Looking tired and stressed, they stood forlornly in our courtyard.

"So tell us, what happened at Nazareth?" Father asked, gesturing for them in sit in the shade of our vines. Mother brought some wine and bread and we gave them time to relax.

"The Nazarenes ran him out of town and tried to kill him!" said Philip.

"Capernaum is now Jesus' only home," said Andrew.

"On the way back to Capernaum, Jesus told us once again to disperse whilst he headed for the hills," Nathanael told us.

We hung on their every word as Philip explained further. "When we arrived in Nazareth, the welcome was lukewarm; they were reticent in their acceptance."

"He tried to have time with his relatives," said Nathanael. "That was impossible, even though we tried to stand guard and turn people away to give him some peace."

"They just mobbed him, always demanding miracles," said Philip. "So he sat by the spring and let the children crowd around him instead."

"He flicked water at them and if they tried the same, he just tickled them until they squealed," said Nathanael. "It was his way of ignoring the men."

Andrew continued. "Even to those who offered him praise, he told them he had not come for cult hero worship."

"After all he has done, he was still trying to be the simple *tekton*," said Nathanael.

"So was he trying to play down their expectations?" asked my father.

"He would only talk about holiness and obedience to God," said Philip, nodding. "He said nothing of the Kingdom until we came to the Sabbath."

"What happened then?" said James and I together.

"There is a makeshift synagogue there now and the leader gave him the leading place and presented Isaiah's scroll," Andrew told us. "But Jesus selected verses from different places to create his bespoke message for the Nazarenes."

"Zebedee, we have all recollected what we heard," said Philip. "That young scribe, John Mark, was with us and we all conferred afterwards over what he recorded."

"We need to find our Rabbi Benjamin and read the scrolls for ourselves," said Father. "Then we can hear the rest of your story."

We all hurried out and found the ancient Rabbi in his vegetable garden. My old teacher's joy to share the scriptures had never diminished and he laid down his tools, straightened his back and slowly walked to the spring to clean his hands with meticulous attention. Inside the synagogue, our steps echoed on the cool stone floor and when Benjamin slowly washed again, we failed to hide our impatience.

"I am overjoyed at your zeal for the scriptures, young men," Benjamin chastised us as he pulled on his silk gloves to handle the parchments. "But with reverence, gentlemen, with reverence."

"The first passage Jesus selected was the one that Nazareth would most want to hear," Philip told him. "He proclaimed to them 'The Spirit of the Lord is on me, because he has anointed me to preach good news to the poor.'"

Andrew continued eager to tell us the details. "But then he omitted 'he has sent me to bind up the broken-hearted' and instead continued, 'He has sent me to proclaim freedom for the prisoners.'"

Benjamin bent forward over the parchment to focus his eyes, but pointed straight to the place. "Ah! Yes, just here."

"And then added in 'recovery of sight for the blind,'" said Philip.

"Then he took that from elsewhere in Isaiah's scrolls," said Benjamin, selecting another with his years of expertise. He laid it out so we could all pore over it.

"He ended with 'to release the oppressed, to proclaim the year of the Lord's favour,'" said Nathanael.

"So, he returned to the original verses," said Benjamin. He moved the scrolls again and then pointed to the verse. "Are you are telling me that this Jesus of Nazareth did not end his reading by completing the verse 'and the day of vengeance of our God, to comfort all who mourn'?"

"Yes sir," confirmed Philip. "It seems to us that he omitted the very verse those Nazarenes would want to hear, that God would vanquish Rome and their tax collectors."

"Then Jesus rolled up the scroll gave it to the attendant and sat down, to show them he would not read any more," said Andrew. "No one took their eyes from him and the silence hung in the air like a storm, willing him to continue."

"So we have never seen a sword in his hand and so far not in his sermons either," said Father.

"Then he told them, 'Today this scripture is fulfilled in your hearing,'" said Philip.

"It was his same message that 'the times are fulfilled,'" said Nathanael. "But not what Nazareth wanted to hear."

Andrew raised his hands. "Everyone from the town was not willing to accept that Jesus really was *their* Messiah."

"Then what happened?" James demanded.

"He must have said something that made everything change?" I asked.

"He started by quoting to them, 'Heal Thyself Physician', to tell them they only wanted him for his miracles."

"And told them he saw no repentance from sins and therefore there would be no miracles, and what's more, it was their fault due to their lack of faith," Nathanael continued.

"So he delivered a rebuttal that they were really the blind that needed to recover their sight," said Father.

"At this point they were starting to stir against him and we thought he would end it there and walk away," said Andrew.

"The Rabbi is just so direct with his challenges," said James, head shaking. "If he sees people are wrong with God, he has no compromise with them."

"That's exactly what happened," confirmed Andrew. "He didn't walk away and just quoted more illustrations from scripture to drive his point home."

"What started the riot proper," said Philip, "was that he told them that Elijah had performed miracles for a foreign widow in Zarephath and also that Elisha had healed the Syrian army commander rather than the any of Israel's lepers."

"It is the same message that God's blessing is for foreigners!" said James. "Will he ask us to pray for The Prefect next?"

Andrew scowled. "He gave blessing to the Samaritans, but the Zealots of Nazareth just erupted in fury. They could not believe 'their Jesus' was telling them that God's blessing was not for them. So they drove him out, all the way to the top of the cliff to throw him off."

"Father," I said, "Jesus told the scarlet woman at Sychar that worship at Jerusalem was not required."

"I will go to Jerusalem for Passover," said Father. "But I believe we heard The Immerser challenge The Sanhedrin with the same message, when he offered sacrifice and forgiveness by The Jordan."

His words rocked me backwards; this had not occurred to me, even as I had been there.

Father brought Benjamin back into the conversation. "Rabbi, would you please give us your view on this use of the scriptures?" he requested.

"My friend, you know that I have never been a politician, like some," replied Benjamin. "I see God's goodness in the scriptures. Whatever the purpose of this Rabbi-Carpenter of Nazareth, I have two judgements." Then, his old and frail voice then became stronger. "First, he did not go outside of the rules of interpretation, and second, I would count his knowledge and use of the scriptures. To be able to go back and forth to selected verses and build such a bespoke message to be … quite exquisite!"

Benjamin's dim eyes peered at each of us in turn as we took in his words. "You say he spoke in Hebrew as well?"

"Yes sir, I far as I can tell, he speaks Hebrew fluently," replied Andrew.

"My, my," said Benjamin, taking Andrew's hand in his gentle wizened grasp. "If your Rabbi should ever come to Bethsaida and if I have not already departed to the place where all speak heavenly Hebrew, I would very much like to meet him."

Father thanked him with the embrace of an old friend and a gift for the synagogue. We withdrew and walked in slow contemplation back towards home for more private discussion.

"So how did you save Jesus from the mob?" asked Father.

"That was impossible because they were so furious," Andrew told us. "We were powerless to help, but then we didn't need to. Jesus somehow just walked out, called us and went on his way."

We stopped and looked at Andrew for more.

"We can't explain how," Philip shrugged. "Perhaps he turned on his power or called on unseen angels. But whatever the reason, Jesus walked right through the mob and no one could lay a hand on him!"

There was a stunned silence as the story finished.

"We all wanted to ask you about this, Zebedee," said Andrew. "We know this Jesus does the unexpected, but to give away to foreigners the blessings of God that we have always thought would be for Israel?"

"We cannot understand this," said Nathanael.

Father nodded. "We have also discussed this since John returned to tell us about Jesus' actions amongst the Samaritans. I have been praying and thinking much about this."

He said no more until we had reached the house and settled again under the vines to escape the summer heat.

Father drew deep breath. "To try and answer your question, the first thing I would say is that the Samaritans count Abraham, Isaac and Jacob to be the fathers of their nation as we do, even if we know they are astray in many other ways. He has told us his mission is to preach the Kingdom of God to 'all sons of Abraham'. Do you recall that?"

Father paused, looking at each of us to ensure we had registered his last statement.

"The second thing I would say is Jesus spoke the truth to Nazareth. The scriptures do indeed say the widow of Zarephath was saved from starvation by Elijah's miracle and Naaman the Syrian was the only one we are told of who was cleansed of leprosy." He raised a hand and gave us his look. "It is not for us to argue with the Law or the Prophets! So, tell me, what else do the scriptures tell us about our prophets amongst foreigners?"

"You need to tell us, Father," said James.

"Think of Jonah, for example. God sent him as a missionary to save the people of a foreign empire. He was a reluctant missionary and didn't want God to bless and save them! Then, consider Joseph in Egypt and Daniel in Babylon and the great blessing their work was to those countries, despite their tyrannical Pharaohs and Emperors."

We all nodded again. Father softened his voice and continued. "My sons and my friends, I want to assure you that the Lord God does indeed bless us and our people in many ways and we need to daily recognise this and give thanks, should we not? But I think we also need to ask ourselves a fundamental question, which is: 'Why does God choose our nation and bless it with his laws and his prophets?'"

I tried to grasp the conclusion, but it was beyond my whit. I wanted to say we were special, but it was safer to wait for his answer than venture my own suggestion; we all waited for Father's careful wisdom.

"I will give you a choice of two. Is it to keep God's blessing to ourselves or to be a force for good in this fallen and sinful world? To take the knowledge of a just and loving God and his laws of goodness out to the nations who also need it?" Father gazed across his contemplative silence and had yet one more illustration for his point. "I suggest that if we think through our history, we find that our problems have arisen when our people brought in the ways of the nations to pollute our land, not when we take the Lord God out to theirs."

My mind began to ease and my guts warmed; my universe could expand again with the mission of my God.

James said, "Thank you, Father, 'The earth is the Lord's and everything in it.'"

"Sir, why then is Jesus rejected in his own country if he brings God's blessing?" Andrew asked. "We all saw the miracles and healings he did in Jerusalem, in Judea and here in Galilee."

"We talked about this on the night we decided to go and see The Immerser," said Father. "Most of the prophets, whom the Sanhedrin tell us to revere, were also rejected by the priests of their own day and why? Tell me why?" He challenged us again to find the answers ourselves.

"Because those prophets did what we have seen The Immerser do and what we now see Jesus of Nazareth does," I said. "He faces people with their sins and challenges them to change."

"Do people want to change?" Father continued to fire his challenges.

"Many people are either too proud or too unbelieving or too hurting inside," said Nathanael. "So they keep truth only in part and they choose not to look inside themselves."

"What of us, if we are to call ourselves his disciples?" said Andrew.

I nodded to him. "This is what we started to find with The Immerser."

"The Sanhedrin did not look for this with The Immerser," said James.

"Many of those in positions of religious or political authority have too much to lose," said Father. "Power and influence, as well as honour, which they count as important to themselves."

Mother had also joined us in the courtyard spinning wool, and took her moment to join the conversation. "This Jesus has chosen to walk an impossible line. He would do better if he learned to win friends and influence people, instead of confronting them like that wild Immerser. I praise God for his prophets, but trouble has a habit of following this Jesus of Nazareth."

We all smiled. James and I heard the concern of our mother and knew her instinct was to protect her sons and their friends from trouble.

Other questions burned inside me. "The Rabbi shows such great concern and compassion for ordinary people, but combines this with facing them with their own sins, not those of The Sanhedrin or the King. Is this what the Messiah is expected to do?"

"To answer that question," said Father, "I would also quote from Isaiah: '*He was despised and rejected by men, a man of sorrows and familiar with suffering. Like one from whom men hide their faces he was despised and we esteemed him not.*'"

We recalled the verses and all nodded again.

"And if I may try and draw my thoughts to a conclusion," continued Father, "what I see in this man, as he preaches his 'Kingdom of God', is both the ability and the manifesto to care for the outcast, the widow and the orphan that our Law and Prophets have always taught us. If he is to complete what The Immerser started, he must feed the people this righteousness and build a following that will make the Sanhedrin an irrelevance, and re-establish the law over and above what the Qum'ran cult ever achieved. Only then could the temple be purified from corruption."

The Second Year and a Half: The Call of the King

17. Impressive Persona

Something unspoken burned inside me, but I waited until the following day when Andrew and Philip had departed.

"Father," I ventured. "I have one further question?"

"Yes, John?"

"Do you now think this Jesus of Nazareth could be The Messiah?"

Father's demeanour held much gravity. "I have been trying to find reasons against him, but in all the prophecies I know, I cannot find anything that does not fit. Yes, I think that Jesus bar Joseph of Nazareth, Son of David, proclaimed as 'Son of God' by The Immerser, could, just could, be The Messiah."

Hearing Father's approval of Jesus was like a torch being lit inside of me. James' face told me the same. I knew that this thoughtful and cautious consideration had been going on inside Father for almost a year, since our time at The Immerser's pool. Before we could speak again, he raised his hands for special attention. "From his actions *so far*, everything he has done fits with what the scriptures tell us about the Messiah, *but* there are still many prophecies that he will need to fulfil about what the Messiah will do among the nations."

"Even now, you are still cautious, Father?" said James.

Father nodded. "The questions in my mind are now: will he explicitly claim to be the Messiah to his own people, as well as telling us that 'the times are fulfilled'? And if so, what will this man do next?"

"I think he must build a following," said James.

"Yes, a kingdom must have people who follow the king," agreed Father.

"Where will that kingdom be, now that he has been rejected in Jerusalem and Nazareth?" I asked.

"I suggest," said Father, "a more important question is: 'what will he ask that following to do?'"

"Where do you think he will lead his followers?" asked James.

"I think we cannot second guess him," said Father. "We can only wait and see, and measure him by the Law and the Prophets in each and every move he makes."

* * * *

As springtime rolled on into summer, I kept Father's words close by as Jesus took us sixty miles back south to Judea. As we toured the villages around Jerusalem at a relentless pace, I saw my Rabbi's popularity continue to climb to superstar status. The speculation in the synagogues and between all those who tagged onto us was as the same in Galilee. It was the same everywhere. Was Jesus an Essene or Zealot? Would he join the Pharisees? Was he Messiah, or was he deluded and dangerous?

But I was now sure he would not align with any one group or another. He would only be God's man, as the prophets of old.

Wherever we went, the Pharisees and synagogue rulers kept a cautious control over their communities, whilst Sadducees sent their stewards to watch our movements through their fields. Meanwhile, the Zealots mingled with the crowds; they seemed to be organised in watches and changed each week. Twice I saw Simon bar Mordecai. I watched him as he watched me, but I did not pursue him, reasoning that now I needed to let him come to me.

Most of all I watched Jesus, that the dust of the sandals of my Rabbi might cover me. He remained indifferent to the praises of the people, refusing to play the cult leader; his only role was the servant of God, the ascetic prophet, his mission always to focus the people and their praises onto his God. He said nothing of Rome.

All the time the people pursued us; they came from far and wide, bringing the sick to be healed. Then we would soon move on again, because crowds attracted the attention of Antipas' scouts or the dust of a Roman cohort as it tramped over the horizon.

Our core group had now grown, but there were those we did not trust. I saw Saul, Chai and others from the entourage of Shlomo and Uri. Jesus spoke only in parables when they were with us. Remembering Father's caution, I marked them all whilst keeping myself anonymous amongst the melee. I saw them sometimes together and sometimes separate in their own parties.

Meanwhile, the wave of popularity carried us along, the pressures were intense, and we all felt it. I knew my Rabbi was being emptied by those who came to him with their pain, whilst the people of power and influence scrutinised him from a distance. When it became too much, our escape was withdrawing to solitary places in the hills until we shook off the flotsam and the spies. Then, Jesus would teach us in plain words from his parables and withdraw for his solitary prayer.

There were two particular newcomers to our core group that drew my attention; I pointed them out to Andrew.

"Do you see the scribe who has joined us?"

"Yes, I first saw him in synagogue, two Sabbaths past," he replied. "He has all the appearance of a scholar. Notice his hands have no calluses. I hope he will carry water and provisions like the rest of us."

"Well, so far the rough sleeping has not detracted from his grooming," I said, looking at the oiled and combed hair and beard of Judas Iscariot.

"What do you make of Thomas?" said Andrew.

"He recites the Law as if he is reading it from a scroll," I replied. "But I wouldn't say the joy of the Lord comes naturally to him!"

Andrew gave a quiet laugh. "Yes, he is the serious type," he agreed. "His style fits that doom-laden stammer and eccentric twitch."

"Except when he recites the Law," I said. "Have you noticed that he never stops or twitches then?"

"No, I hadn't," said Andrew. "Amazing."

"These people have come to us since the riot in Nazareth," I said. "His rejection there has not done any harm."

"I agree," Andrew replied. "It showed everyone that the Rabbi is not a prisoner of his clan and educated people have taken note."

We moved to where Philip and Nathanael we talking with Judas about how they had first met Jesus.

"John and I saw the Rabbi come out of the wilderness," Andrew joined in. "We left The Immerser to follow him and he told us he had spent forty days and nights with the wild animals, protected by angels."

"His actions and words contain many signs," said Nathaniel. "A new Moses in the wilderness, no less!"

"And if this Jesus of Nazareth were projecting himself as a new Moses, to do what Moses did," said Judas, "what would that mean?"

Our thoughts all tumbled out together in reply.

"A new father of the nation?"

"A new nation?"

"A statesman and law giver?"

"To claim a new promised land!?"

"And a stiff-necked people, with a tendency to … g-go astray and w-worship golden idols?" Thomas' deep tones were punctuated with pauses.

"I have been listening to this preaching of the 'Kingdom of God' for some time now," said Judas. "I was there when he drove the moneychangers from the temple, although I kept in the background, waiting to see if this man was a prophet or a revolutionary."

"What have you seen?" asked Andrew.

"It is what he has not done that most interests me," replied Judas. "He has neither preached against Rome nor against the King, as The Immerser did, and there was no blood spilled in the temple."

"That is fine," agreed Nathanael. "But we and every village of Judea await the Kingdom to be restored to Israel and all ask, when will this be?"

"There are two possibilities," said Judas. "Either the Lord God provides an opportunity to step into, or the Rabbi must build a following that enables him to replace the High Priest and his family."

"What opportunity do you think might arise, Judas?" asked Philip.

"If the people reject Antipas and he outlives his usefulness to Rome," said Judas. "This could be an advantage for us. The Prefect would want a civilised alternative that kept the Zealots and their *Sicarii* at the margins."

"The corruption in the temple goes much deeper than just the High Priest," said Philip. "We need most of the Sanhedrin to go."

"The Rabbi needs to build his Kingdom more than in the just the hearts of his people," said Judas Iscariot. "In almost a year, he has only made one spectacular protest and preached a message of hope, but built nothing of substance."

"Next Passover, the Rabbi can replace the whole temple establishment," said Andrew with confidence.

"I tell you, we cannot depose all of the parties and powerful families of Jerusalem," said Judas Iscariot. "That would leave a power vacuum that we could not fill. We need to choose our partners in this new Kingdom and choose with care."

"The Rabbi is his own man," I said. "We have seen him decline all approaches so far."

"That will be good," replied Judas Iscariot. "The Rabbi can ask for a high price when the time comes for powerful allies."

"How will such political bargaining b-bring us closer to The Law and the Lord's blessing?" asked Thomas.

"I think a good strategy would be to target the Pharisees," said Judas Iscariot. "If many of them could be brought over, it would drive a wedge between them and the Sadducees. The priesthood must be returned to the tribe of Levi. What else would you suggest?"

"We would need a generation of hardship in the desert under this new Moses," said Thomas. "The old needs to be swept away and a new Joshua will conquer with a new generation."

I could see some annoyance in Judas Iscariot's demeanour. "You speak of old history," he said. "We have hardship enough now under Rome. We have to deal with today's realities."

"Nevertheless, God does not change," said Thomas. "Neither do stiff-necked p-people."

"You speak with zeal, but it is a shame your speech is not clear." Judas looked down his nose to win his argument.

"Mock the afflicted if you will," said Thomas. "I wear my twitch as a badge of my love for the t-twin brother I lost. For it came to me the day I lost him."

After a few moments, Philip filled the awkward silence. "Do you notice?" he said. "Jesus always wants to teach the people and talk only of God, but most act in ignorance to his teaching and are just waiting for the miracles."

"Yes, I see that as well," replied Andrew. "But remember Nazareth. He refuses to do miracles when the situation is not right. He always needs a purpose or a trueness of heart."

"You're telling me he turned down the support of his hometown?" asked Judas Iscariot.

"Then what is the purpose, I mean the real main purpose, at the centre of his mission?" asked Nathanael.

"The Kingdom, of course," said Philip. "Miracles are done to show the Kingdom of God has power."

"What sort of power and for what purpose?" Judas Iscariot continued his rhetoric.

"God's Kingdom must be free of Roman legions and Roman taxes," said Nathanael.

"What lesson does Hezekiah's story tell you?" asked Judas Iscariot.

"The foreign invader was repelled," said Andrew.

"Only because there was righteousness and not corruption in the heart of God's people," added Thomas.

"Correct, Thomas! A Messiah would unite the nation under him first, in order to deliver us from Rome," said Judas Iscariot.

"What about those Herodians and Sadducees who find order at the point of a Roman sword to be a convenient master?" countered Philip. "Their merchants move freely with less brigands on the roads and more foreign markets for their goods."

"Yes, and more foreign marriages for the convenience of their business," put in Nathanael.

"And more dilution of observance of the Law!" said Thomas.

"Yes, I agree," said Andrew. "Then why doesn't Jesus use his power and free us from Rome as it takes our taxes for their pagan temples? If he did, then all the parties in Jerusalem would not only accept him, but also back him, because it would give them real power in a free Israel.

"Would the factions ever unite, and even then, would they have the might to withstand Rome?" said Judas Iscariot, appealing for reason.

"None of the great prophets of old ever needed an army." I recalled Father's words. "They had God on their side and this was enough."

"Maybe," said Nathanael, after a short pause for thought. "But under Joshua's leadership we conquered this land as a fighting force, as it was promised to us by God."

"So now it needs to be re-conquered again," said Judas Iscariot. "Though not necessarily in the same way. I believe that the Rabbi has between now and next Passover to preach his Kingdom to build a movement of people with the power to sweep aside the High Priest. There will be others who will want to see him deposed, and so we can find allies."

"The parables tell of the Kingdom," said Andrew. "His message has always been the same."

"That is the politics of our situation," said Judas Iscariot. "If the Teacher talks openly about the Kingdom, it will be interpreted as inciting revolution; an alternative rule to Caesar's and Herod's. This is why he chooses his words with care and you must learn to do the same, as I do, if you are going to build the Kingdom with him."

"What of the new nation of the Kingdom?" I asked. "Is your opinion that it will be taken from the existing nation or will it be to lead the existing nation in freedom?"

Judas Iscariot paused. "That," he said, "is a good question, but whichever way, power will need to be wrested from the hands of the Sanhedrin."

So for once, this Judas Iscariot did not have a ready answer and the debate ended, but I knew it was far from over.

* * * *

As we journeyed onwards through the Judean villages, I talked with Andrew in private whenever I could. "Judas is impressive in his speech and appearance, don't you think?"

"He speaks with elders on the same level," agreed Andrew. "He has all the manners and education to win influence."

"He has stature and charisma, too, with those neat robes and hemmed cloak," I said. "I was watching when we entered that last village. Some of the people go to greet him, whilst our Rabbi looks so dowdy."

"He will be invited to top tables along with Jesus," said Andrew. "Your father's name would get you there as well. Why not join him?"

"You know the few whiskers on my chin would count against me," I replied. "Do not suggest this; I need to be discreet as Father told me."

"Yes, I can see that," he said, before adding, "what about Thomas?"

"I like him, he has much knowledge, but neither subtlety nor awareness that his direct manners may offend," I said. "And his speech impediment will always carry the accusation of a source of sin for his affliction."

"He answered Judas well, though."

"Yes, but I don't think he even realises that himself."

"Do you think it will bring more conflict to the disputes?" asked Andrew.

"Perhaps," I said. "But that will not occur to Thomas!"

2/. Drop Your Nets

After a three-day march from Judea, we stood by the lake of Galilee again and, to avoid the dangers of an emperor's welcome, we embraced our farewells in the evening's dusk outside Capernaum. Jesus had told us we should disperse for a while, so that those pursuing us would lose our trail. It also would be a welcome respite from the crowds. The following day, Andrew and I crossed the Herod's border back to Bethsaida. I was much looking forward to fishing with my family and time to discuss all that I had seen and heard. Father and James now often spent their time fishing from Capernaum, instead of Bethsaida, as did fishermen from elsewhere. This caused Simon Peter to demand how so many men thought they could share success in such a small area, unless the fish gathered for sermons as well. I understood his stress, with older parents to support and taxes to pay, but it was just good to be close to Jesus and see what he was doing.

One evening we all set out, Simon Peter and Andrew in one boat and Father, James and I in others with some of our men, with a plan to work together and compress the fish into a kettle. It was now high summer again, my favourite time to be out on the lake. The night was still, warm, clear and almost magical with the flaming torches to attract the fish close to the nets. But on this night, we had no success at all. We returned to Capernaum dejected, despite a beautiful dawn, with Peter muttering that there was not enough fish to go around.

I sat on the seawall, washing and repairing the nets, when Jesus came through the town with the usual large crowd pressing around him. As I had seen so often, their excited adoration was drowning the message of living in God's Kingdom, and as the numbers on the harbour wall grew, they forced my Rabbi to the edge as if they might drown him as well.

Jesus' escape took the form of Simon Peter's boat; he agreed Jesus' request, pushed off and manned the oars. I watched as the sermon continued and Simon gently dipped one oar and then the other to keep the boat in the best position. I reflected on how Simon's good manners contrasted with some in the crowd. On the outside, he might seem thick-skinned and unwelcoming but, in fact, he would offer all the hospitality he could. Jesus had recently healed his mother-in-law from a fever and Simon did not take this gift for granted, though being frustrated by the hordes of people that mobbed his house to be where Jesus was. For Simon Peter, having the Messiah in town was good as long as it did not create too much fuss and intrude into his life, and right now I felt much the same. I wanted to finish my work and go for some sleep.

Jesus finished speaking and, with a mastery of control I had seen before, dismissed the crowd, turning his back to the shore as he sat and faced his oarsman. I heard his voice say, "Thank you Simon Peter, you have been very good to me, but I would like to ask one more thing: put out into deep water and let your nets down for a catch."

At first, Simon Peter had reflected Jesus' smile, but now it dropped from his face as his oars dropped into the water. I froze, knowing Simon and wondering what would follow! At that moment I could read his mind and, with a few expletives thrown in, it said, 'What do simple carpenters think they know about fishing anyway?'

As he tried to keep his manners in order, Simon Peter gesticulated at his empty nets and boat and appealed for reason. He was not afraid to let his feelings show and protested, "Rabbi, we've worked hard all night and haven't caught anything!"

Jesus just sat there, giving him one of his steady gazes, with a little smile that said, 'I know Simon Peter, but do this, please, because I ask you.' So Simon Peter sighed, shrugged his big shoulders and with a voice heavy with resignation said, "But because you say so, I will let down the nets."

As he pulled at the oars, Andrew started to arrange the net. Father, James and I exchanged glances and without a word launched a boat. At the least we need to show our support for Simon, but something else kindled inside me. I had learned that I needed to expect the unexpected when following this Jesus.

Simon Peter had not rowed far enough to be in deep water before they gathered the net up and cast it in a wide arc across the water. As the boat drifted on, I saw the net began to go tight as the brothers pulled, so it closed around anything inside. They started to haul the net, but after just a few pulls, they stopped and looked at each other. We were now close enough to see the startled expression in their faces!

Simon Peter beckoned us with an urgent jerk of his head; both he and Andrew appeared to be struggling to hold the net. Father turned and waved an arm at our men. There were too many other boats around and a shout would betray our catch. James was pulling hard at the oars. Now we were almost with them, we could see for ourselves the huge weight of fish inside the net, wriggling for freedom. It would be impossible to pull the net on board; it was just too heavy and in great danger of splitting.

"Lash the boats together at the prow, with the net between," Father instructed, but I was already there and then joined him and James taking hold of the net to spread the strain.

Jesus had stayed at the back of Simon Peter's boat, but now the situation was under control he joined us as some held the net, whilst others scooped the writhing fish out and into the boat, flapping and slapping around our feet. We were all in high spirits now, enjoying this most fantastic of catches, laughing together as we worked. Then, as it continued, the laughter gave way to gasps and grunts. For a considerable time I continued like this: my back ached, my arms tired, and *still* there were more fish. I was wading in fish now, a heaving mass of slippery silver around my legs. Andrew, still holding the net, encouraged us to keep it up because he could feel the net getting lighter, but I wasn't sure that it was! When we could fill the boats no more and were in danger of sinking, we dug through the fish to find the oars and headed for the nearest shore. It seemed an age as we paddled along, afraid that a single wave could sink us. As the beach came, we all jumped into the shallows, heaved the boats a very little way up the stones and flopped down, knowing that our amazing catch was safe.

It had been a long night and now it was going to be an even longer day, but just then, I could not feel tired. I jumped up and, pulling James and Andrew to their feet, we danced in circles, laughed and clapped each other on the back out of excitement and sheer relief. Then we stilled, aware that Simon Peter had not joined us. He was standing at the water's edge with his big hands loose at his sides, looking at the boats and the mountain of fish and the net, still not emptied. Jesus stood by him.

"All my life, since I was a boy," Simon Peter's voice was a hoarse and emotional whisper. "This is all I have ever done. All I ever wanted to do. Lord, I am but a simple man." He sank to his knees with a crunch of the gravel beach. "Go away from me, Lord, because I am a sinful man."

Jesus reached out a reassuring hand to his shoulder, waited until Simon Peter raised his head, and then said, "Don't be afraid; from now on, you will be a fisher of men." Jesus turned his face to us. "You as well, James and John." he said. "Follow me."

We looked at Father. He nodded, and I knew deep inside me what Simon Peter was now feeling. A power to transform my life was flooding over me, reaching deep into my soul, speaking to me more than any time during my pilgrimage with The Immerser. I knew somehow that we were all feeling it. It is more than a little frightening and yet wonderful, when you know that your life is being turned upside down and will never be the same again.

How long those moments lasted I cannot say, nor can I tell you much about the days that followed, except I had very little sleep. Life was a blur of fish: smoked, dried, broiled and pickled fish.

Both Simon Peter's house in Capernaum and ours in Bethsaida became centres of a huge industry, his family, my family, his neighbours. Caleb and our men worked alongside us with the expectation that the Son-of-David had now come amongst us.

Father called in merchants he knew; neighbours acted as agents to the markets in nearby towns and took their share. The poor and the infirm beggars feasted well. I knew what we were doing; Jesus had not only spoken to Simon Peter in the way he understood, but he was also the provider for his family. For the time when he would be away with Jesus, there was provision, and neighbours would repay what they had received.

Then, at the end of it all, the fish that we had just worked so hard for didn't seem to matter anymore; I was no longer a fisherman.

The day of parting came, with many tears and embraces. James and I, with Father and Mother, had our quiet moment under the vines of our courtyard.

I needed Father's words. "We will always remember your wisdom and caution, Father. What do you have to say to us now?"

Father tried to keep his voice regular and even, as he always did, but on this occasion, he failed.

"I would say that you are doing what every young man dreams of and yearns for, a mission for your life, a quest to follow." He choked and held us close to his chest. "To win our people for the Kingdom of God is something that you will need to strive for, a battle where you must win through. The King has called you and you have answered."

It was a blur of tearing emotions as I hugged my parents and left my old life behind forever.

Jesus was waiting and, as we walked away with him, I told James how I was feeling. "I remember what Jesus said to Nicodemus the Pharisee about being born again."

He nodded. "Yes, I remember every word of what you told us."

"I know what it feels like now," I said. "The old has gone and the new has come. There's no turning back now and life will never be the same again!"

James smiled. "We have new nets to drop now!"

When we came to Capernaum, Simon Peter was quiet, but I could see that Andrew was ecstatic as his feelings poured out of him. "After a year of rising from village carpenter, people said that the Rabbi's mission had come to an end after the double rejection in Jerusalem and his hometown. I was not one of them! Now we know that, far from being over, the mission is just moving onwards to the next stage."

I knew what was going on inside him. His faith was almost childlike in its simplicity; he had seen and he had followed his instincts. Now his brother and his friends were with him, too.

"You were among the first to seek him, my friend," I said.

Andrew continued. "This Jesus of Nazareth will build a movement of people, ordinary people, a living proof that God is doing a new thing in our nation. It will be like your father and that Judas Iscariot have said. At Passover, the Messiah will ride into Jerusalem in glory just like the prophets of old have predicted, and we will see it. We will see him take his place in the temple and the world will see his glory, the Kingdom of God in a nation set free from sin and illness and from foreign invaders."

At that moment in time, I did not disagree, and the surge of expectation ran hot through me as well. Events of the next two years would twist us one way and then the other, but right now, we had made our decision and were following our Messiah into the promise of a new Kingdom.

3/. Blasphemy Spoken

Wild screams interrupted the sermon. I looked for the source as they cried out from the back of the congregation. A man rushed at Jesus and collapsed to the floor before him. The voices came again. First they raged, and then they whimpered. I was close enough to see that they came from the man thrashing around at Jesus' feet. My Rabbi commanded silence and the voices stopped.

Capernaum's synagogue rocked and gasped around us. I heard Jesus' voice through the clamour as he commanded, "Be silent and leave him!" The man convulsed again, his body thrown around as if by some unseen force, then he went limp. Only the rise of his chest suggested life.

The synagogue continued to gabble with excitement as men clambered over each other for a better view. My eyes were locked onto my Rabbi; his actions were almost nonchalant as he helped the man to his feet and spoke gently. The melee parted before him as he lead the man back to his place and asked those nearby to sit close and care for him, whilst they nodded in fearful obedience. Jesus returned to the front, walking with ordinary steps and picking up the scroll again, and looked around with the expectancy of order and quiet for his sermon to continue.

I realised how tight I was holding myself and let Jesus' calm demeanour wash over me. Looking around at James, Peter, Andrew and Judas, their faces told me how I felt. I cannot tell you of another word of that sermon, but Jesus rolled up the scroll and handed the meeting back to a nervous elder. The synagogue stood but nobody moved as we followed Jesus out and back to Peter's house at a suitable Sabbath pace.

After the Sabbath sunset, it all began again. All those who had travelled for days but had been shut outside the synagogue now clamoured at the gate. They pushed and jostled, carrying their sick of many diseases. We stood together at Peter's door, pushing back to bring some order for our Rabbi. Peter's large frame and voice called for order before the man of God. Judas knew how to impress and control with his sartorial presence. He stood in the gate, looking down his nose at the melee, daring the people to disturb his neat robes and oiled beard.

Andrew and I stood with Nathanael and Philip, challenging the people before us to repent in holiness, as we had learned at The Immerser's pool. Were they clean in repentance to come before the prophet, we demanded? Our job was done when a line of some order, if not calm, awaited the attentions of our Rabbi.

I watched Jesus as he laid his hands on each pilgrim in turn; his relentless energy reminded me of The Immerser. Healings and blessings followed the Kingdom message. Again, I heard the wild voices: they called him Messiah, they begged the Son of God to leave them alone, before they were gagged and dispatched at his command.

It was the early hours of the morning before all had been dealt with and I dragged my exhausted frame up the stairs onto Peter's roof for sleep. My one thought, before the stars swam before my eyes, was: had I followed close enough for his dust to cover me? If I felt like this, how did my Rabbi feel? Had all energy and power been drained from him?

* * * *

The next morning we left early. I still felt drained, but I was pleased to be escaping the broiling-pot that Capernaum had become. Once on the road, the debate began.

"We all heard them," said Peter. "Demons in our synagogue."

"Those voices chilled me to the bone," said Nathanael. "They were not of men."

"Demon-possessed people, at synagogue," corrected Judas.

"It is what they said, as much as their presence, that shocked me," said James.

"If they say he is the Messiah," said Philip, "why did Jesus silence them?

"Why should a man of God want the … w-witness of a demon?" said Thomas.

"I heard The Immerser call him the 'Son of God' and people called it blasphemy!" Andrew shook his head in wonderment.

"So demons know the same blasphemy as The Immerser?" I said. "That is, unless it also happens to be the truth."

"What do we call as blasphemy in these times?" asked Peter. "And what is now righteousness?"

"He is only keeping his identity secret until the right time," said Judas Iscariot. "Too many simple peasants are already expecting the Kingdom to appear by miracle after every sermon."

"I have heard the people talk," said Andrew. "They say it is a new teaching and with authority."

"His words had the authority for the exorcism," said Thomas. "He needs no … r-reference from great Rabbis of the past when he teaches the Law."

"Indeed," said Judas Iscariot, "but I think the High Priest would not agree. They will oppose us every day from here to Passover."

* * * *

Our late evening return to Capernaum didn't stop the town coming out to meet us in song, some with branches and garlands. This proclamation of my Rabbi as emperor would not go unnoticed. I looked in the direction of the Roman camp, but the sentry stood quietly, and it seemed that their orders were to monitor and not to confront for the present.

We bunched around Jesus for his protection, clambering and wading through the fervour that crushed around us until we reached the house, but even that was of little sanctuary, as the crowds swarmed again. Pharisees and teachers of the law were already there from all the surrounding villages, accompanied by others from Judea and Jerusalem. It was now plain to me that our movements were being tracked and reported. The most senior men made their way into the house uninvited to listen to Jesus and judge him for themselves. Outside the house, I could hear the immense excitement as people jostled for a piece of the action. Inside was calmer, because important people like Pharisees and teachers of the law were not to be jostled, but we had no space to recline for a meal. I knew that Simon Peter hated this, but he cleared a path for his wife to serve. We had managed to eat a little and

Jesus was starting to speak when a new noise entered the hubbub: the sound of heavy blows on the roof above. Pieces of the ceiling began to fall onto us. It was clear that someone was now digging through it, and those in the centre of the room pressed towards the sides as chunks of baked mud and straw began to rain down. We were trapped: escape from the house was impossible because of the crowds outside, and all I could do was cover my eyes and mouth with my headscarf. Peter went into a ballistic rage, shouting about the house, asking was this the just reward for his hospitality, until he was forced to stop, coughing and gasping in the dust.

A hole appeared and bright sunlight shone down through the fog; the hole became wider as men continued to hack away at it. Then, the noise stopped and I heard shouts of command to pick up ropes and heave. The sunlight disappeared as through came a woven mat with a rope at each corner, lowered into the middle of the room. The figure inside it was the forlorn shape of a thin body, twisted in paralysis. A man looked up at us with the pathos of disease and fear in his eyes for the chaos of his intrusion into such a high-powered meeting of religious leaders.

As he reached the floor, the ropes went slack and faces appeared in the hole, silhouetted against the sky. They apologised with great pleas for mercy. Talking over each other, they explained they could not get their neighbour to Jesus any other way because of the great crowd outside the door.

Jesus showed no regard for the dust and dirt that now covered him and gave the wild-eye paralytic a hand of reassurance.

"Friend … your sins are forgiven."

The room stirred around me as the mood changed, and I knew that these words had been chosen for the Pharisees and teachers of the law. Once again, it was something that could only have been said by a Messiah, a great fake, or a madman.

'Blasphemy!' The whisper went around the room like a bad smell.

Jesus straightened up, looked around at those of high authority and spoke straight into their thoughts, his words delivered in that easy manner of friends at a summer picnic.

"Why are you thinking these things? Which is easier: to say to the paralytic 'Your sins are forgiven', or to say 'Get up off your mat and walk'?"

Silence ensued, but no Pharisee dared to fill it as Jesus gaze caught them each in the eye. "But, that you may know that the Son of Man has authority on earth to forgive sins..." My Messiah turned again to the man at his feet. "I tell you, get up, take your mat, and go home."

We all watched as the man's twisted frame relaxed and straightened, his face wide-eyed in wonderment. He stretched an arm and then a leg as his whole body quivered. He cried out in release, his long groan cutting through the silence.

Gasps came from everywhere as, still wild-eyed and speechless, the man got to his feet, stared mutely at Jesus for a few moments, bowed in thanks and then picked up his mat as he had been commanded. The moment was broken as the men above bellowed their praises to God, disappeared from the ruined roof, and rushed back down the stairs.

I watched the faces of the Pharisees and teachers of the law. They had no answer and, even if they had, it would have been drowned by the ecstatic roars from the crowd outside as the newly healed man walked out through them to embrace his carers. After that, the crowd began to ease as many went with the healed man to mob him for his story.

I sat in my own world, surrounded by the dust and rubble. I had seen this before. Once the people had seen what they came to see, once they had had their 'miracle kick' to excite their otherwise dull lives, they went away satisfied, at least for the moment. The Pharisees and teachers of the law went as well, confounded by the authority of the miraculous; they took themselves off to discuss what Jesus had said and done and what their reaction to him should be. Seeing them go, the remains of the crowd concluded nothing else would happen that day and also left.

I looked towards Jesus; to me, he seemed the least satisfied person of all. Once again, he had emptied himself out of pure compassion for their desperate situation and for the faith that had been shown, and once again, the miracle had gotten in the way of the message. I pondered on how his invitation to join the Kingdom of God had gone unheeded and forgotten. The people were no nearer to their God despite his reaching out to them. Their satisfaction would only be temporary, not the permanent commitment to the Kingdom that my Rabbi invited them into.

I joined with several others as we tried to console Simon Peter, promising to clear up and put his roof back together again.

"Rabbi?" asked Nathanael. "What had this paralysed man done to deserve such a great healing, if his sins were so great?"

"Had he done some great act of giving or pilgrimage with his neighbours?" asked Philip.

"No," replied Jesus. "He had done nothing like these and I did not say if his sins were great or small."

"All I saw in his eyes was fear and desperation," said Andrew.

"Yes, he was only a broken and fearful man," came the reply. "He did not need to be anything else. Men who are desperate of their situation and are broken and humble in spirit before God are the ones who find him."

James put his mouth close to my ear. "Words of blasphemy or words of freedom from sin?"

"I think authority with healing from terrible affliction is not an action of blasphemy," I replied.

I looked across at Judas Iscariot, his scholar's hands were not involved in the clear up; he was sitting with furrowed brow. I wondered for his thoughts for this brand of spiritual politics and the flashpoint that had just been.

4/. The Tax Collector

"He was lucky to leave with his life, never mind the money." My brother's comment was dry and humourless.

Peter's language was too foul for me to describe here, but he spoke it only to the goat, as he rumbled around his animal room. The tax collector had just departed after what I can only describe as prolonged and heated dialogue about the dues on a large catch of fish.

Peter completed his circuit, his expression still violent. "What amount of money?" He demanded to us. "What amount of money can make a man turn his back on his country, its ways and beliefs of the Lord God, to become a paid collaborator for a foreign barbarian?" Peter made to go inside his house, but thought better about it and turned for another lap of the room. "What price for those who made themselves rich by taking money from their own people?" He ranted to the ceiling. "Caesar's thief for the upkeep of a pagan temple; the despicable and barbaric practices of nakedness and orgy!"

The only thing to do was leave him to cool; we went inside the house to continue with the repair of the roof.

* * * *

Some days later, Peter's house was back to normal, even if he was not. The town had mostly left us alone whilst the work was being done and now Jesus led us out again. His life as a carpenter was now impossible; he had left it behind as we had left ours. He no longer told us to disperse during the pressure times; the mission of the Kingdom of God was now full on and today's lesson would be a shocking contrast for us all compared to the broken and fearful paralytic.

As we entered the marketplace and passed the tax collector, I could hear Simon Peter again, darkly muttering about parasites sucking the living out of honest working men. Andrew, James and I walked alongside to calm him with our solidarity. I admit I could find no warmth for these outcasts from our society and regarded them as worse than the foreign invaders that they worked for. So when Jesus stopped at the booth of Capernaum's most hated tax collector, the hunched Matthew, and struck up a conversation with him, we all lingered in the street, wanting to move away as soon as possible.

The short conversation between Jesus and the tax collector ended when Jesus said the same 'follow me' as he had to us. I stood agape as Matthew left his booth, all his money and his puzzled looking Roman guard where they were, and shuffled down the street with Jesus.

It was one of those times when Jesus had a profound effect on one individual. Matthew now hopped around Jesus like a child trying to please his father, begging Jesus to accept his hospitality and bring all his disciples for a banquet that evening.

We grinned and guffawed to each other, expecting that Jesus would cut him down to size and send him packing at any moment. We had seen him deal with self-righteous Pharisees, so this tax collector would be mincemeat!

So then, we all stood frozen in the street, stunned as our Rabbi was gratitude itself and graciously accepted with a huge smile. I cannot describe how a hunchback goes into an ecstatic dance, but Matthew rushed off down the street waving his arms, already calling ahead to his household. Jesus walked calmly on as we shuffled along after him. Simon Peter and Andrew had hanging jaws; it really had been a bad week for them. Nathanael and Philip had open expressions, a mixture of incredulity and disgust. I looked at James and Judas, who both looked as if, for once, they could find common cause.

It was Simon Peter who typically voiced it for us all. "Rabbi, do you think I am so hungry that I will eat a collaborator's food!?"

"This would be a mistake, Rabbi," said Judas. "You would give the priests the opportunity to shame you."

I plumbed the depths of my own feelings again. I remembered how cold I had felt at Sychar, as I saw Jesus offer a place in the Kingdom of God to the Samaritans and how my guts had only been warmed by the light of Father's explanation of the scriptures. Was this just as bad or worse? This was a man who had prostituted himself to the dust-polluting foreign empire and its gods. Was then our God still prepared to be faithful in the face of such infidelity?

The muttering and scowling continued amongst us as we followed Jesus down to the lake and found shade under some orange trees. It was as if he was unaware of our mood, but merely answered the question that none of us had asked by saying, "He is a son of Abraham and as much an heir to the covenant and promises as you are."

After a while to let that sink in, he added, "Which of you would claim to be so righteous that you had earned your place to join this mission?"

No one attempted an answer, and after the afternoon relaxing by the lake to recover from our shock and his chastisement, we were submissive and ready to follow our Rabbi towards Matthew's house.

As we approached, the sound of many people drifted through the air. The courtyard shone with light and warmth as several fires blazed to take away the chill of the autumn evening. It was clear from first glance that a great banquet had been prepared. Many guests had been invited and it seemed like every tax collector in Galilee was there. Jesus was, of course, invited to the top table as the guest of honour and settled there, looking completely at ease. Judas declined and stayed with us, as we accepted the more lowly places allotted to us with minimal courtesy and ate quietly as the party continued around us.

Peter asked, to no one in particular, "Can anyone tell me how this helps to build the Kingdom of God?"

"I can feel the judgemental eyes of a thousand Pharisees and synagogue rulers on me," said James.

I could see them. Some stood at the gate, looking in from the outside, whilst others had been invited to the banquet and had accepted uneasily, out of a need to know what was going on.

After a while, they moved closer to challenge us. "Why do you eat with tax collectors and sinners?"

We squirmed with collective shame and had no answer to give except that we followed our Rabbi.

Jesus, as ever, seemed to know what was going on and walked across the courtyard to give the answer himself. "It is not the healthy who need a doctor, but the sick. I have not come to call the righteous, but sinners to repentance," he told them.

It was the answer I had needed and once more blood flowed into my guts, just in time to digest the tax collector's food.

But these self-righteous men turned to dispute with Jesus and challenged again, "The Immerser's disciples often fast and pray and so do the disciples of we Pharisees, but yours go on eating and drinking."

Peter, still affected by the recent destruction of his roof and ruined hospitality, growled something about 'chance would be a fine thing'.

I saw my brother scowl and he spoke to us quietly, as the Pharisees now focused their vitriol onto Jesus. "Remember, my brothers," he told us all. "The Law of Moses required fasting without food only on Yom Kippur. These Pharisees compete for petty points of who can appear to be the 'most righteous' by making their great display of fasting once a week. Does our God desire displays of righteousness or actual righteousness? What do you think?"

While Jesus was answering them to their face, I marvelled at his grace, his lack of offence, as if only making a point in a civilised debate. "Can you make the guests of the bridegroom fast while he is with them? But the time will come when the bridegroom will be taken from them; in those days they will fast."

My Rabbi was clearly the bridegroom of his own parable. My mother's words about the fate of prophets flooded back into my mind as my guts chilled again. Would he be taken from me?

* * * *

In so many ways like this, we became a national scandal for some and a curiosity for others.

Capernaum was becoming difficult for us, with a Roman cohort and Herod's men always camped close by.

All through the autumn of Jesus' second year of itinerant mission, we travelled the land well beyond Galilee. Constantly under surveillance by Jerusalem, the Herods and Rome, Jesus spoke to the crowds mostly in parables. Often we had to sleep rough and stay hungry for both peace and safety. Times of respite became less frequent, but these were still my favourite times, just a few of us alone with Jesus, when he taught us directly about the Kingdom without the need of his parables. I could live with the disapproval of the Sanhedrin because I felt different and special; one of the Messiah's chosen ones out of our people.

At first, Matthew was an alien figure on the periphery of the group, but Jesus drew him in and we realised that he was human after all. Not skilled with his hands to be a tradesman, but with a head for numbers and procedures, he had wanted the best for his family and the employ of a tax collector had been the only option he had seen for himself. Simon Peter amazed us all by accepting Matthew as one chosen by Jesus, but also as a soulmate. I knew that they both felt the absence from their families and the daily role as a man as protector and provider.

Meanwhile, Judas and Thomas continued to worry about departures from tradition and the incorrectness of our group of men and women together.

"What do you think scandalises the Sanhedrin most?" said Judas. "That we live alongside the women who travel with us, or that Jesus speaks without reference to great Rabbis past, or that we disregard some traditions?"

"All in equal measure!" James grinned back to him. "All of those self-respecting rulers of synagogues would not be seen talking to their wives in public."

"Judas is correct when he says the people don't know what to make of us," said Philip. "Are we breaking anything in the law?"

"Nothing that I know of. All that is being challenged is traditions and people who try and make themselves holier than the Law," said Nathanael. "If indeed that were possible."

Thomas joined us; he seemed to have ears that could hear the word 'Law' at thirty paces.

"But we still go to synagogue and the Rabbi takes his message there," said Judas.

James puzzled for a few seconds. "So the Rabbi does not dispense with the old, when it still has good purpose, but challenges it with the new."

"Does Moses give instructions for synagogue?" asked Thomas, without a stammer.

"No," said my brother, in realisation. "I have never heard a law of synagogue, read at synagogue."

"Then where did synagogue come from?" I asked.

"Perhaps during the exile, when we did not have … t-the temple," said Thomas.

I liked him even more for his humble input. "Thomas, your love for the Law is equal to my father's," I said. "But it seems to me the Rabbi sets the bar of righteousness above even the Law."

"The Law shows us we will always fall short of the Lord God's … p-perfection," said Thomas. "The wrong use of the Law is wrong and … s-should be challenged."

I could see that both Thomas and Judas had the same heart and will for their nation, as did we all, but who would prevail or how could these strands of opinion all be brought together in common purpose? I could not see what our group would become. This was, after all, human nature … or was it sinful nature? Was our group to become separated into factions, no better that the parties of the Pharisees, Sadducees and Herodians? If so, would we become woebegone hypocrites, condemned by our own weaknesses?

On just one occasion, I stole a precious hour and sat alone with my Messiah, that his dust might cover me.

"Your work has been unceasing, Rabbi," I said. "Are you now stronger and more fulfilled or have these past weeks drained you?"

"What do you think gives me strength?" he asked.

"When the Kingdom is extended by your words and actions?" I said.

"No, I am not yet stronger. I am still in weakness, as it was necessary to empty myself. I am fulfilled by doing my father's work, but I must still endure."

"You have emptied yourself? But do not the signs and wonders also empty you?"

"They do, and my Father fills me again, that I may have the strength to continue His work. This lesson of the Lord God's strength though weakness is I would like you to learn as well."

"Yes Lord, I will learn. I would also like to know, when will your Father's work be complete?"

"That is for him to tell me."

"And will you then have the fullness of his blessing?"

"Like every other man on this earth," he looked at me. "I must walk before him and be perfect, in order for my sacrifice to be acceptable in his sight."

He made his Kingdom sound so straightforward and I could never penetrate his mysteries.

5/. Sabbath Confrontation

"The synagogues are divided on account of our Rabbi," said Judas. "You see how the Sadducees look down their noses and keep their synagogue rulers against us.

"It is no more than he told us," replied Matthew. "He brings a sword of division."

"They are either for the Kingdom, or for themselves," said Peter.

"I feel the scrutinising presence of Pharisees always in my face," said Nathanael.

"And I hate this accusation that I am discarding the traditions of our ancestors," said Philip. "It wears me down."

"Then discard only their ... p- petty rules," said Thomas. "Not a jot or tittle from the Law."

"What else would you expect these Pharisees to do when rules are their source of their power?" said my brother. I could see that he had one eye on Judas as he said it.

"It is a stumbling-block," said Judas. "A simple peasant cannot see these things and does not easily leave a lifetime conditioned by religious behaviour and traditions."

I had watched this conflict with the Pharisees all through Galilee that summer and now, as we walked through the autumn cornfields, I could feel it coming to a head.

James' stomach rumbled. "Where would we be without the provision of these noble women? And what risk they take to help us, but it is still forty-eight hours since we ate a square meal. I'm hungry and here we are in a field of grain! I say eat some before the harvest, before it is taken by Rome and they sell our ration back to us!"

He grabbed an ear of corn and rubbed it between his hands to separate the grains.

"You are desecrating this Sabbath, with this ... 'w-work,'" said Thomas, but his voice was not condemning.

"I already was according to the rules of the Pharisees! Has not our journey today been more than the 'Sabbath's day walk' they prescribe, although Moses did not?"

Thomas raised his eyebrows and nodded in acknowledgement.

"So, today my need for nourishment is greater than my need to eat with washed hands," said James. "I feel that is a tradition that I would like to challenge!"

I followed my brother's lead and took some corn-heads. "If I am wrong in the eyes of God, I am sure our Rabbi will tell me!" I said.

"Brothers! The Law favours the poor and hungry to glean the corners of the fields," said James. "I suggest that the moral of the law allows us to take a ration to relieve our starvation, even on a Sabbath." He and Thomas plucked at the corn. Simon, Andrew, Philip and Nathanael nodded and followed.

I watched for a reaction. Some were hesitant, but others followed. The wonder seekers and day visitors, who had recently eaten, didn't follow and remained distant.

Saul of the Pharisees had been with us for a few days, but now walked away, ahead of us towards the next village.

"I think that fly-in-the-ointment needs to make a report," I said to James.

"Perhaps he'll wash his hands from his skin and eat some of the vitals he brought with him, but did not see fit to share," Simon Peter replied with sarcasm.

"He's marching at a un-Sabbath-like pace as well!" Nathanael's voice was filled with dry rhetoric.

"Now we have put our Rabbi into a place of confrontation," worried Andrew.

"I think our Rabbi will have the words we need," replied Peter.

"Seeking confrontation is not always good," protested Judas Iscariot. "We need to win friends and have influence to make our task easier."

"The Rabbi does not seek it, but answers it when it comes," protested Philip. "You didn't expect a Messiah to be a doormat, did you?"

As the fields ended, a reception committee was waiting in the next village. A line of Pharisees, one was large and familiar. I was sure that for Shlomo to journey from Jerusalem to Galilee in person, and not just rely on his spies, meant we were now walking into some twist or plot. Accusing fingers of indignant self-righteousness pointed in our direction as they confronted our Rabbi. "Look at what your disciples are doing. They harvest and they eat with unwashed hands! Why do they do what is not lawful on the Sabbath?"

My Messiah directed them into the scriptures that they were supposed to own, reminding them that Israel's greatest king had gone where only Priest's go, taken the consecrated bread and given it to his followers. Jesus had told our accusers that their bread was our bread, that their understanding of the Law was the opposite of what it should be. "The Sabbath was made for man, not man for the Sabbath," he said without breaking his stride, as we walked straight through their ranks. My brother munched and swallowed with open disrespect. "Have you never read…?" He said, echoing our Rabbi's words towards to our inquisitors.

The village was going to synagogue. Jesus spoke to the women with us, wishing them God's blessing for the scriptures to be opened to them. This sent the local women into a hubbub of confusion as they moved towards their own area.

I watched Jesus' every move as he greeted the local rabbi with all courtesy. The Lord is one, worship the Lord God with all heart and mind and strength, they agreed.

James nudged me and indicated with his head; Peter, Andrew, Philip, Matthew and the others followed his direction. Saul was pulling a man from the place of the afflicted to the front of the synagogue, his withered arm self-accusing of sin and remoteness of God's blessing. I was almost sure I could see his heart banging inside his naked chest. If it was possible for a man to look both hopeful and petrified at the same moment, this man had it. There were only two possibilities for him now: to be restored to God, or to be the scapegoat in a religious power play.

The hapless synagogue ruler stood hopping from one foot to the other. He knew his position was now impossible, stuck between more senior religious men and this radical and powerful young Rabbi. He was now a bit part player in a scene that was to be worked out in his own synagogue. He opened the meeting, went through the motions, and then went for the only option left for him: he invited Jesus to speak to the meeting and retired to a safe distance.

The eerie silence of a tomb descended as Jesus stood. Neither moving to the position of the synagogue ruler nor taking a scroll, he addressed the meeting about the blessing of the Sabbath day. My gaze scanned around the building at the faces of breathless attention from the congregation, the women pressed against the screen and the judgemental demeanour of the Pharisees. My Rabbi told them all that they had gathered there to receive, as their God was at work to feed them, body and soul, on the Sabbath day. Their crops ripened in the fields of God's creation with the sun and the rain and their own Rabbi worked that very day to feed them with God's word, that they might understand his law and have life.

I realised how tight I was holding myself. I looked at the others; all were awaiting the climax that I knew must come.

God's work, our Rabbi told them, was always ongoing, was always creating and feeding and healing and building up. This was the Kingdom of God that would be established and endure forever, for anyone who would enter. He contrasted Satan's work as the opposite; it was to tear down and destroy, to stifle and to enslave in sin and infirmity.

My Rabbi allowed the synagogue several minutes of cool consideration of his words as his expressionless gaze scanned back and forth.

He beckoned the cripple to come forwards. I saw the hope in the man's eyes overcome his fear, but he trembled as he walked to Jesus side.

Jesus addressed himself to the group of Pharisees. "Is it lawful on the Sabbath to do good or to do harm?"

Nothing moved; no answer came. My mind flashed back to The Immerser's pool.

Jesus then polarised it even more for them. Taking a step forward, he demanded, "Is it right to save life or to kill?"

My nerves jangled and my guts squirmed; I knew my Rabbi had moved the issue from the cripple to himself. He had told them that he was doing God's work and to stop it they would need to silence him.

The appalling silence continued. His words could not penetrate the hearts of these Pharisees; to me they became as the Pharaoh of Egypt, hardening their hearts towards God and keeping my people in slavery. Jesus was the Moses to release the people and I needed the Passover of freedom. I looked at the anger etched into his face, and yes, I could even see grief there as well, eyes blazing and nostrils flaring. He was seething with rage at the ignorant stubbornness of these religious bigots.

Yet, his voice to the cripple was gentle and caring. "Stretch out your hand."

The hand twitched and then extended. New muscle grew before our eyes, the arm restored and flexed as the man let out a low ecstatic groan of wonderment.

The gasp that filled the building was that of a thousand people who, having held their breath so long, now found they were desperate for oxygen. It almost drowned out the expulsive grunt of contempt from the Pharisees. Shlomo led them as they stormed out.

"They are shamed in front of the people," said Peter.

"They expected to hold leadership, but are now a shibboleth," said my brother.

"They will use this against him," said Judas.

Jesus called to the synagogue ruler, thanked him for the opportunity to speak, and handed the meeting back to him. The man glowed at being restored to his place and conducted the rest of the meeting well. Afterwards, he threw in his lot with Jesus and extended the hospitality of his house for the evening. We appreciated his courage to step out of line with Jerusalem and told him so.

The next morning the village elders visited to tell us that Shlomo and his Pharisees had made contact with one of Herod Philip's patrols, fabricating for them of a plot against the King, because of the Immerser.

* * * *

As we moved on again, a great multitude from all over Galilee followed us, not caring where we were going. Local villagers were pleased to sell some of their produce at profiteering prices but few had grain to spare beyond Rome's ration. Then merchants saw their chance and trailed the crowds, their camels and mules being mobile markets. James dubbed it our 'circus of madness'. We kept in touch with home and sent letters for pickled and dried fish; our benefactors also continued to keep us alive enough to travel.

This circus continued for many weeks as we continued through Galilee's towns and villages at the time of the autumn festivals. Firstly came the days of Rosh Hashanah. It was the first time I had been away from home for the New Year and it left me homesick for Mother's pumpkin seed pastries.

Then, Yom Kippur saved me. It was like a homecoming to feel like one of my people again as the synagogues welcomed all. Matthew wanted us to reach out, not only to his former colleagues amongst the tax collectors, but to all outcasts from society. I could see something inside him was changing and changing fast in the glow of his acceptance as a son of Abraham. The man that had once turned his back on his nation was now immersing himself in our religion, with the purpose of reaching out to his own. Matthew told us he was now 'sealed by the Lord God's judgement', ready to move onto Sukkot and do what he had never done before: build a booth with his own pilgrim hands. I watched Peter as he assisted, never allowing Matthew's clumsy hands to struggle, but always allowing it to be his construction. The Kingdom came yet closer to me in this brotherhood.

As we journeyed on, Zealots kept in contact and saw their opportunity to warn us of the plot of Shlomo and Antipas, but with the twist that we now needed their protection from the King's Guards. It was the last thing we needed. If Rome learned of association with this warrior band, it would be construed badly against us.

Once again, I saw that Simon was part of the Zealot delegation, so I stood apart and alone in the background to make myself available. He saw me and I was overjoyed that we exchanged a smile and nod of recognition, but he came no nearer and so I knew I could not take the contact any further.

Jesus gave the Zealots the same reply as he had to Barabbas after clearing the temple and it was time to withdraw once again. This time we headed west and south around the lake to be as far from Herod Philip's territory as possible, and in case we had to hop the border to Samaria and flee to where neither of the Herods had jurisdiction.

6/. Tribal Conflict

Home was a wonderful relief to me, but at times, it also felt like a prison.

Jesus had told us to disperse. The winter days had come upon us and the multitudes had ebbed away to their towns and villages whilst the Herods and Rome reduced their patrols.

The sun seemed to rise reluctantly above the Golan and we had slipped back to Bethsaida.

During the first week, the house was full of our neighbours, as they visited to glean every piece of news of our Rabbi. In return, they gave us every possible disputed opinion on whether or not Jesus was a madman, insurrectionist, prophet or Messiah, and what his coming Kingdom would or would not be.

When I escaped the house for some fishing, all that Caleb and the men would talk about was the coming springtime, when the Son of David would call us all to battle for freedom. My recounting of the Rabbi's sermon at Nazareth did little to dissuade them.

In the second week, the north wind blew in from the snowy peaks of Lebanon and our neighbours stayed home. For the first time, we found space for family discussions in the dark winter's evenings around the brazier. James and I told Father and Mother of all that we had seen and experienced. In return, they gave us their perspective on the effect our Rabbi was having from the top to the bottom of the nation.

Father was using his many social and business contacts to know what was happening in Jerusalem and to monitor the political temperature there. He told us that the huge multitudes that had followed us through the autumn festivals corresponded in many less people taking the pilgrimage to Jerusalem. The Chief Priests and the Sanhedrin were feeling their authority ebbing away in the challenge of the radical new Rabbi. The moneychangers of the temple were measuring the lack of pilgrims through their diminished takings.

We told our parents of the scribes that had insulted Jesus to be Lucifer, saying that he used demons to cast out other demons and heal illnesses. Father and Mother told us to expect more of the same.

In the local news, they knew that Mordecai and Esther had had no further contact with Simon, as he remained with the Zealots.

On good weather days, we fished from Capernaum. Jesus continued to preach in the local village synagogues on the Sabbaths; his compassion for all who sought him was undiminished. Still he would disappear for days and nights of prayer, the half-starved, vagabond ascetic going back to his desert of struggles and discipline. We took turns to go with him, carrying some firewood and blankets to survive the winter nights. He told us his very private things: the pressures he felt, the fears he had, the need for prayer and a refilling of virtue. He told us he needed to endure, to fulfil his mission. We would talk about our hopes and fears for our nation. I began to see I had a role, not just in the mission, but in the life of my Messiah, as the human companion that he needed.

Winter, I decided, was my new favourite season, when I could be with my Messiah and not share him with a demanding multitude of others.

It was after Chanukah when Jesus called all of us together again at Capernaum. As we walked from Bethsaida, James and I discussed our surprise that Jesus had not waited for the days to lengthen a little more, and how this must be something new and significant. We arrived in Capernaum and found a further twist: a small group of Zealots had left their winter hideout to make contact again. It was the Barabbas we had seen in the temple and my erstwhile friend Simon was there again. He looked thinner and rougher than when I had last seen him and the scar across the palm of his hand told of a ceremonial blood-brotherhood.

"Greetings, Rabbi," said Barabbas. "You see I come with just a few men, to listen to your wisdom, to talk and assure you of our support to build the Kingdom of God you preach."

My mind flashed back to that night on our roof in Jerusalem when Nicodemus delivered his well-prepared message. Here was another man from another powerful sect that wanted to recruit my Rabbi into their politic.

Barabbas continued, indicating to Simon. "My young compatriot tells me that he knows one of your disciples well and that you choose good people for the Kingdom. I would like to assure you that I also choose with care."

"Greetings, Barabbas," Jesus gave his cordial welcome. "I remember that we spoke before, when you had seen my zeal for the Lord God's temple, and you have remembered well what I said about seeking the Kingdom of God."

"Indeed I do, Rabbi, and my interest is not only the purification of the temple that you did so well, but also the purification of the whole land, that we would live long in it." replied Barabbas.

"And this is what you have come to talk about?"

"I have come to find common cause with you and plan our campaign together for Passover," agreed Barabbas.

"Are our kingdoms the same, Barabbas?"

"That is why I suggest we talk; we should find a more private place."

"The Lord God has sent me to invite all children of Abraham to claim their place in the Kingdom," Jesus assured him. "You are welcome. God seeks all men and, as you will see, I have a former tax collector who now follows me."

Barabbas wrinkled his nose, but said, "He shall be welcome to us."

So, to my surprise and I suspect also many of the others, Jesus agreed we would withdraw to a place of sojourn in the hills. I gave Simon a broad smile of welcome, but I was sure that there would be a twist here somewhere. I was now confident of Jesus' character; I could not imagine my Rabbi was about to cleave to those who would foment insurrection, so what could his purpose be? How far would my Rabbi go to win people for his Kingdom?

It took a few days for other disciples to join us and by the time we were together, Jesus had already departed alone towards the north. Without him to set the tone, we were on edge as we walked with the Zealots. These men were all battle-hardened fighters, but at least we outnumbered them. The conversation was perfunctory as we moved towards the pre-arranged place at the foot of the mountain. I knew where Jesus would be, up the mountain in prayer, and he descended with the dawn as our camp awoke and stirred into activity.

Jesus addressed the Zealot leader. "Barabbas, you asked me about our intentions for a spring campaign."

"Yes, Rabbi, we are one in purpose to restore Israel to its people," said Barabbas. "Some of my men require your blessing to heal illness and injury and are ready to stand with you."

"I will continue to preach the good news of the Kingdom of God to all who have ears to hear."

"As we approach Passover, the people's expectations of freedom will grow." Barabbas appealed to us all with his palms upturned. "Passover must bring freedom from slavery and the people will remember your action to clear the temple a year ago. They will expect more this year and they must be given a lead to follow."

"I need to choose twelve who will be sent to their nation with the Kingdom message. They will be my Apostles."

It was as I had seen with Nicodemus; Jesus had passed over the invitation to join any group with a political agenda and then stated his own.

"If this was your purpose during this sojourn, then you should continue, Rabbi," smiled Barabbas. "I did not come to impede your progress."

An alarm sounded within me, and I whispered to James, "Will our Rabbi reveal all his plans to this man?"

James returned a grimace and a shrug of doubt.

Jesus just smiled in return and turned to us, his message ever the same. "The Kingdom of God is at hand for you; in the days ahead, I will send forth twelve of you to do all that you have seen I have done in God's name. You must preach the good news, heal the sick, raise the dead and cast out demons. It is time to prepare you for the next stage."

Then came the names: "Simon, called Peter, Andrew bar Jonas, James and John bar Zebedee," I gasped, lightheaded. I was sure my feet would rise from the earth as I followed the others to his side. "Nathanael, Philip, Bartholomew, Levi called Matthew, Thomas the twin, James bar Alpheus, Simon bar Mordecai," the name hit me like a thunderbolt, "and Judas Iscariot," finished Jesus.

I looked at Simon. Trancelike, he walked out of the ranks of the Zealots towards Jesus with slow steps, as if drawn by some inexorable force. Every set of eyes followed him in captivated silence. The Zealots stood rooted to the spot with jaws hanging.

Jesus indicated a place between us and laid a welcoming hand on Simon's shaking shoulder.

Barabbas recovered and cried foul, "Rabbi, I did not come here to steal your disciples and you have no business taking mine!"

"I have invited him to seek the Kingdom of God as I have done with any other man. It is his choice to leave or remain, and yours as well."

"We have a covenant in blood," barked Barabbas, raising a scarred palm towards us. "See his hand and mine!"

"And if he and I have covenant in spirit before God, it is more powerful and permanent than yours," returned Jesus.

The arteries in Barabbas's neck bulged as his face flushed and in a second, his sword was in his hand. His companions followed. "Simon is mine, and I will take him!"

"Our kingdoms are not the same, Barabbas. In the Kingdom I have been sent to build, his bondage is by choice. The blood in God's Kingdom is that by which men are saved, not bound." Jesus took a few steps forward and delivered a challenge in a voice oh so gentle. "So are you going to slay me, Barabbas?"

We gathered protectively around him, with Simon in our midst; a few of ours had drawn swords as well. "The times are fulfilled. Repent and receive the Kingdom of God." Jesus extended his constant invitation with open hand across to the Zealot band.

"I am a son of Abraham and I will see Israel restored and cleansed of Rome's tyranny!" Barabbas proclaimed, but he knew he had lost. "God does not send a passive Messiah to bring freedom for our people." Then, with a final defiance: "We will meet again in Jerusalem!" He turned on heel and stomped away, with his men following in his wake.

"What a steal! What a subtle manoeuvre!" Judas sat as a man of letters does and told us all of his new enthusiasm. "I had thought that this carpenter of Nazareth did not have the mettle, the necessary ruthlessness to be an effective leader, but this was excellent."

"And what do you think of the result, Judas?" asked James. I could tell he was using the moment to explore Judas Iscariot's full opinion.

"Why, a politically balanced party of course. We now have representation from all the main areas and extremes of our nation, from tax collector to zealot, one a collaborator with the foreign empire, the other committed to its violent overthrow and therefore every shade in between." Matthew looked on with a much-pained expression, but said nothing. "We can use this to reach out to all and tell them they have a place here!"

"Has that been the Rabbi's appeal in his mission to date?" questioned James.

"You miss the point, James," argued Judas Iscariot. "The Rabbi has talked of the next stage of the mission of the Kingdom. This is what will happen this year, you will see."

"I remember what the Rabbi said about the wineskins," said James. "He has asked us to leave our old lives behind, not to bring them with us in order to attract others with the same baggage."

"Parables and concepts are all very well. The reality is that we need to recruit people to build this movement and create real political change."

I watched the faces of the others as they listened to the dispute; none of them had seen fit to join it. All now saw that this was a contest for leadership and direction within our Twelve. All waited to see in which direction it would go, and when and if Jesus himself would intervene.

That night, I sat under the stars and prayed for the right direction to come to me. James came and sat beside me. "Four months to Passover," he said.

"Is that enough to build the power to replace the High Priests?" I said. "Judas speaks so much like Father. At times, some of his views are very close."

"There is a difference," he replied. "Judas has it all worked out, but Father would not be so prescriptive."

7/. New Wineskins

The days lengthened towards Passover, and my Messianic chariot hurtled forwards, the rocks breaking under its iron wheels. Desire, Expectancy, Power and Freedom, their eyes wild, with foam-flecked flanks and thundering hooves, straining at the bridle, pulling me along. The new grass was soft under my feet as we Twelve and the wider group gathered again. The multitudes began to gather again; the unspoken clamour for freedom was deafening in my ears.

Meanwhile, Capernaum was ringed by legionaries and Herod's Guard camped within the town.

Jesus led us out, but towards the north. The multitudes from every town and village of Galilee pressed all around us, humming with a delirious excitement. We decided it must be a clever bluff and we would soon double-back for Jerusalem. The masses thought the same, even as Songs of Ascent began amongst them.

Jesus stood where the ground rose behind him, the multitudes spread before us on the wide grassy plateau. After he had dealt with their maladies, he sat them down and called us Twelve to his side. The representatives of Rome, Herod and Jerusalem bullied their ways to prominent positions in order to measure his every word.

My stallions came to rest as he started to speak, his first big set-piece sermon of the new season.

I watched my Messiah. What was he feeling now, with a hundred thousand eyes of both adoring public and jealous enemy examining him? He had prepared for this moment through hours of prayer and solitude. How much had the healings already emptied his virtue? What now did he have to give?

He turned his face from the crowd and spoke to us as if we were the only ones there, but his voice carried, clear and strong, in the still warm air for the people to hear.

"Blessed are you..." he told us multiple times. We were blessed because we recognised our poverty of spirit, our need for God, because we mourned for our people, because of our humility, our mercy, purity, yearning for peace, and even because the world would persecute us, as they had persecuted the prophets before us, for all of this.

We sat almost an hour listening as our Rabbi was meticulous in the delivery of each statement, illustration and parable of his sermon. Once again, it was all his own words, with reference to neither the current priesthood nor the great Rabbis of the past. The new Moses held authority over them all, for those with the eyes and ears to perceive it.

"My life is now an open and illuminated book for the scrutiny of them all!" I whispered to James and Simon.

James nodded agreement. "We are objects of virtue in a show cabinet."

"When I sought spiritual enlightenment with The Immerser," said Andrew, "I did not expect to become this object of pitiful curiosity and amusement."

I reflected on what a profound statement that was from Andrew. I looked at the crowd as Jesus continued to direct their attention to us. Did they want to become hungry vagabonds like us, or did they just want entertainment for their dull lives? Did they desire a bloody revolution, or freedom delivered for them on a miraculous plate?

Now Jesus turned to Saul and the group of Pharisees: not one little dot or pen stroke would be removed from the law until everything had been accomplished and heaven and earth were gone. The new Moses was here to fulfil the old Moses, not to destroy.

Thomas purred his approval.

To the people, he proclaimed the commandments were great in the Kingdom of God, but that unless their righteousness exceeded that of the Scribes and Pharisees, they would not have entry to this kingdom that he preached.

The people murmured their amazement and I saw Saul and Chai despatch one man from each of their group to report back to Jerusalem.

Jesus turned away and climbed onto the higher ground. A few of our number rose to follow, but Peter told them Jesus needed time to rest and be alone. The multitude was restless for action as they watched him leave.

The Roman cohort exchanged places with a fresh one from Caesarea. They made no move towards us, so we lit a fire to eat, discuss and dispute into the night.

"This was a call to return to the true law of God," Judas Iscariot told us. "We must throw off the petty bindings of the Pharisees and the spiritual denial of the Sadducees."

"Yes, indeed, Judas," replied my brother, "but to me, it was also more than that. He told us to be perfect, just as God in heaven is perfect. This was the Lord God's word to Abraham."

"I heard him examine the very thoughts of my heart and mind," murmured Matthew. "My bad thoughts were 'hatred', my appreciation of a woman other than my betrothed, was 'lust'. My sinful emotions closed the door of the Kingdom in my face!"

"I too have thought my fellow man a fool," said Nathanael. "I stand in danger of the fires of hell!"

"Have hope, my brothers!" exclaimed Philip. "He has showed us the way. Leave a gift at the altar, go and make peace with a brother in foolishness, and then return to make the offering."

"And when I pluck out my sinful right eye and throw it away, how do I make peace with that and return it to its place?" asked Andrew.

"He cannot mean this literally?" said Nathanael.

"No, I do not think so," my brother smiled in reply. "The Rabbi is not suggesting self-mutilation; his parable tells us that if we have sin in our life, we need firm and decisive action to cleanse ourselves."

"Then please tell me, simple man as I am," said Peter. "What am I to take for real and what is spiritual, lest I gut and pickle myself like this fish, to preserve my un-sinful parts for the Kingdom?"

Simon and I chuckled to each other. Peter he never knew how funny he was, even in the middle of all this intensity.

Thomas' heavy tones entered the fray. "I must say that the key point of law for me was the … c-correct context of: 'an eye for an eye and a tooth for a tooth.'"

"Pah! So we will wait for someone to strike you on both cheeks!" scoffed Judas Iscariot.

"Then so you shall!" Thomas looked back at him. "Fool-for-the-Kingdom as I obviously am!"

Thomas' retort came as if from the mouth of our Rabbi, delivered with righteous accuracy, and every head turned. "His words told me that it is not mine to respond with personal revenge, but to rely on the Lord God's law to be my avenger!" Thomas completed his strike to the discomfort of our learned comrade Judas Iscariot.

"So what of those that use this very verse to promote our resistance to the oppression of Rome?" challenged Philip. "Are we to be doormats to them also?"

"It has nothing to say of that," Thomas was deliberate and sonorous in reply. "It speaks of the civil order and society within our nation. I do not suggest it can be applied to matters outside our people, such as our relations with the barbarous foreign hordes, who know nothing of the law."

James and I exchanged looks. Thomas had been as fluent as I had ever heard him. His currency had just risen within the Twelve at the cost of others, and yet he seemed oblivious.

"Thomas," said my brother. "You have shown us a mind like a meat cleaver for the separation and application of points of law."

Judas Iscariot attempted to retrieve his status. "Your insight is challenging, Thomas. So I have another question for us all: if a Legionary of Rome forces you to carry his equipment for one mile, will you then offer to carry it a further mile, as our Rabbi suggests?"

I baulked at the very thought of marching with their legions. This 'law of burden' that they could impose on us, their dust choking my breathing, as their presence choked our freedom. In the silence, I knew every man felt the same.

"But think of the effect it would have on those b*****ds!" The voice had spoken at my side, but in the silence it carried to all who were there. It was our young Zealot speaking in his rural vernacular. Simon sat beside me with his head down, a mischievous grin on his face, talking to himself rather than anyone else. "…to tell a legionary that I carried his burden, not for him but so that I could proclaim the greatness of my God to him."

Simon realised we were all looking at him and raised his flushed face, but I saw a bright resolve in his eyes, and he continued undeterred: "Imagine the sense of victory if a legionary was forced to listen, or even if he just told me to get lost and preferred to carry his own bags!" He grinned at us, as he imagined his moment of conquest.

Everyone sat with blank faces and blinked back us. I decided that if Simon had spoken, so could I. "Yes, I can imagine that. The dust of his feet would not choke me to proclaim our God as the Lord of the whole earth! This is what the great prophets did when they stood before kings and rulers." Now they all looked at me. "To walk before God and be perfect, as he told Abraham."

"Tell me then, young philosopher, what does this mean?" Simon Peter addressed his challenge at me. "Just what does it mean to be perfect in God's sight?"

"He told us: the sin is in the thought, in the heart and mind first, before it is committed to an action," I said. "That is the time to pluck it out and throw it away."

"Can a man do that?" asked Judas Iscariot. "Which of us here has ever kept the law to perfection? Which of us could always be pure in heart and thought as he has told us to be? I say this is not possible for mortal man."

"I do not disagree, Judas," my brother replied. "So my question is: Where will this 'better righteousness' come from? How can he give this to us, and how could we ever accept it and keep it?"

"After Passover, we'll have the power to enforce it and make the people understand," insisted Judas Iscariot.

I got up and moved away, my guts squirmed with frustration. I knew something was wrong, but could not express it. The sermon had not been a manifesto that could be written and enforced; I believed it was a living manifesto that could only be written on our hearts and minds.

I found myself a quiet place to lay and gaze at the heavens and their twinkling lights. I churned it all over. How could I explain it, when I struggled to understand it myself?

My Rabbi had always said 'he who has eyes, let them see and he who has ears, let them hear'. We had accepted an invitation to the Kingdom; it had not been imposed on us. We, the poor and wretched, the blessed, the persecuted; we had to *be* the political manifesto. We had to live it, not just obey it.

* * * *

"The Rabbi's mother is outside," Andrew came to tell us. "All his brothers, too, saying they have come to take him home!"

The melee in the street quietened to hear Mary calling for her son.

"Jesus, I need you come and take care of me and your sisters. Remember your duties to me."

"Tell her she is dear to me," Jesus indicated to Andrew to relay his message, "but now I have many others to care for."

Mary kept up her insistence. "Remember you are but a poor *tekton*, my son. I praise God he has blessed you with miracles, but it is not your place to stand on mountains and preach great sermons of law. The adoration of these people has caused you to take leave of your senses: you are not a new Moses!"

The family joined in. "Jesus, my brother, this is going too far. Do not listen to the whisperings that this talk of God is true!"

I stood at the door with Andrew, relaying the calm refusal Jesus gave us. "They have the same fears as we did," I said. "That their brother is the madman or the fake."

"Or that he will join the *Sicarii*," he agreed. "It cannot be easy to accept your brother is the Messiah."

"Is it any easier for us?" I asked him. "To be appointed as the twelve spiritual sons of the new Moses, The Messiah?"

"How can we be successors to the twelve sons of Israel?" asked Nathanael.

"Judas was correct," said Philip. "What a mixed and disparate group we are."

"Is the Messiah going to build his new Kingdom on us?" said Matthew. "Us, the foundations of a Kingdom that would never be conquered and last for eternity?"

"Have faith, my brother," Thomas spoke with his usual gravity. "Think of those twelve sons of Israel, of their ... m-mistakes, weaknesses and jealousies and even betrayals."

"Yes," said Peter. "It is so."

"Then comfort yourself," said Thomas. "Our God is wondrous, if for nothing else but that he chose to work out his purposes through the most ordinary of men!"

I decided that I liked Thomas even more.

Simon was now always close to me. Jesus had put him into my care. He had much to get used to, and I worked hard to give him the brotherhood that he needed to replace the one he had left behind.

"You will hear much eloquent debate of the Law," I said, "but look at what you see; Jesus walks among the poor and needy. He chooses you and me rather than the Scribes and the Pharisees; we are new wine for a new wineskin."

Simon Peter came up to us. "I have something to say, Simon bar Mordecai. A question for my young friend John to witness."

Simon stood mutely to receive as Peter towered above him. I stood too.

"I do not want to see your *Sicarii* pointed at the throat of my brother Matthew. What he was is now past. Once I hated him and his kind, but now his place is beside me in the new Kingdom of our Lord."

"I have my past as well," answered Simon. "I will accept my place in the Kingdom under the rules of my King."

As I watched, they looked each other in the eye and my big friend nodded his acceptance.

"I would not have cared for the life of any tax collector," Simon added, "but my real hatred was for the steward of the Sadducee who held us in bondage and took our crops for such little reward, whilst they sold it onto Rome for such handsome profit."

8/. Passover and the Roman

Desire and Expectancy lay wounded amongst their stablemates as my Messianic chariot dragged to a broken standstill. My Rabbi had now told us that he would not lead us to Jerusalem for Passover!

There was too much potential for conflict with the Sanhedrin, and an armed uprising by Barabbas and his *Sicarii* was likely. The people could even run wild and spark an intervention by Rome.

We were instructed to take Passover with our families and communities as we had always done and come together again in Capernaum afterwards. After a brief visit to his family, Jesus collected a few provisions and disappeared again towards the hills. I watched him depart in speechlessness.

Once again, we Twelve dispersed and James and I sailed our boat back to Bethsaida in abject silence. After a family conference, it was decided to close the house. Father and Mother would come with us and we would all travel with our friends and neighbours in the community pilgrimage I had always enjoyed so much. Following a day of preparation, we departed en masse. The very old sat in the carts wedged in with rugs and cushions and tents; the very young ran alongside until they were exhausted and then clamoured to sit with the old. If I tell you that from our roots, from the days of the patriarchs of our nation we were a pilgrim people, trekking to our Holy Land, I hope you will understand what all this meant to me. The excitement of packing and travelling together had always been part of my Passover, being part of the great throng of people going down the Jordan to Jericho. Then we would sing on the long climb to Jerusalem; the Songs of Ascent would roll out across our land. The pace would always quicken as we got closer, as we strove onwards, for the first glimpse of the city and the temple.

I had so many memories of years past, but this year was different. As we travelled and camped at the overnight halts, we listened to the talk around us. Would the radical young Rabbi be there with his new teaching? Would he confront the temple order again? Would the Kingdom be proclaimed and freedom come to us at Passover, as it must? Did Rome sniff a rebellion in the air?

We listened but kept our council, taking the temperature of our nation, measuring their perception of the events that would unfold before us. We exchanged occasional words as we marched; in the evenings, we discussed nothing except the joy of the pilgrimage, as voices do carry far in the still night air.

In Jericho, there were more legionaries than in previous years. I knew they were watching for an unusual movement of people. As we got to Jerusalem, the legions were camped on the Mount of Olives, their cohorts already patrolling the main routes.

At the city gate, I was amazed to find Joash and Yossi beside me. Was it by a fortunate happenstance, or a God inspired coincidence, I asked myself? We took the cleansing of the Mikvah together and embraced for memories of the Immerser's Pool.

Their news was that his disciples were allowed to have contact with The Immerser, to take food to his cell and to relay messages; Seth remained on vigil outside the fortress gate at this time. They also knew that Antipas would have The Immerser brought to his private rooms to have him preach from the Law and the Prophets. Release was too much to hope for, at least whilst the adultery with Herod Philip's wife continued, but Joash and Yossi were nonetheless optimistic. They wanted to know where our Rabbi was. Our reply that we had been instructed to disperse for Passover left them more than perplexed, but they assured us they would inform their master.

As we made our way through the thronging streets of the city, Pharisees stood on the main corners, and in the temple I saw Shlomo with Saul, directing operations. In the temple courts the moneychangers plied their trade, but with the Temple Guard standing close by, I took it all in.

Rome and the Sanhedrin, as well as my family and I, were all braced for trouble and when an uproar rolled through the streets on the Sabbath, it came as no surprise.

The roof was the best vantage point, where we could observe out of trouble.

"It comes from the direction of the Sheep Gate," said Father, "but it is not an angry noise."

"Look, the legionaries remain on the walls, just watching," said James.

As we watched, the flow of people towards the source of excitement began to reverse into a procession shouting the praises of God and heading up to the temple, so we went down to the street.

Father called to the passing throng. "Friends, please share the reason for your joy."

"A healing at the Pool of Bethesda!"

"A cripple of years now walks and carries his mat."

"The angels of the Lord have spoken!"

We all looked each other. "Your Rabbi is here," said Father. "Go to the temple and see what you can find out."

James and I followed the crush through the tunnels and into the Temple Courts. The healed man gave his testimony and got only condemnation for carrying his mat. I moved close enough behind Shlomo to hear his conclusion. "The accursed Nazarene is here, he has a safe house somewhere," he commanded to the Temple Guard. "Find him!"

* * * *

Father and Mother filled our house with hospitality. When they were not welcoming guests, they visited others, both business and social acquaintances. We were just another family at the most important festival in our national life, bringing our sacrifices to temple and trying to avoid the situations where tempers boiled over in the streets.

As the festival week progressed, I saw fewer Pharisees on the streets, the Temple Guard retired to less conspicuous places, and I felt the tension ease. The temple's fears of Jesus repeating the upheaval of the previous year ebbed away and on the last and greatest day, the city relaxed to roast the Passover lamb and Rome's legionaries patrolled with less intensity.

Many relatives joined us for the Passover Seder. We ate the lamb and the Matzah and Father proclaimed each cup in its turn, and when the youngest amongst us opened the door, Elijah was not there. We sighed and Elijah's cup remained, for next year in Jerusalem, as we had always reminded each other.

After our guests had departed, I climbed to the roof where a year ago Jesus had challenged Nicodemus to a new life. I looked out over the city and I interceded in prayer for my former Rabbi, The Immerser. Had my nation missed the Elijah that had been amongst them, but now lay in the King's dungeon?

Passover concluded with no further disturbances. I knew my 'Nazarene' had remained elusive.

Next year in Jerusalem: what would it bring for me, my family and my Messiah?

As we journeyed home, Desire and Expectancy still walked beside me. They had recovered, but Expectancy was now hobbled, unsure if he would ever run free.

I moved amongst the returning pilgrims, listening to their despondency. Where was their Lord? Why had he not visited them at Passover? Why had his prophet not met them in the temple as he had a year ago? How long must they wait for the Lord's Messiah?

We had been back in Bethsaida for a week when a letter came from Capernaum. Jesus was gathering the Twelve together again. Father told us he expected Jesus to continue from his great sermon, to again proclaim the Kingdom and build his movement of people on the foundations of his twelve chosen Apostles. For James, I, and the others, it would be like life in the arena, with every eye looking on to judge our worthiness of life or death. We knew our mission now: to follow our mysterious Rabbi and be worthy of the life we were called to, even the impossibility of walking before our God to be perfect.

Then, Father told us that he and Mother were now committed to our Rabbi's Kingdom. They would travel with us when they could and support us from home with food and finance when they could not. I held Father's hands, pressed my forehead against them and wept tears of grateful emotion. We prepared the provisions and a boat and left the next day for Capernaum.

* * * *

We arrived to find the town embroiled in controversy, with half its population gathered in the marketplace and with the local synagogue leader and elders meeting with Jesus on behalf of a Roman centurion.

Simon Peter and Andrew were there, standing behind Jesus. James and I pushed our way through the surrounding mass and implored our comrades to tell us what was going on.

"This man's slave is sick," Peter explained above the babble of the speculation around us. "Very sick, and he has impressed on our elders to ask the Rabbi for healing."

"He loves his slave much," commented Andrew. "We all know these Roman officers do with their servants."

"Whatever force has this centurion brought to bear on your elders," replied my brother, "I cannot imagine it will sway Jesus."

"It's not like that; there is no threat," replied Peter. "We know this because the elders came to us first, to ask for a private audience with Jesus, but then word got out and this happened!"

"I don't understand," questioned James. "Why do the elders speak on behalf of this Roman?"

"He paid for the synagogue to be rebuilt," was Peter's terse reply.

We listened to the debate. It was calm and measured in front of the people, but we knew that the stakes were high and that there was a distinct possibility that someone – elders, synagogue leader, Roman or Jesus – could be disgraced in a very public manner.

The elders were telling Jesus about the synagogue and that this Roman had come to love Israel and our God. The Centurion had been included in the Passover, the alien amongst them as the scripture commended, and they deemed his request worthy of Jesus' consideration.

"We have already seen that he will extend God's blessings to those outside Israel," Andrew reminded us.

"Yes, but never in public and at the request of others," James whispered his reply. "What will matter more, the individual and their circumstances or where they come from and what they stand for?"

Jesus had now replied, for the benefit of the crowd and the elders, stating that he preached a Kingdom for all sons of Abraham, but that he also respected their request and would agree to meet the Roman and make his own judgement.

He and the elders now stood together and, with the unhurriedness that was required, arranged themselves in order of seniority and moved away. The crowd parted and then bunched in behind us. We all knew that the next few minutes had the potential for unrest. There would be many in the crowd who would be against the Roman, no matter what his supposed worthiness of blessing.

But then the Centurion stood in the street before us as an ordinary man, dressed in plain linen with nothing to tell of his rank and position and, with a humble dignity, announced to my Messiah and all gathered there that he, the servant of Rome, was not worthy of having the Lord of Israel enter his house. He told everyone how he understood authority and command, he knew his situation and that he had faith in the judgement and word of our Rabbi.

The Roman had claimed my Lord was his Lord and at that moment, I did not know what I felt; my mind was spinning and my feet would not move. It was the ultimate humbling of this gentile, this erstwhile enemy of my people. His gods lay fallen at my feet, but was I yet ready to share mine with him?

Did I believe his faith was genuine, or was this just a worship of convenience?

I regarded this man of stature and authority; he had humbled himself on behalf of his slave, for the love of a fellow. James and I looked at each other; he raised his eyebrows at me in an expression of positive expectation of what would follow. "It is almost like the man lowered through the roof," he whispered. "A declaration of need, of compassion, even for this gentile; I think it will win the day and our Rabbi will respond!"

"Win the day?" I said. "Which side are you on?"

"The Kingdom side!"

"I'm not ready for this," I hissed in reply.

Jesus addressed the Israel that surrounded him and told them that this was a faith he had not found amongst them, but it was sufficient for the Kingdom. I felt the silence chill around me as Jesus paused to let his statement sink in, before continuing to challenge his adopted hometown to a stronger faith. In His Kingdom, he told them, many peoples from east and west would eat at the banquet of our fathers, but others who supposed themselves to be sons of the Kingdom would find themselves shut outside in the darkness.

I felt every man around me stiffen with the tension. "Nazareth, again!" Andrew's voice trembled. The crowd murmured and shuffled with menace around us; the elders had faces of stone but continued to stand with Jesus. I watched my Messiah as he stood with purpose and turned his gaze around to meet eyes of the whole crowd. His authority over the masses held firm, the moment passed, and the tension eased.

Turning to the Centurion, Jesus told him that what he asked would be done for him. The man turned for his house without another word. How much had just been drained from my Messiah for the servant of Rome? I struggled with my inmost being.

The elders thanked Jesus for his forbearance; he graciously thanked them for their good judgement. The crowd dispersed to dispute the events of the day. I felt the sweat, sticky under my armpits and prickle down my back. I also heard Judas Iscariot, as he voiced his displeasure. "Why does he need to force the situation to a confrontation with our people?" he appealed to the rest of us.

9/. Living Manifesto

"Matthew, my brother," said Peter. "I would be overjoyed if you were able to stand straight. We should ask the Rabbi for the Lord's face to shine upon you and heal you."

"Thank you for this great kindness. I have thought of this also," said Matthew, in halting speech. "Yet I am not sure."

"You are not sure of what?" asked Peter. "You have seen many blessings and healings given."

"I was called to follow, just as I am," said Matthew. "My soul was healed, my place within my people was restored to me, but healing of my frame was not necessary."

Peter looked thoughtful, albeit somewhat rebuffed.

"The Rabbi called me to follow," said Matthew. "I did not need signs of the Kingdom to understand that he had given me my portion."

"The Lord created us body, soul and spirit," said my brother. "I am sure he wants you to stand before him as a whole man."

"I do not doubt that," replied Matthew. "One day in the Kingdom I am sure it will be so."

"Why not now?" asked Peter. "Your healing would tell of the wholeness of the Kingdom."

"I agree, Peter my brother," said Matthew. "Your care for me is wonderful in my heart."

"But…?" said James.

"If I stay as I am, the timid, who dare not ask for blessing, will know that they too can have their part in the Kingdom. My frame can reach out to my people as my words never could."

"Would you not want to be straightened?" asked Andrew.

"Yes, I would," said Matthew. "He told me to seek first the Kingdom and all the rest would follow.

Would the people see a normal-bodied former tax collector, or a man accepted by the Lord God despite how he appears and what he once was?"

"How long have you been thinking of this?" Peter asked.

"I think ever since Barabbas wanted his men to be healed," said Matthew. "He wanted blessing for his fighting men."

I left Matthew, Peter, Andrew and James to their discussion and wandered away with my own thoughts. Judas has seen a politically correct balance; Matthew and Simon saw an individual invitation.

Our Rabbi had once healed Peter's mother-in-law, but would he heal his own if we asked?

If we were all perfect specimens, would that help us to appear as an elite, a sinless elite?

Or an elite as the Sanhedrin was an elite?

Was Matthew right, did we represent God's invitation to all, poor and wretched and blessed?

* * * *

The following day, the rest of the Twelve arrived and, in the meantime, so did Seth and Yossi, Joash having remained close to The Immerser.

Jesus chose to receive them in the evening and made space for them amongst the crowd. We all knew that there would be a Kingdom message.

"Rabbi, we bring greetings from our master, The Immerser," opened Seth. "We pray for God's blessing upon him as he languishes in Herod's dungeon."

They both look hesitant, as if they had something difficult to say.

"What message do you bring from your Rabbi?" asked Jesus.

"Our master, The Immerser, asks to know," they requested, "are you the Expected One who was to come or should we expect someone else?"

"The Immerser has the same question that we have heard on the lips of the nation," my brother spoke in hushed tones. "Why did the Rabbi not take Passover in the Holy City? Why did he take no action this Passover as he did the last?"

I nodded, remembering the murmurings of the people on the return journey, their expectations exhausted.

"Yes," agreed Andrew, "The Immerser knew his mission and he needs to know that his mission is fulfilled, or if he should still be preparing the way for the Messiah to come."

Jesus stood and walked a few paces into the centre of the street and turned a circle, his arm indicating the people who awaited his attention. "Go back and report to John what you hear and what you see: the blind receive sight, the lame walk, those who have leprosy are cured, the deaf hear, the dead are raised, and the good news is preached to the poor. Blessed is the man who does not fall away on account of me."

We all exchanged looks and nodded. These words from Isaiah's scroll were familiar from many Sabbath's past, and once again, our Rabbi had added his own interpretation.

"Once again, he tells us that he is the fulfillment," said Nathanael. "He is doing what the prophets have foretold the Messiah would do."

"Just not what some people expect him to do," added Philip.

"He did that at Nazareth as well," said Andrew.

"I hope we don't get the same result," said Judas.

"I know it now more than ever," said Peter. "The times are being fulfilled, in our time."

"What did you go out into the wilderness to see? A reed swayed by the wind?" Jesus demanded from the crowd. "If not, what did you go out to see? A man dressed in soft clothing? No, those who wear fine clothes are in king's palaces. Then what did you go out to see? A prophet?"

A pause hung in the still evening air; to me, it seemed as a gulf between the man of God and his adversary, between the rock of purpose and the king swayed in the winds of sin.

"Yes, I tell you, and more than a prophet. It is the one about whom it is written: 'I will send my messenger ahead of you, who will prepare your way before you.' Truly, I say to you: among those born of women there has not risen anyone greater than John the Immerser. Yet he who is least in the Kingdom of God is greater than he. From the days of John the Immerser until now, the Kingdom of God suffers violence, as violent men take it by force."

“The Kingdom is at hand, if these people would take hold of it,” said James.

“The Rabbi warns us to beware the violent men of force,” said Judas. “The message is not good for The Immerser.”

Jesus was still addressing the crowd. “For all the Prophets and the Law prophesied until John. And, if you are willing to accept it, he is the Elijah who was to come. He who has ears to hear let him hear.”

I did have ears to hear it. Father’s quiet and careful wisdom had been correct. John the Immerser was the Elijah that preceded the Messiah. The Messiah had come, the signs, miracles and wonders as his evidence, as they would be again this evening.

* * * *

Soon thereafter, we were following our Rabbi out of Capernaum again, to where we knew not until we arrived, but this prevented neither the ongoing dispute about the healing of the Roman’s servant, nor the speculation of where we were going and what our Rabbi’s lesson would be.

Judas Iscariot speculated on how the healing could be used for influence amongst the Sadducees. Peter and Matthew discussed The Immerser’s imprisonment and our freedom. Thomas wanted to discuss how Moses would see it. Andrew said that it was now time for us to call our Rabbi ‘Lord’. Many from Capernaum came with us and others joined on the way as we headed south around the western shore of the lake, through Gennesaret, Magdala, passing by Tiberias, until we came to Nain. I had already learned that our Rabbi did nothing at random and looked ahead with great expectation.

Out of Nain’s gate and heading for the burial ground came a funeral with all the passion of the accompanying mourners and a sizeable crowd. At its head I saw one woman, clad in black and in despair, with neither husband nor sons beside her.

“This is why he has brought us here, I am sure of it,” I told James. “Her loss is everything.”

Thomas was nearby. "Are all this entourage here to ... s-support this woman or to await the opportunity of her land?" His tone of voice revealed his level of his suspicion.

Sure enough, Jesus led us to meet the procession and hailed them to pause. The next we knew he had instructed them not to weep, and spoke to the young man as if he was alive and then, lo he was!

Emotional overload took over: the woman in hysterical gasps of bewildered joyous relief, the erstwhile mourners in confusion. Thomas lectured them about their responsibilities to widows under the Law of Moses, with neither pause nor twitch, until they melted away in fear of the judgement they perceived was now upon them.

We stayed long enough to be courteous and accept hospitality. Then, as the funeral day ended and the news spread feverishly through the district that God had visited his people, we departed. In the next days, we crossed the Jordan to the east, out of Antipas' territory and into the Greek cities of the Decapolis. This had the effect of leaving most of the crowds behind; the scouts of the Pharisees and Sadducees elected not to have the dust of foreign soil on their sandals either. For me, it was blessed because I could walk close with my Messiah and ask him: how much virtue remained untapped and why did he call himself the Son of Man?

Here, amongst the Gentiles, it was again a different lesson: an insane demoniac from the tombs of their burial area was delivered from his indwelling possession, whilst their unclean animals were driven to mass drowning by the same demons. These people were also convulsed with fear, albeit different from the mourners of Nain. They begged us to leave, lest the rest of their disgusting practices and animals were lost, whilst caring nothing for the messenger, his message or his miracles.

What my emotions were during these times, I am not sure I can tell you, because I could not make much sense of them myself. My own chariot and stallions had taken me nowhere at Passover and now the alternative chariot my Messiah was driving had taken me on this giddying ride, where the power and the miracles had gone to new and dizzy heights – the sick had been healed, the dead raised and the demons cast out.

As we crossed back into Antipas' Galilee and headed back towards the lake, Jesus helped us make sense of it all. "What have I shown you in these past days and weeks since we gathered in Capernaum?" he quizzed us all.

After a pause, Peter was the first to speak. "You have shown us greater signs and miracles than ever before!"

"And what did the signs point to?" came the next question.

"In Nain, you fulfilled the Law, without needing the Law," proclaimed Thomas. "The land was restored to the family by the raising of the … d-dead without the need of being redeemed in by the clan, or redeemed by the jubilee year."

Jesus seemed satisfied with that answer and moved on. "And what about the Roman? Was it right to give God's blessings to him and his slave?"

"We should do this more, to gain their favour," said Judas Iscariot.

"Did God see that man as an oppressor of his people, or as a man prepared to humble himself and admit his need of our God?" asked Philip.

"Or, are both of those things true at the same time?" put in Nathanael.

"Yes, indeed, those are good questions," our Rabbi confirmed. "What then did you see at Gadara?"

"The legion of evil fled before you!" said Andrew. "A legion of five and a half thousand in that one man!"

"And found its place in the foreign swine," said our young Zealot, revealing a growing confidence to express himself beyond his young years.

"What picture does this give you, when all is put together?" asked Jesus again.

"I think you took us to Nain and Garada with a purpose, because of the centurion of Capernaum," said James.

Jesus said no more, challenging us to work out his purpose and fill the silent space he had left for us.

"Rabbi, I would like to pull together all these words," I ventured. "You are showing us that whatever was done for the gentile, it was a token of blessing from God, but what was done in Israel was greater. At Nain, it was a fulfilment of the Law and the Prophets and the Kingdom that you preach. At Gadara, you showed us what we have always been told, that our land is blessed, whereas outside on foreign soil, much evil and chaos has its place?"

Jesus smiled with a small nod of his head.

"You spoke well, young philosopher," acknowledged Peter.

I flushed with embarrassment, but inside I glowed all the way back to Capernaum.

We took a boat to cross the lake; it was escape from all who pursued us with Messianic fervour, whether from adulation or suspicion. It was also time alone with our Rabbi, but I still braced myself for arrival in Capernaum.

10/. The Shame Trap

One night in Capernaum became infamous as 'the banquet from hell' and its shock waves rippled around Galilean society for years afterwards. In order to understand what happened there, I need to take you into the culture and customs that are central to the ways of my people, as the mast and sail are to one of our fishing boats.

Following the tour to Nain and the Decapolis, we had returned to Capernaum, where the elders and the whole town came to meet us. It was a welcome for a Messiah, or a Caesar, for the world to see.

Saul of the Pharisees and Chai of the Sadducees were on surveillance duty as usual and Rome was ever ready to maintain order. That same Centurion had his job to do, after all.

In Galilee, the village elders and many synagogues welcomed us, but the long tentacles of power from Jerusalem held many local Pharisees against us. On the opposite extreme, the Sadducees were dismissive and aloof, being closer to the Herodians in the richer synagogues of Sepphoris, Tiberias and the other cities.

These two parties of rival theologians now began to work together against my Rabbi, waging their war of words designed to discredit him and twist any controversy to their advantage. Their chosen weapon in this warfare was now more subtle than the 'prince of demons' jibe: now they adopted the calculated insult with the purpose of bringing shame upon my Rabbi.

Perhaps the most extreme of these calculated insults came at the house of Simon, a Pharisee of Capernaum. A banquet had been arranged in pious righteousness, inviting access for the poor and the beggars, who stood at the gate as we arrived, awaiting their turn.

"I still feel out of place at these times," Andrew confided in me. "Life did not prepare me for society banquets."

As soon as I entered the Pharisees' courtyard, I could feel a trap had been set here. The steward stood over the washing with little demeanour of welcome, then lowered his gaze to overlook my Rabbi, and the foot-washer proceeded to the next man.

"See how they have ignored the Rabbi," said Matthew. "How can we be worthy to be here without him?"

Peter bristled. "The Pharisee thinks he can shut the door in our faces!"

"Steady, Peter," said my brother. "I suggest we follow the Rabbi's lead and see what happens."

I looked at the steward face: it told its own story, of a man who had been given the job of delivering the insult.

Jesus stood alongside us as the servants attended to our feet. I watched the steward become even more awkward as Jesus refused to react and play into his hands.

"He's giving them every opportunity," said Andrew.

"This is gross," said Judas. "It should not be endured."

"Do we leave then?" asked Philip.

"How can we stay?" said Nathanael.

"That would be a greater … s-shame in front of these beggars," said Thomas.

"It's what they want," said Simon, his lip curled in defiance. "I'm not backing off."

Jesus entered the house and Peter went to follow. "If he stays, then so will I," he said.

Our host had assumed that his omission of all courtesy would leave my Rabbi dangling in isolated humiliation, but he had miscalculated. I followed Peter and my Rabbi's filthy feet across the threshold. Once inside, I could see that many of Simon's senior colleagues from Jerusalem were present.

"Shlomo is here," said my brother.

"He's leading the plot," said Judas. "The sole objective is to pour a public humiliation upon the Rabbi; a shame for us to share in as his disciples."

Simon the Pharisee greeted the most distinguished and oldest Rabbis, where Shlomo held court amongst them, and their huddle closed against the most powerful Rabbi in the room.

"What now, Lord?" said Bartholomew.

"Follow me," came the usual reply, and my Rabbi proceeded uninvited into the dining area and reclined on one of the most luxurious couches. James smiled at me, and then at Peter and Andrew, with the same mischievous smile that I had seen in the Sabbath cornfields, inclining his head for us to follow. Peter replied with a grunt of agreement. Now we walked straight by the servant with the hand-washing vessel and found places at the lower tables for ourselves, as close to Jesus at the top table as we dared.

I knew that we had blown away every standard of accepted behaviour. Our actions felt more than awkward, they flew in the face of everything my upbringing had taught me. Where I would have stood to await the oldest and most respected as they settled themselves; now I reclined with unwashed hands and watched these men file into the room. Their confrontation with our Rabbi's filthy feet sticking out from his threadbare garment showed in their faces. Shlomo's own expression was thunderous.

"Look at our host's face," murmured my brother. "He is not concerned because now he has all he needs to condemn our Rabbi for his gross impoliteness and disrespect; he believes his trap is closing."

"We shall see," replied Peter. "Our Rabbi always has the right words!"

Judas had maintained his etiquette at a high table and sat with face of stone.

As ever, my guts churned within me at the tensions I was feeling; I was sure the evening was a smouldering torch that would yet burst into full flame.

The needy were last to enter, waiting their turn to gather some morsels and leave, except one figure, which broke their ranks and moved towards the top table. As she came nearer, I recognised this woman. Mary of Bethany had followed us since we had passed through her village near Jerusalem some months before. She was another scarlet woman, who had already confessed many sins of passion and had found acceptance from my Rabbi in that confession. Mother had befriended her, but warned James and I that her emotions were both variable and vulnerable and that Mary would always see our Rabbi as a challenge that she wanted to possess, but would struggle to understand how she could love him.

What happened next turned the night on its head. An emotional noise, a stifled sob, came from beneath her veil as she came closer to Jesus. She was now just in front of us and I could see her eyes were fixed upon his feet and the story they told. Mary knelt beside the mired feet, touching them and sobbing to herself. My mind went back to the scarlet woman at Sychar and I somehow knew what this Mary was feeling. She had met a man who had shown her value and respect, whereas all others had taken what they could from her, and now she was seeing that man being publically insulted by those who would accuse her. That knowledge was railing inside her.

What she then did sent a wave of shock around the room, for she removed her veil and let her hair free for all to see. I gasped as much as any other; I had never seen a woman's hair before. I had never expected to until my wedding night and now, there in front of me, it fell in soft curls across her face, framing it in the flickering light. It went on, cascading down over her shoulders. I was enraptured as much as I was shocked. I felt the blood rush to my groin; I tore my eyes away and studied the food on my platter, lest my eye caused me to sin and I needed to tear it out to maintain my place in the Kingdom. The room was hot around me. I dared not look at my brother or my compatriots.

Only Mary's soft sobbing broke the pregnant stillness and my ears could not block out her presence. After many long breaths to regain my composure, I could look again and see what was happening. Then I understood her action; the veil had been removed to let her tears fall free and now this was her offering to my Messiah, with her own tears and hair, to do what our host had refused to do, to wash his feet and remove his shame.

I looked at Jesus, his composure unruffled as he reached for another tasty morsel like nothing was out of the ordinary. Every eye around the top table smouldered against him, willing him to do what they expected and expel this scarlet woman from their company, not least because she had dismantled their self-righteous game plan.

A small bottle of perfume appeared from beneath Mary's garments. This too went onto the feet, for a further caress with her magnificent hair and then kissed with tender lips. I studied my food again and chewed with mechanical monotony.

The silence, excepting Mary's sobs, was as appalling as any of the others I had known in this past year, until it was broken by a few words from my Rabbi.

"Simon," Jesus addressed our host. "I have something to say to you."

"Say it, Teacher!"

I thought the reply sounded a little strangled, but did Simon the Pharisee have any choice?

It was a simple parable that drew Simon into a trap of his own making, about two debtors, one who owed little and the other who owed much. If the debts were cancelled, which of the two would love their creditor most for the forgiveness they had shown?

Simon the Pharisee judged correctly that it would be the one who had been forgiven the most and thus pronounced his own judgement.

"The one who loved little and will be forgiven little is you," my Messiah told him.

And to the scarlet woman, Jesus spoke in the same direct manner. Yes, her sins were indeed many, but now her shame had been cancelled out by the faith that she had shown and the honour she had done for him.

The room riled and rumbled against my Rabbi again, just as it had after the man who came through Peter's roof was healed of his infirmity and his sins.

"He has the words!" Peter confirmed to us all with satisfaction.

Mary arose, her hair defiled but her face at peace, and returned to a place with the needy, where people fled from her path.

Jesus spoke with all courtesy to thank the Pharisee for his hospitality and his care for the poor and needy. Then, proclaiming they needed his attention also, he rose from his couch. I tried to follow without haste, but every nerve within screamed at me to leave that room.

"We were all defiled," said Bartholomew. "The Rabbi's feet and your unwashed hands defiled the meal and that woman defiled her own hair."

"Well, they should have washed his feet then," said James.

"They wanted him to wash his own feet," said Judas.

"Or force him to leave in humiliation," said Matthew.

"Our God raises the poor and humbles the mighty," Peter reminded us.

"The Lord God turns back on their own heads the ... c-curses of the unrighteous," proclaimed Thomas. "The Pharisee received only the humiliation he had planned for others."

"Shlomo has suffered deep public offence," said my brother.

"They will all lick their wounds and look for vengeance," said Judas.

For many nights, I lay on my back as the stars swam in and out of focus. How could he be God Almighty and forgive sins? How huge indeed was God's grace that it did not diminish the sins of Mary, but magnified them only to cancel them completely. They were shame upon shame, and yet were now blotted out.

In my mind, I could hear my father quoting from Isaiah's scroll: 'he took our sins upon him'. That is what my Messiah had done for Mary of Bethany. She had sprung the trap and yet he had deflected the anger for her onto himself.

I prayed to my God to ask him if I needed to follow my Rabbi in this association with the scarlet woman, so that she might feel his love challenge her.

11/. The Growing Divide

The dizzy chariot ride went on. I felt I would lose my soul unless I could keep some perspective of my own life. Time had been a blur during the past three months since my Messiah had called me to be an Apostle.

Unable to sleep, I watched the summer day dawn. As the sun broached the horizon, I asked the rays to illuminate the world of my second summer since I had first left home to seek The Immerser.

The times were being fulfilled, but they were flowing fast through my fingers. I still yearned for Passover and freedom and the questions of how it could happen were still before me. Passover: next year in Jerusalem? Where would my Messiah take me before then?

I spoke with my brother, Matthew and Peter. "If we are 'Apostles', then he is preparing us also 'to be sent', just as he has told us he was sent for this?"

"When first he said it," James replied, "I was sure it would happen at Passover. Then, after his great sermon, I was certain of it. Now we have to wait, another year, another Passover!"

"In his great sermon on the mountain, did you not feel yourself being separated from our own people?" said Peter.

"This feeling of separation grows in me too," said Matthew. "It is almost bereavement now; will our people soon become unreachable?"

* * * *

It was late one evening, when the crowds had dispersed, that Jesus said to us again, "Let us go once more to preach the message through the towns and villages of Galilee. That is why I was sent."

All through that summer, it was the same: an incessant and exhausting pace, teaching, parables, healings. With no place to call home, we were all fugitives relying on remote places and safe houses and the escape across the lake in the night.

It was during a night-time escape across the lake that one of the most incredible events took place. Whilst Jesus lay exhausted and asleep in the stern, the wind changed direction and came out of the southern desert hot and angry as it funnelled up the Jordan. We fishermen knew the danger and rowed for the nearest shore, but the squall enveloped us, the wind clawing at the waters until they towered above us, swamping our boat as we shook and screamed at Jesus that we would all be drowned.

He stirred and spoke the words, "Quiet! Be still!" The storm died, the wind bleeding away to the sigh of its own demise. Then he turned to us in a voice, with surprise, quite even and calm, "Why are you so afraid? Do you still have no faith?"

Afraid? We were all terrified, and backed away from him to cower like small animals at the other end of the boat.

Later, we stood in silence around a roaring fire, our clothes steaming dry, as Jesus was again in exhausted sleep.

"Why did he speak to us like that?" said a downcast Philip. "Any man would be frightened for his life in that storm!"

After a pause, Bartholomew said, "Perhaps because we should have had the faith to understand that God would protect us because we are part of the mission of his Messiah?"

"We should simply not be afraid of losing our life," said Nathanael.

Another pause, as we all considered this.

"Is that why the wind and waves obeyed him, then?" asked Philip.

"Can anyone else think of another reason?" asked Bartholomew.

"What about you, young philosopher?" Peter called to me. "I am sure you have been thinking. What do you say?"

I cringed with a little embarrassment. "I agree with Bartholomew," I said. "It was a parable enacted for us. He did it for us, to show that we should not fear if we are with him."

"And is there more than that?" inquired Peter.

I gathered my words; "We have seen that his words have power. He speaks and it is done. He had already told us 'we are going to the other side', therefore we should expect it to be just so!"

Another pause, and so I continued. "Do you believe he is the Messiah, Peter?"

"Of course, why else would I be here?" said Peter, with a gesture to our wretched condition and barren campsite.

"Then he is of God?"

"Yes, he is the Lord!"

"And the Lord God Almighty created this world like the scriptures tell us?"

"Yes, it is so," agreed Peter.

"Then the creation is his, it is his to command and so it is the same with his Messiah! At the beginning of creation, when the earth was formless and void, the Lord God said, 'Let there be light' and it was so. He spoke the word and it was done with neither argument nor conflict, and in the same way his Messiah spoke and the waves were put into their place. In both cases, order was established from chaos."

"I will no longer call him 'Rabbi.'" Peter's voice was soft as if awestruck. "From now, I will always call him 'Lord.'"

"Take care you don't say that in the Centurion's earshot or you head might not stay on your shoulders for long," said my brother drily.

"Then why does the Lord not calm the raging of the nations and bring order to our nation and cleanse us of Rome?" Judas looked down his nose at me.

It was Philip who came to my aid. "The Immerser already asked that question when he sent his disciples to question the Rabbi about the lost Passover." Then, he added, "I am sure he will; it is only a matter of time. He asked us to follow, that was all."

* * * *

We returned to Capernaum, where the welcome had its usual fervour, almost crushing us in their midst as we tried to form a protective phalanx around Jesus. Desperate people awaited him as usual, but on this occasion, it was no ordinary person, but a synagogue leader, called Jairus, who tore his way through the crowd to slump on his knees before my Lord and beg for immediate attention for his dying daughter. We had not gone more than two streets when Jesus was then ambushed in the chaos by an unclean woman, who momentarily grabbed a handful of Jesus' cloak. He halted the whole crowd and amazed us all by asking who had touched him, because power and virtue had been drained from him.

By the time that was all done, a servant of Jairus' household had arrived to tell his master that it was too late for his daughter. My heart went out to this decent man as he dissolved in helpless grief.

We picked him up and I heard Jesus tell him not to worry, only to believe in the resurrection of the dead. By the time we arrived at Jairus' house, there was a bunch of rent-a-mob mourners already plying their trade. They scoffed and ridiculed as Jesus told them the girl was just asleep, but then with authority I had never heard on the lips of any man, my Messiah spoke! Every word rolled out with the thunder of command and this mob shuffled for the gate, wondering why they had ever come.

Peter, James and I accompanied him to the inner room, whilst the others sealed the house. The girl looked as pallid and lifeless as I had ever seen, but the colour returned and she awoke to Jesus' command, even looking bewildered at her parent's emotions. Again, it was Jesus' expressed wish for the parents not to speak a word about him, but give glory to God, and we departed.

We took some back streets to Peter's house. I tarried at the rear with Simon and watched Judas Iscariot as he walked with head down, his jaw muscles clamping.

Later that evening, I found a quiet moment with my brother. "Did you observe Judas after the girl was raised?" I asked.

"Not really," he replied. "I was too overwhelmed by the pace of events and my swirling emotions to protect the Lord from the crush. What did you see?"

"I saw a man who thought his place should have been with us in the inner room," I said.

"I see," he replied.

"Judas is trying to influence me and Simon with his opinions. He sees us as young and impressionable, but opinions in the group have not been in his favour recently, have they?"

"No, and if the Rabbi wanted to send a signal for the direction that he wants opinion to follow, then this would be a way of doing it." My brother's face was thoughtful.

"But how would a scholar like Judas Iscariot take that, being amongst the likes of us?" I asked.

James looked at me for my conclusion.

"I think he has taken it as an action to exclude him on purpose, as a calculated rebuttal, perhaps even as an insult."

My brother pursed his lips and nodded agreement at my scenario.

* * * *

It was autumn in Galilee again. We took Yom Kippur in Capernaum and then, as the population returned from the pilgrimage of Sukkot, the day that James and I had anticipated finally arrived. Apostles we were, and now it was our time to be sent to our people.

"An autumn campaign! What king has ever before marshaled his forces for an autumn campaign?" My brother shook his head in slow wonderment.

"Our God is … l-like no other god," said Thomas. "His King is like no other king. You should not … b-be surprised."

"I feel like a fledgling on the edge of the nest, about to leap into the void before me," I told them both.

The last eighteen months had been training for this moment: listening to my Messiah preach and teach, watching him in action, seeing the reactions of the crowds and the parties of the Sanhedrin.

Now he called us together, much as a leader does to his troops before battle, and he gave us a motivational speech like no other. It was the battle for the hearts and minds of our nation. We were not being sent to Gentiles or Samaritans. Our weapons were words of truth and law and compassion of heart.

He told us that we had power and authority, a Messiah's power, to heal the sick, raise the dead and to drive out demons, as we preached the Kingdom message.

We were to have nothing to live on, no money in our belts, no bags to encumber us. The message we preached would bring us a welcome of peace. If our message was not welcomed, we were to leave, shaking the dust from our feet against those who did not have ears to hear, and leave them for the Lord God's judgment.

Once again the dividing lines were drawn: if people did not choose the Kingdom, then they would be against the Kingdom and our people would no longer be our people.

We hung on his every word. What would our reward be in the Kingdom, for our endeavors in his name?

He told us. We Apostles were sent out 'like sheep among wolves'. We would need to be 'as shrewd as snakes and as innocent as doves' and, because he was our Rabbi, we would be flogged in the synagogues. If we were dragged before the Gentile rulers, we would proclaim the Kingdom also to them. The Holy Spirit of God would be our advocate and our source of comfort as we fled from one persecution to another.

Then, he prepared us to be sent on our way in twos. Jesus took the wider group away with him and we Twelve remained. We would all meet again in Capernaum.

I was paired with Simon bar Mordecai, my brother with Andrew. Peter noted with a smile that Judas had been paired with Thomas and said he would pray for them both!

"I feel naked, apart from my Messiah's words," I told Simon.

He grinned at me; adventure danced in his eyes. At that moment, my companion seemed better prepared than me, and I needed his reassurance.

"You heard the deal," he said. "We acknowledge him as Lord before men; he presents us before his Father in heaven. But to disown him cuts both ways as well. We expect no peace when we love him more than we love our own. We lose our lives to find our true life in him. I have done this; I left my own. My destiny was an outlaw's death and now he is my life."

I knew that for all my knowledge of scripture and fine words in our debating, I could not match this simple confidence that now exuded from my mission partner.

We set out with the dawn, Simon and I heading west. It was important for me to head away from Bethsaida and any thought of home and comfort, as we walked with rising sun on our backs.

"Now what will Rome and the Sanhedrin do?" exclaimed Simon with glee. "Let's see if they can keep track of us all now, as we spread across the land."

"Let's keep our mind on the mission ahead of us and the Kingdom we must proclaim," I cautioned. "He told us not to worry about what is behind."

Simon considered this for a moment and then reversed his previous words. "Yes, if we can do what we have been sent to do, they will have no problem following our trail of signs and wonders! Bring it on!" He grinned at me again and I was so glad he was there.

12/. Much Grief

They arrived laden with grief, Joash, Seth and Yossi, proclaiming the death of their Rabbi. John the Immerser was no more.

We offered food and wine but they would not eat and so we sat them down and gathered around to hear them. I looked for my Messiah, but he was not among us. Then, I saw him sat with his back to a wall and his eyes closed.

My brother drew Andrew and I to the fore, knowing of our time together with The Immerser's disciples. We sat by them as they rocked back and forth with the weight of their news. Andrew held Joash's arm as I reached out to Seth and Yossi. "My brothers, will you share your grief with us that we can bear this burden together?" Andrew asked.

"The servants told us," Joash began. "We had got to know them well from all the times we had visited our Rabbi. So they told us everything." He choked off in sobbing.

"It was the King's birthday banquet, with all his officials from Judea and Galilee. They were high on wine and the princess, Salome of Herodias offered to dance." Seth was still as he muttered his words with his head down.

"Queen Herodias had plotted it," snarled Yossi. "The scheming whore needed to remove the accuser of her adultery!"

"Antipas promised the princess up to half of his kingdom as his price for the dance to continue," said Joash. "But the girl said her price was the head of The Immerser, delivered on a platter to their banquet on the King's word!"

"Antipas was trapped by his own shame, the wine and the Queen's manipulation," Seth voice was a hoarse whisper of emotion.

A collective groan rose amongst us, all reached out their hands and placed them on the shoulders of our friends.

"We took his body," said Joash, before choking again.

"And his head," groaned Seth. "We buried them together at Qum'ran, where the community mourned with us this week past."

Yossi was on his feet now, as his grief raged at the sky. "The greatest prophet in four hundred years, his life snuffed out like a candle, the price of a voluptuous temptress and her striptease!"

All could see that Yossi was now fighting mad as his arms flailed about him. Peter rose and nodded at Andrew before moving to embrace Yossi against his large frame. Yossi's fists beat against his back, but Peter did not flinch, and Andrew closed from behind to complete the press. As Yossi tried to break free and run, the brothers held him tight for several minutes, until his body sagged between them and his grief tailed away into helpless sobbing. As they continued to hold him, we all gathered closer, held Joash and Seth and wept with them. Then Jesus came and sat amongst us and we sang dirges and psalms deep into the night.

My former Rabbi had been the messenger. What now for my Lord? What now for me?

It was soon afterwards that a servant of Joanna came to Jesus, sent by his mistress with a warning. The news of our preaching the Kingdom all over Galilee had been reported to Antipas and now, in a crisis of conscience, he was torturing himself that The Immerser had been raised from the dead. Not only were his patrols being sent out to track down the Immerser that Antipas supposed to be resurrected, but the King himself was also touring all the places where John had preached his repentance of immersion and was working his way up the Jordan towards Galilee.

Everyone's arms were in the air as we gathered around Jesus, giving opinion of what to do. The majority wanted to withdraw to where Antipas could not find us. This meant either south into Samaria, where we would get little assistance, or east into Herod Philip's territory.

Father approached Jesus and offered our house in Bethsaida. It offered many options if further escape was needed: across the lake, into the Decapolis, or even a double back over the border to Capernaum.

Jesus accepted that he could over-winter with us and lie low in Bethsaida, with much gratitude. He would continue to tour alone or with a few of us Twelve and promised my parents to keep their house safe. His plan was to make short visits to Capernaum to continue to preach the Kingdom and maintain contact with his family, before withdrawing across the border to Bethsaida again. The Twelve and the wider group would not travel together and risk attracting attention, and return to our occupations and families. We would lead our pursuers on a dance as they strived to find our whereabouts.

When in Bethsaida, I glowed at the honour of having my Messiah at our home to talk with him and share his strains and stresses. The draining and filling never stopped. I would hear him leave the house in the early morning, as he went to start his day in solitary prayer before a day of preaching and healings. After darkness had fallen and he could not be recognised, he would return exhausted; eat whatever Mother put before him and fall asleep on the mat by the brazier. We would put a pillow under his head and blankets over him and there he would stay. Sometimes he allowed James or me to go with him and other times he would appear in Bethsaida's marketplace, as always calling on all there to repent and take hold of the Kingdom of God for themselves, before disappearing again into the winter dusk.

Father told us the assassination of The Immerser was weighing heavily on our Rabbi and he had a plan to encourage Jesus to break from his intensity. He shared it one day, when Andrew was with us.

"That day Benjamin searched the scrolls for us," said Father. "He asked to meet the Rabbi if he was ever in Bethsaida. I think now would be a good time."

"How do we make that happen, Father?" asked James.

"Andrew, you are the key because you were at Nazareth," said Father. "This evening, when Jesus returns, tell him how Bethsaida's oldest Rabbi helped you understand his sermon at Nazareth. Tell him he is the Rabbi of your boyhood and that Benjamin has asked to meet him."

So our plan was made, and that evening as Jesus ate by the brazier, he agreed to rest the next preparation day. We would all visit Rabbi Benjamin to talk of his sermon at Nazareth.

* * * *

As we approached Benjamin's house, through the overcast autumnal streets, the windows glowed with warmth. Once inside, many lamps burned, the brazier was stoked, and aromas of spices and sugared almonds and fresh baking teased my nostrils. All the goodness of recent harvest had been prepared, as much as Benjamin could muster. We approached a table of fresh bread and pressed oil, smoked fish and stuffed vine leaves, cakes and figs and good wine.

Our ancient Rabbi rose from his chair as his housekeeper introduced the young Rabbi who proclaims the Kingdom of the Lord God. After a long round of embraces and every courtesy had been exchanged, we waited for Benjamin to lead the prayers and settle again. The housekeeper served and withdrew. With such a banquet, we gave praise for every morsel and talked of the Lord God's provision and blessing on our land. It was only proper that the business of the evening could wait.

When it came, Benjamin spoke in his fluid Hebrew and I struggled to keep up, but I knew that he was testing my Rabbi rather than me.

"Thank you for accepting the invitation of an old man," Benjamin began. "I have long been hoping to talk with you. Tell me about the Kingdom you preach."

I leaned back and watched as Benjamin sat close to Jesus and searched his face in the lamp's light.

"It is no more or less than you already know, from the Law and the Prophets," replied Jesus. "How could I ever pretend to tell this to a man of your great age and wisdom?"

"You are gracious to me," said Benjamin. "However, we both know that it can be a matter of interpretation. I have heard of your interpretation at synagogue in Nazareth from your young disciples."

"How does that seem to you, Rabbi?" said Jesus.

"Do you ask me for my interpretation of the scriptures, or my interpretation of yours?" asked Benjamin.

"I invite you to tell me whatever you think is right," said Jesus. "Speak with all truth, as we must before the Lord God."

"It seemed to me that you confronted men with the truth that they need, but would rather not be told," said Benjamin. "They need the truth in order to be saved, though they would prefer a more comfortable message."

"Do you think they would listen more if I gave them the message they desired?"

"Of course they would! Do not kings have courtiers that tell them what they want to hear?" said Benjamin. I saw, by the lamp, a challenging light flickering in his eye, as he added, "You might also benefit by surviving to speak another day."

"You suggest my life is worth more that the truth, Rabbi?" asked Jesus.

"If you are truly the Messiah, then Israel needs your Kingdom to last forever, to fulfill the Law and the Prophets. Is that not your purpose and your destiny?"

I could not remember when I had seen this old and gentle Rabbi so animated as he leaned forward, almost hawk-like in his chair. His olive skin glowed in the light as his probing questions were like an interrogation of my Messiah. I looked at Father, but his face was impassive as usual, as he also worked hard to follow the Hebrew.

"My destiny is only what my Father has willed for me," said Jesus. "I am called to walk before the Lord God and be perfect. As was His call in the covenant with Abraham."

"Then what is your mission? How can you fulfill this spotless life?"

"To fulfill the Law and the Prophets as you have said. You are quite correct, Rabbi."

"I ask you for your interpretation, then," said Benjamin. "How are the Law and Prophets to be fulfilled?"

"By removing the curse of Eden, to restore the tree of life; so that all men may be free," Jesus was now quiet and matter of fact as he fed our old

Rabbi another theological morsel to chew. Benjamin's eyes continued their dissection of each word and every expression. Jesus continued. "Before the temple offered any sacrifice, the Lord God gave us Passover. Please tell me, how do you interpret its message, Rabbi?"

"The blood of the spotless lamb delivers us from slavery to life!" Benjamin confirmed.

Jesus nodded, an unspoken reply, and gently held one bony hand between his own.

For the first time, Benjamin paused to consider. I could see him striving to put the pieces together, as I had tried to do so many times. "The Lord God pronounced the curse," he said in slow and thoughtful speech. "Therefore only the Lord God can remove the curse, no other is worthy to open that scroll."

"Your understanding is great, Rabbi," said Jesus, with a pause. "I had no doubt of it since I entered your house; here your peace has filled my soul."

"Forgive me, Lord, you flatter my understanding but you need to help me understand more," said Benjamin. "How … how will the Lord God fulfill that purpose?"

"You know the answer; you have always known it, Rabbi," Jesus continued to hold Benjamin's hand. "The sacrifice has to be perfect, without spot or blemish; that is what the Lord God requires."

A cloud passed over Benjamin's face as he sat back in his seat. I saw his shoulders droop, his eyes relaxed into the far distance, his jaw hung open and his small frame quivered.

"Yes, Lord," he said, slowly. "Perfect! To be the perfection that a mere son of Adam could never achieve." His eyes focused back onto my Messiah. I cannot describe the expression that his face then beheld, except that it had both horror and wonderment in equal measure. Suddenly, Benjamin grasped Jesus' hand between both of his; his voice was trembling as he said, "Now, I know for myself that you speak of truth that men do not want to hear."

"May the truth keep you in eternal life," said Jesus, with utmost gentleness.

It was then I saw tears well up in Benjamin's eyes, as he turned to us and spoke in Aramaic. "All my life I have wondered if I would ever know this moment, but now it is here, I think I have lived too long."

"Of course not, my dear friend," said Father. "We will need your wisdom for many years to come."

The light had gone out of Benjamin's eyes. His trembling continued. "Thank you for the grace you have brought to the house of an old man," he said. "I need to be alone now with only your words, and regret I must ask you to leave."

"Of course, Rabbi," said Jesus. "Your hospitality has been wonderful. May the Lord God bless you and keep you, may he turn his face towards you, be gracious to you, and give you peace."

"I do not want to leave you in distress, Rabbi," said Father. "May I, at least, tarry with you a while?"

"Thank you, but I do not wish you to see an old man weep. Please go now."

I had heard enough stress in Benjamin's voice to know it was time to leave, but I did not understand what had happened here this night. I glanced back as we reached the door, Benjamin sat hunched over the table; his wizened frame shaking as a pool of tears fell in front of him.

As we walked up the gloomy street, I knew Andrew would speak; he would not be able to contain himself. "Forgive me, Rabbi, my Hebrew is not sufficient to understand. What has happened to cause Rabbi Benjamin's sadness?"

"Your Rabbi is a man of great understanding," said Jesus, very evenly. "Of such men the Kingdom is made, but great knowledge can be a heavy burden to carry."

Could I put these pieces of the Kingdom together, as Benjamin had? How could I carry this burden with him and my Messiah?

The Third Year: Into the Storm

17. Power Declined

"How long can the Lord keep up this intensity?" said Peter.

"I think he cannot rest until his mission is fulfilled," said Andrew.

"Even a Messiah is still human," said Judas. "All I see in him is stress."

"I agree, Judas," said my brother. "He is the only prophet in Israel now."

"He told me enough to know he and The Immerser had been together since at least their youth," I said.

"Is the mission to be more than humanly possible?" said Matthew.

"How is that possible?" said Bartholomew.

"I don't know," said Matthew. "But a king who reigns forever is not mortal."

"He bleeds, like the rest of us," said Judas Iscariot.

"Can this emptying and filling he speaks of end with becoming so fulfilled with good works that he escapes this life, as Elijah did?" said Philip.

"Can that achieve the perfection he speaks of?" said Nathanael.

"Abraham believed the Lord's word," said Thomas. "That was … c-credited to him as righteousness, not his works."

"I am sure the Rabbi does not lack in believing the word of the Lord!" said Andrew.

"He is more relaxed alone with us," said James. "I think he needs us close to him, as well as being sent out for him."

"We will see the tension grow when the springtime comes," said Judas Iscariot.

As winter mellowed and the north wind from the snows of Lebanon lost its bite, my body welcomed the growing warmth of the sun, but my spirit again began to feel the stress. It would not be long until the attention of the multitudes was upon us and the pace of the mission would accelerate with the demands of Passover and freedom once more.

My four white stallions came to find me again. Although Desire had never left me, Expectancy now stamped his hooves again, snorted impatiently and champed his bit. Power moved in his stall, kicking at the door, whilst Freedom brooded at the thought of ever being released. My nation waited in expectation for their Messiah to come and deliver the Kingdom and the freedom they yearned for.

It was still early springtime when we Twelve gathered again with the boats at Bethsaida, and Jesus took us across the lake to the east and away from the lakeside towns. Many people were now busy by the lake and in their vegetable gardens and anonymity proved impossible. The word spread and other boats soon followed us loaded with human cargo; I could see others following on the shoreline by foot. Men, women and children, whole families leaving everything and following with only the clothes on their back. By the time we had crossed the lake to the far shore, some had even beaten us there and swarmed forward, as an impromptu welcoming committee.

Whatever time I had hoped for with my Messiah now vanished, as more caught up with us and followed us into the hills. Jesus sat down in the fresh spring grass for the people to come to him.

"This relentless work gives me painful memories of The Immerser," said Andrew.

"It is more training for us," said my brother. "We will be sent out again, I am sure of it."

"He teaches me compassion," said Matthew. "When the people are like sheep without a shepherd."

"It has always been the way," said Judas. "Most wander through life with little meaning."

"Remember, Moses sat as judge for all the people from … d-dawn 'til dusk," said Thomas. "His father-in-law told him that unless he appointed others to share the burden; he would only … k-kill himself under the strain."

I tried my utmost to share my Messiah's burden. We all did, and all day we marshalled the crowds. Before I took them to him, I told them his message was to repent and have eyes to see the Kingdom. I told them to look beyond their lives to the eternal Kingdom, to disregard their immediate needs and embrace true repentance, if they wanted to be immersed in the spirit of their God. To my chagrin, I was only a servant of my master. Even if my message was the same as his, it did not come from his lips. I could not deliver the freedom they believed they needed; I was only a mere underling, with a few wisps of beard on my face.

It was another exhausting day, with hardly a moment to sip water from my skin.

"They will not leave," said James. "Their expectation of the Kingdom is too great."

"It is still weeks to the Passover," said Peter. "We cannot do this until then."

"He gives them no reason to leave," said Nathanael.

"They give him no break to eat, but expected blessings unending," said Philip.

"I see him being drained again," I said. "His teaching is more intense than ever, the compassion for the sick incessant."

It was late in the afternoon when Jesus tried to force a change and moved on up the hill, but the people followed, still refusing to leave. Messianic fever and the coming Passover were a binding that we could not break.

As we climbed, it was Nathanael who first voiced what we were all beginning to worry about. "He seems oblivious that the night is almost here."

Peter, James and Judas joined Nathanael. "What can we do now, Lord?"

"The women and children are in thousands. Are they going to spend the night in the open and with no food and little water?"

"You must send them away."

"They will need to scatter into the countryside and different villages and buy something to eat."

We stopped and looked out over the great crowd following us upwards and it was then our Rabbi asked us all, "Where shall we buy bread for these people to eat?"

"Eight months wages would not buy enough bread for each one to have a bite!" Philip was aghast at the practicalities. "Are we to go and spend that much money for them to eat?"

"How many loaves do you have?" Jesus replied. "Go and see."

I looked inside myself for some spiritual food, some satisfaction for the people, as we started to search through the crowd, calling for food.

"He's set us a challenge," I told Peter. "You remember he has told us to pray for our daily bread. There is a meaning here that I am trying to catch. Did you hear it in his question?"

"Tell me when you find it, young philosopher," replied Peter. "My bread has always been baked."

Andrew brought to Jesus a boy who clutched at his barley loaves and two small fish. "Lord, there are others who have food but are hiding it, but how far will this go among so many?"

Jesus replied, "Have the people sit down in groups of about fifty each."

Was this to be a test of faith for the people as well as for us? I went with the others as we moved out into the crowds, calling instructions in our Rabbi's name.

The men ranged across the hillside and arranged themselves in seniority before my Messiah; groups of fifty or a hundred were easy to count when in ranks and files. Expectation hung in the air, voices buzzed and rumbled, as we made our way back up to where he sat. I turned and counted: there were about one hundred groups of men sat in order on the ground before us, with the thousands of women and children to the rear and at the sides. It looked like an army arranged in formations, laid out for parade or even for battle, and at that moment fear clutched at my heart.

I knew for certain that this was a great moment, but that great disaster was also possible.

Jesus stood with that pitiful small basket of food in his hands, raised it towards the heavens and raised his voice giving thanks to God for his provision for them. Then, breaking the barley loaves and fish with his hands, Jesus started to hand it out first to the small boy and then to each of us. As the food continued to flow from his hands, all the others started to call the people forward to come and collect it. The women came with baskets and headscarves; they were the first to see the miraculous multiplication of the boy's small basketful, as it continued to grow into a feast that filled their own baskets. In their growing excitement, they jostled to receive the food and then scurried away to be the first to deliver it back to their men-folk and tell of the miracle food that they carried.

The excited gossip in the women became a growing murmur of approval among the men. I heard what they were saying. "Surely this is the Prophet who is to come into the world," they told each other as they ate their fill of the blessed bread and fish. As the women retired to the rear, we now faced the regiments. Senior men rose to proclaim thanks to God for his Messiah and the rest of the rank and file followed in, growing crescendo as they began to surge forward.

I could see it all now; the stage was set for the power play that the nation was looking for. Springtime, when kings went to war, Passover beckoned; an army of men, laid out in rank and file, their bellies filled and ready to march.

"Peter!" my brother cried out. "They will carry him every step of the road to Jerusalem!"

"He must seize the moment," said Judas Iscariot. "We have fed them what Rome and the Sanhedrin have taken from them."

"King by mob rule?" said Nathanael. "Is this a Messiah's way?"

The others stood rooted in indecision.

My Messiah was way ahead of us, holding up his arms, as if to still the crowd's advance. He suddenly became a Messiah that most had expected, as he barked orders. "Gather the pieces that are left over. Let nothing be wasted."

Then to us, hissing urgent instructions to run for the boats and go. Then, his voice of command again. "Go and gather!" His voice was loud and the sweep of his arms dramatic and the masses were controlled again.

Fear was rising within me, but I started to work on the piles of pieces that still surrounded us. We had to stop the crowd's advance and I began to gather with my hands, still calling for baskets. I knew I had to take the lead. For once, the few wisps of beard on my face were to my advantage; this was less of a humiliation for me than the older men. In this act of service, the women ran to join us.

The hundred companies of men stopped their surge forward, confused to see what the Messiah's disciples were doing; some even contributed uneaten food they still had. The senior men also called out for food to be collected for the march to Jerusalem.

We fled, huffing and puffing down the hill with our loads. I heard the crowd still and quieten behind us as Jesus spoke a dismissal to them. We pushed other boats off as well, to prevent pursuit, and clambered aboard our own. I looked back. He was climbing alone into the dusk; the multitudes milled around in confusion, their excitement punctured.

We rowed hard until the shoreline disappeared in the fading light and then paused for breath, to take account of what had just happened or had so nearly happened to us.

"That was frightening," said Matthew, gasping at his oar.

"Had he seen that would happen all along?" said Bartholomew.

"Or was it such quickness of thought to control the danger?" said my brother.

"He always has the words," said Peter.

"I was not against a march on Jerusalem," said Judas. "But it was a master stroke of crowd control."

I sat against the mast and thought it through; whichever way, the crowd had been confused and halted by the diversion that Jesus had put us to. As they awaited and expected orders from the new king, we Twelve had made our getaway.

Simon joined me. "I have learned much today," he said. "I saw the Messiah dismiss his self-appointed army. Whatever kingdom he is planning, it will not be to overthrow the Sanhedrin on the terms of a mob."

2/. Bread and Rations

As much energy went into our disputes as into the oars as we rowed for a long time, without making much headway into the wind and swell.

"The Lord gave us that task of feeding the people on purpose," said Philip. "He didn't need us to help him."

"He asked for loaves and I just did what he asked, finding that boy," said Andrew, his voice belying the need to justify himself.

"Did he try not to act because he foresaw the danger?" asked my brother.

"We are but fools; we are simple Galilean peasants, I tell you!" In a stunned silence, Peter continued, "Why do you think He asked us to find something for the people to eat? Because he knew what would happen if he fed them and became their YHWH Jireh!"

"Yes, that is the reason," said Judas Iscariot. "How else would the people react, when he gives them what Rome has taken from them, and with Passover on the horizon?"

"He already told us to pray for our daily bread. Was this also a parable, with his meaning being to give the people spiritual food, like the teaching he gives them?" asked Matthew.

"I don't know the answer to that, Matthew my brother," said Peter. "I only want to follow and do what I see our master doing and the next time I see him performing any miracle, I will ask him if I can do the same. Then I cannot be wrong!"

"We have failed him," Thomas' judgement was depressing. "After all he has ... t-taught us about the difference between law and traditions. We could have fed them in families ... b-but we failed because we are still children of our traditions and not of the Kingdom."

"Thomas, thank you for your insight, what you say is true," said my brother.

"Failure will stay as failure if we do not learn from it, unless we learn from this," said Nathanael.

"We have entered a new phase of the mission," said Peter.

"We have all seen the difference since the murder of The Immerser," I said. "He faces both the King and Sanhedrin alone now."

"Then why did he not seize the moment, take the crowd with him and march?!" exclaimed Judas. "The timing is perfect for the start of a campaign that would take us to Jerusalem."

"Perhaps five thousand was not enough?" suggested Philip.

"Pah! More would have joined on the way," argued Judas. "The opportunity was there and I think he could have taken it."

"And when we reached Jerusalem, how would we get past the legion?" said Bartholomew. His question was a leveller for us all.

"Approach from the other side," said Andrew.

"The Antonia would see us coming and signal the legion to fall on us," said Bartholomew. "Bad idea!"

"We send a delegation to the Tribune," said Judas. "Inform him we do not rebel against Rome, but only come to finish what our Prophet started in the temple two years ago."

"You expect a Roman to say, 'alright, as long as you don't make too much disturbance'?" said Matthew.

"Why don't we just walk by, hand-in-hand, with olive branches in our hair!?" Peter was loaded with sarcasm.

For few moments, only the rhythmic creak of the oars and the wind and waves filled the silence.

"My father, Zebedee of Bethsaida, always told me to remember that so many of those great prophets of old did not need an army," said my brother. "They had the Lord God on their side, and for them, that was enough."

"Then I hope he also told you about Joshua, conquering the land, taking each city in succession, The Saul and David ridding the land of the Philistines," returned Judas Iscariot.

"I am not seeking to argue with you, Judas," said my brother. "I am recalling what the scriptures tell us about Elijah, Elisha, Isaiah, Jeremiah and the many other prophets, who were not heads of our nation like the men you refer to. Their first concern was to speak the word of God and the word of God sometimes won the battles against the foreign armies too, if we take the examples of Elisha and even King Jehoshaphat."

Judas Iscariot was not about to be persuaded. "Think also what the people did to so many of those prophets for their efforts," he replied. "Persecuted, flogged, dropped into pits and often killed. Who wants to die a prophet's death? Who wants to be at the mercy of powerful men, when can have power ourselves?"

My brother held his tongue. We looked at each other and both knew that further dispute might make Judas' argument sound appealing to some of the others.

Matthew diverted our attention to a more immediate task. "We need to change shifts with fresh rowers if we are ever going to get across the lake against this wind. We still have more than halfway to go!"

We rowed on through the darkness with a single torch burning in the inky blackness. It was sometime later, in the fourth watch of the night, when a sharp cry of both surprise and fear halted our oars in mid-air. All eyes followed Philip's pointing arm. The hairs stood on the back of my neck, as illuminated by the flickering torch, a cloaked figure glided across the water a little way from the boat.

A chorus of horror rose from among us. "Pull!" shouted someone, but our oars dipped in panicked chaos and clattered against each other.

Someone shoved in beside me and, two to an oar, we tried again.

"Together!" my brother yelled. "Dip. Pull!"

The blood was coursing through my veins as every sinew strained when, several strokes later, a hand lay on my shoulder. "Wait!" said Andrew's voice. "Listen!"

A familiar and friendly voice relieved our terror as it came to us across the wind and waves. "Take courage. It is I; don't be afraid."

We halted again. Those of us at the oars gasped heavily, but Peter stood, holding the mast and called back, "Lord, if it's you, tell me to come to you on the water."

"Our big friend means to fulfil his promise and do whatever he sees his Lord doing," said Matthew.

No one argued; everything was now possible with our Lord.

"Come," Jesus replied, and so I felt the boat rock as Peter stepped over the side. A further step and he turned to look at us in amazement and triumph. The boat lurched and dipped dangerously, as all aboard clambered over each other to see for themselves. Peter took a few steps more and all was well, until the wind, as if with demonic mischief, raised a wave that slapped squarely against him. His eyes left his Lord to regard the waves and his faith failed him. In his moment of fear he sank, crying out to be saved.

Immediately, Jesus was there. "You, of little faith," Jesus chided him gently as they walked back to the boat. "Why did you doubt?"

The wind died down, and I could not work out why the shore that had seemed so far away now seemed suddenly quite near. We all embraced our Lord in welcome and worship. I saved a moment for Peter, who sat in the stern looking as if he had been burgled by a tax collector.

"Why do I doubt?" he asked me.

"You had more courage than I and others who stayed in the boat," I told him.

He harrumphed a reply, but I knew he appreciated it.

* * * *

The next day, when I awoke in Capernaum, the quiet was unusual and pleasant. We had had a few precious hours of peace to eat and then sleep. After all, each of us had a basket of bread and fish to toast on the brazier. Most of Capernaum, it seemed, was still on the far side of the lake or otherwise sailing on the lake, looking for their miracle maker and the Passover that they desired.

By midday they had found us again, a brooding people, ill at ease from their hopes dashed on the hillside the previous day. The senior men demanded to know when and how we had returned, as if trying to make sure they were not left behind again.

My Messiah's answer was, as ever, to his agenda rather than theirs; they really wanted a free meal rather than his word, he told them.

"He has told them the truth they … h-had not asked for," said Thomas.

"Do not work for food that spoils, but for food that endures to eternal life," Jesus continued. "The Son of Man will give you this bread. On him, God the Father has placed his seal of approval."

My mind flashed back to the woman at the well of Sychar and the living water giving eternal life.

"These are the people we need, their support can carry us forward," reasoned Judas Iscariot. "The Rabbi builds a relationship with them, only to tell them, 'no more'. It needs more that this to build a kingdom. Why do we not feed them again?"

The senior men in the crowd wanted to know much the same, but behind the question, I could see their attitude was quite closed. They had presumed wrongly of the march on Jerusalem and had felt the shame of rebuttal in their error and now sought to justify themselves.

"What must we do to do the work God requires?" they demanded.

Jesus answered, "The work of God is this: to believe in the one he has sent."

The next question was almost truculent. "What miraculous sign will you give that we may see it and believe you? What will you do? Our forefathers ate the manna in the desert. As it is written: 'he gave them bread from heaven to eat.'"

Jesus said to them, "I tell you the truth, it is not Moses who has given you the bread from heaven. For the bread of God is he who comes down from heaven and gives life to the world."

"Sir, from now on, give us this bread," they chorused.

Then my Messiah declared to them all that he was the bread of life and with him they would never go hungry or thirsty. They had seen him, but still they did not believe.

Yes I thought, it was Sychar over again, different people, different place, the same message. It put these people from my own nation alongside others from another nation, whom I had once feared and despised.

I heard them mutter and grumble that they knew his parents and his home, so how could he claim to come down from heaven?

But Jesus would not leave it there, telling them to stop grumbling, teaching them of what was written in the Prophets.

The argument amongst them was no worse than ours, but they began to leave, saying the teaching was too hard and they would not follow any more.

"Yesterday, many of these people tried to make him king on their terms," said James. "Now, a day later they refused to allow the Lord to be their king on his terms."

"They did not want unfathomable parables," said Judas Iscariot. "Only the conquering Messiah to remove the legions of Rome and give them the bread of their own land, instead of the dust. What is so wrong with a kingdom like all the others of the world?"

At that moment, Jesus walked back to us. "You do not want to leave too, do you?"

Peter answered, "Lord, to whom shall we go? You have the words of eternal life. We believe and know that you are the Holy One of God."

"Have I not chosen you, the Twelve?" He regarded us. "Yet one of you is a devil!" It was a reply that rocked us all backwards.

"Is he trying to get us to leave?" asked Philip with open shock.

"We will be as Gideon's little army," said Andrew forever faithful. "There is a victory to be won."

* * * *

Much later, James joined me under the starlit heavens to contemplate the day that had been.

"The bread," I said. "What was the purpose of the bread and the fish never ceasing?"

"Brother," he looked across at me. "If God gave you a gift, perhaps it was wisdom in these matters. What do you have to say?"

"In Isaiah's scroll," I said. "'A kingdom, of the increase of His government and peace there will be no end.' Like the bread."

"Yes, very good," He replied. "I also have a point."

"Yes?"

"It taught us and the masses that he would not lead a march on Jerusalem, because one day we know that we must go there."

"Simon got that as well. I was so pleased to hear it from him," I said. "There is another question I wish even more that I could find an answer for."

"Which is?"

"Who is the devil amongst us?"

But James slowly shook his head; we could only look towards the stars for answers to that one.

3/. Total Withdrawal

The politics of freedom and Passover continued in heated debate.

"Rome will support whatever they see is most reliable," said Judas. "They know Antipas is unstable and if his murder of The Immerser is seen as provoking a bad reaction in the nation, they will remove him as they removed his brother."

"So you are saying that the Rabbi should foment a rise of the people, to remove the King?" said Bartholomew.

"It would be seen as vengeance for the … d-death of his cousin," said Thomas. "Moses forbids that."

"If he is the Lord, then it is written: 'vengeance is mine, says the Lord,'" replied Judas.

"He doesn't need to provoke anything," said Andrew. "The people would have carried him."

"Rome has always preferred a puppet ruler," said Bartholomew. "It's more convenient for them than direct rule."

"They have always balanced the power of the temple with the Tetrarchs," said Matthew. "They know too much power in one place is bad for them."

"Except when they have it all," said Simon, by my side.

"The day will come when we will go to Jerusalem, in that Barabbas was correct," said Judas. "Tell me on what basis of power will we do that, if not the will of the people?"

I looked at James. If he didn't have a reply, then Peter surely would and in his usual no nonsense manner, a bigger argument would be sure to start.

However, it was Thomas that spoke first. "David refused to … r-remove King Saul by bloodshed even though his men urged him to rid himself of the sleeping … t- tyrant at his feet." His slow and heavy tones delivered another leveller from the scrolls. "I believe it will also be so with the Son of David."

It ended there, but I knew the truce was only temporary. The stress of trying to work out our destiny with the Messiah would continue to foment within us all.

I was relieved when Peter spoke some peace. "For two years we have experienced opposition from all the ruling classes, and we have been carried along by this wave of adulation from the people. So now the Rabbi has disappointed them and turned away some of the would-be disciples amongst us. This is nothing new; he has already been thrown out of his hometown, healed a servant of Rome and kept his miracles hidden."

"The agents of the Sanhedrin were in that crowd, as usual," said my brother. "They will report back that the Lord did not lead a rebellion."

"Do you think they will be less concerned that the Rabbi is a threat to them?" asked Bartholomew.

* * * *

The next time we left Capernaum, that hope was soon to be dashed. The main body of Pharisees from Jerusalem now joined the fray with the local ones. Seeing the opportunity to drive a wedge between Jesus and his adoring public, they attacked whenever the opportunity arose for them.

It was the start of a year of intense opposition, when our travel would become even more frenetic. The events of that spring and summer changed me forever and yet even these would not be the last in the presence of my Messiah. I know I have told you that before, but the change was an ongoing challenge for my young life to endure.

He took us south across the lake and landed at Gennesaret but, as ever, the Pharisees were well informed and it was just before Passover that a group of senior men from Jerusalem found us.

I shrank into our group and studied each of those that confronted us. As usual, I could see Saul; he had brought other senior Pharisees, but not Shlomo. I had not seen him since that evening at the house of Simon the Pharisee and I could imagine him brooding in Jerusalem.

In our vagabond existence, ritual washing was not always possible. Once again, the Pharisees seized upon this to make their accusation. "Why do your disciples break the tradition of the elders? They don't wash their hands before they eat!"

In my Messiah's current intensity, he threw the challenge back into their faces. "And why do you break the command of God, for the sake of your tradition?"

They stood stunned by his bluntness.

"God said, 'Honour your father and mother'. So why do you nullify the word of God for the sake of your tradition, when you put monetary gifts into the temple's coffers, that should have gone to support elderly parents?" His tone was dismissive, as he delivered his teaching without breaking from the meal. "You hypocrites! Isaiah was right when he prophesied about you: 'These people honour me with their lips, but their hearts are far from me. They worship me in vain; their teachings are but rules taught by men.'"

I looked around at the faces of the others and we all looked at the thunderstruck faces of the men of authority. Having given this crushing rebuke from both the Law and the Prophets, Jesus rose from the meal and called to the crowd.

"Listen and understand," Jesus told them. "What goes into a man's mouth does not make him 'unclean', but what comes out of his mouth, that is what makes him 'unclean'." The rebuke continued as he proceeded to teach the crowd in direct opposition to the Pharisees' challenge about the 'unclean eating'.

Dark thunderclouds passed across the faces of the senior Pharisees; I was sure that if looks could kill, they would have slain my Messiah there and then. The crowd stayed quiet and neutral, content to be onlookers without commitment that could get them into trouble. Jesus returned to our meal, the Pharisees stalked away and the crowd dispersed.

Peter, Philip, Nathanael and my brother all looked at each other and then, as Nathanael inclined his head towards Jesus, most of us gathered round him.

"Lord?" said Nathanael putting quiet concern into his voice. "Do you know the Pharisees were offended when they heard this?"

"Every plant that my father has not planted will be pulled up by the roots." Jesus' reply to Nathanael's careful understatement was almost as dismissive and blunt towards us as it had been to them. "Leave them; they are blind guides. If a blind man leads a blind man, both will fall into a pit."

Peter persisted. "Explain the parable to us."

"Are you so dull?" Jesus confronted us with a choice between material traditions and inner spiritual truths. Like the Pharisees, we retreated and dared ask no more.

"It is no worse than John and I heard from The Immerser," Andrew told us all. "He denounced those from Jerusalem as a 'brood of vipers, trying to flee the coming wrath' to their very faces!"

I realized that this was quite true. Up until now, Jesus had been much more restrained in his criticism than the firebrand Immerser. Now that seemed to be changing, since the Immerser had been eliminated. Had my Messiah given up on ever being able to win the hearts and minds of the Sanhedrin? I thought back to the rooftop meeting with Nicodemus. Was that really almost two years ago? Nicodemus had told Jesus then that the Sanhedrin knew that he must be from God, on the evidence of the miracles that he had done. Yet they were still unable to let go of their traditions and their status to accept my Messiah for who he was. I could feel the last vestiges of my respect for the elders of my nation ebbing away from me; it was the bereavement that I had heard Matthew speak of.

We moved on again, this time by foot. There were days of marching: leaving the lake behind, heading north with Jesus striding out before us, leading us along unfamiliar roads, through the hills where he had never taken us before. I realized we were leaving Galilee and the Herods' territory altogether.

Judas Iscariot voiced his opinion. "This is the opposite direction to where we should be going."

"We will not be in Jerusalem for Passover," said my brother.

Many of our travelling group turned back at the border area. Father and Mother embraced us, telling us to follow our Messiah, as we were young and strong, but the journey was too much for them. I watched them go back towards home and family and Passover, and sat by the wayside with Simon and John-Mark beside me, held in moments of despondent indecision.

"A large part of me yearns to go with them, back to all that is familiar," I said.

Simon embraced me; I cannot tell you how grateful I was. "We are again like Gideon's little army," he told me. I turned and looked after my Messiah, I followed and we walked on together.

The Roman Province of Syria lay before us, as we started to descend the slopes facing the great sea. The ports and great trading cities of Tyre and then Sidon lay ahead.

I saw my four white stallions again: Desire hung his head over the door to his stall, Expectancy lay despondent on the straw and snorted his disgust, Power paced and kicked his door, whilst Freedom stood motionless and morose. My feeling matched those of Expectancy; I was unsure of whether to walk close to my Messiah or to lag at the back in lost hopelessness. Never before had I been away from my family or from Jerusalem for Passover. A few short days ago, I had felt my relationship with the elders of my nation ebbing away; now my whole nation was being torn away from me. I regarded my feet as they shuffled through the foreign dust. I told myself that I had accepted that we were to be a new nation without the baggage of the old, but I had never expected to be away from the blessed land that God had given us, away from everything familiar, to be treading foreign soil at Passover. Passover! How could freedom come at Passover if we were never there? My stomach felt cold within me.

"Why are we here and where are we going?" asked Andrew.

"Is this a total withdrawal?" Philip asked us all.

"And why is he moving so fast?" said Judas Iscariot. "We have no pursuit. Is he running away from the Herods, or from the Sanhedrin, or from Passover itself?"

"I really don't know," James shrugged. "Our Rabbi told us to go only to the lost sheep of Israel and so I cannot think why we are in this foreign territory."

"Perhaps he has some important teaching for us that needs solitude that we will never find at home," suggested Bartholomew.

"These regions should not be … f-foreign to us," Thomas wagged his finger. "This was once Israel's land, the territories of Asher along the coast to Tyre, Naphtali in … t-the hill country and Dan up to the source of the Jordan Valley."

"I agree, Thomas," said Judas Iscariot. "This was David's kingdom as well."

We all nodded, grateful for this crumb of comfort. This was still our promised land.

My feet moved easier, as I strove to catch up, this was once part of David's kingdom and my Messiah was from David's line.

And what can I tell you about the Passover Seder? I hardly want to speak of it. We Twelve found hospitality with one of our own in this foreign land, but my Lord was not there, he was away in his wilderness. I felt as if a void had opened in my soul as another Passover yearned for freedom.

It would be another year in the wilderness, only to follow the dust of my Messiah's sandals.

4/. Face of Stone

It was the usual ignorant melee who pushed and shoved for a glimpse or a touch of my Lord and then made their way outside again to the babbled debate in the street. We had scouted a house in this Phoenician village that would offer hospitality and slipped Jesus in, to keep his identity secret. Even here, it only worked for a short time, and to our exasperation, the local people came to the house in droves.

We waited for it to pass, but there was one Greek woman who did not go away.

"Lord, Son of David, have mercy on me!" she implored from her knees. "My daughter is suffering terribly from demon-possession."

Jesus did not answer a single word to her, but as an hour passed, this woman's persistence began to wear us all down. Judas, James, Peter and I went to Jesus, stepping between him and the woman.

"Send her away, Lord, all her crying is getting on our nerves. Did we not come here for some peace?"

His answer was terse, as if it were a lesson we should have already known but he needed us all to learn over again. "I was sent only to the lost sheep of Israel."

The woman's pleading continued and when it came, Jesus' response was one of the most crushing I had ever heard; it relegated this desperate woman to a lower place where she deserved no blessing. "Let the children have their bread first, it is not right to take it and toss it to their dogs."

I expected her to shrink away or dissolve into tears, but to my amazement she remained, unbowed. Returning his cold stare with a steady gaze of her own, she answered, not with the same loud emotional appeals, but with a controlled voice of certainty.

"Yes, Lord, but even the dogs eat the crumbs that fall from their masters' table."

I heard Jesus' exhale and saw his features soften to compassion and, yes, I saw even admiration in his eyes, as he now answered her in warm and soft tones. "Woman, you have great faith! For such an answer, you may go. Your request is granted. The demon has left your daughter."

Relief and joy spread across the woman's face in equal measure. Her body relaxed as her eyes rose to the heavens and then, with great sobs of emotion, her head bowed in reverence before Jesus. Without another word, she got to her feet, before pushing her way back through the crowd, scolding them to let her pass. I followed; I had to see for myself, as she scampered down the street and into a house. I lingered long enough to see her come dancing out with a small girl cuddled in her arms. The image stayed with me all night.

The following morning, as we left the village, our disputes reached new heights.

"Why did he compromise?" asked Judas Iscariot. "She was not a child of Abraham to deserve the blessing of our God."

"I agree," said my young friend, the Zealot. "Why not just send her packing?"

"Maybe, but she called him 'Lord' and our master rewarded her faith," said Peter. "Did you not see how straightforward she was in belief from the start?"

"She accepted her situation to be called a foreign dog," said Nathanael. "But she also pleaded her right to the crumbs that fall from our table. I admired her answer and her determination, Gentile woman or not."

"It was far better than the lukewarm commitment we have seen from many in Galilee," said Peter. "What about those who have turned away from the Lord, just because they do not like some of his teaching?"

It was characteristic Peter; I loved that he was always ready to back my Messiah. He was again the father that I needed then. I knew he might struggle with some of the teaching and meanings of parables, but he knew commitment and belief when he saw it.

"I still say it was a compromise," argued Judas Iscariot. "A man of God must know his mission and stick to it."

"I agree with your principles, Judas." I knew my brother was trying to manage the group's harmony as he spoke. "However, I would ask you which is the greater principle of the Kingdom: is it faith and belief, or is it national boundaries? If it was the latter, then how does a Messiah conquer the world with a kingdom that is ever growing?"

For once, Judas Iscariot was not able to dispute the argument. I watched as my brother now stepped into the centre. This was the moment to assert himself in the leadership struggle within the Twelve. It would require all his powers of diplomacy. "We discussed this issue of our God blessing other nations once before, two spring-times ago, before we were called to the mission." He addressed everyone. "It was my father, Zebedee of Bethsaida, and our Rabbi Benjamin who opened Isaiah's scrolls for us. John had seen our Lord reveal his glory to a Samaritan woman and then Andrew, Philip and Nathanael has seen him rejected in the synagogue at Nazareth. They rioted because he told them God would not bless them with miracles, as Elijah had done with the widow at Zarephath." He paused for effect, before adding, "We are now in the region of Zarephath."

"So what did you think back then?" asked Bartholomew.

"We did not know what to think at first," replied James. "We greatly struggled with this issue."

"Then, I thought it was wrong," said Andrew. "But Zebedee of Bethsaida reminded us about other stories from the scriptures."

"Which scriptures?" asked several voices, some inquisitive and some demanding.

"Think of Daniel in Babylon," said James. "His diligent work was distinguished above all others. No corruption could be found in him and he prophesied to the Babylonian and Persian kings."

The others were pensive, knowing that this wisdom had come from men of standing and trying to remember when they had heard this at synagogue.

"Joseph did not bow the knee before Pharaoh, even under the threat of death," continued my brother. "You all know how God interpreted the dreams and Daniel used the wisdom that God gave him to save thousands of Egyptian lives as well as those of our fathers, from the famine that swept the land."

Judas Iscariot had subsided into sullen silence, and I joined my brother. "If that is not enough for you, my brothers, I pray you remember Jonah, sent on mission to the people of Nineveh, idol-worshipping aliens as they were. Our God cared for them because, as he told Jonah, they were a city of people, who didn't know their right hand from their left."

"So you are telling me that it is all to be given away to the Gentiles?" protested Judas Iscariot. He knew that he was losing the argument and his influence was waning.

"No, Judas," replied James, "not given away for free. Only where a person has faith and gives commitment, the Rabbi shows us that such faith can cross the boundaries of race and nation."

"And how do we judge that faith?" asked Nathanael. "Our Lord can do it, but how can we?"

"We are still disciples and so we must learn," said Peter. "I do not have your reasoning of the scripture, sons of Zebedee, but I can follow my Lord and do what I see him do."

"I remember now what he said," Philip exclaimed in a moment of inspiration. "The Lord said 'let the bread be given *first* to the children', so at the very least she could have claimed that her turn would come."

We all looked at Philip, casting our minds back to these words. Judas Iscariot moved away, it had been the final nail against his argument, but my brother called him back.

"Judas, you are the learned politician amongst us. Tell me, do you not think that our Rabbi must walk this political tightrope by necessity? He cannot yet reach out to the foreign nations for his Kingdom to fill the world without disgrace here at home, and yet he cannot refuse genuine faith and commitment in the Lord God."

"I will think on it, James," was Judas Iscariot's reply.

Jesus continued to stride out in front, taking us yet farther north to Sidon. There were many exhausting miles ahead as we then headed east to the source of the Jordan before followed the young river back down to Galilee.

There was just a moment when we stood at the farthest point of ancient Israel, when I saw something different in the face of my Messiah. It was as he turned south to face Galilee; he seemed to raise his gaze beyond it, to Jerusalem, and tremble. It was the face I had seen when he came from the desert, betraying a determination within him, knowing that one day he had to go that way and face whatever lay ahead for him there. I stood close to him, wanting to wrap my arms around him, and from that moment I could not leave his side, watching the emotions that crossed the face of my Lord. I knew he needed my companionship; he was being drained more than ever before as he drove himself onwards, to walk before his God and be perfect.

But which of us was the devil he had spoken of?

We walked to the south again, back towards Galilee and towards home, yet also back to those who were rejecting us. Now that Passover fever had passed, we expected Capernaum, but he took us around the east bank and down into the Decapolis, another land of Greeks that had once been part of the greater Israel. My Lord, the Son of David, was to walk the lands of his great ancestor's kingdom.

Not all who lived there were Greeks, and our own people soon found us as the news spread that the prophet from Nazareth had come to their territory. The masses gathered and I stayed as close to him as I could. Simon was with me as we shared this burden to support our Messiah. He had not changed what he was doing; the Kingdom of God was preached and demonstrated in miracles here, as it had been in Galilee.

There were always boats willing to take us and once again, we headed across the lake and landed at Dalmanutha on the western shore and back to Antipas' territory. Any respite we had gained in the foreign lands was now lost as the Pharisees closed in with their accusations and challenges.

Again, it was a force of both local and Jerusalem Pharisees. I was stunned that they could follow our movements and know our destinations and talked to my brother about this.

Were there spies amongst us? Yes, we had always known that, but were they now so close to our inner circle? How could they guess our destination?

How could spies get the message ahead of us to enable the opposition to move so fast? This time, it was Judas who answered it for us. The Pharisees were not racing ahead of us to our destination; they were simply at every town and village around the lake waiting for us. They were organized and had mobilized all of their forces against us, Judas Iscariot told us. He was right; we were just a fly to be swatted, buzzing around them but never out of their reach. It was Judas Iscariot's moment to lecture us about the need to grow our movement in number and organizational structure, like Moses had in the desert and Jehoshaphat had done with his judges. How else could the Kingdom grow to fill the world?

Thomas gave his approval of the scriptures; it brought Judas back into esteem within the Twelve.

In Dalmanutha, it was both Pharisees and Sadducees waiting for us. "Give us a sign in the heavens," they demanded from my Lord, that they might believe he was the Messiah, the Son of God.

I stood close to Jesus, hearing his deep sigh, telling his interrogators they knew how to interpret the weather from the appearance of the sky, so why could they not interpret the signs of the times on the earth in front of their noses? He turned to the miracle-seeking crowd and told them, if a wicked and adulterous generation looked for a miraculous sign, none would be given except the sign of Jonah.

I looked at the faces around me. It was a statement that puzzled both our opponents and followers. Since Nazareth, I had understood that Jesus did not do 'miracles to order', but what did the 'sign of Jonah' mean? To emerge after three days within a monster? It made no sense to me.

The only place I now felt secure was in the boat. There was no home for me now: always to be moving, crossing and re-crossing the land and the lake again, but moving on, inevitably towards Jerusalem and the great and final battles to come.

5/. Death Foretold

Another day east of Dalmanutha and we came to the great sea. Now Caesarea lay before us; the great galleys of Rome lined its harbour.

"Romans and Samaritans," said Philip.

"Days of marching from Gentiles in the east to Gentiles in the west!" commented Nathanael.

"The Lord seeks the Sons of Abraham to the ends of the earth," said Peter.

It was high summer again and, through the long and hot days, we had traversed the country from the Decapolis and across all of Galilee.

One evening, around the fire, talking over the day's events as usual, Jesus raised his voice, "Who do the people say I am?"

We offered answers of the various things we had heard.

"Some say John the Immerser."

"Others say Elijah."

"Still others say one of the prophets."

"But what about you?" he asked. "Who do you say I am?"

We all looked at one another, knowing the answer and yet, at this moment, we were being asked to declare the most fundamental and world-changing truth.

It was Peter who answered. Who else to declare the straightforward truth that we all needed to hear? "You are the Messiah, the Son of the living God," he said, in a voice that was steadfast and certain in conviction.

"Blessed are you, Simon, son of Jonah, for this was not revealed to you by any man, but by my Father in heaven," Jesus replied. "And I tell you that you are Simon and on this rock I will build my church, and the gates of Hades will not overcome it. I will give you the keys of the Kingdom of God; whatever you bind on earth will be bound in heaven and whatever you loose on earth will be loosed in heaven."

I exchanged a meaningful look with my brother, and moved around the fire towards him.

"Why now?" I whispered. "We have been with him for all this time. Why does he say this now?"

"Jerusalem must be ahead," James quietly replied.

Anyone could see Peter was walking on air from the approval he had received.

"He tries not to look too pleased with himself, but fails badly," I told Simon, who grinned back at me.

"I can't say I blame him," he replied.

Those closest to Peter smiled and clapped him on the back, but tried to bring him back to earth.

"So Simon Peter, you answered well," said James. "Do not get too carried away, remember that the Rabbi reminded you of your simple roots, son of Jonah, and that this answer came from the Father in heaven rather than from your head!" he added with a teasing twinkle in his eye.

"Oh! So you must keep me humble, must you?" answered Peter.

"Of course!" James grinned back at him. "You should keep me humble too, if I am ever given such a blessing."

"I am just pleased to follow my Messiah," said Simon Peter with a nonchalance that a child would have seen through. "For him, I must be Peter the rock, as he told me when I first met him."

We all laughed, pleased to see our friend so happy, but knowing it would take some time for Peter to come down.

The fire was left to burn low and so we wrapped our cloaks around us to settle down for the night. I lay awake for several hours, looking up, thinking about God in heaven and what Jesus' reply had been to Peter's declaration of faith and Messiah.

The following day, as we walked on to the next village, I asked my young Zealot friend to give me some space and chose a quiet moment to walk close to Peter. I knew that my opinion and closeness to Jesus would have Peter's respect, but I still needed to be very careful with the honour of my elder.

"Simon Peter, you remember what the Rabbi said about the building of his church?"

He looked at me as if to say, 'of course I do', except the wary look in his eyes showed he knew I wanted to say something.

"Tell me, young philosopher," he replied with raised eyebrow. "What is the full meaning of what my Messiah told me?"

I continued with all the diplomacy and grace that I could muster. "I do not think this is a burden that you must bear alone. This is something we all must share in, as our responsibility to the Lord and to the building of his Kingdom."

From a corner of my eye, I saw my brother smile with approval and he drew a little bit closer. I was grateful for the support his presence gave me.

"Firstly he called you 'Simon' and not 'Peter'. Secondly, he said 'on this rock I will build my church'. Well, what do you think the Lord was referring to? What was the rock on which his church is to be built?"

Peter shrugged his big shoulders just a little; I had calculated that he could not say it would be him alone, without being very conceited. To my relief, he responded with an equal measure of grace. "I rely on you to tell me these things, young philosopher."

I continued with care as Andrew, Philip and some of the others drew near.

"You had made a great and important declaration and that drew the Lord's response to all of us," I said.

"That he would build his church on all of us?" Peter was trying his best to be helpful.

"We must all have our part to play," I replied. "However, I do not think this was the Lord's real meaning."

"What was it then?" asked Andrew. "What do you think is the rock that his church will be built on, if not us?"

"I believe it is the declaration itself, the declaration of his name and his title. That is what Peter did; he declared that Jesus of Nazareth is King, Lord and Messiah. Do you see that this declaration is our part of building his Kingdom, something we all must do?" I surprised myself at the conviction I heard in my own voice.

"Why, then, did he tell us again not to reveal this to anyone?" asked Philip.

"It can only be that the time is not yet right," I said. "He is telling us this now, to prepare us for whatever is ahead."

"He must take his place in the temple so that all men can see his glory," James reminded us all. "I am sure then his name will be proclaimed throughout the world!"

"I do not disagree," said Nathanael, "but first I need to see the Kingdom restored to Israel."

I knew Nathanael was right, but I still could not see how that was going to happen. Any vision of the future remained opaque to me.

Over the next few days, I felt an increase in the tempo as we continued across the Plain of Sharon. If Peter's declaration had been a watershed moment, then nothing prepared me for the earthquake that followed. It was around another evening fire that Jesus confirmed he had to take us to Jerusalem. A joyous rumble of enthusiasm erupted from all of us gathered there, we would see the Kingdom restored and the world would see our Messiah's glory! Then, as we quietened, Jesus had not moved: he stood beside me, head lowered, somehow shrunken and cowed and, then, in the awkward void that followed, he told us that Jerusalem was where he would suffer and die at the hands of the elders, chief priests, and teachers of the law.

I heard his words, but it did not seem real to me. My Messiah could not die, how else could his Kingdom never end? He said something else about being raised on the third day, but in my state of numbness, I could not make it out. I looked at the faces around the fire; all were blank and furrowed in disbelief.

Peter was standing at Jesus' other hand and it did not take him long to react. I followed as he took Jesus to one side and began to rebuke him, saying, "Never, Lord! This shall never happen to you!"

It was then I saw my Lord's eyes; they were quite unnatural in the flickering firelight, they looked straight through Peter and away to Jerusalem. His reply was spat out, in a voice laden with angst and confrontation. "Get behind me, Satan! You are a stumbling block to me; you do not have in mind the things of God, but the things of men."

Somehow, I reached for Peter in the shocked silence. As I held his arm, our legs had collapsed under us and I didn't know where anything was anymore.

Jesus still stood above us, with his face to the south and Jerusalem, and what I saw in my Messiah's distant eyes was the same as I had seen when we stood at the farthest northern point of David's kingdom. The face was set like stone and his mind in another place, as if a tremendous battle were going on within him. Was he being drained or made perfect? I needed to know, but I could not understand.

The others gathered around Peter and tried to comfort him, telling him that Jesus had not looked at him as these words were said. It was little comfort. Peter knew he had done something wrong, but why had it produced such a reaction?

Jesus returned to us from his state of trance. I saw his face, still purposeful as he began to speak anew, in quiet tones. "If anyone would come after me, he must deny himself, and take up his cross and follow me. For whoever wants to save his life will lose it, but whoever loses his life for me will find it. What good will it be for a man if he gains the whole world, yet forfeits his soul? Or what can a man give in exchange for his soul?"

Then, he told us, "For the Son of Man is going to come in his Father's glory with his angels, and then he will reward each person according to what he has done. I tell you the truth, some who are standing here will not taste death before they see the Son of Man coming in his Kingdom."

I was not alone as I lay awake that night, and for many nights thereafter, in silent wonder and puzzlement at these words. Was he Messiah, fake or madman, as were had first feared? We debated, but got nowhere.

I considered my companions, this group of ordinary men, in much the same way as I had done when we Twelve were called, just before his great sermon. We had been plucked from such mundane lives, and had denied ourselves of homes and livelihoods, and yet they were still being called to something more. Just how could a man lose his life, but keep his soul? This was in the hands of God himself.

I could hear the stress, the renewed intensity in my Messiah's voice, and see it in his manner. I knew that we all felt it; small groups in hushed voices replaced our large disputes. The intensity was building all the time and I wondered what would come in the days to follow. In the meantime, Peter needed companionship. If something had been needed to bring him down to earth after his triumph of a few days earlier, then this was it in heaps.

We moved on again, walking inland and back into the hills of Samaria, and had crossed Antipas' border when Jesus announced he needed to take Peter, James and I away with him for a time of separation. The others had gotten used to this since Jairus' daughter had been raised to life almost a year ago, although my brother and I knew that Judas Iscariot still found it hard to accept the close inner circle that he thought he should be part of. I could still see anguish in Peter and hoped this would be a time of restoration for him. He had shown commitment above all of us. My guts jangled and my heart vowed to always stand by him and show the commitment that he had.

6/. Harbinger

Just three of us followed Jesus as he climbed; the breeze from the great sea was a welcome relief to the sweat on my brown.

"North to the source of the Jordan, then east to west and now Mount Carmel," said Peter. "I will follow the Lord to the ends of the earth, but it is hard on the legs for me!"

"It is as if he must claim every stone for Israel," said my brother.

"Then there will be many more stones," said Peter. "My legs will need prayer."

"This takes me back three years to my discipleship with The Immerser," I said. "It feels more like a wilderness for spiritual restoration than counting its stones."

Peter paused for breath and we turned to look out over the vista. To the west, the great sea sparkled away to the horizon; to the south, Samaria and Judea stretched before us.

"Are we here because we can see all of our blessed land?" said Peter. "Or is this for the ends of the earth to see the Lord's glory?"

We turned to climb after our Rabbi again and found him on a small area of plateau, already standing with arms raised towards Jerusalem.

"The time must be near," said my brother. "This must be a moment for preparation."

"For him or for us?" said Peter.

"He needs us close to him, more than ever," I said. "I am sure this is why we are here."

What happened then I have never been able to put fully into words, but it seemed to me that my spirit quickened within my breast and my pulse was racing faster than I had ever known, the blood pounding and rushing through my brain. My mind and body felt relaxed, and yet at the same moment, all of my senses were on full alert, as Jesus led our prayer. He had said some of us would not taste death before we would see him in glory, and right then I could have passed from life to death and been happy. I was not sure if this was trance or reality, but my Lord was different before me, a vision of white light, vivid and moving. I wanted to run for both joy and terror, but knew not where I could go and was unable to move anyway. Two other figures appeared, also dressed in lightning, and joined our prayer. When each had prayed for the King and the glory of his everlasting Kingdom, they sat and talked and my trance (if that's what it was) became more like reality, and I could follow the conversation between my Lord and our visitors, whom he addressed as Moses and Elijah.

It was too much to comprehend; time seemed to have no meaning. Was the Kingdom now come upon the earth?

The visitors talked to Jesus of his destiny in Jerusalem and how the perfection of his departure there would bring about the fulfilment of the Law and the Prophets.

'Departure'. I hated the word and wanted to run again, but could only sit with petrified attention.

Then the conversation was ending, with Moses and Elijah saying their farewells and Peter on his feet, waving his arms. "Master, it is good for us to be here," he garbled. "Let us put up three shelters – one for you, one for Moses and one for Elijah."

He was filling the void of terror we all felt as the cloud descended around us. I collapsed to my knees and then my face at the presence of power as a voice spoke, deep in tone, vibrating my chest cavities. "This is my son, whom I love," it said, "with him I am well pleased. Listen to him."

Then, I was relaxed and light; James reached out and shook me. "The Immerser's pool," he reminded me, "just like the voice at the Immerser's pool. The Son of God!"

I cannot tell how long we all stayed on the ground, breathless and overwhelmed, and yet a deep peace had now replaced my terror. The breeze was light on my face and the sky open above me. Peter's words somehow now made sense to me; the booths would be our meeting place with the Lord God as we had entered his realm.

The light faded and the stars appeared. My Lord, once again restored to the garb of a simple Galilean peasant, sat smiling and reassuring, allowing the time that we needed to pass.

In the morning, Jesus talked to us about our experience. "Don't tell anyone what you have seen until the Son of Man has been raised from the dead."

Peter asked, "Why do the teachers of the law say that Elijah must come first?"

"To be sure, Elijah comes and will restore all things," replied Jesus. "I tell you, Elijah has already come and they did not recognise him, but have done to him everything they wished. In the same way, the Son of Man is going to suffer at their hands."

Now it all fitted together for me with certainty. The Immerser and the Elijah of old, my father's wisdom, the voice at the pool and here on the mountain, the Messiah and the Kingdom. Only one piece I could not make fit: what did 'rising from the dead' mean? My Messiah was in the prime of his life and at the height of popularity and power. I had seen him raise people from the dead; what was the spiritual meaning of this new parable? As we descended the mountain, I just needed to find it.

"This is Elijah's place," said my brother. "Do you think the Lord will cut all that is false from our nation, as Elijah's did with the Baal's?"

"You think that is why we are here?" said Peter. "Will Elijah join us again in Jerusalem and slaughter the moneychangers at Passover?"

"Their blood could not be allowed to pollute the temple," said my brother. "But they could be driven out first."

"Gehenna would be the place," said Peter, coldly. "A symbol for all the people. Elijah's fire. Their worm would never die and their smoke would rise, instead of their false evening sacrifice."

I had never heard Peter talk this way before and it shocked me. What had the power on the mount prepared us for? Within me, the cloud of glory was meeting the dark cloud of an end game in Jerusalem.

"Jerusalem at Passover," said my brother. "It must be this year now."

* * * *

We rejoined the others and were flung back into earthly reality; they were arguing with some priests from Jerusalem and a man was screaming for attention for his possessed child. A large crowd was looking on but, as soon as they saw Jesus, we were fighting them back as they mobbed around him.

The possessed child was yet another reminder how powerless we all were compared to our mighty Messiah. Faith the size of a mustard seed would have done it, but none of us had it. As we moved on again, inland and back to Galilee, the first big dispute for some time erupted amongst us all. It was born out of the shame of our inadequacy; we all needed to prove our worthiness of a place in his Kingdom.

Jesus divided us into smaller groups and we passed straight through Galilee at a fast pace, unlike our earlier preaching tours of the villages. Our night-time halts were always remote and again Jesus told Peter, James and I that he would be betrayed and handed over to the Sanhedrin. It just added to our sense of powerlessness and our need to talk ourselves up.

We slipped into Capernaum again at night and the next day, inside Peter's house, Jesus asked us all what we had all been arguing about on the road.

No one volunteered the answer. Our dispute had been about which of us could be considered the greatest among us. What was more, I suspected that Jesus already knew the answer to his own question, as he fetched a child from play in the street.

We gathered in the main room and he called each of us Twelve to him and told us again about the principles of the Kingdom of God and the rules and manners that governed it. If you want to be first, you must be the servant of all, he told us. I had spent three years worrying about my youth and the few wisps of beard on my face and now, unless I changed to be this little child, I would never enter the Kingdom of God. Jesus' eyes roved across us and I squirmed under his gaze.

From the height of the transfiguration experience to the humility of a child, glory had been revealed to me, life after death was vivid and powerful, and the point of entry stood before me with scuffed knees and dirty hands.

* * * *

Within days, the attacks resumed. Collectors of the Temple Tax came calling, asking Peter if his Rabbi paid their tax. It had to be just another conspiracy to find a reason for accusation of disloyalty to the temple. We had no money, so Peter was sent fishing and came back with a fish and the fish had four drachmas for the tax. Like the child, the small issues were not neglected whilst the Kingdom was built.

We moved on, yet again south across the lake, made landfall in the Decapolis and continued on foot down the Jordan. I congratulated myself on having already worked out where we were going, as we came to Peraea and this time the eastern border of David's kingdom. My Messiah was continuing to seek out the children of Abraham in the land that had been given by our God.

For a few days, we travelled and gave our message without hindrance. Our swift movements and changes of direction had wrong-footed our enemies and left them behind. We visited the places where The Immerser had done his work and the people flocked to us as usual.

"The Sanhedrin cannot stop our message," said Judas. "Our movement keeps growing."

"We just need to keep winning hearts and minds for the Kingdom," said Nathanael.

"One by one," said Philip.

"Will it be Jerusalem this side of winter?" said Bartholomew.

"We must be there at Passover this time," said Matthew.

Meanwhile, my other questions were still unresolved, what would 'rise from the dead' to bring the Kingdom. I told myself that my Messiah would reveal all in due course, I just had to follow, and one early morning found space with him for the first time in weeks.

"You care for so many, Rabbi. Are you full or empty at this time?"

"My Father will send angels to strengthen me if I ask him."

"Do you ask him?"

"I pray for his daily bread, as I said you should pray," he replied. "He gives me the portion of virtue and strength I need each day, to do his will."

"Does the virtue fill you to walk before him in the perfection he asked of Abraham?"

"Your care for me is of great comfort, John bar Zebedee. I will need it in the days ahead."

"How can you give me the better righteousness you once spoke of?"

"You must pray for the word of God to give you speech and the heavenly host to be your guard also."

"Yes, Lord," I said. "As the deer pants for the water, we all await the Kingdom."

"We should pray now," he said and lay prostrate.

It ended the conversation. I could never reach the point I was seeking and the mysteries still eluded me.

It did not take long for the temple's forces to find us again; Pharisees came forward with technical questions about legalities for divorce, whilst local people wanted their children kissed and blessed. Taken together, it was an amazing melee. After just a few weeks, Jesus reversed our direction, back to Capernaum for rest and supplies.

7/. Invasion Force

My Messiah was the most withdrawn that I had ever known during those summer days in Capernaum; I felt as if I could no longer reach him.

Most of the time, he was away for prayer; when he was amongst us, he said little. When the people came to seek him, we had to turn them away. We told the town elders and synagogue rulers he was not there.

The waiting was impossible and we all filled the time with whatever we could. Fishing was now my pastoral exercise, as much as to sustain my family, but it was so good to see Caleb and the other men again, even if their clamour for stories of the Son of David was exhausting. Peter and Andrew were much the same, throwing themselves into the task of restocking the larder for both their family and Matthew's. Meanwhile, Matthew visited his former colleagues and did a superb job of negotiating our taxes to practically nothing.

Nathanael, Philip, Bartholomew and the others went to old jobs or found employment from the market place. In all these ways, we reduced the attention on Peter's house, but I visited often, looking for my Messiah. When I did see him, his warm smile was still there for me, but so often his face was the one I had seen as he put Satan behind him. I knew deep in my jangling guts that the road to Jerusalem could not be far away.

* * * *

It was late summer when that day finally came. He announced with little emotion that he would be flogged and killed. I still needed to find the meaning of this parable and I could see that he was holding himself within.

The contrast with his mood, the sense of relief amongst us, was palpable, with much speculation as to if we would be in Jerusalem for the autumn feasts. The news spread and our numbers grew.

Father and Mother were with us, many other relatives of the Twelve as well. Our wealthy benefactors supplied us and the local elders and synagogue rulers joined us. We were the army that would march on Jerusalem. Our Lord told us that no longer would we be walking the extremities of our land, now we would walk through the very midst of Galilee and Samaria. Yes, Samaria, the ancient lands of Manasseh and Ephraim, was now to be symbolically claimed for the Kingdom, as Tyre, Sidon, the Decapolis, Caesarea and Peraea had been already.

I was walking to Jerusalem with my Messiah and the determined resolution in his face told its own story. Every step he took was that of a man walking into a storm, battling against it as he went deeper in. I felt my own mood become more stressed as I followed in his dust.

"Lord, the people expect so much. You are always drained and I see much stress in your eyes."

"Thank you for your care for me, John, but do not worry, my Father will always sustain me."

"When will your Father fill you with the perfection that you seek?"

"I did not say he would. You misunderstand that I must reach this perfection for myself."

"I am sorry, Lord, you told me the Father fills you with what you need. How did I misunderstand?"

"The Father fills me for the good works of the Kingdom, which is for others, not for me."

"Lord, when you take your throne, how much more will these good works go out into the world?"

"To reach the perfection the Lord God requires, my nature must be that of a servant, in human likeness."

"I know that obedience to the Law is required, Lord, and when you take you place in the temple, the Sanhedrin must be obedient to you."

"The Kingdom will be proclaimed for them to enter and every man must choose whom he will serve."

"Will that be this year in Jerusalem?" I asked.

"It will be at the time my Father has set," he replied.

"Lord, these past two years, we have waited for freedom at Passover."

"Freedom is for anyone who finds me."

"Lord, there are many things I do not understand!"

"Do not worry; I did not need you to always understand. I asked you only to follow."

My four stallions were harnessed to the chariot but did not want to be driven and I did not know whether to charge or if we would withdraw again.

Behind us, shadowing at a careful distance, was a cohort with Capernaum's centurion doing his duty. I yearned to know the thoughts within his mind. Was he compromised between beliefs and loyalties? Could he even be a protection for us?

In the days of that march, people from every village, town and city of Galilee either wanted to join or made excuses not to join us and my Messiah dealt with them all.

A rich Sadducee was told to sell all he had, another would-be was told to go and bury his dead faith, whilst others fell away as the commitment of many was tested.

"The Rabbi has his winnowing fork in his hand," said Philip.

"The good seed will be with us," said Nathanael. "The chaff will be blown away in the wind of mediocrity."

"It was never like this with the Zealots," said Simon.

"We are a better army," said Andrew. "A chosen few."

"We are living Gideon's story," said Thomas, as clear as the day.

"Well done, Thomas," said Matthew. "He will whittle us down to the ones that have the courage the Lord God requires."

"He will prepare us for whatever lays ahead," said Peter. "He has the words."

"Soon it will be Samaria and then onward into the heart of Judea," said Judas.

"The Sanhedrin will know we are coming," said my brother. "But not where we are coming from!" He grinned at me.

"The parables and illustrations pour out of him," I said. "These healings and deliverances come as if the Lord had so little time to complete so much. I worry that it will drain him to exhaustion."

* * * *

Crippled men were healed on the Sabbath and Pharisees met us everywhere. Again, some used the prince of demons taunt, others invited him to a banquet, but Jesus did not meet their standards of ceremonial washing and the same conflict and insults flew around. Another dinner party from hell ended as Jesus pronounced woes, trice over, onto his hosts.

"My brothers, it is the Pharisees who are now the kingdom divided against itself," said Peter. "At the very least they have run out of new ideas for insults."

"The Pharisees do not worry me now," I told my brother. "It is what he tells us. What is the Sign of Jonah? A monster to swallow us all makes my guts twist in nightmares."

"The story had a good ending," said my brother.

"Then what is the meaning of being arrested, beaten and handed over to the Roman authorities."

"I don't know either, but there has always been an answer for these things."

Then some Pharisees came to us with a warning to make our escape and go elsewhere; Antipas' Guard was looking for us with orders for arrest. The news was bad, but the source of the warning itself was a chink of light.

As we left Galilee, messengers were sent ahead into a Samaritan village to ask them to prepare for the Messiah and his disciples, but all that came back was a shameful rebuttal.

"After all you have done for these people, Lord." I was enraged, and James, too. "You shared every blessing with them, as if they were us."

"This is only because we go to Jerusalem and they want to play games about holy places," said my brother. "Lord, we should teach them about unholy places, let us rain fire on them as Sodom."

"And Gomorrah," I said. "Just give us permission to pray curses upon them."

"Sons of Thunder," he shook his head at us. "I will say to them what I said to Israel; let the dead bury their dead. You should both know I do not act as you have willed."

I followed meekly behind, pondering my emotions, as we moved on to another village instead.

"So we got the rebuke, rather than the Samaritan villagers," I said to James.

"We reacted to defend our Messiah's honour," my brother replied. "Yet a Messiah seems to have no regard for his shame."

"He has nothing to prove," I said. "We have been growing a siege mentality with the pressure upon us and the unknown ahead of us."

"We are making excuses," said James. "Whatever the pressure on us, it is but a jot compared to him."

As we left Samaria behind, many were shaking the dust from their shoes and it was now that my Messiah made his next move. As he had sent us Twelve out into Galilee, now he handpicked seventy-two of us to go before him into Judea, to every town and place where he would preach the Kingdom.

"Another autumn campaign," said my brother. "Except now it's not Galilee!"

"Even as I shake Samarian dust off my feet, I feel as if the Judea I am entering is yet another foreign land," I told him.

Simon squeezed my arm so tightly that I winced, the sheer adventure danced in his eyes again. "Judea lies before us," he told me. "It will be you and me to preach the Kingdom, heal the sick, raise the dead and cast out the demons."

"The Kingdom is at hand," I said. "The message will bring one of two responses: either acceptance or rejection."

"Blessing or damnation!" he agreed.

"We must be organised as well," Judas told us. "A plan, so that we do not cover the same ground."

"We must ignore the challenges of the Pharisees," said my brother. "They will come, but do not get pulled into their disputes and waste time.

Remember what the Lord told us about pearls before swine. Speak only of The Kingdom, shake your sandals, and move on as he has taught us."

Once again, we got the full eve-of-battle speech from our Messiah and this time it reminded me of Sychar, all over again, as well as Bethsaida.

The harvest was plentiful; we workers were a few lambs among wolves, as we took nothing with us except his message and our peace. If we were not received, we were to shake the dust from our feet and leave hungry.

I had long ago learned that my Messiah had no middle way, as he denounced the indifference of the cities of Galilee that had treated him only as a freak show, a street entertainer, a bottomless pit of blessing, wonder and miracles, and yet had returned no commitment to him.

He ended telling us that those who listened to us listened to him, and he who rejected us also rejects him and the Lord God that sent him. To be rejected by God, I thought, that was hell indeed!

As Simon and I walked away, I knew I would not see my Messiah again until we all united at Rosh Hashanah. The fledgling on the nest had to fly and, in those following weeks, there were times that I never wanted those days to end. I now felt mighty in compassion; I was sure that I viewed the world as my Messiah did and that I was worthy of him.

My four stallions came to visit me as we walked between villages; they were in step with each other. Desire cantered easily along with Expectancy, heads and knees prancing high, and Power, who now looked less muscular, nuzzled Freedom encouragingly. I shared them with Simon and always told him what they were doing, that I wanted to run with them and felt as if I would never tire.

Their presence helped my skin grow thicker and we preached the Kingdom to the Pharisees and moved on. They viewed us with aghast suspicion and I knew they hated that we disregarded their challenges and jibes. They had no answer for the name we proclaimed.

Every morning Simon was shaking me awake with the dawn, telling me there was a kingdom to build.

He seemed unstoppable, but I held him back for prayer, morning, noon and night, telling him if our Messiah needed his daily portion, then so must we.

8/. Triumph Brought Down

"Lord, even the demons submit to us in your name!" Every one of us breathed these words in quiet awe.

Most of the seventy-two were already there when Simon and I had arrived with the sunset and joined the excited party of many voices. Spirits were high, with stories being told and retold over again, as we crowded around Jesus. All of us eager to impress, to reward his faith in us, to prove we were worthy of the Kingdom, and for us in the Twelve to prove to ourselves that we had removed the shame of previous failures.

In this New Year, I was sure that all things were possible, and that our conquest of Judea would continue.

In reply, our Lord told us of things even more fantastic: that he had once seen Lucifer fall like lightening from heaven. That he had given us authority to trample on snakes and scorpions and to overcome all the power of the enemy; nothing would harm us. Yet most of all he told us to rejoice that our names were in 'the book of life' even more than the submission of the spirits.

"I have not seen him so happy and relaxed in many months," said Judas.

"Not since the news of The Immerser's murder," agreed Andrew.

"His fantastic stories of victory over Lucifer are like that day we first saw him come from the wilderness," I said.

"Our failures are … b-behind us now," said Thomas.

"Thomas, you also have more joy than I have ever seen," said Peter with a grin and a huge embrace. "There is nothing against it in the Law, you know."

"The Lord's joy is from our elation and success and I am overjoyed at his approval," said Nathanael.

"As if our spirits are soaring together," said Philip.

Then my Messiah raised his voice, above the volume of our excitement, and to me his words seemed to echo off the sky. "I praise you, Father, Lord of heaven and earth, because you have hidden these things from the wise and learned and revealed them to little children. Yes, Father, for this was your good pleasure."

I was a little child again, the child I wanted to be. I glowed inside.

Our mission was going from strength to strength and, after the months of feeling under siege, I could now see the Kingdom advancing before me.

Taking the Twelve of us aside, he told us, "Blessed are the eyes that see what you see. For I tell you that many prophets and kings wanted to see what you see, but did not see it, and to hear what you hear, but did not hear it."

We rejoined the others. I revelled in it all, just being part of a huge mass of people who sang and danced together, as we and our Messiah partied late into the night.

* * * *

I woke the next morning still buzzing on the elixir of success. Simon and I sat with James and Andrew, exchanging all the stories of our missions. It was then that Mother came to us, saying she needed to talk to the Lord. James and I followed behind her, exchanging questioning looks, as she knelt before Jesus. We did the same.

"What is your request of me?" he asked.

"I ask, Lord, that you grant for one of these two sons of mine to sit at your left and the other at your right, when you come into your Kingdom."

I was stunned; my childlikeness was being undone by a power grab of the worldly politics that our Rabbi had always shunned. In my mind's eye, I could see inside Mother's head: Judea lay at our feet, the very demons had submitted to us in His name, so the Sanhedrin and Jerusalem would be next, and then Rome.

I heard a despondent sigh from James, which told me he could see the same. A trap had appeared before us, born out of our mother's ambition, but to refute her request would be a shame to her and a lack of ambition on our part.

"You don't know what you are asking," his voice was severe. "Can you drink the cup from which I must drink?"

"Yes Lord, we can." Our voices spoke together.

"Then you will indeed drink from my cup, but your place in the Kingdom is not for me to give."

His words were given with such finality that no other question was possible. In the silence that followed, Mother rose, but her head stayed low so as not to look into the eyes of the Lord. We were the same as we followed her in retreat.

It did not take long for us to receive a deputation from the other ten; from the start, it did not look comfortable.

"Apparently you both count yourselves as above the rest of us?" questioned Nathanael.

James replied with slow caution. "How is that, my brothers? What can we have done to offend you?"

"Your mother speaks on your behalf, perhaps?" probed Philip.

"And asks for your place in the Kingdom to be above ours?" The look in Peter's eyes told us that we needed to be straightened out for our own good and at that moment he became my other big brother.

Judas Iscariot stood in the background for once and I could sense that he was again the shrewd politician, letting others do the condemning for him.

"We can only ask our Rabbi for his judgment upon us," my brother humbled us both. "If we have been weighed in the balance and found wanting, we will of course take any admonishment he prescribes."

As we all approached him, I was sure Jesus already knew what was coming, as he surveyed us with a raised eyebrow to invite our question.

"So my 'Boanerges'; my young sons of thunder!" He addressed us with a twinkle in his eye and at that moment, I remembered the wedding at Cana and that he had once also been subjected to a mother's ambition. I prayed he would understand and that we would not be badly shamed, that he would turn the frail water of our human ambition into his wine.

He asked us if we wanted to be like the rulers of the Gentiles and lord it over each other. I was not sure that I could think of a worse question, than to be invited to compare myself with the cruel and venial Pontius Pilate.

The other ten were appeased as we were told again the greatest amongst us would need to be the servant in his Kingdom. However, it did not end there: the Twelve were told to prepare to return to Galilee, to be at our home synagogues for Yom Kippur, and to serve there, in welcome of the most poor and marginalized. It would be a hard march to get there in time.

The remainder of the seventy-two and the wider traveling group would continue in Judea.

As we headed north, I trailed at the back, and James with me. We didn't speak of it, but I believed this was an unscheduled diversion of our mission. We should still have been proclaiming the Kingdom in Judea but now Jesus needed to bond us, the Twelve, back together again.

"So, after all Mother's enterprise, her request could not be granted," said James.

"The Lord's words were more of a rebuttal to her as to us," I said. "Then she had to endure Father's chilled silence; that was there for all to see."

"I think they will leave the mission for a time and go to Jerusalem for Yom Kippur and Sukkot," said James. "That will be good for them."

"We have glimpsed something new of the Kingdom," I said. "Our King does not have all authority, at least for the places of honour."

James considered this. "The law has also shown me that rights and responsibilities go together, but the Lord's words gave us no rights to the Kingdom that we tried to claim."

"Has Mother's ambition dealt us nothing but trouble with no guarantee of reward?" I said.

"I am sure there will be reward enough," said James. "Remember what the Lord said about the cup of cold water."

"Yes, I am sure of that too," I said, "but I was talking about position and authority. I thought we had become the twelve pillars of the new Israel?"

"It will always be a future of some knowns and unknowns," said James.

Andrew fell back to join us. He knew we were hurting. "Judas is telling them all that he is in favour of this return to Galilee. He says the doubling back on our tracks is a good tactical move," he said.

"I can see his point, but I'm not convinced this was indeed all part of the overall strategy," I said. "It weighs heavy on me that we are the cause of this."

I sat long into the night to pray to the God that I could not see, beyond the starry host that I could see and yet who was as close to me as my Messiah.

* * * *

Back in Capernaum, Jesus' brothers were with us at synagogue for Yom Kippur. They were urging him to go back up to Jerusalem for Sukkot, telling him that this is what he needed to promote his public life. I was amazed at how out of touch their comments were and how naive they were of the dangers he faced. Jesus told them to go ahead and do their religious duties without him and once they had departed, told us he would be going in late to hide in the masses and to start collecting supplies.

I was concerned for Peter and Matthew, neither of them were built for another sixty miles in just a few days' march. To my relief, we took a boat across the lake to reduce the walk and then followed the main route down the Jordan valley. We could merge with the main flow of the pilgrimage and be inconspicuous coming up the Jericho road with the masses, rather than coming in from Samaria on the Damascus road again.

Nothing was ever lost for my Messiah and we got a constant flow of parables during those days: a rich fool, a serving master, a great banquet, a cheating steward, a Pharisee and a tax collector, and a beggar and rich man in luxury and torment.

"These stories get more outrageous," said Judas. "Will he tell these to the people during Sukkot?"

"I'm sure he has more," said Peter. "He always does."

"Perhaps he gives us a foretaste now," said Nathanael.

"You mean so we are not so shocked in the temple?" questioned Philip.

"If masters leave top table with bags of food for their servants, the Kingdom will stand the world on its head," said Andrew.

"It is no more than the servant-leadership he has taught us," said Bartholomew.

“The parables are different,” said Judas. “He is projecting a picture of the Lord God, not us. That is why I say they are outrageous.”

“Perhaps tax collectors will give rebates too!” said Peter, with a playful elbow into Matthew’s ribs.

“Very likely,” agreed Matthew. “Except Caesar won’t!”

“He will, if the Messiah rules the world,” said Simon.

I loved these times when we were together, without the pressures of the mission.

“Indulge me to be … s-serious for one moment,” said Thomas.

“Must we, Thomas?” said Peter, his eyes dancing with gentle mischief.

“Yes you must,” said Thomas, looking peeved. “The Kingdom is a serious matter.”

“You are right, Thomas, please go ahead,” said my brother.

“The Lord God gave us a promised land. He has given us the Law and he has given us the Sabbath. His Messiah is a …. v-vagabond peasant. He is a God not like any other gods, when did he ever not serve his people? Why is that any less … out-outrageous than a serving master or one who has compassion on a cheating … st-steward?”

Peter was smiling, his voice gentle with appreciation. “Thomas, you are wonderful. Truly wonderful.”

Thomas held his arm, shaking it gently. “Does that mean you think … m-my interpretation is good?”

“Yes, Thomas, it is good.”

Then, suddenly, Thomas had thrown his arms around Peter, his voice cracked with emotion. “You are to me like the brother I lost!”

I watched as the smiling brotherhood closed around them; hands were gently laid, voices affirmed.

“El-Shaddai,” said Bartholomew.

“YHWH-Jireh,” said Matthew. “He will provide.”

“Oh stop it, Thomas,” Peter sniffed and gulped. “Now you’ve got me going as well.”

9/. The Safe House

There was only one conversation amongst us: would the Lord risk Jerusalem at Sukkot?

On the long ascent from Jericho, our debate continued in between each song, but the rejoicing around us carried me along. Then, when it seemed as if we would go straight into the Holy City with the masses, we broke away just two miles short, where a house opened to us in the village of Bethany. It was the home of sisters Martha and scarlet Mary of the magnificent hair, who had travelled with us for over a year; their brother Lazarus also lived in the village and soon became a generous friend.

"Was this his safe house two years ago, I wonder?" said James.

"It would explain why Shlomo could not find him in Jerusalem," I replied.

"A base to work from almost under the noses of the Sanhedrin," said Matthew.

"This could mean a great deal of trouble for these people," said Judas. "We must be careful to keep our movements unnoticed."

"The Lord kept our home safe last winter," said my brother. "We will need to know the way here at night."

"And make sure we are not followed by Saul or Chai," I added.

"They work so hard to feed us," said Peter.

"Your wife has done us the same honour, my brother," said Matthew.

"They are well known in Jerusalem society," said Bartholomew. "How great is Martha's love for her sister and what a different life she could have had."

"What opposites they are," said Matthew. "Yet the Lord honoured the emotional one that listened to his teaching rather than the one that fed him."

Simon, John Mark and I sat a little apart. "The legions have camped high amongst the olives as usual," said Simon. "They will have a cohort at every gate."

"I still hate their dust, but their oppression is not what I fear so much now," I told him. "What a journey I have been on in these past three years. I am now more afraid of the rulers of my own people and what they would do to the Lord."

"Would the Sanhedrin really hand The Lord over to The Prefect, like he has said?" asked Simon.

"If they did, there is no reason for a charge against him," I said. "No one has ever seen a sword in his hand."

"We need the people to remain peaceful," said John Mark. "Any disturbance would be the excuse the Sanhedrin need; they can play on The Prefect's fears."

* * * *

The next morning Jesus told us he would go to the feast, but alone and in secret, and sent us on ahead to mix with the crowds. We all knew where we would be able to find our Lord; all we had to do was to wait in the temple.

James and I found Father and Mother at the house and reunited with much joy that we had the house to stay in, as usual.

"The city is awash with rumour and conspiracy theories," said Father. "If you move through the crowds, you will hear the whisperings for yourselves. Some say he is a good man, others that he's a deceiver."

"From the days before the feast, the Chief Priests and Pharisees had their disciples watching the gates and the main street corners," Mother told us.

Father nodded. "Uri and Shlomo have their forces organised. The people do not talk of the prophet from Galilee near those in authority. Jesus of Nazareth is the unmentionable name."

Once in the temple, we worked in small teams. James, Andrew, Simon and I stayed close enough to keep a watch on our Lord. In the initial days, we saw him spend long times in prayer and it was not until halfway through the feast that he went to the centre of the temple courts and started to teach the people. After a hurried conference, we divided into pairs and stationed ourselves around him, but close to any Priests and Pharisees, that we might hear their words. Simon and I were together again and, knowing we were unrecognised by Shlomo and Uri, we could stand close, listen, and then move back to the others.

When he spoke to the massed pilgrims, the Law and the interpretation flowed from him as I had never heard before. It was as exquisite as Rabbi Benjamin had said. The Jerusalemites were amazed all around us. We listened as they asked themselves where an ordinary Galilean peasant had gotten such learning from. This was the one the Sanhedrin wanted to kill, so why were they not acting?

He was the same gaunt man we had always known, but he didn't look like a Messiah to them.

I fretted for his safety, but I could also see that my Messiah seemed in control and at ease with himself. He was where he wanted to be; he knew the whisperings of the crowd and answered their unspoken questions and, even more, he answered the shadowing forces of the authorities.

Speaking of God, truth and Moses, he asked why they were trying to kill him. Some shouted back he was demon-possessed, demanding who was trying to kill him.

He spoke of miracles, circumcision and healing the whole body, and judgment, until some of Shlomo's men came through the crowd to seize him. I clasped Simon, holding my breath, but they could not seem to get to Jesus. He just always seemed to elude them.

Andrew appeared next to us. "It is like it was at Nazareth," he whispered. "They cannot touch him."

The whisperings of the people changed. "When the Messiah comes, will he do more miraculous signs than this man?" they asked.

We knew the Pharisees had heard the new whisperings and gathered with the Chief Priests, who had mobilised a group of the Temple Guards. I nudged Simon and Andrew. "Look, what will happen now?"

The guards came into the crowd, looking for any excuse of error or blasphemy to take Jesus by force, but my Messiah dealt with them with such grace that they could only stand there, too awestruck to move, like tongue-tied children before an elder. Simon and I embraced in relief.

Andrew was triumphant. "As my brother always says: 'He has the words.'"

So it continued through each remaining day of the feast. Jesus appeared in the temple courts and disappeared again. His enemies watched him, but could not corner him, and on the last and greatest day of the feast, Jesus stood among the crowds and called out in a loud voice, "If anyone is thirsty, let him come to me and drink. Whoever believes in me, as the scripture has said, streams of living water will flow from within him."

"The Jerusalemites have the same questions as we did three years ago," I said to Andrew and Simon. "Are these the words of a Messiah, a madman or a fake?"

"Some say he is the Prophet, others say he is the Messiah," said Simon. "That will rattle the Sanhedrin."

"They are divided," said Andrew. "Some put their faith in him, asking if any more miracles could be done by a Messiah, others wanted to seize him."

"I heard Nicodemus trying to reason with Shlomo and his fellow Pharisees," I said. "He was asking how the Law could condemn a man without first hearing him to find out what he is doing, but he was soon shouted down with insults. Go and do your homework, they told him, a prophet does not come out of Galilee."

One day some in the temple said they believed, but it was just another trap and Jesus told them they were trying to kill him. It climaxed with a dispute about the true father of the nation and claims of deity. They tried to stone my Messiah, but again he slipped away. On the way out, we paused by the Pool of Siloam and Jesus restored sight to a man born blind. It kept the Pharisees and Priests busy for the next two weeks, trying to deny and discredit the healing.

Judas Iscariot warned us that this was too far, too much. If the people caught Messianic fever, all could be lost in an uprising that would be swept away by Rome.

At the end of the week, we walked away unscathed; we Twelve and our Lord had escaped the great cauldron of a Jerusalem festival. The pilgrims went home and Rome's legionaries marched in their suffocating dust back to Caesarea, until the next time.

With much gratitude, we said our farewells to Martha, Mary and Lazarus, and met up with our larger group. Many of the seventy-two were still active in Judea, preparing the way for the Messiah. Jesus took us again through the towns and villages, always moving on, to stay ahead of the opposition and protected by the fascination of the crowds that followed us.

The Pharisees countered us everywhere they could with technicalities of the law, telling the synagogue that Jesus could not be his own witness, therefore his teaching could not be valid.

* * * *

Three months after Sukkot, we split up to infiltrate Jerusalem for Chanukah and did it all again. Jerusalem was much the same as we had left it, a city divided against itself because of my Messiah. Some people believing, others challenging and opposing.

One day, Jesus walked in the temple area of Solomon's Colonnade and the Jerusalemites gathered around, baiting him, asking how long he would keep them in suspense and to tell them plainly if he was the Messiah.

"This is a trap," Judas told us. "The priests have set this up, we must we ready to pull him out and get back to the streets."

"Yes, I can see this too," said Peter. "They know he will tell a straightforward truth, and they will use it to condemn him."

"Then, there will be others waiting with a pile of stones outside," said James. "Whichever exit they try to push him towards, we must take another."

It happened just as we had predicted. Our Messiah answered that he had already told them exactly who he was, then went further and asserted deity again: he and the Father in heaven were one.

The trap sprung, death to the blasphemer was proclaimed, but as they closed on my Messiah so did we, and he slipped away between us. The flashpoint had passed without a struggle and we all melted into the crowds and met again in the evening's dusk on the Mount of Olives.

"They will never imagine or tolerate that a man could be of God," said Andrew.

"What else do they expect the Lord's Messiah to be?" said John Mark.

"They cannot see further than the next pile of takings," said Simon. "How can you expect them to see goodness?"

"I have still not worked out the spiritual meaning of why he had told us he would be arrested and killed," I said.

"No matter, it was like Nazareth again," said Andrew. "Our Lord was impregnable, untouchable."

After all of this, we descended back through Jericho and withdrew to Peraea for a respite. This was back to where The Immerser had first done his work. It was wonderful, just like the old days, as the people flocked to us from everywhere we had ever heard of, as well as other places we never had.

I listened to their talk, as they found the spiritual enlightenment they had been seeking. "John the Immerser never performed a miracle," they said, "but everything he said about this man was true."

The borders of my Messiah's Kingdom were continuing to grow.

10/. Power Displayed

There was a feeling of unfinished business back at Jerusalem. It hung over me like a thundercloud, and lightning flashed from that cloud every time my Lord talked about his coming death. Like the sign of Jonah, it was a parable that I could not fathom and for which my Lord had offered no further explanation. I discussed it with my brother, next with Thomas, for his understanding of the Law. Lastly, I talked with Judas Iscariot, who told me that our movement was dying for lack of influence, whilst we went hungry on the edge of the desert. I got no further; the cloud remained impossible for me to penetrate.

One certainty remained: as the days grew warmer, Passover was now just over the horizon. The sound of the hooves and the jangling of the bits and bridles of my four white stallions came into my ears every day.

One day in the early springtime, a servant from the house of Martha and Mary found us. His message was urgent: their brother Lazarus was dangerously ill and they were appealing for Jesus' return.

I stood close to my brother. As we both watched Jesus' face, I saw one of those a faraway looks in his eyes as he considered this news.

"This sickness will not end in death," he told us all. "No, it is for God's glory so that God's Son may be glorified through it." He withdrew for prayer, and we welcomed the tired and distressed servant with as much hospitality as we could and gathered around him to discuss the matter.

"The Lord will return soon, my friend," said Peter. "It was one of his statements that mean something significant will happen soon."

"Did you hear how he did not call himself the 'Son of Man'?" said my brother. "Instead it was 'so that God's Son may be glorified'?"

"Without the presence of the people, we will be vulnerable, so close to Jerusalem," said Judas. "We don't need to take that risk."

"We have all seen that he can heal at a distance of many miles," said Nathanael. "Perhaps it is not necessary to go back."

"Perhaps the healing is happening right now," said Peter, as we regarded the figure of our Lord walking towards desert solitude.

The servant was perplexed, torn between remaining and departing. We knew he would have considered it his duty to take Jesus back to his mistress, but now that did not seem possible. We assured him that Jesus cared deeply, for Martha, Mary and Lazarus gave him food and gathered around him in prayer for the return journey, up the difficult road from Jericho, and he departed in the haste with which he had appeared.

For two days, we remained by The Immerser's pool and it seemed that the return to Bethany was not needed. For me, they were restless days. I still felt that something important was developing in my cloud because of that remark that 'God's son may be glorified'.

When Jesus emerged from the desert with the dawn, we all gathered round and he gave us the simplest of statements: "Let us go back to Judea."

"But Rabbi," we protested together, "a short while ago the Jews tried to stone you, and yet you are going back there?"

His answer was a mysterious as ever. "Are there not twelve hours of daylight? A man who walks by day will not stumble, for he sees by the world's light. It is when he walks by night he stumbles, for he has no light."

We all paused, searching for the meaning. "Lord, are you telling us we can already see what we were going into?" asked Nathanael.

Then he told us plainly, "Our friend Lazarus has fallen asleep, but I am going there to wake him up."

Peter replied, "Lord, if he sleeps, he will get better."

"Lazarus is dead, and for your sake I am glad I was not there, so that you may believe. But let us go to him."

Silence fell as we all took this in before Thomas's heavy tones broke it for all of us. "Let us also go, that we may die with him."

"Do you think this could be a trap of the Sanhedrin?" asked Judas.

"The servant would have told us," said Bartholomew.

"Unless they held his mistress hostage," said Matthew.

"It doesn't need to be a conspiracy," said Judas. "It could be the opportunity the Chief Priests are looking for. The family is well known in Jerusalem and Lazarus' passing will bring many mourners."

"Do they know this was our safe house?" said Matthew.

"We cannot know," said Peter. "But if we return and half of Jerusalem sees us there, then they will know for certain."

As we started to march, I juggled it all in my head: 'God's Son may be glorified'; Lazarus is dead and yet my Lord is glad; for our sakes that we might believe!

We passed through Jericho without pause, and all the way up the long climb on the Jerusalem road, the thought would not leave my head was that we had tarried for two days whilst Lazarus had slipped away from our world. Ahead of us one man's death was already certain, what now for us?

We stood on the edge of Bethany in the early evening, dusty and tired but waiting to assess the situation. Nathanael and Philip walked ahead; we needed to know just who was in the village, what danger would there be for us, but also get to our safe house.

Our scouts returned with the news. "Many visitors from Jerusalem are there," said Nathanael. "Much comforting and mourning with personal friends, but the local rabbi has gone now."

"Lazarus had already been in the tomb for four days," said Philip.

Andrew stood at my elbow. "Would we have got here in time if we had left immediately with the servant?" he said.

"We will never know," I replied.

"What will the sisters say now?" said my brother.

"Look," said Simon. "One of them is coming!"

The figure of a woman came towards us; it was Martha. I watched her slow and deliberate steps as she held herself together under the heavy burden of her grief. She stood before our Rabbi and they regarded each other, Martha trying to find the words, Jesus giving her the time to compose herself to say them.

Her voice came tired and strained, as she was trying not to sound accusing, the lump stuck in my throat. I heard her clutch at straws of hope, wanting to ask but not daring to ask for something, she knew not what; not daring to believe what she wanted to believe. "Lord, if you had been here, my brother would not have died. But I know that even now, God will give you whatever you ask."

"Your brother will rise again," Jesus told her.

Still holding herself together and searching his face with her eyes, Martha answered with the hope of eternity with God. "I know he will rise again in the resurrection at the last day."

It was now I heard emotion crack into my Lord's voice. "I am the resurrection and the life. He who believes in me will live, even though he dies, and whoever lives and believes in me will never die. Do you believe this?"

"Yes, Lord," she told him. "I believe that you are the Messiah, the Son of God, who was to come into the world."

With this ultimate statement of faith, she turned and walked with slow dignity back to the duties with her guests.

It was not long before another veiled figure came towards us, this one with shambling steps and hanging head. Mary did not come alone, but brought many from Jerusalem with her to witness what happened as she reached Jesus. Her knees buckled and she and her emotions collapsed at his feet pouring forth the same words as her sister, except this time her voice assaulted us in great accusing sobs: "Lord … if you … had been here, my brother … would not … have died!"

Those who had come with her dissolved into a fresh weeping and it was now that my Lord's emotions also cracked in a way that I had never seen before, as if something was tearing away inside of him. "Where, where have you laid him?" he almost stuttered.

Some men stepped forward. "Come and see, Lord," they replied. Their women scooped up the distraught Mary and led us towards the tomb.

My Lord was now weeping uncontrollably and suddenly it seemed as if everyone was there: Martha again, the whole village, so many from Jerusalem, and on the way, they discussed the weeping Messiah.

"See how he loved him!"

"Could not he, who opened the eyes of the blind man, have kept this man from dying?"

The tomb was a prestigious cave, with a great stone across the entrance. Jesus was now supported by Peter and Nathanael, but shocked everyone to the core as he cried out, "Take away the stone." Nobody moved and all looked in horror.

It was Martha who answered for us all; I stood in awe that this woman of substance could be always so in control of herself. "But Lord, by this time there is a bad odour, for he has been there four days." Just how she could have uttered those words that described the now decaying brother that she had previously known so warm and loving, I could not tell. I sat slumped on a rock.

But now my Lord had his voice of command out, even amongst his grief. It was the same one I had heard when he dismissed the mourners of Jairus' daughter. "Did I not tell you that if you believed, you would see the glory of God?"

James pulled me. "We must act and take the lead."

I pulled Simon and, to my relief, Peter and others followed. We levered and heaved the stone away and retreated, gasping and trembling.

Then my Lord, who had always done the miracles so privately and sworn so many to secrecy, stood front and centre and, with almost dramatic gesture, looked up to the heavens and called clearly for all to hear, "Father, I thank you that you have heard me. I knew that you always hear me, but I said this for the benefit of the people standing here, that they may believe that you sent me." And then, in a still louder voice of command: "Lazarus, come out!"

All heads swung around; all eyes fixed the black void of the gaping doorway, and then a movement flickered and a thousand voices gasped and gagged and shrieked, as a figure clothed head to toe in the wrapping of the grave came unsteadily through the low entrance and into the light, struggling to remove the cloth from his eyes and head.

Many instinctively backed away, but the two sisters embraced, squealing in delight, and then clasped Jesus briefly, but so hard that he winced.

"Take off the grave clothes and let him go," Jesus told them, and they ran, Martha crying and Mary howling with delight, to embrace their living brother. Most of the crowd followed, just wanting to see and touch and talk with the living Lazarus.

11/. Ruthless Challenge

"At last!" said Judas Iscariot, bubbling with excitement. "The Lord has displayed his power for the world to see. With so many witnesses, this will be reported in every house of Jerusalem and every village of Judea."

"And done so publicly when so many miracles have been private or hidden," said Bartholomew.

"The Sanhedrin has no basis to resist him now," said my brother. "But that doesn't mean that they won't!"

"Passover will be the climax of the mission," said Judas. "Who can deny this miracle, this sign of resurrection after four days in the grave!"

"Yes indeed," said Matthew. "I agree with Judas, this was a calculated demonstration of his power under the very noses of the Sanhedrin. A fantastic power play; let them try to deny this!"

"Will they just step aside?" said Bartholomew. "I cannot see it being that easy."

"No, they will never do that," said Judas. "They will seek a deal on the basis that Levites must continue to minister at the altar."

"Even though some of those … Ch-Chief Priests make that false claim for themselves," said Thomas, with evident disgust.

"Yes, Thomas, I know that," said Judas. "Once the Lord sits in the temple we can deal with that and work those pretenders out of their positions."

"Whilst they will try many intrigues to remove us, being non-Levite peasants!" said Peter. "That would leave the Lord alone."

"Will that ever happen?" asked Matthew. "Will light co-exist with darkness?"

Andrew had other thoughts. "The Lord was so emotional," he said. "I have never seen him out of control like that before. If this was so planned, why had he not been able to prepare himself, knowing that death was only a temporary sleep and that he brought life?"

"I think it is because he waited," said my brother. "I saw the look in his eye when the servant came to us. He knew and yet he waited on purpose."

I nodded in dumb agreement, yet I trembled and my guts chilled deep within me.

They all looked at my brother and then understanding dawned first in Matthew's eyes. "Yee-ess, we have all been thinking that this was a great and incredible blessing for Lazarus and his family, but if I were to play the devil's advocate for a moment I would ask, 'was it really a blessing or a rather cruel exploitation'? As Rome's taxman, I used to understand such things well!"

My eyes met with Matthew's in a deflated mixture of mutual horror and wonder.

"We know he can heal at a distance. I'm sure he could have done it again," James continued in hoarse tones. "So he chose to let Lazarus endure suffering and physical death by waiting two days in the desert. The Lord planned for Lazarus to be the ultimate sign in him as the Son of God, just as he told us. That is why he was so broken: he was faced with the grief and suffering that he knew he had allowed happen, because he had to put the Kingdom before his friends."

"Lazarus will now endure physical death twice," said Matthew. "Once just past and once more at the end of his life; to dust we shall all return. But how many men will have to endure that twice!"

I regarded the circle of shocked faces, even Judas looked completed bereft.

"Is the building of the Kingdom so important?" asked Nathanael. "That it has to be so ruthless!"

"He has always been so compassionate on the needy," said Philip. "How does this fit?"

"We have seen him be compassionate on the lost, but Lazarus was not lost. He knew and he believed. Lazarus was already safe for eternity," my brother continued. "We must look through our Lord's eyes, what he has taught us is that only eternal life and death matters, not physical life and death in this world."

"We have never seen him compromise anything," Thomas now joined in. "Moses put the same ... ch-choice to our ancestors in the desert: 'I set before you the ways of life and death! Choose life!' The choice is life or death, heaven or hell, glory or torment. There is no compromise, because there is nothing else, no middle ground!"

Now it was Peter who joined the defence of his Messiah. "Lazarus may have suffered for the Kingdom and perhaps so shall we, but he has been a great fisher of men and his reward will be great in heaven!"

"Yes," said Matthew, almost to himself. "Think of the lost facing eternity in godless darkness and needing rescue. Faced with that, nothing else matters. That is what I knew as I left my tax booth."

* * * *

That night I watched the Lord's canopy overhead and asked him: was this the biggest moment of the past three and a half years, the most enormous game-changer of my young life? Life or death, what would now happen at Passover? Surely, freedom could wait no longer.

The next day, James and I went up to the city, taking Simon with us, to visit Father and Mother who were wintering there to be closer to us. We walked against a tide of excited and chattering Jerusalemites, hurrying to Bethany to see Lazarus for themselves. Inside the city, the talk was of nothing but Lazarus. Many of those who had been at the tomb to see him raised proclaimed they had put their faith in Jesus of Nazareth as Messiah.

In stark contrast, we found Father and Mother without joy. Rather than sharing the excitement, they received us in deep sorrow at the intransigence of the Sanhedrin.

"I have visited the temple and talked with friends," said Father. "Last night the Chief Priests and many of the Sanhedrin met in crisis debate. They are in fear of both the people and of the Roman Prefect taking their position and power."

"They know that they are losing authority because the people hold both The Lord and The Immerser as prophets," said Mother.

"The Chief Priests are today's Pharaohs," Father shook his head. "My heart bleeds to say it. They are as hard-hearted as Egypt, wanting only to keep the people under their power."

"Lazarus is in danger," said Mother. "The Sanhedrin would remove him if they could."

"More than that, some of them have plotted death for Jesus," said Father. "They have prophesized that one man needs to die for the safety of the nation."

"The Lord keeps telling us he will be handed to the Prefect to be flogged and killed," I said. "What is the meaning of this?"

"They cannot lay a hand on him," said James. "They have tried so many times but he is untouchable."

"The Kingdom must last forever and the world will see his glory," said Simon. "What else can happen?"

"I have no answer for this," said Father. "I believe he is The Messiah and we need freedom in so many ways. We have expected it these past two Passovers. I cannot tell if it will be now or not, but I can tell you that in times past some have tried by force and failed."

It was then Father turned to Simon. "Young man, I have news that may be difficult for you, but be assured that your parents were well when I last saw them."

I saw Simon stiffen in concern and found that I had taken a step closer to support him.

"Did you hear of an incident in the temple?" said Father. "Some Zealots from Galilee incited the people to revolt."

"We heard that they were dragged to the street and The Prefect had them slaughtered, along with their sacrifices," said James.

"Not all of them; the leader was taken alive." Father regarded Simon and held his hand as he spoke. "It is Barabbas I speak of, he is now incarcerated in the Antonia."

For a few moments, Simon said nothing, but then nodded. "Yes, I once followed Barabbas and this would have been my destiny also." He turned his hand to show the scar. "Barabbas no longer has a hold over me."

Father patted Simon's shoulder. "I am truly pleased to hear that."

"Pilate knows about the Messianic fever," said Mother. "His spies have informed him of the radical Rabbi from Galilee that was drawing huge crowds and whose followers were spreading his word through Judea."

"The Prefect is also expecting the Lord to make his move at Passover," said Father.

Promising to keep us informed with messages as much as they could, Father and Mother embraced us all with tears, but also with much hope that everything the prophets had written would soon be completed well.

Back in Bethany, we reported all Father had told us.

"Everyone is looking for you Lord," said Peter. "They seek the Messiah, but they do not understand you."

"Beware that they seek the Messiah, but not his Kingdom," said Judas.

My Messiah, I thought to myself, they would kill him if they could get to him.

"Jerusalem is a tinder box waiting for … t-the torch to set it aflame," said Thomas.

"It is not safe here, we are a danger to this house," said Jesus. "Dear Martha, you have loved and cared for us, but we must bid you farewell for a while."

This wonderful woman still gave us as much food as we could carry. We each embraced Lazarus and turned again for the Jericho road. This time we went to the very borders of Peraea, to the desert edge, and a remote village called Ephraim.

It is not easy to make a living in a place such as Ephraim in wintertime. Goat herding was an occupation that gave me much time to think and pray. Peter and Andrew made fishing trips to the Jordan. Many of the dwellings benefitted from a carpenter's skills.

This was our hideout for a time, whilst the inevitability of Passover loomed ever larger in all of our minds. Would we return to Jerusalem for Passover?

A messenger from Father arrived. My brother received it and the rest of the Twelve crowded around to hear the news from Jerusalem. It told us that multitudes were already arriving from all of Judea, moving in from the country early for their ceremonial cleansing before Passover, the city was full and thousands were already camped around the walls. Hundreds of thousands from every Jewish outpost on the empire were now flooding in as usual, catching the mood and demanding for news. Jerusalem awaited only the Galileans.

The messenger himself continued to tell us of the gossip in the streets and temple courts, the question on everybody's lips: where was Jesus of Nazareth? Would he come to the feast or not?

Father's message ended that the Chief Priests and Pharisees had given orders for the arrest of our Lord. The Tribune of the Antonia, alarmed at the unexpected early movement of masses into the city, had sent to Caesarea. Pontius Pilate was already encamped with two legions and more were expected.

12/. The Scent of Death

In the week before Passover, thousands found us at Ephraim and the village expanded into a tent city.

Jesus moved us down to The Immerser's Pool, where tens of thousands more awaited. Our numbers were being swelled daily with the masses coming down the Jordan.

"Last year we had only five thousand," said Judas.

"It was nothing compared to this!" exclaimed Andrew.

"They still want to carry the Lord into Jerusalem," said my brother.

"He is their Galilean Messiah," said Peter.

"Did he withdraw from the five thousand because he could see ahead to this?" asked Nathanael.

"I still think it was because the moment was wrong," I said. "The Lord wants order in his Kingdom, not a mob rule."

"He is the Lord and he will enter the Holy City on his terms," said Peter. "He will rule there for eternity."

"How will he control these multitudes now," ask Matthew. "They will become even more delirious on the ascent."

"With this 'people's army' under his control, we will be an irresistible force," said Judas. "Now we can replace the Sanhedrin, we can sweep into the city and take the temple as ours."

Judas Iscariot's ambition was clear, but I was not comfortable. Simon was beside me, and for his sake, I whispered, "He should not say the 'Temple can be ours'. This is the ambition of so many conquerors, the temple must ever be the Lord's." I was relieved that Simon pursed his lips and nodded in return.

"Yes, The Sanhedrin can be replaced, but how do we get into the city?" said Matthew. "What of the legions? If we march down the Kidron Valley with these masses, it will be what Rome has prepared for and fears most."

"Well we cannot enter in secret with these all around us, as we did at Sukkot," said Thomas using his gift for the straightforward and obvious. "How do we get … p-past the legion?"

"We have not come this far for Pilate to unleash his legions. The slaughter would be great and the hills would bristle with crosses," Peter's grim voice reminded us all. "This cruel Prefect will not hesitate."

"Pilate has waited years for revenge, since he was forced to back down and remove those effigies of Caesar from the wall," Matthew told us. "We would deliver what he wanted, the excuse he has waited for!" His warning chilled us all.

"We can do it if we time it right," Judas told us. "If we move on the eve of the Sabbath, when all are in preparation and get inside the city before the gates close, we can then move from the inside after the Sabbath. We can split up and all incite the people from different places."

Judas Iscariot had it all worked out, the consummate politician that he was. I looked at James for a response. We did not need another internal dispute now; the moment needed my brother's diplomacy.

"That could be a good plan, Judas," said my brother. "I cannot imagine that the Lord has not prepared for this time in thought and much prayer. He will reveal his plan when the moment is right and we need to be ready for all possibilities."

"So many questions to be answered," I told Simon and John-Mark beside me. "How will he control the people, so this is on his terms, not theirs? How can the legions not be agitated? How do we get inside the city? How will he take the temple, as we know he must?"

"You have many worries, my friend," Simon told me. "Your cleverness is the source of your dreads. The prophets tell us he will take his throne in Jerusalem and the world will see his glory. What else do you need to know?" He threw an arm around my shoulder, a stout farm boy's arm of reassurance, and at that moment, I was so grateful. His simple words of faith and certainty were what I needed, as I returned his man-hug embrace.

As we left The Immerser's Pool, innumerable thousands pressed all around us, with yet thousands more in front and behind; their hymns of joy were unending and it seemed to me ever more zealous, with each step towards Jerusalem. Yet my Messiah still had time to answer the call of a blind beggar, who shouted to the 'Son of David'. Roaring for attention, even above the crowd, the man threw his cloak aside, groped forward through the masses and received his sight. When passing through Jericho, the diminutive chief tax collector made a shameful ascent of a sycamore-fig tree to catch a glimpse. Jesus stopped the crowd and exposed the taxman's undignified position and gave him dignity. His tree spoke of faith, as much as the blind beggar's cloak. The hated taxman accepted forgiveness and Jesus accepted his hospitality for the night and quashed the disapproval of the locals.

Once again, I had seen my Messiah reach out to both the oppressed and the oppressor: both had been on the outside, both had been invited into the Kingdom, both had responded.

* * * *

The next morning, as we started the ascent to Jerusalem, the mass expectation of the Kingdom appearing in some immediate miracle was at fever pitch. It was time for some serious crowd control, with a long parable about a man of noble birth leaving for a distance country and leaving his servants in charge of his lands. My own world grew a little darker; was this the spiritual meaning of the question I had not been able to answer? Was my Messiah going to leave me?

In the crowds, I saw many carrying branches cut from the Jericho palms. Now these branches to would herald their Messiah, my Messiah, all the way to the conquest of his city.

The Songs of Ascent began and I sang them as never before, with the hoof-beats of my four stallions always in my ears. They were the backbeat, a foreboding drumbeat to battle, whilst in the foreground the dispute and speculation of my comrades continued as to what awaited us in Jerusalem, and how and when our Lord would restore the Kingdom to Israel.

Yet amongst all this, the thing that I most held dear was that I was going to Passover in Jerusalem with my Messiah. It was all I had yearned for during these past three years.

We arrived in Bethany six days before the Passover Seder. Tomorrow was the Sabbath and it was as late in the preparation day as possible. My Lord's timing was immaculate. The Sanhedrin would know we were there, but for now would not be able to touch us.

News came from Father that the Chief Priests had turned up the pressure even more now, with a plot against Lazarus' life because he was the cause of so many going over to Jesus' side.

Outside the house, the masses continued to gather. Jerusalemites had found out Jesus was there and were hastening to see him, also Lazarus. Some were even Sabbath breakers, trailing in after dark.

We did not move up inside the city as Judas Iscariot had imagined. Instead, at Lazarus' house, it was an absolute joy to gather around his Mikvah. The contrast with the dust and sweat of the Jericho road made my transition through this symbol of purity and holiness more special. I felt yet closer to my God and his Messiah.

That evening, Martha served a great dinner in Jesus' honour, but as he reclined at the table with the restored Lazarus alongside, it was what Mary did that dominated the moment.

As I have already told, Mary was capable of the unexpected and the outrageous and this evening was no exception. Standing behind Jesus, she opened an alabaster jar and poured the heavy scented embalming oil over his head and body. We all watched as it ran over his body and she rubbed it into his hair and impregnated his clothes. It was worth a small fortune; the pungent scent would linger weeks both in the house and on my Lord.

Some protested and Judas Iscariot, in particular, objected that the money could have been given to the poor.

When Jesus spoke up in her defence, it was not Mary's actions that jangled my guts in fear, but my Messiah's words that she had done this beautiful thing for him to prepare him for burial. I still could not see through to his meaning. I heard his words but wanted to blank them out, just as I wanted to blank out the overpowering aroma. For almost four years, I had seen my

Lord do anything he needed to. How could he who had brought life to the man reclining alongside him now talk of his own death?

That perfume became a prison from which I could not escape; to me it became the scent of death.

Outside the house, I joined the others of the seventy-two and our wider group, and the thousands that had pushed the limits of Sabbath rules to be close to my Messiah. Inside the house was claustrophobic; the heavy perfume was too much for me.

What would the morning bring? Pilate already had one revolutionary leader incarcerated inside his fortress. What would he and his legions make of a Messiah who would come to the Holy City, heralded by hundreds of thousands, and claiming an everlasting throne?

The Sanhedrin, so afraid to lose their power, with men on every street corner, watching and waiting for the man of whom their leaders had already prophesied death.

I knew everything was now in place for the great and final power play; the battle climax was at hand.

My speculations agonised inside me. All I needed was for the Kingdom my Messiah had preached to become reality.

The 'Final Week': Battle Climax

1/. Triumph or Tears?

My fitful sleep was broken by the excited hum of a hundred thousand voices; the Galileans were breaking camp, whilst thousands more were arriving from the direction of the city.

My brother emerged from the house. "The Lord will not go up so close to dawn, it would be seen as an aggressive act that could bring the legions upon us."

I went inside and joined the prayer; it was a prayer for calm, for joy not tension, for control not riot. In long periods of silent reflection, it was prayer for us as much as for the masses outside.

All through the morning, we could hear the crowd grow as more arrived, gathering in a huge and joyous mass.

"They expect that the Kingdom will be restored to Israel this day," said Judas. "The Lord cannot disappoint them."

"They will hail the Messiah into the city," said Matthew. "It will be no less than they would for Caesar, except out of fear."

It was late morning as we followed Jesus out and into the sunlight, and the hum swelled to a low roar of excitement from the awaiting army that now stood on the hillside as far as my eye could see. I expected to be mobbed but it was not so; they awaited the Messiah's command.

The Messiah greeted them in the name of the Lord, that his face might shine upon them and give them peace.

He told them that he needed a steed on which to ride into the Holy City and that we would wait whilst it was brought for him. Two were sent ahead to the next village, but those of us close enough heard him say 'donkey'.

Gesturing for us to follow, the Messiah started to move among the people, smiling, pronouncing blessings of grace, unhurried, statesmanlike, moving to the head of his army.

The two returned, leading a mare and its colt, bringing murmurings of confusion and wonder from the multitudes.

We threw our cloaks over the colt's back. Jesus sat astride and, as the mare was led in front, it began to plod. The walls of the Holy City had always thrilled me at every Passover, but never before had this sight been accompanied by the Messianic joy flooding from the crowds, as they began to spread their palm branches and their cloaks before him. Praise to God erupted whilst his Messiah sat impassive beside me; the colt plodded onwards.

"No armed revolutionary ever rode a donkey's colt," said my brother. "This beast is our ticket past the legion."

Judas Iscariot was in raptures. "This is a stroke of genius, Rabbi. You have defused the moment."

"How could he ever lead a charge on that?" Simon grinned beside me.

"And how could the people ever charge ahead, without him?" My brother's smile was as broad as the sun.

"I pray it is so," said Bartholomew.

"I pray that the Tribune does not ... th-think we are a cover for a band of Zealots in a ... s-suicidal bid to free Barabbas!" said Thomas. "Pray! Keeping praying!"

"Relax, Thomas," said Peter. "The Centurions will laugh when they see, and who cares if they do!"

As I walked alongside, for just a moment it was a much smaller thought that claimed me: whoever could ride an unbroken colt anyway? It made no protest, as if angels had anointed it with heaven's peace, to allow a rider on its back for the first time and not flinch at the masses that jostled around it.

I looked ahead at the massed tents of Passover pilgrims in the Kidron. Tens of thousands more now jostled for a view as our procession approached. Above the Kidron, shields and armour flashed in a throng of activity on the Mount of Olives. The legion was being called to readiness, banging sword against shield to intimidate us and we were going to walk by right under their noses, as if butter would not melt in our mouths!

The great sea of Passover pilgrims began to part before the plodding colt, demanding to know who was the man being given the emperor's welcome.

The crowds proclaimed his name: the prophet from Galilee, the Son of David, the one who came in the name of The Lord! Hosanna!

James caught my eye and pointed towards the city walls. "They are closing the gates."

"The city will be under a lockdown," said Matthew.

"Imagine the turmoil within the walls as the people hear this noise," said Bartholomew.

My gaze shifted to the Antonia fortress; its turrets bristled with spears, as it exchanged signals with the legions to our right.

"Whatever happens now, we are in the middle of it," I called to James. "The only possible escape is to remain close to the Lord."

Beside me, Simon was ecstatic and then I decided this was the place for me, as well. Desire and Expectancy danced and pranced beside me, Power had now taken the lead and Freedom cantered in his wake, confident that his time was near.

I looked at the others. Thomas was still in sonorous prayer and chanting psalms, Judas Iscariot looked triumphant, Andrew and James were living the moment, Nathanael, Philip, Bartholomew and others were close together, singing praises with the crowd and swept along like me.

"The Lord is acting out the same Kingdom message as he always preached," James shouted us all above the tumult. "The invitation is given, but the Kingdom is not imposed."

Yes, my brother had it correct as usual. The Messiah would enter Jerusalem in a triumphant procession; it was a public offer of himself as King, but on his terms.

"His offer is directly to the people," said Judas. "The Kingdom will remove the Sanhedrin."

All of a sudden, Power seemed out of place. My imaginary stallion needed to be of a different kind and yet, in my heart, neither could he be a donkey's colt. Uncertainty gripped me, my guts churned as usual. There were still mysteries I could not fathom.

The crowd bunched up as we came to the steep and winding pathway to the Golden Gate. It had remained open and here the Pharisees met us, complaining that the children spoke blasphemy with their Hosannas.

My Messiah's reply was cool and dismissive: the stones themselves would otherwise give praise.

Judas Iscariot was more direct. "Is that the best you can do, whinge about the children? Move along or be swept aside!"

It was now that I realized my Lord was weeping. "Oh Jerusalem, Jerusalem. If only you had known this day, even you, the things that make for peace! But now they have been hidden from your eyes."

I moved close and rested my hand on his arm, but his lament continued in prophecy of destruction yet to come. Where was the Kingdom now?

The Pharisees were forced ahead in an undignified trot as we entered, with tens of thousands from Galilee pouring through the gate behind us.

"We're in!" exclaimed Judas Iscariot. "The Tribune will know better than to provoke a riot in here."

"He knows he can watch our movements from the Antonia," said Peter. "They will isolate us by closing the tunnels."

Across the outer courts with the shouts and praises all around, I watched the Chief Priests and Temple Guard. Even now, I was hopeful that they would come forward in welcome; we all knew many priests had believed and come over to us since Lazarus.

Frustration welled up inside me. "James," I said, "see how they cling to their places of authority."

"What authority?" said Simon beside me. "How the mighty have fallen!"

"Praise God for a bloodless … r- revolution," said Thomas and resumed his chanting.

"Now I know Father's despair," said James. "They are not of the Kingdom to which I belong."

The outer courts opened before us. "If there is going to be a flashpoint, it is now," said Nathanael.

The moneychangers and sellers stood close to their tables. Some were still, some of them collected up their money. The crowds around us grew quieter as the Messiah dismounted. All watched and waited as he walked slowly past them.

"I know what he's thinking," said James.

"I know what they are thinking, too!" said Andrew. "Memories of their humiliation of three years ago will still be raw in their minds."

"One word," said Judas. "All it needs is one word or gesture and the people will follow the Lord and sweep all before them."

I looked up to where Rome's soldiers watched from above, spears and bows and arrows bristled out from every part of the Antonia Fortress. It was a deliberate and intimidating show of strength by the Tribune. With one word from him, those spears and arrows would come raining down upon us.

Would either of those words be spoken? Meanwhile, thousands still poured in behind us.

"I pray this will not come to blood," Simon whispered to me. "These soldiers know that if the Lord is just waiting for enough followers to enter, before he made his move, then the battle in this confined space will be fierce and dangerous."

We all stood close. "Everyone here remembers the ferocity with which the Lord cleared this place three years ago," James told Peter, Judas Iscariot and the others.

"This must be the moment," said Judas. "He can dismiss the Chief Priest in front of the people; we can take power, if we act now. The Sanhedrin today and Rome another day! The Lord must use his power!"

So all eyes were now on my Messiah: some expectant, some hopeful, some resentful, some fearful.

Jesus led us on across the inner courts. It was a long tour of the temple. For more than an hour we followed, puzzled as our Lord walked around, looking at everything in detail.

"It is as if he's inspecting the holy objects," said Matthew. "Or looking for something which cannot not be found."

"Why doesn't he act?" Judas asked more than once in exasperation.

"Our part is to wait for his command," said Peter to the rest of us. "He has given our Sanhedrin the opportunity to accept him as he has come to them, in peace. It is for them to act and accept him."

We continued to follow our Messiah as he walked past the Chief Priests, looking into their faces, past the groups of Pharisees and the Sadducees and those from Herod's court.

"They look at the Lord down their noses," said Peter. "But they cannot meet his gaze as an equal."

"Those Sadducees try their best to ignore him," said Nathanael.

"Let them try and ignore the people!" said Philip.

The tense standoff continued as we walked on, all around the temple area and then up towards the Holy of Holies, and there Jesus stood for a long time with his arms raised in prayer; we stood with him. My Messiah was in control of his emotions and his display held the masses in peace.

Finally, he turned to us, the Twelve and the wider group. "It is late," he told us, but loud enough for the watching parties and crowds to hear. "There is nothing here for us. Let us go now."

Voices of authority called for early preparations to close the temple and the guards moved to their positions. The tension eased all around us as we moved back across the inner court. I watched as the traders began to smile and talk amongst themselves, confident that their business was now safe.

Jesus led us back through the masses still thronging the outer courts, out through the Golden Gate, across the Kidron and up the Mount of Olives, right through the camp of the legions. Andrew and I knew this move from years ago and told the others to look for any potential spies following.

2/. Not Fit For Purpose

"Why are we here? What did we achieve today?" Judas Iscariot asked us all.

"If he is the king our nation has waited hundreds of years for, why has he not taken his place?" asked Nathanael.

"You saw the way he masterminded our entrance this morning," James reminded them. "Was that for nothing?"

"When has he ever acted without purpose?" Peter asked us all. "The Lord offered himself in peace, he does not suit the Sanhedrin's idea of what a Messiah should be, but I do not think it ends here."

"They still regarded him as an impostor; false miracles from a false Messiah," said Philip.

"They fool themselves, as it is convenient to them," added Bartholomew.

"What do they know of the Law?" said Thomas. "Those that have purchased their … p-position ever since that mongrel Herod would sell it to them."

"The remainder of Passover week is ahead of us," said Matthew. "We wait for its fulfilment at least!"

I had watched Jesus' expression as we left the temple. Now he was walking ahead of us saying nothing.

"See how angry and despairing he is," I said. "It reminded me of that Sabbath he restored the man with the withered arm, when Shlomo stormed out."

From the Mount of Olives, we watched to make sure there was no pursuit before returning to Bethany in the dusk. Mary and Martha welcomed us with their usual joy, but it was a quiet evening as many of us kept our thoughts to ourselves or talked in small groups.

"He still hates the sight of the traders on the take, when the people need to be fed the goodness of the Lord," said James.

"He must still take his place in the temple so the world will see his glory," said Andrew. "How will this happen? Are we to expect a direct action from the Lord God? Will the Kingdom just come to pass now?"

"We can only wait until tomorrow and follow our Lord," declared Peter.

As they debated, I moved to recline next my Messiah, the embalming oil held me in its aromatic spell as my mind again went back over the years I had spent with him: at Matthew's banquet of the tax collectors, my Lord's words were that his followers would mourn when the groom was taken from them. I shivered, trying not to imagine that, in some way, he could soon be taken from me. I was holding onto every moment I could spend with him.

It was a restless night and next morning the mood was the same. All through early morning prayer, my guts wound themselves in knots with anticipation of the day ahead. We had all learned, over the course of the past three years, that Jesus would talk with us when the time was right. For now, no one asked hard questions, and tried to prepare for whatever lay ahead.

This morning it was just us and a few others on the Jerusalem road, and then Jesus did the unexpected sort of thing that I had gotten used to. Leaving the road, he took us to a fig tree, announcing that he was hungry.

"But Lord," said a bewildered voice, "it is not the season for a fig tree to bear fruit."

We all stood by, exchanging expressions of puzzlement, as his search through the leaves was almost melodramatic, before he stood back and told the tree. "May no one ever eat fruit from you again!"

"That was like a curse," I said to my brother. "I am sure those leaves started to droop."

"There is a lesson for us here somewhere," said James. "A parable has been enacted for us."

As we continued along the road, Nathanael said, "I think I have it! What did he spend so much time doing yesterday in the temple? Was it not searching?"

Now the significance of the actions exploded into my mind, but my brother beat me to it. "Searching for fruit!" he said. "Spiritual fruit, the good fruit of the works of the Lord God, and there was none!"

In the next instant, Judas Iscariot was with us. "It is a temple as unfruitful as that tree and the people give much and get nothing in return but a system that prevents them from reaching their God."

"And the Lord has ... j-just cursed it!" added Thomas' condemning tones.

"Did you not see his tears?" I said. "The Holy City was not prepared for the coming of its Messiah."

I felt the sudden and drastic change in the mood and regarded the faces around me; no longer were we individuals following in our own fears and uncertainties. I knew what lay ahead this second day of Passover. We were heading for an unfruitful temple where The Sanhedrin was only interested in maintaining their power and spiritual growth was impossible.

Today was the day when freedom would be proclaimed. Power snorted and whinnied his agreement, whilst Freedom cantered around me in delirious circles.

We climbed the steep path with deliberate strides and through the Golden Gate. My Lord quickened his pace and we bunched closer to him. "Last evening the traders spent time celebrating," he told us. "They believe that the Son of Man and his people dared not challenge them, and today they are confident in their business."

"And they are totally unprepared for what is coming!" Judas Iscariot volunteered to finish on our Lord's behalf.

"Lord, set the people free," said Peter. "Proclaim the year of the Lord's favour."

"We are with you, Lord," said my brother. "Lead us and the people will follow."

"Same as usual," said Simon next to me. "You proclaim the Kingdom, I'll take the action! Let's turn their shambles back into a Temple for the Lord!"

Jesus led us straight in and we took the outer courts by storm, driving everything before us.

Simon rampaged on ahead of me and I can testify that when Simon bar Mordecai hit something, it stayed hit. As I followed in his wake, I saw all the frustration of years of the injustice that had impoverished his parents and his farm came pouring out of him. Money tables were flung, spinning into the air, and when they broke under his fists, he brandished a splintered leg across the faces of the traders.

Most of the seventy-two were now with us; Galilean voices proclaimed the Messiah was here to take the temple and we rolled across the vast acreage of the temple site. In the chaos, doves burst from their cages to fly free, lambs stampeded to a good escape. The traders were thrown out; their screams of indignation and howls of protest drowned, Temple Guards and priests were swept aside.

It was a straight repeat of three years earlier, my Messiah with whirling knotted rope cleansing the temple, but this time I stood alongside him with my brothers-in-arms, clearing out the detritus and shouting at them above the chaos, the same rebuke time and again: "Get out of here! How dare you turn my Father's house into a market!"

As the dust settled, Jesus turned us to the people. We stood with our Messiah to proclaim the Kingdom was come for all to see and enter.

"The Lord God wants your obedience not your money," said Matthew. "To obey is better than to sacrifice."

"Did not you find forgiveness in the repentance the Immerser proclaimed?" shouted Andrew. "The only sacrifice you needed then was your shame and your sin."

"Give this money to the poor, the orphan and the widow; this is the Law and the Prophets," proclaimed Thomas, as smooth as silk.

I took my turn. "This is the Kingdom before you, take hold of it for yourself!" My Messiah had taken control of the temple; the world could now see his glory.

We moved out amongst the Passover pilgrims and invited them to come before the Messiah and into the presence of their Lord.

Jesus had calmed himself and now sat and taught them from the Law. The masses of people hung on his every word, amazed at his teaching. The blind and crippled came to him and he healed them. The Messiah in peasant's garb, speaking in their common everyday Aramaic.

"There is no concealment now as before," said my brother. "The Lord shows his miracles for all to see."

"The Chief Priests cannot deny it and they can do nothing about it either," said Judas.

I watched them sulking in the shadows, I could see the bulk of Shlomo and Saul in with the Pharisees; they had lost the control of the temple and they had lost control of the people.

My Messiah sat there in the middle doing their job; *He* was now the high priest teaching the people about their God. The incense rose from the altar before God and still the heavy fragrance went forth from my Lord and pervaded the temple.

We all sat around and brought people to him, as we had learned to do during the tours of Galilee, but now we were here! The temple had been conquered. I was sure I walked on air this day. Simon and I could not stop grinning or clasping hands.

"The Sanhedrin will be ever more desperate to find … w-ways to kill the Lord and remove his … th-threat to their power," Thomas reminded us.

"They cannot, because the people would revolt against them," Andrew replied.

"They will try to discredit him, to shame him in front of all the people," Judas told us again. "They will manufacture a proof that he is not the real Messiah, but an impostor. They must make him into the madman with demons that they have accused him of being. We must be on our guard to counter their intrigues."

All day I watched the robed figures in the shadows, their gestures animated and expressive of their desperation.

I looked up at the Antonia; it bristled with spears as it had yesterday. Signals went out to the legion on the Olivet, but as the day progressed, they became less.

"What will The Prefect make of this?" asked Nathanael.

"He will monitor and contain, but not provoke," said Matthew.

"He'll wait and see which way it goes and prepare to back the winner. If it keeps the people happy, it makes his role easier," said my brother.

"I still say he will be pleased at an opportunity for revenge," said Andrew.

"He may be content with more taxes," said Peter. "You can be sure he will calculate that if there is less given to God, he can get more for Caesar!"

"That can wait for another day, my brothers," said Philip.

"Today we should attend to the Lord's Kingdom," said Nathanael.

All day and into the evening, my Lord continued with the people and well beyond the statutory closing time. There was no way any of those who called themselves rulers of the people could assert their authority on this day. The Temple Guards hung around looking redundant; some even gave up and departed.

When we departed late into the evening, I could see Shlomo, Uri and the Chief Priests still arguing about their plans into the night. We strode up the Mount of Olives. It had been a glorious day, my Lord had taken possession of his Temple and no one could oppose him. I was sure that I now basked in God's glory, made available for all to see in teaching and healing.

I felt untouchable, and yet as I walked at the rear, the same mysteries remained for me and I could not escape that heavy aroma, that scent of death.

I found Judas Iscariot was next to me, his brow furrowed in thought as he spoke to himself and much as he spoke to me. "Why have we left the temple again? Why not seize power with the support of the people, depose the Sanhedrin once and for all and be done with it?"

"Perhaps that is for tomorrow?" I offered.

3/. Tricks, Snares and Woes

The Temple Guard did not want to look my Lord in the eye and the traders fled before him. Early on that third day of Passover, nobody stood in our way. The Messiah took possession of the inner courts and the people gathered around him.

I watched as the forces gathered against us, assembling amongst the columns: Chief Priests, Pharisees, Sadducees, Herodians were all there in large numbers. Their tribal rivalries and theological differences were put to one side in common enmity against my Messiah.

"They are not about to surrender power without a fight," said Judas.

"Today they look prepared," said Nathanael. "They have plans."

"They will have worked hard all night on their scheming," said Philip.

"The Chief Priests will be first," said my brother. "They need to reclaim the temple or they are lost."

He was right; they spoke for all the people to hear: by whose authority had the Galilean usurper challenged their authority?

"And if he tells them the truth, they will call him out for blasphemy," said Peter.

My Lord had his own question for the judgement of the people: was the immersion of repentance for sins from a man or from God?

All eyes swung back to the priests, who withdrew a little way to argue amongst themselves.

"It is like the interrogation at the Immerser's Pool again," said Andrew in my ear.

"What will they say?" Judas Iscariot mused aloud, with evident sarcasm, for all to hear. "What if it were from God?"

"Then why did the Sanhedrin not accept it?" Nathanael answered for him.

"So therefore it must be from man?" Judas Iscariot's mocking tone continued.

"All the people held The Immerser was sent by God," said Andrew, springing to reaffirm our former Rabbi.

"So the Priests would lose even more face before the people," James finished with a smile of admiration. "What a surprise, they don't have an answer. So why should The Lord answer theirs?"

Jesus delivered his dismissal with an airy finality and the people's voices rumbled around us in support.

"That's put an end to the questions of the Chief Priests," Peter said with satisfaction.

"He saw through their duplicity from the start," I whispered to Simon, who nodded with enjoyment.

"They were not interested in knowing about The Lord's authority, only in trying to discredit it."

"Didn't he turn it back upon their heads so beautifully?" said Philip. "If they could not make a judgement about the first great prophet to arise for four hundred years, what right did they have to make any judgement about Jesus of Nazareth?"

However, my Messiah's response had not ended there. It was a parable about a man planting a new vineyard and renting it to some vinedressers of shameful behaviour, who beat the servants and then murdered the son of their landlord for their own greed and profit.

As the parable unfolded, the whole assembly knew who those tenants were and eyes turned towards the priests, but the punchline was also for the people: the owner would return to take his justice with the tenants and give his vineyard to others.

The people around me recoiled with exclamations of 'shame' and 'no' and 'may this never happen!', but it didn't drown out the silent fury of the priests.

Judas Iscariot groaned and let his exasperation show for all to see. "Why does he have to say this now?" he appealed to us all. "We need the support of these people to complete the conquest. These people need to know their Messiah will rid them of Rome, not be threatened that the land will be taken from them!"

"We saw Nazareth." Philip and Nathanael stood together. Andrew nodded. "The Lord has always chosen to confront people with what they don't want to hear, regardless of the consequence. He is not about to change his ways now, Judas."

As Jesus returned to his teaching, I watched the different parties despatch agents to move amongst us: spies to infiltrate the crowd and act as if they were honest truth-seekers. It was not difficult to spot the Herodians, Rome's puppets with fine clothes and jewellery. They brought their politically charged question in honey-coated words of false flattery.

"Rabbi, we know that you speak and teach what is right, and that you do not show partiality but teach the way of God in accordance with the truth." I saw Jesus smile, a minimum of smile. "Is it right for us to pay taxes to Caesar or not?"

"A clever trap, they have him now!" exclaimed Judas. "Either way they will shame him as a traitor to the people for paying, or betray him to Pilate if he refuses!"

"He has the words," Peter reminded us. I hoped he was right.

My Messiah was gracious at their concern for correct payment of taxes. Why not look at a coin and see whose money it was? They needed to do their civic duty, as well their duty to God, he told them. I knew his one-liner to 'give to Caesar what is Caesar's, and to God what is God's' would live long in the memory of the people.

"Hah, what an answer!" Judas exploded from his fears in triumph.

"They cannot trap him." My brother shook his head in admiration and amazement.

I breathed again in relief, as the lords in fine clothes melted away from the crowd.

"See, they go to contemplate their responsibility to those who rule them," Matthew told us.

"Miracles are not needed here," said Peter. "Truth will always expose false arguments and the politics of self-interest."

"This is a hundred times better than The Immerser's Pool," said Andrew. "The Lord is not dealing with just the messengers; he's dismissing the leaders in the middle of the temple."

We grinned at each other, but I was still fearful and alert. I knew it was not over yet and I watched to see what would happen next, as Jesus kept talking to the crowds and responding to their needs.

Perhaps it was inevitable that it would be Uri and the Sadducees who would head the next assault to shame my Lord before the people. Uri did not risk himself, but as a general in the battle preferred to send Chai and his other disciples with their well-prepared theological trap. Starting with the pretence that Moses would approve, it was a riddle of seven brothers who all married the same woman, but each died in their turn. So who would this woman be married to in the resurrection?

"What a surprise, a question on their favourite subject," said Thomas. "Greek … l-logic to deny the resurrection, in spite of all that is written in our scriptures."

"Very good, Thomas!" said Peter. "I've never heard you do condemnation with sarcasm before. Let's see what The Lord has to say about it."

My Lord's reply was but a seamless part of his teaching the people; marriage was only for this age, he told the people, it didn't apply to the age of the resurrection. In the age to come, God's children would not be dead, just as the angels lived in the heavenly realms.

He turned to the Sadducees. "To God, all are alive and you are badly mistaken!" Gasps of amazement and adoration erupted from the crowds all around us.

"What a punchline," said Judas.

"See how the people are enjoying this duel being played out before them," said Philip.

"Some of these Pharisees are enjoying it as well," said Nathanael. "Listen to them revelling in the shame of their rivals."

It was then that one Pharisee stepped forwards alone. "Of all the commandments, Rabbi, which is the most important?" he asked.

"That's the first genuine question that I've heard all day," said Peter. "It will get a straight answer."

"Hear O Israel, the Lord our God, the Lord is one," said my Lord. "Love the Lord your God with all your heart and with all your soul and with all your mind and with all your strength. The second is this: Love your neighbour as yourself. There is no commandment greater than these."

The Pharisee of integrity concurred that this was more important than all burnt offerings and sacrifices and was told in return that he was not far from the Kingdom of God.

"Good! At last!" Judas enthused. "We find common ground with the best of them as partners to sweep the rest away!"

"Truth is always a good common ground, don't you think, Judas?" my brother replied. "I believe the Lord tells us that principles always go ahead of circumstances."

"What now of these … Pha-Pharisees," said Thomas. "They have stood back and watched as others have attacked the Lord and have seen him despatch them one by one. Will any of them dare … t-to question him?"

As we continued to sit around our Lord and the people with us, it became clear there would be no further challenges.

"The other Pharisees will not engage," said Judas. "They are hiding behind the one good answer that was given."

"Can they see the Kingdom he has preached these three years or prefer to live in their own?" said Matthew.

The answer was not long coming, but it did not come from the Pharisees, as my Messiah brought forth the issue on which everything else hung.

"How is it that the scriptures say the Messiah is the Son of David?" he appealed in the direction of the Pharisees. "David's own Psalm tells us: 'The Lord said to my Lord; sit at my right hand until I make your enemies a footstool for your feet'. If David calls him 'Lord', how then can he be his son?"

The people hummed their amazement and looked towards the Pharisees as they had at the Sadducees.

"So Pharisees, will you not speak?" said Judas in rhetoric. "Either answer or be shamed as the Sadducees were. Is Jesus of Nazareth who he says he is? Is he the Messiah of God!?"

"And those times you said our Lord had no authority to forgive sins will come tumbling down about your ears!" said Peter.

No response came. Shlomo, Saul and their party stood mute and perplexed under the pressure of the crowds.

"The people remember all the times these Pharisees have lectured them in righteousness and taken advantage in their authority," said Andrew.

"Humbled by the greater wisdom of a man in clothes like mine," grinned Simon, as he almost danced on the spot.

"More than that; the people want to believe he is the Messiah," said my brother.

Turning his back to the Pharisees, my Messiah spoke to his adoring masses, loud and clear. "The teachers of the law and the Pharisees sit in Moses' seat. So you must obey them and do everything they tell you. But do not do what they do, for they do not practise what they preach. They tie up heavy burdens on men's shoulders, but they themselves are not willing to lift a finger to move them."

Just when I thought he would stop, my Lord's condemnation become more explicit. He listed out their sins and his damnations of them for all to hear. It was something that all who heard it would never forget; an attack of such verbal savagery that the whole temple stood transfixed like moths attracted to the flame that would burn them, yet they were unable to turn away and escape.

"Woe to you, teachers of the law and Pharisees, you hypocrites! You shut the Kingdom of God in men's faces, you yourselves do not enter, nor will you let those enter who are trying to..."

I lost a sense of time but it must have continued for twenty to thirty minutes, the Pharisees cowering under the force of the Messiah's terrible verbal beating. For all their strict adherence to the Law, they were stripped of their moral authority in front of the people. I counted the woes. Seven times, with seven different reasons, my Messiah pronounced the words, "Woe to you teachers of the law and Pharisees, you hypocrites..."

I could feel myself also cowering as he denounced their lists of petty rules, their false outward zeal, their practice of oaths, their demonstrative giving whilst neglecting justice for the poor, their greed and self-indulgence, their outward posturing and then the outright accusation of arranging of the deaths of innocent and righteous men. Then, with echoes of The Immerser, he called them a brood of vipers and predicted their eternal destiny in hell. Every word seemed to sear into my consciousness.

As the echoes died away, the temple was but a scene of transfixed statues. Then I saw my Lord burst into tears and again lament over all that was Jerusalem, telling them how he had longed to gather them all to him as a mother with her children, but they had rejected all his efforts and now they would not see him again.

Silence fell like an abyss. He walked away across the temple; I could still see tears glistening on his face.

4/. Destruction Will Follow

We remained moths still trapped by his flame, until Peter pushed and prodded us all out of our trance and we followed in the direction he had gone. We fanned out in the crowds and found him by the treasury where all filed past to pay their taxes. Simon, Andrew, Thomas and I sat with him, watching the offerings being thrown into the temple chests as the others talked and watched for the Temple Guard.

"See this woman?" He indicated a small and aged woman. From her ragged clothes I took her to be a widow, her position between life and starvation would be a fine balance.

"Moses wrote the Law for the care of such as these," Thomas affirmed. "She should be provided for with alms from these chests."

As we watched, two small copper coins were given and I saw Jesus smile for the first time that day. He called us all together to tell us she had put in more than anyone else. Out of her poverty came faith in her God. He rose to go.

"He has found the fruit he was looking for," said Nathanael.

"Someone who knew their life was safe in the Lord God," agreed Philip.

"None of the Sanhedrin showed us that," said Andrew. "Will this finish tomorrow?"

"He told them they would not see him again," James reminded us all.

"Look at him," said Bartholomew. "It is as if he is saying goodbye!"

We followed our Lord as he took us around the temple, walking, pausing, touching, and moving on.

The whole wider group crowded around us in high spirits; they had seen their Messiah vanquish all his enemies in a long day of battle.

"Look, Teacher! What massive stones! What magnificent buildings!" said some.

As a boy, I had often marvelled at those foundation stones, some forty feet long and twice as high as a man, great ashlars of Jerusalem stone that gleamed in the sun.

Jesus' reply was cool. "Do you see all these great buildings? Not one stone will be left on another; every one of them will be thrown down." He said nothing more, as if he had slipped back into his lament.

As we walked across the Kidron and up the Mount of Olives, the shock subsided a little and our disputes began.

"I heard him once tell the Pharisees he would destroy the temple and build it again in three days," Andrew told everyone.

"A new temple then for the new Kingdom," said Nathanael.

"A new time to ride in and restore the Kingdom," put in Philip. "Not on the donkey next time!"

"If it comes to pass, I do not think we can be its new priests," said Thomas. His thoughts had turned to the legal practicalities, as always. "That is for the Levites; we must be Twelve tribes in a different way."

My steps grew slower and I slipped behind. I could think no further than the next forty-eight hours of Passover. I found myself again at the rear with Judas Iscariot, who also had no desire for the debate but shared his reflections with me.

"Why cannot he seize the moment?" Judas Iscariot demanded. "Have we again come all this way in triumph to walk away and leave it all behind?"

I had no answer and remained silent.

"He never misses an opportunity to miss an opportunity," Judas persisted in his exasperation. "All this power and we are still itinerant beggars, awaiting a prophet's death!"

"The people have made him their king already, Judas," I said.

"It is not enough!" countered Judas Iscariot. "There is part of him that is still the naïve peasant of Galilee. He will never succeed on his own, but I can make this happen. He must be made to fulfil what needs to be done, to be put in a position where he must use his power."

"Judas, this is not your place!" I was astonished at my own response, but he had already turned away, back down towards the city.

I followed him down the path. "Are you telling me you are going to put yourself above the Messiah?"

He gave no answer.

"Judas, do you believe he is the Messiah, or are you like the Pharisees saying he is not the Messiah you want?"

"No man is perfect before God; Moses was not alone, with Aaron beside him. I can be the Aaron that speaks to Pharaoh and to the people. I have not come this far to see the Kingdom unfulfilled."

"Moses was not the Messiah," I called after him. For a moment, I watched him go. I felt cold; I turned to hurry after the others.

I caught them up near the summit and stood for a while, where I could look out over the temple as the smoke of the evening sacrifice ascended as prayer to heaven. All Jerusalem was laid out before me and I wondered where Judas Iscariot had gone. I thought of my parents down there and wondered how I could ever return there if my Messiah now refused to.

James pulled me into the group, they had decided answers were needed and a deputation was required. Jesus was sitting, looking out over the city as I had done, his mood still melancholy as we gathered around him.

"Tell us, Lord," asked Peter, "when will these things happen?"

"And what will be the sign that they are about to be fulfilled?" My brother added.

He continued to look out over the city and after a while started to speak to us. We were not to be deceived or allow ourselves to be alarmed at rumours of pestilence, death, destruction, famine and earthquake that were all part of the world. But we would be hated for being of him and, yes, a prophet's death would await in a world where love diminished and evil increased, but the Kingdom and the Lord God's saving grace was always there for us.

I tried to think beyond Passover and imagine great ages to come. How long was this mission, this battle, going to go on?

His next words then took me back these four years, to that evening meal on our roof to escape the legion's dust. He spoke of 'the abomination that causes desolation' standing in the Holy Place; when it did so again it would be time to flee to the mountains. History would repeat its circles and a great tyrant, scheming and deceptive like the first one had been, would one day come to Jerusalem to glorify himself and use our Temple for his own egotistical and political ends.

I felt as if the very reason for my life was draining away from me as my Lord continued; great distress, false prophets and false Messiahs, signs in the heavens as the very stars would fall from the sky.

Was it possible to walk through such a world and not have worries, to believe that my life was held in the palm of my God's hand, that he was still in control of my destiny and not the tumult that would surround me?

When would it happen?

The day and the hour were already known, but not by him, he told us. No, not even my Messiah, only the Lord God of heaven knew this. This was not for us to know, our part was to know that we had been given the signs to look for, to hold our own destiny in our own hands, in covenant with Him.

For he would return for us, at that unknown hour. He told us of his own special dawn in parables of warning and reassurance.

That day, when he had chosen me as one of The Twelve, played through my mind. To be sent to my nation, I recalled my emotions as a priest of the new Kingdom. Now I shuddered. I had had enough explanations now, but my Lord was not finished and I was again the moth trapped by his burning light.

Parables, it was more parables. Forever we had wanted to know when the Kingdom would be restored to Israel and now we were being told the answer was to be ever watchful and prepared for its arrival. There were no compromises, there never had been, and even the Gentile nations would come to know this and their people be separated, like sheep and goats, for eternal glory or darkness.

Darkness. I now needed some modicum of darkness, to crawl away and escape this burning light that illuminated the future of my world, but just before I escaped, my Lord delivered a punchline that hit me like a knife driven deep into my bowels. In that voice of calm but cold certainty, "As you know, the Passover is two days away – and the Son of Man will be handed over to be crucified."

A new wave of embalming aroma washed over me like nausea.

I crawled away a small distance and lay on my back, looking up through the gnarled branches of the ancient olives. A cold sweat prickled my skin as the night fell and the stars appeared twinkling above. What could, what would cause them to fall from the sky?

* * * *

The fourth day of that Passover week was the one I have always wanted to forget, to erase from my mind. It dawned bright and clear, but the sun was dark in my eyes. On this day, I had no Passover joy, no hope of freedom. My eyes studied my Lord's every move and expression until I could not abide any longer.

He had arisen early for prayer as usual, but made no move towards Jerusalem. I had known that he would not return, but it was not possible to prepare for the empty void that was this day.

All of us, the Twelve, idled at a loss of what to do with ourselves. Yesterday we had commanded the very centre of power, a force that would guide our nation to a new future; today we were again ordinary people going through the familiar routines. Judas Iscariot vocalised it all for us, but nobody was up for the dispute.

I watched my Lord; we all watched him. Today, he asked Martha and Mary for work he could do with his hands, jobs in their house and garden. He was happy with tools in his hand, singing idle songs to himself.

I shared my thoughts with my brother. "Judas Iscariot called him a naïve peasant from Galilee and left us last night. He has some plan to force action from the Lord."

"Judas Iscariot has always had his own mind on these things."

"Do you think The Lord wants to be back in Nazareth again?" I asked. "After all we have seen, is there a part of him that does not want to be The Messiah?"

James nodded his head. "I believe he has always known his destiny, but what a burden it must be to carry the hope of the Kingdom restored to Israel!"

Simon spoke up. "Having come this far, that destiny must be worked out this Passover."

"The next two days will tell us," agreed James.

"I need to escape from the aroma of that oil," I told them. "Will you come and visit our parents?"

So we asked for our leave and walked back down the Jerusalem road. Simon was now welcomed by my mother as one of us. It was a wonderful relief to be a family again and I realised that I was doing the same as Jesus of Nazareth was doing, just needing to be with people who loved me.

I tried to engage Father about the words of my Messiah, but he would not. I had never known him to not have an answer for me.

We went up to the temple; it took us even longer than usual in Passover's teeming masses. On every street corner stood the Sanhedrin's men, on every tower and wall were Rome's. The pilgrims milled and meandered; we knew who they were looking for.

Inside the temple, the atmosphere was surreal. The Priests, stripped of their authority with such savagery the previous day, went through the religious motions. The Temple Guards looked as redundant as ever: they had not been able to keep order all week and now there was no disorder to worry them. The traders were like dogs, sniffing around the edges, not daring to set up their money tables as they sat in the sun. It was a nothing day of confused emotions, a brooding atmosphere, calm before a final climactic storm. Even here, I could not escape; it was as if the aroma of that embalming oil followed me still.

5/. Elijah's Cup

The last two years of unfulfilled Passovers had left a void in my life and today I needed that emptiness to be filled to overflowing. Tonight I would eat the Passover with my Messiah; the promise of freedom and life in his Kingdom that would never end.

Today I would take Simon's advice, and believe and trust that all would be well. Today, I decided, would be different from all other Passovers; I just needed to let it happen.

The dawning in Bethany had been quiet. We gathered at Lazarus' for prayer and the cleansing of his Mikvah, where I caught a scent of the embalming oil again. My Lord isolated himself for further prayer and our disputes began again. What else would we ever do on this Passover day!

"Will he proclaim the Kingdom amongst us tonight and then to the people tomorrow?" Nathanael asked us all.

"Why did he not stand in the temple and proclaim the Kingdom already?" asked Judas Iscariot.

"There can be no Kingdom when he weeps over Jerusalem," said Bartholomew.

"What he told us amongst the olives was destruction with many chapters yet to come," said my brother. "Famine and plague are not short and inconsequential."

"This must be for the Priests and Rome," Judas Iscariot told us. "Like Pharaoh, they will not listen until their power is broken."

"But it was we who were told to run for the hills, not the legions!" said Nathanael.

"That could be for our safety, whilst the legions are being erased," suggested Simon. "The Lord told us not to be alarmed."

"May they indeed be erased," said Judas Iscariot. "But he told us 'the abomination of desolation' would stand again. This cannot be allowed to happen!"

"Then the temple is destroyed," said Matthew. "Not one of those great ashlars left upon another and yet a greater temple must be built."

"He told the priests that if they destroyed it, he could raise it in three days," said Andrew.

"That's different to it being destroyed by enemies who will throw up earthworks and lay siege," replied Philip.

"Well, he could still raise it in three days!" protested Andrew.

"If the abomination of Rome has polluted the temple, I say destroy it all completely and not just the high altar this time." Nathanael's passion was getting higher.

"Solomon's temple was greater," mused James. "Yet it was not the first. Are we to return to the Tabernacle of Moses?"

"The Lord has always … b-been the new Moses to me," said Thomas.

"But we are not Levites to be new priests of his new temple," protested Nathanael.

"We bring a sword to divide the people, my friend," said Philip. "We have been the new wine and the new skin."

"I say again that I was separated from our people by his great sermon on the plateau!" put in Matthew.

"We shake the dust from our feet as testimony," agreed Peter. "That is our sword."

I saw Judas Iscariot move away. He had decided that this dispute was no longer relevant for him.

"He said nothing of the destruction of the Law!" Thomas was on his usual form. "Of that we can all give thanks."

"Not until heaven and earth pass away," reminded Nathanael.

I screwed up my courage to ask the question I dared not ask myself. "None of us says it," I said. "The one thing we dare not speak of: when he tells us of his death or how he will be taken from us. Tell me please that this is but a parable."

"I believe *He* is the Lord God's Messiah," Peter reassured me. "He told me himself. He will reign forever, a Kingdom that shall never cease."

"Then what is this parable?" asked James bar Alpheus, the quiet man amongst us.

"I will get out of the boat and sink again, if that's what it takes to find out!" proclaimed Peter. I loved him all the more for saying it.

"And what about when he says he is going where we cannot follow?" asked Philip.

"He has always gone up mountains and out to deserts for longer periods than we can," said Peter. "Have no fear."

"What of the false messiahs that will come? Does that not worry you, that many of our people will be lead astray and oppose us?" asked Nathanael.

"How long will this mission need to go on before all this is accomplished?" asked Andrew.

"Not even he knew the hour of the Kingdom," said Matthew.

So it went on, all things were possible with our Messiah. Every new scenario we imagined had to be argued through, and yet the possible answers only multiplied in front of our eyes.

Jesus returned; it was time to ask where he would take the Passover.

* * * *

As Peter and I walked towards the Holy City, anticipation grew inside me and my four stallions trotted happily along with my every step. Excitement bubbled out of Peter as he talked to himself in wonderment. "A man carrying a pitcher! With all the water carried by women, how does he know there will be one man?"

"He has all knowledge and can do whatever he wants to," I grinned back at my big friend. We spotted our man amongst the heaving masses and he led us to his master and a sumptuous room.

This was a wonderful few hours, Peter and I singing hymns together, exchanging stories of former Passovers as we prepared the Passover lamb. All those wonderful familiarities that I counted off in my mind, the candles, the bowls, the parsley and salted water, the boiled eggs and horseradish and the wine and the unleavened Matzah.

Jesus arrived with the others, bringing more high spirits and recollections. I breathed in the warm light, the aromas and the relaxed chatter. Our great act of theatre was about to begin. We tucked our garments into our belts, ready to run into freedom.

The wine filled our first cup, to proclaim the Lord would take us out. He would give us salvation from our labour of slavery on this Holy Day of freedom.

"How eagerly I have waited to share this Passover with you, before I suffer," he told us. "I will never eat it again until the Kingdom comes." If I had ever hung on his every word, this evening would magnify it a hundred-fold. "I will not drink this cup again, until I do so in the Kingdom of the Lord God, so take this and share it amongst you."

And so our first cups remained untouched, this evening we would share his; this would indeed be a Passover like no other.

As we dipped the parsley into the saltwater of our tears, Matthew spoke up. "Who will be our youngest child tonight and ask us why we do this?"

I knew that it was either me or Simon, and all eyes turned to us. I waited for Jesus to make a choice, but to my surprise, Simon replied, "I will be that child for you, my brothers, if you will agree." There was a general murmur of approval.

Now Jesus spoke again, tearing the Bread of Affliction; it became his broken body to be shared among us as the first cup had been. How often had I promised him I would follow and share?

We raised the second cup, deliverance from servitude to the foreign oppressor, and Simon took his cue. "Why is this night different from all other nights?" His Hebrew was not cultured but adequate and I nodded encouragement to him.

"Why on all other nights do we eat bread with yeast, but on this night we eat only unleavened bread?" The others also murmured, encouraging him onwards.

"Why on all other nights do we eat all kinds of herbs, but on this night we eat bitter herbs?

Why on all other nights do we not dip herbs at all, but on this night we dip them twice?"

He stumbled a little, but these words were inside all of us, from ever since we could remember.

"Why on all other nights do we eat in the normal way, but on this night we eat with special ceremony?"

I smiled, sharing his relief as he finished with a little triumph and our Lord took up the story, the story we all knew so well. Together we lifted the second cup and listed out each of the plagues with drops of wine.

All those wonderful old familiarities continued, the lamb bone, the boiled egg, the Matzah dipped in the horseradish.

"Once we were slaves but now we are free!" our Lord proclaimed.

"Once we were slaves but now we are free!" we chorused in reply. Every other year I had passed from sorrow to joy, from darkness to light. Now, it was the other way.

It was then that Jesus rose to his feet behind me. I felt him move away and turned to see him remove his outer garments and take a towel and pitcher and basin.

He started with me, taking off my dirty sandals, to wash and dry my feet, before moving on around the room as we all quietened and watched in amazed silence. Peter protested and drew his feet away.

Jesus looked him in the eye. "Unless I wash you, you will have no part with me."

"Then, Lord, not just my feet but my head and hands as well!"

"The Lord bless you Peter, my brother," called Matthew. "You are out of the boat and determined to walk and even run all over again."

All laughed, but all knew there was a new act of theatre amongst the old. Jesus allowed himself a broad smile. "A person who has had a bath needs only to wash his feet; his whole body is clean. And you are clean, though not every one of you." He settled beside me again.

We filled the third cup, and now it was Elijah's cup, filled with all its promise of redemption as my people passed through the Sea of Reeds. Was I safe from pursuit and did my promised land lie ahead?

Expectancy lead the charge as my four stallions thundered through the room. I wanted to climb aboard, yearning to be there and not tarry any longer in the nearly-but-not-quite-Kingdom where I was dwelling.

"I tell you the truth, that one of you will betray me this night." A fog descended over me and the heavy oil started to suffocate again. My brain did not want to register his words. A piece of the Matzah hit me. Peter mouthed at me, "who is it? Ask him who!"

"The one who dips the bread with me," he answered, handing it to Judas Iscariot. "Go quickly and do what you must."

Judas Iscariot departed and I did not want to know anymore. I looked at the sacrifice, the Passover lamb. The Immerser had proclaimed 'Lamb of God who takes away the sins of the world'. Benjamin's tears, I could dip my parsley in them now. It all echoed round and round inside my head, the lamb's blood, as death passed over our forefathers. I tried to shut it out of my mind but I could not; my Lord, the Passover lamb.

The fourth cup, thanksgiving and hope, I had none of either. Where now was the Kingdom that would never end? I could not see it.

Simon rose to take his last act of the evening, but he never got to the door. Jesus reached across to the unoccupied place and lifted the brimming cup, Elijah's cup, the cup that had always remained at my every other Passover.

"This cup, which is poured out for you, is the new covenant in my blood." I watched transfixed as he poured it out. "But behold, the hand of the one betraying me is with mine on the table. For indeed the Son of Man is going, as it has been determined, but woe to that man by whom he is betrayed."

Around me a new dispute was starting. I knew my brothers were as lost as I was. Trying to fill a void of uncertainty, they argued over which of them could be the greatest, a self-protection to ensure they could not be the lowest.

He started to speak to us in that voice of calm certainty; the one I had first heard when he came out of the desert. It was time for the Son of Man to be glorified. He was going where we could not follow and as we remained, his new commandment was to bear each other in love and comradeship.

Peter rolled onto his knees, demanding to know where his Lord was going and proclaiming that he would follow to the death. With the same certainty, he was told that he would deny his Lord repeatedly before a rooster called at dawn. Peter subsided.

Do not let our hearts be troubled, he told us. How could that be? It was an impossibility for me.

Thomas wanted to know the way. He was told that his Lord was the way.

Philip wanted to see the Father. He was told he had already seen him.

We would not be alone; the Spirit of Truth would always be with us. I had never felt so alone in a room full of friends.

Nathanael wanted to know what had changed that all this glory would be revealed to us and yet not to the world. Surely the world needed to see that glory?

But it was more and parables and teachings, new commandments for new covenants in a world that would hate us. Prophecies and prayers and future glory, but all I wanted was to have something, just a token of certainty for the moment of now. All my familiar certainties of the Passover had now been ended forever in the dawn of an uncertain new world.

My Messiah led us in a hymn before we left the safety of our room for the darkened streets. He held our hands as we walked towards the gate. As we crossed the Kidron ravine, Peter was still protesting he would always be true. Or would Simon bar Jonas be sifted as wheat? Simon? He was no longer Peter the rock for me, and another of my certainties departed.

Now, in the darkness, I could feel his anguish. The voice was no longer calm and certain, now what I heard was strained and quavering, beseeching us all to stay and not fall into temptation. Stumbling a few steps further, I saw him pitch forward and remain face down. He was pleading, begging over and over, and then 'yet not my will but yours be done'.

I was spent. Emotional exhaustion claimed me and I fell in and out of consciousness, I could not keep watch with my Messiah as he had asked.

Then he was shaking me awake, flaming torches ringed the garden, Temple Guards and Judas Iscariot.

"Judas, are you betraying the Son of Man with a kiss?"

The guards gathered round. I could see their swords and clubs drawn. In their torchlight, I could see my Messiah's face patterned with blood.

"Who is it you want?" he asked them.

"Jesus of Nazareth."

"I am he."

The same words that had repelled them in the temple did so once again. For a few moments, my spirit soared as he challenged the guard again and they did not lay a hand on him.

Everyone stood in confrontation and then, it all changed.

He did not walk through them. Their hands fell on him. Rope bound him. The guards were a wall between us. Their flaming torches were the stars that had fallen, from my sky.

6/. Night Without End

John Mark fled naked past me, his empty robe left in a guard's grasp. In the confusion of running shadows and torchlight-punctured darkness, I followed Peter's large form and found James besides me. The Temple Guard were called back and did not pursue us.

The torches started to move away, back down the path towards the city. We all knew we had to follow.

"They will take out their revenge on him," said Peter. "Every humiliation they have suffered before the people will come out!"

"They must be taking him to the house of the High Priest," said James.

"We cannot get in there," said Peter. "It will be a rigged court, the family of the high priest, Shlomo, Uri and their like." His voice quivered with a fear that I had never heard from him before.

"There are others who can get in," said James. "We need Nicodemus and Joseph of Arimathea and any other friends we can find to argue for him."

"Go for them," said Peter. "I will follow the Lord." My brother hurried away.

"I may be able to get in," I mumbled. "Watch for me." The streets were still busy as pilgrims made their ways back to their dwellings; I pushed through them to catch up with the procession of torches. They led me not to the High Priest, but the house of his father-in-law. My father's standing and reputation with my best educated dialog would be my pass into this house. Fear seemed to have left me now, I had once promised my Messiah that I could drink from the same cup as him and he had told me that I could. I followed the arrest party into the inner rooms and, when I knew the layout, went back for Peter.

I hoped to pass Peter off as an acquaintance of my father, but he was not good at such subtleties and his accent was the cause of questions. I left him by the courtyard fire, protesting he was not involved in the Galilean revolt against the temple, and made my way back through the house. In the midst of priests, guards and servants, I was so alone. I was in the lion's den with my Messiah and yet I had no urge to run.

The interrogation began and my Messiah stood in the centre of the rigged court that Peter had predicted.

"I have spoken openly to the world," Jesus replied to their charges. "I always taught in synagogues or at the temple, where all the people come together. I said nothing in secret. Why question me? Ask those who heard me. They know what I said."

The scowls and sneers confirmed it was a reply they hated because these men could neither admit they had been there to hear my Lord themselves, nor dare to bring witnesses from the people that had adored the teaching and healings. I winced as they struck his face, but my Lord was unbowed in his reply. "If I said something wrong, testify as to what is wrong," he told them. "If I spoke the truth, why did you strike me?"

I made my way back to Peter. "This is not the full court, just a brutal softening-up process."

"Then they will take him to the High Priest next. This buys them time to gather the Sanhedrin after Passover. A secret plot so they can summon those who hate the Lord."

We followed again, through the streets and into the house of Caiaphas the High Priest, and through all the fake witnesses and false testimony, my Lord stood in mute condemnation of their proceedings. I knew it was his testimony against theirs, The Messiah did not recognise the authority of the court.

Frustration boiled over and the High Priest intervened from his throne. "Are you not going to answer? What is this testimony that these men are bringing against you?"

The silent repose remained, and I saw real fury rise in the High Priest's face as he pointed at his prisoner. "I charge you under oath by the living God: Tell us if you are the Messiah, the Son of God."

As the echoes of the charge ebbed away, I held my breath. Then I heard him speak, calm and clear, "Yes, it is as you say, in future you will see the Son of Man sitting at the right hand of the Mighty One and coming on the clouds of heaven."

All those times that he had told us not to reveal who he was flashed across my mind, and now my Lord had confirmed it to those who plotted to end his life.

With a cry that shattered the stillness, the High Priest tore his robes. "He has spoken blasphemy!" he raged. "Why do we need any more witnesses? Look, now you have heard the blasphemy. What do you think?"

"Death!" shouted Shlomo.

"Crucify!" proclaimed Uri.

"Death!" chorused the Sanhedrin. "He is worthy of death!"

Now the brutality really began. I slumped against the wall quaking with cold fear and shock, but I could not leave. My blindfolded Lord was being thrown around the room, as spittle and punches, insults and taunts rained upon him. "Prophesy to us, Messiah," the dulling blows landed. "Tell us, who hit you!"

It was then that I saw the face of Judas Iscariot across the room. It was colourless in horror, the expression of a man who realises he has made a huge miscalculation and was now a redundant observer in a situation out of his control.

I was numb, incapable of feeling any more.

The High Priest called his minions to heel, issuing orders, telling them the false Messiah and blasphemer must die that coming day in order that the city would have the Sabbath to calm down.

I left them plotting and dragged myself out of that room. I needed Peter; I needed his big fatherly steadfastness. I needed him to share my trauma; it was more than I could bear alone.

In the courtyard, an argument blazed around him as hot as the fire: the High Priest's men accusing, Simon Peter in vehement denial, cursing and swearing at them and at himself. I stood there trembling in helplessness, and then the arrest party emerged from the house with Jesus in their midst. Peter froze, his curses gagged in his throat at the sight of his Lord bloodied and bruised. I was sure that for a fleeting moment their eyes met and it was then that I heard the cock. Peter charged out of the courtyard and into the darkness. I knew what had happened. It was the last I saw of him on that night.

Now I was alone, so alone, the fire did not warm me.

The Chief Priests were giving instructions to the guard to take Jesus to the Prefect's Palace and plotting the case they would present. Judas Iscariot was trying to push himself into their midst, imploring, trying to reason with them, offering a money bag, telling them to let Jesus of Nazareth go as he was guilty of no crime. The money was refused, so Judas Iscariot emptied it onto the courtyard stones, where the silver coins bounced and rolled away. I watched as he tried to turn back time, to undo what could not now be undone. His deed of betrayal of innocent blood would now hang around his neck forever.

His confession of his sins was dismissed as his own responsibility and he, who had styled himself to be the astute operator, now knew he had been just a pawn in the game of others. He disappeared into the blackness; it was the last I saw of him on that night as well.

On that interminable night, truth and justice had no interest, the currency that mattered was power and I was powerless. What I felt then as I left the courtyard, I cannot tell you, it must have been desolation and emptiness, but I can only remember numb. Just numb.

Then a voice called my name and out of a shadow stepped the stocky figure of my partner in mission; he would now be my partner in grief. We embraced in silence. His brawny hug was crushing in its angst; the warmth of another human being was beautiful and comforting. We hurried through the dark and empty streets in the direction of the palace.

In the cold and grey beginnings of dawn, we could see The Prefect's Gate and wrapped our cloaks tight about us, sinking into the inky shadow behind a wall to watch the next episode of tragedy unfold before us.

"Pilate's spies will have told him of a Messiah and a threat to the Sanhedrin," whispered Simon.

The gate opened and legionaries stood around their Prefect for the priests to present their accusations. "We have found this man subverting our nation. He opposes payment of taxes to Caesar and claims to be Messiah, the one anointed by God, a king."

I watched as Pilate walked around my Lord, determined not to be hurried by the Sanhedrin's pressure. "Do you expect me to believe this miserable specimen of a man, this brutalised and emaciated peasant, is a threat to the might of Rome?"

"He has disturbed the whole of Jerusalem," countered the priests. "We cannot be responsible if the people are incited to riot!"

"Is he not the one that disturbed your temple?" Pilate's tone was mildly accusing. "He has turned over your tables, not mine."

"He is no friend of Caesar."

"I'm quite sure he's a loyal Jew." I now heard sarcasm and dismissive in Pilate voice. "May I assure mighty Caesar of your friendship, O noble priests?"

"You are no friend of Caesar if you set this man free! You have ended the rebellion of those that came before; we bring you this one for that same reason. Is that not loyalty?"

"Then why not show your true loyalty and deal with this peasant yourselves?"

"We have no right to kill a man."

"That didn't stop you killing that one called Zechariah between the temple and the altar," retorted Pilate.

Back in the shadows, we watched this cold duel fought over our Lord's life.

"He knows their game," Simon spat. "He cannot allow the Sanhedrin to make him a scapegoat for this!"

"He does not want to do their dirty work," I whispered in return. "But he will do what he has to do to keep the peace or it will be worse for him in Rome."

"He was defeated over those effigies of Caesar," hissed Simon. "Another defeat would be for Rome as well as him."

Now the priests really started to bully The Prefect, their strident voices carrying to us in the cold night air.

"You need our help to keep the peace!"

"There are over a million in Jerusalem, all expecting the Messiah and conquest!"

"Could you contain them without us?"

"You have one rebel leader already, he had only a few followers; this one has multitudes."

We listened as The Prefect continued to dismiss the charges and then, with a despising look, Pilate went back inside ordering his guard to bring the prisoner. I knew my Lord's fate hung in the balance and my heart hung there with him. Simon and I waited in agony and cold. Only where our torsos touched did there seem to be enough warmth for both of us, I was so cold without and within.

When Pilate emerged, we strained our ears to hear him. "I can find no basis for a charge against him," he told the Priests. "However, having found he is a Galilean, I will send him to Herod, as Galilee is his jurisdiction, not mine."

We stumbled on together, dodging down the alleys and over walls to keep sight of them, the next chilling act of the nightmare dragging us along also as its prisoners.

Once again, we were condemned to hide in the shadows and imagine the worst of what those of Herod's court, so exposed and humiliated in the temple just a few days earlier, were doing to our Lord.

When he reappeared, dragged between two of Herod's Guards, I could not see his face for the blood and the shape of a crude crown, a briar of thorns, which had been impaled into my Lord's scalp. Draped on his body was an elegant scarlet robe, a fake-royal cloak. My Lord was now a gift-wrapped offering from the puppet king, to the Roman Prefect.

A corner of my cloak was forced into my mouth as Simon stifled my sobs and whimpers, lest they revealed our hiding place. He held me tight, pulling my face into his shoulder, whilst burying his into mine. Pain, pain in my side, his fingers dug into my ribs, then I realised my fingers ached for the same reason. We both released and for a wordless moment regarded the shocked expression of the other. The sound of the solders faded down the street and we shambled after them.

7/. Judgement

There were no longer shadows to hide in. The city was waking as Pilate struggled to impose his authority over the Chief Priests, telling them Herod had returned the prisoner without charge.

My hopes rose, be it ever so little, but the men of the Sanhedrin knew only one word: "Crucify! Crucify!"

The Prefect tried again to dismiss his assailants. "You take him and crucify him; I find no basis for a charge against him."

The response was already prepared. "We have a law, and according to that law he must die, because he claims to be the Son of God."

We saw our Lord taken back inside, but the Chief Priests kept up the insistent barrage from the gate, shouting, "If you let this man go, you are no friend of Caesar. Anyone who claims to be a king opposes Caesar."

I cannot write the expletives that came from Simon at that time, and now it was for me to hold him back. I felt him shaking with rage as I dragged him away and we slumped down in the street where a small patch of early sunlight could warm us.

"What now?" I asked. "What will Pilate do?" I was too numb to think for myself.

"They will take the Lord to the Antonia. Remember, they have Barabbas already."

My brain started to function through the fog of shock that hemmed me in. "Pilate has two dangerous prisoners. He knows both have thousands of followers that could incite the people to riot."

Simon and I played out the scene before us that day. "So, he will calculate which is the greater danger to him and his legions."

"Yes, but his own pride and arrogance means he hates the corner the Sanhedrin have forced him into."

"To do their dirty work, those vermin." Again, Simon fell into a rage of the vernacular; I could feel anger building within him.

People were now starting to stream past us; news was spreading fast. The city was in the same fervour of speculation that we were.

"Come on!" I rose and pulled at Simon to follow. "The Praetorium. Pilate will take The Judgement Seat and offer a prisoner to the people."

"The Lord or Barabbas!"

"I know, Simon, but for the first time this night, I now feel as if I can do something, I can pray." I held his face in my hands, forcing his eyes to meet mine. "Will you pray with me that even now the people will see the Kingdom before them and they can choose their king?"

He said nothing, but nodded and his arm fell across my shoulders.

But we could not get near. The Temple Guard had erected a human barricade and their shields and spears threw us back. They did their work with cold efficiency, pushing people in the fringes, whilst at the front to make their voices heard were the Zealots, the Pharisees and Sadducees.

The scene was set, and an unholy alliance of freedom fighters and Sanhedrin called to the Prefect to fulfil the custom of the release of a Passover prisoner.

"Do you want me to release to you the King of the Jews?" responded Pilate.

"Away with this man! Crucify, Crucify!" the mob shouted. "Release Barabbas to us!"

"Why?" Pilate challenged them. "What crime has he committed?"

"Cru-ci-fy!" was the single raging torrent of an answer as the Zealots became a riotous mob, flinging dust towards the eyes of the Prefect's Guard as they moved forward to meet the angry uproar.

As Pilate washed his hands in final protest and withdrew, and Barabbas walked free into the crowd of cheering Zealots, all hope now drained from me. I looked at Simon. His jaw was jutted forward, his teeth and fists clenched, his eyes on Jesus as he was taken back inside.

Then by some miracle of the most appalling kind, Judas Iscariot stood before us.

"This is all wrong!" he blurted. "Why doesn't the Lord use his power? They could not lay a hand on him in Solomon's Colonnade. Their stones would not strike him. You told me how he walked through the mob at Nazareth! Why doesn't he do this now!?"

"So you had it all worked out, didn't you?" Simon snarled back in his face. "You, who always fancied yourself to be better than the rest of us. You, who tried to impress me with your educated speech. You, the great scheming politician that knew how to seize power from the Sanhedrin and Rome. You fomented this brew and it's exploded in your face. How are you going to build your kingdom now!?"

The veins in Simon's neck were bulging and his face coloured up as I held his muscular shoulders, trying to pull him away.

"It's not my fault if he doesn't use his power!" Judas Iscariot protested.

"You have betrayed the Messiah!" Simon yelled into his face. All the grief-trauma pent up inside him released and, shoving me aside, he flew at Judas Iscariot.

Judas was screaming and terrible animal noises came from Simon as I tried to pull him away. I was shouting for help to the crowd that circled us, and then strong arms pulled us all apart and we sat regarding each other in the dust and filth.

Great whoops of emotion came from Simon before he crumbed into helpless sobbing. "Forgive me, Lord! I have failed you!" Then he was gone, shoving his way through the crowd.

Judas looked horrendous. An eye was gouged, and an ear and mouth were torn, as blood flowed over the oiled beard and onto the torn and soiled robes. He held a hand of crushed and broken fingers. "Didn't use his power, not my fault!" he gibbered, and then he was also gone.

I lay there alone; once again, I was so alone. How long I lay there I cannot tell, but the crowd moved away and left me. The Praetorium was emptying, the final scene would move to the place of the skull. I could not yet escape; I still needed to be with my Messiah.

At the gate of the Antonia I found the women, those faithful souls who had provided for us at the height of our mission, still faithful as they huddled in shared grief.

Around us was a baying wolf pack, relatives of the victims of criminals also due for crucifixion that day, mixed with vengeful Pharisees. A great howl went up as the gate opened and the execution party came into view, the legionaries driving the mob back with the jabbing butts of their spears.

My Lord had been scourged, his flesh in tatters. He collapsed and again I heard him as he wept for Jerusalem. We came to the place; as the hammer blows drove the great spikes through flesh and bone, I felt every tortured scream driven through my guts. The great crosses were hoisted upright and dropped into their stands, bringing cries of agony as the crucified bounced on the spikes, tearing the holes larger in hand and foot.

It was then I saw her. She looked so small and frail, so trembling, and about to break. Mary, mother of Jesus, crushed with grief. I wanted to run, anything but to look into those tortured eyes, but we were prisoners of the moment together.

"A sword." It was all she would say. "The angel, he told me a sword would piece my heart also."

Then, my Lord spoke to me for the last time that day, and told me to take his mother away as my own. It was then I saw my own mother. How long she had been there, I could not tell. For a moment, her hollow eyes met mine and then she joined the other women, gathered around Mary, forcing her to leave.

Finally, I was released; he had given me permission to leave him. Even then, there was no light. I had returned to the night, within and without darkness, and cold was growing around me. The mob were pausing from their abuse of the crucified to gaze bemused at a darkening sky as it hid the midday sun.

It made no difference to me. My night would never end.

King of Heaven and Hell

1/. Earthquake

My emotions were already deceased and there was no reason for the rest of me to remain living. That Sabbath was the most wretched day of my life, alone with Peter, back in the upper room now barren, bereaved, bereft.

Peter was a broken man. Thrashing around in his nightmare of personal failure, he kept recounting the moment when Jesus' eyes had met his own as the cock crowed. When awake, he tore his clothes, when he slept, he thrashed about and cried out like some of the demoniacs that Jesus had healed. I was sure he was close to complete mental breakdown.

Perhaps the reason I could stay with Peter and not go mad myself was that my own numbness remained. I had also lost any feeling of belonging; I had lost all feeling. I knew Father and Mother were within a Sabbath's walk, but I had no desire to see anyone.

All that day I ate and drank nothing, but lived on the four years that I had known him. I had been part of demonstrating the reality of His Kingdom with miracles, and now my mission had gone; its king insulted with a thorny crown and killed in the cruellest way imaginable. The Messiah, the hope of the nation, foretold by the prophets, awaited for hundreds of years, the power and grace I had lived with, was gone.

Nothing remained. My mind went over that nothing for the thousandth time and found a great emptiness, a gaping hole in heart and mind numbed by shock and grief. It was a grief from which I had no hope of recovery. Peter and I were together in this one thing, like me his night would never end.

Outside I could hear the muted sounds of the city at Sabbath, restoring normality and order. Once the Sabbath was over, the future of the Twelve would be short. We would be rounded up and the wrath of the Sanhedrin would fall upon us. Death or exile?

Even if we were spared, there was no escape. What future did I have, anyway? Could I ever go back to what I was before, back to the nation I was no longer part of? I had shaken their dust from my feet.

I had lost my life with my Lord.

As that Sabbath ended, Peter and I fell into fitful snatches of sleep once again. I saw many hours through that night. As the dawn cracked across the grey sky, I felt a little giddy. The floor moved under my body and for a few seconds the earth continued to move and rumble before it quietened again. Outside was a hubbub of voices and some screams as I made my way to a window. The walls and towers of Jerusalem were still standing.

I sat again and watched the first rays of dawn start to lighten the room. What would the day bring and how could I face it? Peter said nothing.

Something hit the outside door, a voice was calling and fists beating. I stiffened in fear before realising it was not the heavy pounding of the guard, but the lighter more frantic beating of small hands, and the voice was a woman's voice, a voice I knew. It was Mary Magdalene. As I opened the door, Mary fell onto the floor at my feet, her hands still beating their frantic tattoo. She twisted her head upwards, words coming with great gasps of breathlessness emotion.

"The Lord … Lord's tomb … stone … rolled away … body gone … not there! Angels … said he's risen … He's gone … not there!"

Peter was beside me now and the other women were straggling up the street, in the same state as Mary.

"Where?" demanded Peter.

"Legionaries … ran past us … like rabbits … in fright." Mary's story still tumbled out.

"Where?" demanded Peter and I together.

Mary pointed and gasped out the name of the city gate and the place of Arimathea's tomb. Peter set off without another word and I followed, running past the other women, bare feet pounding on the hard stone pavements, out through the gate and on. I fell more than once but hardly noticed it and ran ahead, leaving Peter to wheeze his large frame in pursuit.

My lungs gasped at air as my feet sped across the grass and into the garden of tombs and then, faced with the black opening and discarded Roman weapons, I stopped.

The garden was peaceful and undisturbed now, what had happened here? Once again, I was alone and afraid of what I would find, afraid of what I would not find. I needed Peter now. He lumbered up, passed me without a glance and entered where the great stone had been rolled away. I followed him into the cool dampness, where the heavy breath streamed out of our mouths and echoed off the walls. I did not dare reach out into the darkness, not knowing what I might touch, but stood still as my eyes began to adjust to the darkness.

"The grave clothes! Peter, do you see them? Look how they are folded." My excitement was rising within me. "Look Peter, look. No grave robber would have gone to such trouble, neither would the soldiers!"

"I see them. So tell me, what does this mean? Where is the Lord now?"

"I can believe. I can believe a miracle has happened here, like so many we have seen before."

"Maybe," said Peter. "Maybe." After a few moments more, he moved back through the entrance to the sunlight outside. "Maybe," he said again. "That makes no difference to me now!"

"How can you say that?!" I protested. "If he's alive, the mission will go on! Think what it would mean!"

Peter turned and began to walk away. "It will be fine for you; you can carry on with him. I cannot. There is no place for me in the Kingdom of God. I promised him my life and failed. When it came to the choice, I denied I even knew his name; it can never be the same for me."

I followed, protesting. "Peter, we all failed him. We scattered like sheep and left him in his hour of need and what is more, he knew we would. We all share that guilt!"

"Not like me," Peter replied. "You didn't promise like I did, you didn't deny like I did. He didn't look in your eyes as the cock crowed like he looked at me."

I stood and watched Peter's back as he trudged away. I had nothing more to offer him. I needed to remain in the garden; it had offered me hope.

The early morning sunlight warmed me and I noticed the birdsong, I couldn't remember the last time I had heard it. I turned back a little way, looked at the Roman spear and shield lying there, thinking through the morning's events beginning from the earthquake. I regarded the open tomb and the darkness within, for a few fleeting moments I thought I saw Freedom, my stallion, standing there. Was I hallucinating due to exhaustion, or had a still small voice spoken a shaft of light into my abyss?

A voice called my name. It was Mary Magdalene also returning and, like me, lingering in hope. We could not be together for long – understand that in my culture this is not possible. She looked at me, eyes examining me from beneath her veil.

"Do you believe me, John bar Zebedee?" she demanded.

"Yes, your testimony is good," I reassured her. "I saw the others coming up the street; do they follow you here now?"

"No, they have gone to Bethany and to seek out the others. What will you do now?"

"I need to go to my family," I told her. "I need to share this as well; I need other people to believe with me."

She nodded understanding. We wished each other the Lord's blessing and parted.

I walked slowly in contemplation at first, and then my steps grew faster. I needed to see my family. I dared not think they would not be at the house and the relief of finding them, Father, Mother, James and Simon as well, was too much for me. I collapsed into their embrace and let the trauma of the past two days and nights drown me in its emotional dungeon depths, only now to send me soaring to speculative heights. I would challenge any man to live through what I had done and not do the same. Father, James and Simon took turns to hold me through the helpless quaking with my head in my hands, endless cups of hot sweet tea and many attempts to speak. Simon filled in many parts for me and then found the freedom to confess his assault on Judas Iscariot. After several hours, I could make sense to myself and to my family and I could re-enter their world.

In the silence, as Simon and I ended our account of the Passover night and crucifixion, I looked at Father.

"John," he began, and cleared the emotion from his throat more than once. "John, the last time you came here, you asked me a question I could not answer, because I dared not contemplate its meaning. You asked me why The Lord was making such constant references to his own death."

He paused, holding himself, before he could speak again. "I could not answer, but now I will try. Although, as the Lord lives, it is a mystery I cannot yet fathom. After that evening with Rabbi Benjamin, I could not rest until I knew the reason for his distress. He resisted at first, but in the end he took me to Elijah's scroll and the verses that tell us, 'He was pieced for our transgressions, he was wounded for our iniquities. The chastisement for our peace was upon Him and by his stripes we are healed.'"

Father paused for breath, the lines of emotion etched across his face, before he could continue. "Benjamin had understood that The Lord would be our Passover lamb, spotless and perfect. It was his destiny to break the curse of Eden. It is as if we … we ate his flesh and drank his blood, to free us from its slavery."

We all sat, unmoving. I think it was for a long time.

In the silence, I relived the evening of the Passover Seder in every joyous and agonising detail.

Was it only three days past?

Later, James asked, "What should we do now?"

"I think you should all gather at the room where you shared the Passover," said Father. "The women are already about this task, to find the others. And then you must wait."

2/. Beyond Belief

The room was filled with brooding disbelief rather than the spark of hope that I yearned for.

I thought of the women, their breathless excitement and hope that had filled their eyes, but all I could feel was the weight of the mood of my companions against me. I wanted to take each of them by the hand and beseech them to believe that anything was possible with the Lord, yet I had neither the will nor the emotional energy to confront their wall of despair. Like me, each had been through their own nightmare in the past three days; their belief had been shattered, now to be required of them again.

We were brought together by the absence of any other alternative, yet the reality was beyond belief. Our ever-hospitable host had left some food, but no one was touching it.

Returning to this room also meant that I had to face Peter, but now I found him changed again, still disturbed but now alert and sitting bolt upright with his back to the wall. All he would say was, "I have seen him. He was here. The Lord was here."

It grated with the others.

Andrew, full of anguish for his brother, asked me if I thought this was an hallucination brought on by his state of mind and lack of sleep.

Nathanael and Philip were the last to arrive; no one had been able to find Thomas.

"Did you bar the door behind you?" demanded Bartholomew.

"Yes, yes," came the terse reply.

"Where are the others, will they follow and reveal where we are?" asked Matthew.

"The others are scattered. Some are already leaving the city. They have their own problems," said Nathanael.

"And we have all come here in our twos and threes," affirmed Bartholomew.

"Why are we here, what are we hoping for?" demanded Philip again.

"Peter and my brother have seen the empty grave, as have the women," said James.

"The Sanhedrin is already peddling the story that we are the grave robbers! I have heard it!" exclaimed Matthew.

"The guard had discarded their weapons as they fled," I said. "I was the first there after the women."

"It makes no sense, why would any man go through with such a fate when it was in the Lord's power to avoid it?" said James bar Alpheus.

"He gave us many warnings that he would be handed over and killed," my brother reminded us all.

"Are you saying that the Lord God willed this for His Messiah?" asked Nathanael.

"He prayed this in Gesthemene," Peter spoke from the other end of the room. "For his father's will be done and not his own!"

"Then how will his Messiah reign forever?" Nathanael bit back.

"My father had the word of Isaiah from our Rabbi," I said. "'He will be pieced for our transgressions and crushed for our iniquities.'"

"Then I need your father to come and explain this for us," came the reply.

I felt cowed; they were all under the strain to believe what they wanted to believe. It held us all in its grip.

Every one of us started at the sound of hammering on the outer door. It was not a woman's fist this time, but a heavy man's fist, then two. Then all relaxed in relief, the voices were familiar.

"Cleopas and Amos!" exclaimed Nathanael. "They were leaving the city the last I saw of them."

Andrew and Simon hurried downstairs and then reappeared, each almost carrying the gasping and exhausted pair back with them. Their news poured forth in breathless chaos before they had even slumped onto the floor.

"We have walked and talked with the Lord!"

"He broke bread before us."

"Then he disappeared."

"We did not recognise him at first, as he walked with us."

The sentences became longer as they both regained some breath.

"At first he was but a stranger who knew nothing of Jerusalem in these past days, asking us to explain our forlorn."

"And then he told us we were simple and slow in belief not to know the Lord's Messiah would rise from the dead."

"Then he expounded every scripture I have ever heard."

"All of Moses and the prophets."

"Yes, all of those that testify of the Messiah."

"Our hearts were bursting within us!"

"The miles seemed to pass so easily under our feet then!" finished Amos.

"Where did you break bread?" my brother asked.

"Emmaus, we had stopped for the night," replied Cleopas. "We asked him to stay, though we still did not know it was him at that time."

"He was going on alone," said Amos. "We persuaded him to stay and talk more with us."

"It was then, as we reclined at the table and he gave thanks and broke the bread, that we saw him for the first time."

"But then he disappeared from his place."

"You have run the seven miles back from Emmaus at this hour of night?" asked Nathanael.

"If my heart fails me now, I believe in the resurrection!" returned Cleopas with a radiant smile.

It was then that the light in the room seemed to change. All of us looked around. There was another figure amongst us, and then his familiar voice said, "Peace be with you."

We were all frozen in time and space.

"Don't be worried," he almost chuckled, and I saw that easy smile that I had always loved and known him by since the start. "Why do I look into your eyes and see all these doubts rise in your hearts? Look at my hands and feet and let your eyes believe what they see. It is me as you have always known me."

He started to move amongst us. "Touch me and see. A spirit does not have flesh and bones, as you see I have."

I reached for his hand; I wanted this moment to last forever. The hand was warm and the skin was soft, the calluses that had been there were gone, only the scar of the great spike remained. I closed my eyes and put my forehead against his chest. It was warm. The robes were new and fresh. The embalming oil was gone. I felt the heartbeat; it was life, and it was human. He was my Messiah. It was an incalculable mystery.

Nobody had yet spoken and now my Lord smiled a winsome smile and almost tut-tutted at us all.

"Have you any food here?" he asked.

I cannot remember who proffered the piece of broiled fish and honeycomb, but he reclined and ate it in that ordinary way that he always had.

I studied him. He was different. It was not just that when I had last seen him he was caked in dried blood. He was altogether different; the strain lines that had built up these past four years had gone from his face, the straggling grey hairs had also disappeared, and his head and face were full with sleek hair and beard. When my forehead had been on his chest, there was smooth muscle laced across the bones, not the emaciated gauntness I had seen pinned to the great beam of the cross. My Messiah was not just alive; he was restored.

"Where is Thomas the twin?" he asked us. "You should find him so that you are all together, and I can talk with you all again about what the scriptures say and how it had to be this way for me. Why did you not believe the reports of the women? Their testimony agreed with each other and with the empty grave, did it not?"

Then, having delivered this rebuke, he smiled and said to us all again, "Peace be with you! As the Father has sent me so I am sending you." Walking amongst, us he acted out a small piece of theatre, breathing on us and saying, "Receive the Holy Spirit. If you forgive anyone his sins, they are forgiven; if you do not forgive them, they are retained."

As Jesus came to Peter, a strangled gasp came from somewhere deep within him. Peter held a trembling hand out in front of his face, as if Jesus was a fearful beast that needed to be kept at bay. Jesus beckoned him to come. “Peace be with you.”

At that moment, Peter was anything but peaceful. He seemed like a man being drawn inexorably to his doom, as with his arms still held out in front of him and uttering unnatural speech, his steps were as if in slow motion.

Jesus held his hands and told him, “I will go ahead of you into Galilee. Meet me there, Simon.”

With that, he wished us God’s blessing and departed from his place. The room seemed to me a little dimmer, but as if his peace now pervaded the whole house like a gentle music. We all reclined, talking in little quiet groups, as if afraid to break it. Surreal; it was still beyond belief, and yet I could believe.

Much later, I found a rooftop and tried to think about the consequences of my Lord no longer being held within the boundaries of normal time and space, but it seemed that those thoughts could wait for another day. After three tortuous nights of sleeplessness, the slumber I now fell into was deep and blessed, without a dream or image of the previous horrors.

3/. Breakfast on the Beach

"Galilee, why did we have to come back … t-to Galilee?" Thomas asked us all. "The Kingdom must come first to Jerusalem; then it can spread across the world."

Nathanael threw a stone into the lake. "For all we know, he may be clearing the temple out again right now," he speculated.

"Maybe, but I think not," replied my brother. "Everything he has done, since he first said 'follow me', has been to train us in the ways of the Kingdom. I feel sure we must wait for that next stage."

"I think we all needed a little time to recover from that Passover week," said Cleopas.

I watched the wind blow ripples across the lake's surface, enjoying its springtime warmth as I always had done, and reflected on the past two weeks since the emotion of that first resurrection Sunday. I felt just as delirious now as I had then.

"I was in a nightmare that would never end," I said. "Now I am in a dream that I never want to end."

"It is a strange feeling, this 'being back home'," said Andrew. "These last four years home has been wherever The Lord was."

"All my surroundings are familiar and yet somehow still foreign," said my brother.

"I remembered what you told me that day we walked away from the boats," I said. "We would never be the same again."

"He set me apart for the Kingdom," said Matthew. "I will be an alien in my own land, unless I can win my land for the Kingdom."

Matthew was right; there was a feeling of unfinished business in the air as we waited for Jesus to make his next move.

Peter was, as usual, restless without anything to do, and paced the harbour wall, mending nets and hanging them in the sun. It was the Simon-Peter I had always known. Whilst others were content just to talk and share the memories of all they had seen and done with Jesus, Peter needed more than memories.

It did not surprise any of us that after brooding for most of the morning, he announced he was going fishing. We all agreed to join him; it would be good to be back on the lake together, with more memories of our Lord. I was also grateful to spend the afternoon preparing the boats and nets, the torches and the oil, slipping easily back into the old routines. Then, as the dusk of the day fell around us, we pushed the boats off and set out for a night's fishing.

All night we sailed and rowed calm waters, casting the nets, searching for the shoals of fish. We refuelled the torches and hung them over the sides, cast the nets again and drifted along, pulling the net so that it would draw around anything in the cool, dark depths.

All would have been good, except that we did not catch anything all night and as the dawn came, Peter let out a long sigh to tell everyone that his frustration was now reaching new heights. He pulled in the net one last time and without sight of a fish, we made for the shore.

The spring morning was breaking with clear skies and the Lord God's creation sang to me as I had never heard before. In a few moments, the rising sun would burst out from behind the huge mass of the Golan to warm us. To the north, I could see the snow-capped mountains of Lebanon.

It was still too early for many people to be out and about, but as we neared the shore, a man called out to us, his voice clear across the still water. "Friends, haven't you any fish?"

"No," we answered back in chorus.

"Go away," muttered Peter. "There are no free breakfasts to be had here."

The man called again. "Throw your net on the right side of the boat and you will find some."

For a moment, no one moved, and then Peter stood. James joined him and they gathered the net out of the bottom of the boat so as to cast it out once more. No one asked 'why are we listening to this stranger?' For some reason, at that moment, it just seemed a natural thing to do.

The net fell in a good, wide arc and, as Peter and James started to haul it back in, the ropes went taut. I also grabbed a rope and others followed, but the weight was too much.

One look told me that Peter was in the same place as me, we were transported back to that summer morning almost three years ago when Jesus had finished his preaching and asked Peter to put out to deep water.

"It is The Lord!" I said. Peter was already ahead of me, the boat rocking from his flying leap. James and Nathanael took the oars and rowed after him, towing the net full of fish.

As we reached the beach, the delicious smell of the fire with baking bread caught my nostrils.

"Bring some of the fish you have just caught," the young man said to us.

He was different again. Our eyes darted at each other, asking the same unspoken question that could be read on all our faces. 'Who is this? Is it him?' No one dared say it, because really, we knew it was the Lord. I studied him to work out what had changed and realised that he was younger than when I had last seen him. I was now looking at a man not much more than my own age.

He took the bread and the fish, gave thanks, broke it and shared it as he had always done. I was being served a banquet by the King himself, who sat beside me and talked about how there was nothing like fresh, hot bread and fresh fish for breakfast, on an open beach, with a clear spring morning, as reward for a long night's fishing.

As we finished eating, Jesus said, "Simon son of Jonah, do you truly love me more than these?"

"Yes, Lord. You know that I love you."

"Feed my lambs," came the reply.

Simon had returned to being 'son of Jonah, the fisherman'. I knew there must be more to come.

Three times Jesus asked Simon Peter for his love and on the third time, he said it with a word for love that, in my language, is a bond that can never be repaid, a love that could not be deserved, as only a Father could have for his creation.

Peter flinched' I knew the reason. For each of his three denials, there had been a demand for commitment, each stronger than the previous one. Peter groaned and raised his arms and let them fall again as he said, "Lord, you know all things; you know that I love you."

Jesus looked at him with his steady gaze. "Feed my sheep." Then he continued, "I tell you the truth, when you were younger you dressed yourself and went where you wanted, but when you are old, you will stretch out your hands, and someone else will dress you and lead you where you do not want to go."

I put an arm across the shoulders of my big friend, not so much to comfort him but to congratulate him. "We came to Galilee for restoration; it was the same for me at Yom Kippur."

Then Jesus stood and said to Peter that simple phrase that he had said those three years ago. "Follow me."

I followed, too. Although I knew my jealousy was wrong, I needed every moment. I knew the time was coming for my Messiah to leave me as he had always said.

For a moment they turned to look at me, but then continued and I kept a respectful distance.

4/. Close and Personal

In due course, my time also came. We walked together, my Messiah and me, to a quieter place where we could sit with our backs to the trunk of an ancient olive tree and enjoy its shade as the day's temperature rose. I had to know everything. What had Pilate said to him? What had he endured in Herod's court? All the traumatic details, I had to know what he had been through.

"Lord, why did it have to be this way?" I said. "Why could you not just restore the Kingdom to Israel?"

"Are you asking why I could not be declared king in a temple or palace instead of having it declared above my head on the cross?"

I paused to take that in. "Lord, the world needs to see your glory to believe in you, so it is better for you to be king in the temple."

"Yes, you are not wrong, but for two days the world could see my glory in the temple. It was not the glory the world expects."

"So you will go there again, for the all the world to see?"

"Things must happen in their prescribed order. First, I had to humble myself to the powers of this world, in order that I could triumph over them and over death itself. With God, it must always be this way. Do you remember how the scriptures say that Moses was the most humble man in the world?"

I nodded.

"And how David admitted his adultery with Bathsheba, instead of using his power to cover their shame?" His eyes left me for the distant horizons. "When we first met, I told you that I was in weakness. Can you believe that now I am in strength?"

"Yes, Lord."

"The way to be a leader in the Kingdom of God is to be a servant first. I have told you this many times, with the instruction to deny yourself and take up your cross. This was the way of The Immerser that you saw in the desert before me, the way I had to follow and the way you must follow too."

"Yes, Lord," I said. "I know it must be this way for me."

After a while of silence, I dared another question. "Lord, if you were not in the tomb, where were you for those days of … of your death?"

"I descended into hell, to preach to the spirits in prison there. This was also part of my mission."

I shuddered with cold. "Lord, what is…"

"What is hell like? Is that what you want to know, John?" he finished the question for me.

"Lord, I want to know what you went through, because I think I understand that you went through it for me."

"For you and for every part of the Lord God's creation; the thorns grew from the curse of Eden, so I had to bear them to redeem the dust of the earth itself." He gestured his hand at the fields in front of us. "Do you see this world, John? We see good and evil, all mixed together every day, do we not? Some men always lust for riches and power, others are more worthy and seek truth and justice. Rulers and authorities may be far from perfect, but without them to enforce law, all would be disorder, would it not?"

I nodded.

"All the kingdoms of the world will strive and will endure for their time. One day Rome will demise to settle in its own dust. But there is one kingdom that cannot be allowed to prevail, a kingdom that would swallow all of the others if it could. Its ruler once offered them all to me in a grand deception."

I looked at him, as his freckled youthful visage gazed into the distance, and asked, "Your adversary in the desert, Lord?"

He nodded. "The Lord God is winning his creation back to himself, at all costs."

"Lord, were you that cost?"

"John, I want you to imagine this world with only the evil and with nothing of good, no rule of law, no justice, just disease, corruption and chaos."

"That's not easy, Lord, but I'll try my best."

"Now think about how this world was in the beginning. Before the disobedience of Adam and Eve, man did not need to work the land for it to bear its crops; he did not battle with thorns and thistles like he does now."

"But Lord, even now the Lord God still blesses and sustains this world," I said. "The sunshine and rain falls on the righteous and the unrighteous alike, in order that the land bears its crops."

"Yes indeed, but now imagine a place where God did not do his sustaining work, a place where he could not, because all evil and sin had been given to that place." He paused for me to consider this, much as my father would have done. "Imagine a place where the crops grow weak without water or light, strangled by the thorns. Then, they are taken away before the eyes of the people, devoured by beetle and locust. The people themselves slowly decaying with eternal pestilence."

I nodded, that I was following his pictures.

"A place without law, and without anything to sustain it. There all existence would be forever diminishing, fading away and yet never reducing to absolute nothing."

I looked at him, trying to take all his words into my consciousness.

"Now, imagine the dwellers of that wretched place, having once known another place that they had lost. In that other place, they could have made a simple decision to live their lives in a different and better way, in the way of humility and justice that we just spoke of. Having failed to make that decision, they saw fellows who had made a different choice leave for a place of eternal blessing, more than they had ever known. The lost, having made the choice against their God, got their wish and entered the place where God could not be."

"Is that hell, Lord?"

"In such a place, those people linger in hopeless and eternal torment, knowing they were but that one choice away from the place of eternal blessing; the Lord God's total sustaining presence, just as it was in Eden, when man would walk and talk with his creator."

"Yes, Lord," I said. "Yes, that would be hell indeed."

"Man was designed in God's image, to live. You once asked me how I could walk before God and be perfect."

"Lord, I understand why Rabbi Benjamin wept. The sacrifice needed to be without spot or blemish." I began to tremble, and he put an arm across my shoulders.

"Tell me of any fears you have, John, we are here to talk about these things together. Anything you need to know."

A gentle silence continued between us for a few moments.

"Lord?" I said.

"Yes, John?"

"You will be going back to your father soon, won't you?"

"Yes, I must go."

"But you will return to redeem the earth, the very dust, as you said?"

"The day will come when no man shakes the foreign dust from their sandals, because all lands will be blessed."

"On that day, will the Lord's Messiah reign for all people to see? When will this be, Lord?"

"It is as I told Benjamin. My destiny is only what my Father has willed for me," he said. "I am called to walk before the Lord God and be perfect."

"And you have called me to follow first and understand second," I sighed, "as knowledge can be a heavy burden to bear."

"Yes, John. I ask you to follow still. The Lord God is redeeming all things to himself. In those days the dust will no longer yield thorns and thistles, from the labours of man. The Tree of Life will grow in abundance; its leaves for the healing of the nations."

I nodded.

"But right now," he said, with a certain finality, "it is time for us to return to Jerusalem."

5/. 'Til Death Us Do Restore

As we walked, we recounted to each other and to ourselves all those memories of the last four years: the power and grace; the wonderment; the experience that had defined our lives.

It was as we approached Jerusalem that Jesus came to us again, joining our chatter, the joy and the laughter of friends together, without the masses that had always been there before.

We visited Bethany to share a little time with Martha, Mary and Lazarus, and many of the wider group of disciples found us there. Then he led us all on up the slopes of the Mount of Olives, with its panorama over the city. I knew the time of parting was near, yet now I did not fear it.

As we looked out over Jerusalem, the question we had asked him so many times came forward again: "Lord, are you at this time going to restore the Kingdom to Israel?"

Desire and Expectation cantered towards me.

He smiled that relaxed smile for us all and, with the merest of rebukes in his tone, told us again, "It is not for you to know the times or dates the Father has set by his own authority."

We had to wait, Power would come and the Freedom of his spirit.

They also cantered towards me; I knew that I would ride them to the ends of the earth.

He did not disappear this time; I think it was gentler for our sakes. Still giving assurances and blessings, he was taken up and away.

I walked forward; some reached out after him, and others fell to their knees, as his shape grew smaller.

Two dazzling figures had joined our throng, asking why we stood looking into the sky. Then, in a whirl of dazzle they were also gone and we stood, as no one wanted to disturb that moment.

For how long I cannot tell you, but it was Peter who broke the silence. "I need you to help me understand one more matter of the Kingdom."

We all looked at him and waited for the question.

"Where will this Kingdom be now that the King has returned to his heavenly Kingdom?"

"I think this Kingdom has no borders or boundaries," said Nathanael. "It will be wherever we make it."

"Do you remember he once told us that it was inside us?" said Andrew.

"Yes, so he did," replied Philip.

"We have seen a world that wanted to recruit our Lord into its factions and claim him for their own kingdoms," said my brother.

"He told us to always be as one," said Bartholomew. "One day he will end all those factions."

"The Law of his Kingdom endures," said Thomas. "Until the world itself endures no longer and has no … f- further need of it."

"He invited me to join the Kingdom and I did," said Matthew. "I am still a Jew, but now I am more than that, and in my heart I am still ready to follow my king to where he has gone. In one sense, I am already there. I am still part of that Kingdom and my Messiah has commanded me to invite others as he invited me."

There was a murmur of agreement to Matthew's words.

"Yes, we are in the Kingdom now, but not yet fully as it one day will be," I said.

"Then tell me, will this land of our forefathers still have the Lord's blessing in its place amongst the foreign dust?" asked Peter. "Will the Kingdom ever be fully established on our blessed land?"

"Yes Peter, I am sure of it," said James. "The Lord has fulfilled many prophecies, but there are still others to come. One day, at the time we are forbidden to know, he will ride in to take his throne."

"How will it be?" some of the others asked. "Tell us how it will be."

After a pause, my brother said, "John, do you remember what old Benjamin of Bethsaida used to teach us about his favourite verses from the scrolls of Ezekiel: the Glory of the Lord returning to the temple?"

"Tells us, sons of Zebedee," Peter said with a warm smile. "We were not all good at our studies as young boys; tell us how it will be."

"It is early in Ezekiel's visions that he sees the Glory of the Lord leave the Holy of Holies and move to the threshold of the temple," said James. "Then a little later, the Glory leaves the temple threshold and moves to the east gate of the temple, before it moves on again and leaves the city altogether and goes to the mountain on the east of Jerusalem."

"Which is where we now stand," said Peter.

They all nodded at the significance of this place where we had spent much time.

"Then almost at the end of Ezekiel's scrolls," I continued, "the Glory returns from the mountain of the east to take its place again in the centre of the temple."

"It is as the angels told us, then," said Peter. "He will return in the same way as he departed."

"But do we still wait for Elijah to come first, to herald his return?" asked Philip.

"The Immerser was of the spirit of Elijah," I said. "But he was just a foreshadow of the day when the true Elijah will appear once again, just as the Kingdom is also a foreshadow of the Kingdom that he will bring with him one day, in all its fullness."

"I have seen Elijah, with Moses. It terrified me at that time," Peter told us all.

We all turned to look at the sky again. It was too fantastic to be true, and I knew it was still beyond belief for some who stood there with me.

In those moments, I said no more. The time would come to share what my Messiah had shared with me, but right then, I kept it to myself, like a naughty child with a secret present. After all, I told myself, knowledge can be a heavy burden to bear!

After a further time of stillness, Peter brought us all back to the present. "That is all I need to know," he said. "He has sent us out again. Once it was just us, the Twelve; then it was the seventy-two, now we are sent to the world."

Andrew said, "John and I heard The Immerser when he said 'He that comes after me will baptise with the Holy Spirit', and we have now been told to wait in the city until we receive this Holy Spirit."

Someone asked, "Why did he never marry and leave a succession?"

"He left us as his succession," came a reply.

"Yes I know, but why not leave a blood heir for the Kingdom?"

"There would inevitably be competition for a blood succession," answered my brother, "as there was after King David himself."

"Yes, it would take us back to what Moses had to do in the desert," confirmed Thomas.

"There is no law against royal succession, Thomas," said Peter.

"No, indeed," said Thomas with much gravity. "It will amaze you that, for once, I do not talk of law … b-but of nationhood. We were but a … t-tribal society until Moses sat as judge to end the cycles of blood revenge and give birth to the nation."

Peter sighed. "Thomas, your insight is a truly wonderful blessing."

It was as we started to walk down the slope I heard them come over the crest behind me, the hoof-beats in unison, the harnesses jangled, the chariot wheels rumbled on the ground: my four stallions were ready for their work. They drew up beside me, tossed their heads and snorted in welcome. They were, like my Lord, different from how they had been. Desire was calmer and more measured, no longer champing his bit, though Expectancy was still ready to lead them on to new horizons. Power was a yearling, a colt dancing before me on gangling legs. Then there was Freedom, sleek and lithe. I walked along the row and stroked their necks as they nuzzled me, jealous for my attention. I stood in the centre, looking down the great shaft to where it joined the chariot. I thought of the ride I had endured so far, the exhilarating, stomach-churning, gut-wrenching, white-knuckled ride with my Messiah.

"Freedom," I said. "You did come at Passover, like I knew you must." In reply, he blew horsey breath down his nostrils at me.

It was only now that I truly realised there was no way back for me. Whatever the future held, my life was no longer mine alone. I walked around, letting my fingers run along Freedom's smooth flanks and then swung myself up into the chariot.

I grasped the reins with both hands.

Appendix 1

Timeline – the four Passovers and events of Jesus' ministry

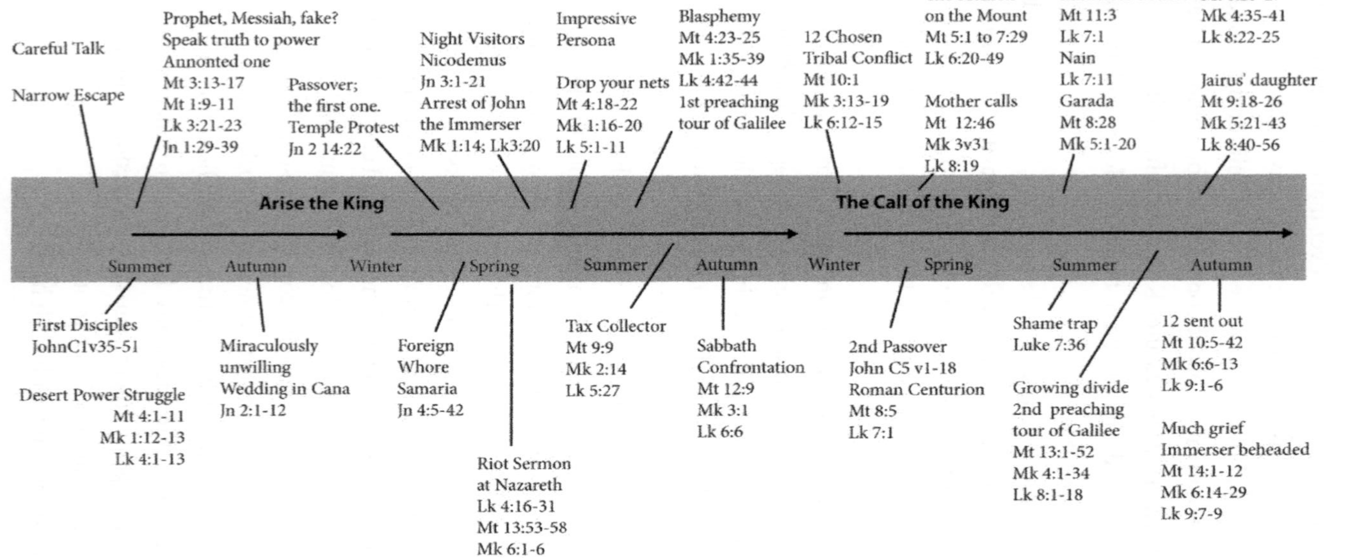

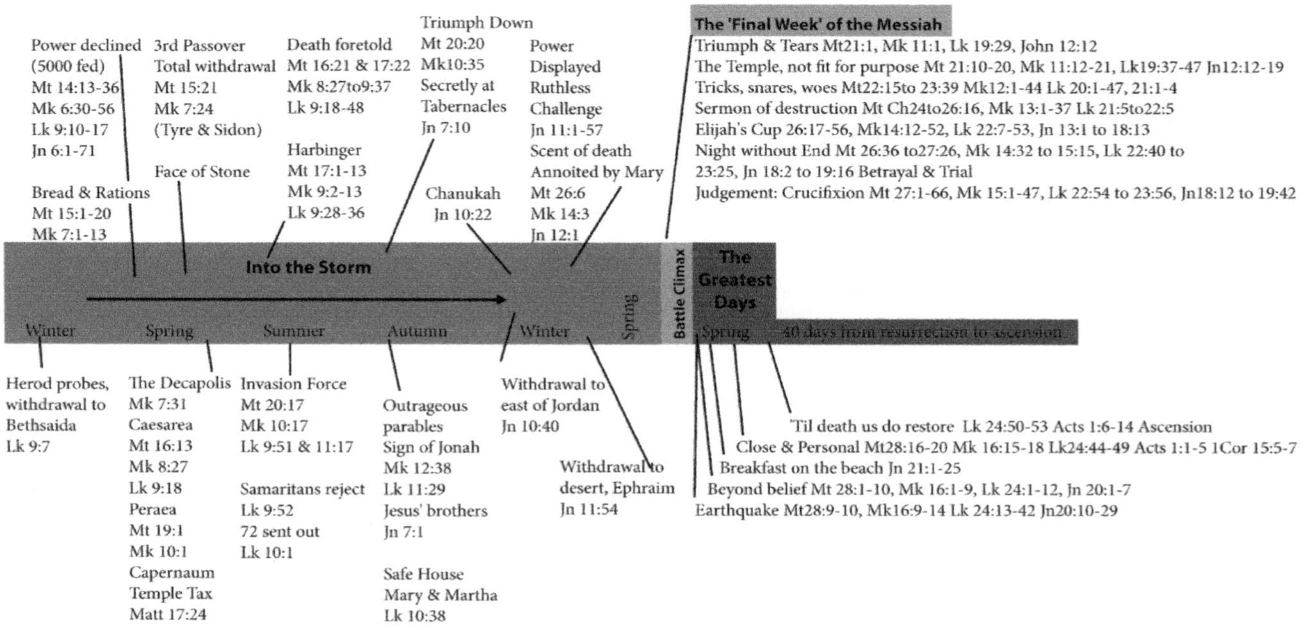

Power declined
(5000 fed)
Mt 14:13-36
Mk 6:30-56
Lk 9:10-17
Jn 6:1-71

Bread & Rations
Mt 15:1-20
Mk 7:1-13

3rd Passover
Total withdrawal
Mt 15:21
Mk 7:24
(Tyre & Sidon)

Face of Stone

Death foretold
Mt 16:21 & 17:22
Mk 8:27to9:37
Lk 9:18-48

Harbinger
Mt 17:1-13
Mk 9:2-13
Lk 9:28-36

Triumph Down
Mt 20:20
Mk10:35
Secretly at
Tabernacles
Jn 7:10

Chanukah
Jn 10:22

Power
Displayed
Ruthless
Challenge
Jn 11:1-57
Scent of death
Annoited by Mary
Mt 26:6
Mk 14:3
Jn 12:1

The 'Final Week' of the Messiah

Triumph & Tears Mt21:1, Mk 11:1, Lk 19:29, John 12:12
The Temple, not fit for purpose Mt 21:10-20, Mk 11:12-21, Lk19:37-47 Jn12:12-19
Tricks, snares, woes Mt22:15to 23:39 Mk12:1-44 Lk 20:1-47, 21:1-4
Sermon of destruction Mt Ch24to26:16, Mk 13:1-37 Lk 21:5to22:5
Elijah's Cup 26:17-56, Mk14:12-52, Lk 22:7-53, Jn 13:1 to 18:13
Night without End Mt 26:36 to27:26, Mk 14:32 to 15:15, Lk 22:40 to 23:25, Jn 18:2 to 19:16 Betrayal & Trial
Judgement: Crucifixion Mt 27:1-66, Mk 15:1-47, Lk 22:54 to 23:56, Jn18:12 to 19:42

Into the Storm

Winter | Spring | Summer | Autumn | Winter | Spring | **Battle Climax** | **The Greatest Days** Spring | 40 days from resurrection to ascension

Herod probes,
withdrawal to
Bethsaida
Lk 9:7

The Decapolis
Mk 7:31
Caesarea
Mt 16:13
Mk 8:27
Lk 9:18
Peraea
Mt 19:1
Mk 10:1
Capernaum
Temple Tax
Matt 17:24

Invasion Force
Mt 20:17
Mk 10:17
Lk 9:51 & 11:17

Samaritans reject
Lk 9:52
72 sent out
Lk 10:1

Outrageous
parables
Sign of Jonah
Mk 12:38
Lk 11:29
Jesus' brothers
Jn 7:1

Safe House
Mary & Martha
Lk 10:38

Withdrawal to
east of Jordan
Jn 10:40

Withdrawal to
desert, Ephraim
Jn 11:54

'Til death us do restore Lk 24:50-53 Acts 1:6-14 Ascension
Close & Personal Mt28:16-20 Mk 16:15-18 Lk24:44-49 Acts 1:1-5 1Cor 15:5-7
Breakfast on the beach Jn 21:1-25
Beyond belief Mt 28:1-10, Mk 16:1-9, Lk 24:1-12, Jn 20:1-7
Earthquake Mt28:9-10, Mk16:9-14 Lk 24:13-42 Jn20:10-29

Gregorian Calendar Weeks and Months

Weeks	41	42	43	44	45	46	47	48	49	50	51	52	1	2	3	4	5	6	7	8	9	10	11	12	1
Months		October				November				December				January				February					March		

Jewish calendar with main religious festivals

Weeks	1	2	3	4	5	6	7	8	9	10	11	12	13	14	15	16	17	18	19	20	21	22	23	24	2
Months		Tishri				Heshvan					Kislev				Tebeth				Shebat					Adar	

Jewish Week	Religious Festivals	Day of Month	Significance
1	Rosh Hashanah (Feast of Trumpets)	1st (Jewish New Year)	Important Biblical Day
2	Yom Kippur (Day of Atonement)	10th	Important Biblical Day
3	Sukkot (Feast of Tabernacles)	15-22nd	Pilgrimage Festival
12	Chanukkah (Festival of Dedication / Lights)	25 -30th	Pilgrimage Festival
23	Purim (Feast of Esther)	14th	Importany Biblical Day

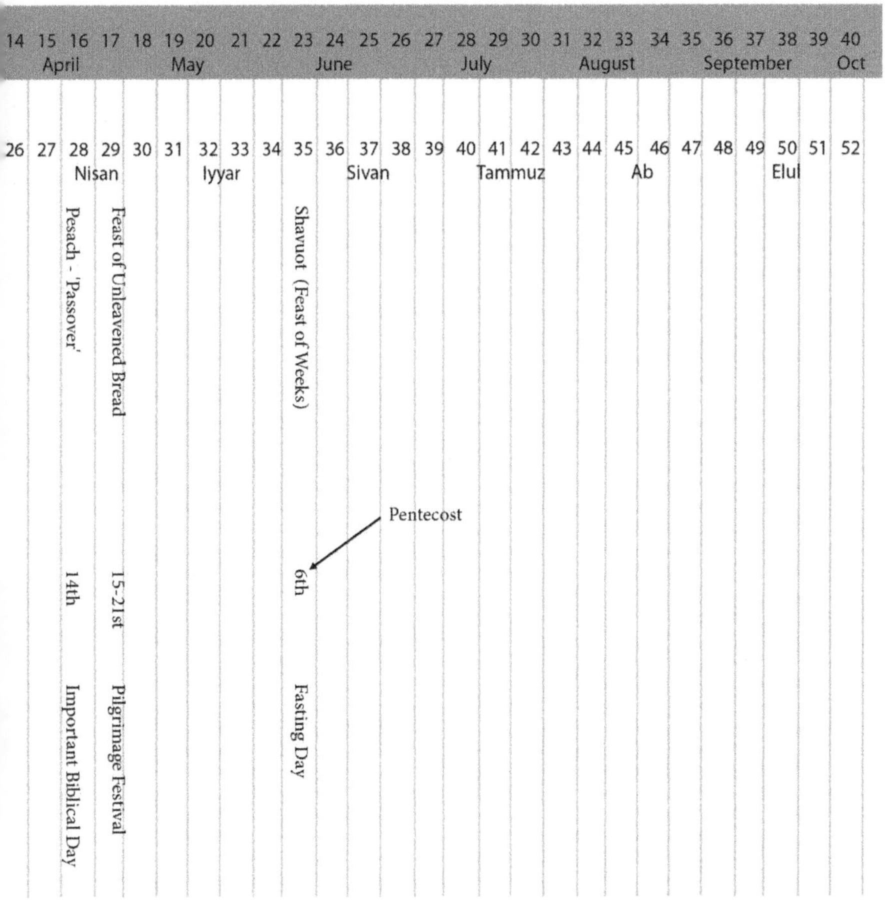

14	15	16	17	18	19	20	21	22	23	24	25	26	27	28	29	30	31	32	33	34	35	36	37	38	39	40
	April				May					June				July				August				September				Oct
26	27	28	29	30	31	32	33	34	35	36	37	38	39	40	41	42	43	44	45	46	47	48	49	50	51	52
		Nisan				Iyyar					Sivan				Tammuz				Ab					Elul		
		Pesach - 'Passover' 14th Important Biblical Day	Feast of Unleavened Bread 15-21st Pilgrimage Festival						Shavuot (Feast of Weeks) 6th Fasting Day																	

Pentecost → 6th